*continued . . .*

# THE SCEPTER'S RETURN

## BOOK THREE OF THE SCEPTER OF MERCY

# HARRY TURTLEDOVE
## writing as
# DAN CHERNENKO

A ROC BOOK

ROC
Published by New American Library, a division of
Penguin Group (USA) Inc., 375 Hudson Street,
New York, New York 10014, USA
Penguin Group (Canada), 90 Eglinton Avenue East, Suite 700, Toronto,
Ontario M4P 2Y3, Canada (a division of Pearson Penguin Canada Inc.)
Penguin Books Ltd., 80 Strand, London WC2R 0RL, England
Penguin Ireland, 25 St. Stephen's Green, Dublin 2,
Ireland (a division of Penguin Books Ltd.)
Penguin Group (Australia), 250 Camberwell Road, Camberwell, Victoria 3124,
Australia (a division of Pearson Australia Group Pty. Ltd.)
Penguin Books India Pvt. Ltd., 11 Community Centre, Panchsheel Park,
New Delhi - 110 017 India
Penguin Group (NZ), cnr Airborne and Rosedale Roads, Albany,
Auckland 1310, New Zealand (a division of Pearson New Zealand Ltd.)
Penguin Books (South Africa) (Pty.) Ltd., 24 Sturdee Avenue,
Rosebank, Johannesburg 2196, South Africa

Penguin Books Ltd., Registered Offices:
80 Strand, London WC2R 0RL, England

Published by Roc, an imprint of New American Library, a division of Penguin Group
(USA) Inc. Previously published in a Roc trade paperback edition.

First Roc Mass Market Printing, July 2006
10 9 8 7 6 5 4 3 2 1

*To Anne and to Russ*

# CHAPTER ONE

Down in the southern part of the Kingdom of Avornis, spring had come some little while before. It was just now reaching the capital. The city of Avornis had had a long, hard winter. It wasn't as bad as it could have been—the Banished One hadn't tried to bury the city in snow and ice, as he had a few years earlier—but no one who'd been through it would have called it mild.

Today, King Lanius was glad to be able to leave the royal palace without a hooded fur cloak that reached down to the ground and sturdy felt boots with wool socks inside them to keep his toes from freezing. His breath still smoked when he did go out, but the icicles had melted from under the eaves of steep-pitched slate roofs and all the snow was gone from the streets, leaving those that weren't cobblestoned (which was most of them) calf-deep in stinking mud.

A few of the oaks and maples around the palace showed the buds that foretold new leaves. Some of the season's earliest birds perched in the mostly bare branches. The songs they sang sounded relieved and perhaps a little surprised, as though they too had trouble believing winter might be over.

Prince Crex and Princess Pitta, Lanius' son and daughter, stood beside him. They were happier to get out of the palace than he was. Snowball fights and snowmen were all very well, but they'd had to spend most of the winter indoors, and that had chafed at them. If the smell from those nearby muddy streets bothered them, they didn't show it.

Pitta pointed to one of the birds in the closest oak. "What kind is that, Father?" she asked, confident Lanius would know. People were always confident Lanius knew any number of small, mostly useless things. They were usually right, too.

"The one on that second branch there?" he asked, squinting toward it—he was a bit shortsighted. His daughter nodded. He said, "That's a goldfinch."

"How come it isn't gold, then?" Crex asked.

And Lanius knew that, too. "They're only gold in the later spring and the summer and the first part of fall," he answered. "The rest of the time, they're this sort of greenish yellow color. But you can tell what they are by the song they sing." He whistled a few notes of it, not very well.

He wondered if Crex would ask why the birds were gold only half the time. *He* would have, when he was a boy. But he'd always been wildly inquisitive about everything. He still was. Crex—and Pitta, too—had only ordinary children's curiosity.

He smiled down at them with a strange blend of affection and exasperation. Most ways, they took after their mother's side of the family, not his. Queen Sosia was King Grus' daughter, and Grus was as practical and hardheaded a man as had ever been born. Lanius did not like his father-in-law very much. How could he, when Grus had grafted his family onto Avornis' ancient royal dynasty and held in his own hands most of the royal power? That Grus' hands were extremely capable made matters no better. If anything, it made them worse.

Crex and Pitta even took after that side of the family in their looks. They were solidly made, where Lanius was tall and on the scrawny side. His beard had always been scraggly. Crex didn't have one yet, of course, but Lanius was ready to bet it would come in thick and luxuriant, like Grus'.

The children looked more like their mother than they did like him, too. Lanius laughed at himself. That wasn't so bad. He was ordinary at best, while Sosia was a nice-looking woman. Her brother, Prince Ortalis, was darkly handsome. Ortalis' problems lay elsewhere. In looks, he and Sosia both resembled Grus' wife, Queen Estrilda. The one who looked like

Grus, all nose and chin, was his bastard boy, the Arch-Hallow Anser. Yet Anser was as good-natured as Grus was tough. You never could tell.

"I'll bet the moncats would like climbing the trees," Crex said.

Lanius laughed again, this time out loud. "I'll bet they would, too," he said. "And I'll bet they'd get away if we ever gave them the chance. That's why they stay inside the palace, and mostly inside their rooms."

Mostly. They were supposed to stay in their rooms all the time. The Chernagors had brought him his first pair of moncats from an island somewhere in the Northern Sea. The beasts were much like house cats, except that they had clawed, gripping hands and feet like a monkey's—hence the name they'd gotten here. They also added a monkey's sharp cleverness to a cat's unreliability. Lanius sometimes thought it was a good thing they'd never figured out the bow and arrow, or they might be the ones keeping people caged up.

Pitta echoed that thought, asking, "How does Pouncer keep getting away all the time, Father?"

"If I knew, sweetheart, he wouldn't do it anymore." Lanius was a thoughtful as well as an honest man. After a moment, he shook his head. "I take it back. He wouldn't do it *that way* anymore. He'd probably figure out some other way pretty soon, though."

Even by moncat standards, Pouncer was a pest. Somewhere in the room where he was kept, he'd found a secret way out. There were ways through the palace, too, ways too small for a man to use but perfect for a moncat. Pouncer would hunt mice in the royal archives and sometimes give them to Lanius as prizes. He would show up in the kitchens, too. Sometimes he stole food. More often, though, he ran off with silverware. Lanius had never figured out why—probably because the moncat was inherently a nuisance. He was particularly fond of big, heavy silver serving spoons. Maybe he planned to pawn them to pay for his getaway. That made as much sense as anything else Lanius had come up with.

"I can climb a tree like a moncat," Crex said, and started for the nearest one. It was an old oak; its branches didn't begin until well above the level of Lanius' head. Crex might have been able to get up into them anyway. He was much more agile than his father had been at the same age. Whether he could come down after going up was a different question.

Lanius didn't try to tell him that. It would have made no sense to him. What the king did say was, "Oh, no, you don't, not in your robes. Your mother and the washerwomen will scream at you if you tear them up and get them all filthy."

"Oh, Father!" Crex sounded as disgusted as only a small boy could.

"No," Lanius said. Crex didn't care if Sosia and the washerwomen yelled at him. But they wouldn't yell just at him. They'd yell at Lanius, too, for letting Crex get his clothes filthy. That was the last thing Lanius wanted. There were times when a king was a lot less powerful than his subjects imagined him to be.

King Grus knew he would never make a wizard. That didn't keep him from watching as Pterocles shaped a spell. Nor did it keep Pterocles from explaining as he worked. The wizard, a man who wore his breeches and tunic as though he'd fallen into them, liked to hear himself talk.

"Spells of foretelling have their risks," Pterocles said.

"The biggest one is, they're liable to be wrong," Grus put in.

Pterocles laughed. "Yes, there is that," he agreed. "But that mostly depends on how the magic is interpreted. The principle underlying the spell is sound. It is based on the law of similarity. The future is commonly similar to the present, for the present is what it springs from."

"Fair enough," Grus said. "If you can, then, tell me whether the Menteshe will go on with their civil war this summer."

"I'll do my best," the wizard answered. When he laughed again, much of the mirth had leaked from his voice. "The Banished One is probably trying to see the same thing."

Grus grunted. That was too true for comfort. Civilized folk, led by the King of Avornis, worshiped King Olor and Queen Quelea and the rest of the gods in the heavens. Centuries before, the gods had cast the Banished One out of the heavens and down to the material world below. He still burned to resume his place and take his revenge, and the Menteshe nomads in the south gave him reverence instead of Olor and Quelea and the other gods. Here in the material world, the Banished One was something less than a god. But he was much, much more than a man.

"If you find your magic vying with his, break yours off and get away," Grus said.

"You don't need to worry about that, Your Majesty," Pterocles said feelingly. "I will. I'd be lucky to come off second best in a meeting like that. I'd be lucky to come off at all."

He set three silver coins on the table in front of him. One was minted by Prince Ulash, who for many years had been the strongest Menteshe chieftain. Ulash, a man of courage and intelligence, would have been dangerous even without the Banished One's backing. With it, he'd been doubly so, or more than that.

The other two coins were shinier and more recent. They'd been struck by Sanjar and Korkut, Ulash's sons. Neither prince was willing to see the other succeed their father. They'd been fighting each other for years now, and the Menteshe to either side had joined in the war—at least as much to plunder what had been Ulash's realm as for any other reason.

Both Sanjar and Korkut had even appealed to Avornis for aid. That was a pleasant novelty for Grus; the Menteshe were more in the habit of raiding Avornis than appealing to her. The spectacle must have infuriated the Banished One, but not even he seemed able to stop the nomads from squabbling among themselves.

Pterocles put Sanjar's and Korkut's coins on top of Ulash's so that their edges touched. He sprinkled a little dirt over them. "Dirt from the south bank of the Stura," he told Grus. The Stura was the last of the Nine Rivers that cut across the rolling plains of southern Avornis from east to west. Its southern bank was not Avornan territory at all, but belonged to the Menteshe.

To Grus, the dirt looked like . . . dirt. He didn't say anything. He trusted Pterocles to know what he was doing. So far, the wizard had earned that trust. Pterocles began to chant. The spell started out in modern Avornan, but quickly changed to the old-fashioned language only priests, wizards, and scholars like Lanius used these days.

As he chanted, the dirt began to swirl and writhe above the coins, as if caught up in one of the dust storms so common in the lands the Menteshe ruled. The coins struck by Sanjar and Korkut sprang up on their edges and started spinning. Round and round they went, faster and faster.

"Does that mean they're going to keep fighting?" Grus asked. Without missing a word or a pass, Pterocles nodded.

Suddenly, it seemed to Grus that *three* coins were spinning on the tabletop. He thought Ulash's silverpiece had gotten up from where it lay to join the dance, but it was still there. He wondered if his eyes had started playing tricks on him.

Pterocles' incantation slowed. So did the spinning coins— and there *were* three of them. The dirt and dust that had floated above the table settled back to its surface. Sanjar's coin and Korkut's settled down on top of Ulash's so that their edges touched once more.

The last coin, the one that appeared to have come out of nowhere, wobbled over and lay down covering parts of Sanjar's, Korkut's, and Ulash's. Pterocles raised his hands above his head. He fell silent. The spell was over.

Grus picked up that last coin. No Menteshe had minted it. His own craggy features, stamped in silver, stared back at him from the palm of his hand. He held the Avornan silverpiece out to Pterocles. The wizard stared at it. "Olor's beard!" he muttered. "I never thought—"

"Does this mean we're going to get mixed up in the fighting south of the Stura this year?" Grus asked.

More unhappily than otherwise, Pterocles nodded. "I can't see how it could mean anything else, Your Majesty. It wasn't part of the sorcery I planned. Where it came from . . ." He gathered himself. "Sometimes the magic does what it wants to do, not what you want it to do."

"Does it?" Grus said tonelessly. He looked at the image of himself, there on his palm. "Is the magic telling us that we ought to get mixed up in the nomads' civil war, or just that we *will* get mixed up in it?"

"That we will, Your Majesty," the wizard answered. "You

may take that as certain—or as certain as anything magic can point out. Whether we will become involved in a big way or a small one, whether good or bad will come from whatever we do—whatever *you* do—I can't begin to say."

"If I order my men to move against the Chernagor city-states in the north instead—" Grus began.

"Something will happen to make us fight in the south anyway," Pterocles broke in. "You're bound to leave garrisons down by the Stura, to beat back whatever Menteshe raiders come over the border. Maybe some of your men will chase after the nomads. Maybe it will turn out to be something else. But we will meet Korkut's men, and Sanjar's, on land that once belonged to Ulash. So much, I would say, is clear."

"And will we win?" Grus kept looking at the coin he held. "My silverpiece came out on top, after all."

"I'd like to say yes, Your Majesty," Pterocles answered. "I'd like to, but I won't. I simply don't know."

"All right. I'd rather have an honest answer than a lie trotted out to make me feel good . . . I suppose." Grus laughed. He supposed that was funny, too. But then the laughter froze on his lips. "If the Banished One is trying to look ahead, too, he'll see the same thing, won't he?"

"If he doesn't, Your Majesty, I'd be astonished," Pterocles said.

"Huzzah," Grus said somberly. Fighting against the Menteshe south of the Stura would be hard enough anyway. No Avornan army had successfully pushed south for more than four hundred years. How much harder would it be if the Banished One knew the Avornans were coming ahead of time? *Well, we'll find out.*

Beaters and royal bodyguards surrounded King Lanius, Prince Ortalis, and Arch-Hallow Anser as they rode out of the city of Avornis to hunt. Chainmail jingled on the guardsmen. The beaters—Anser's men—wore leather, either left brown or dyed green. They looked like a pack of poachers. If they hadn't served the chief prelate of the Kingdom of Avornis, most of them probably would have been in prison.

Anser cared more about the hunt than he did about the gods.

Grus' bastard son always had. But he was unshakably loyal to the man who'd sired him. To Grus, that counted for more than religious zeal. And Anser, along with being unshakably loyal, was also unshakably good-natured. There had been worse arch-hallows, though Lanius wouldn't have thought so when Grus made the appointment.

"Well, let's see how we do today," Anser said, smiling in the sunshine. "Maybe you'll make another kill, Your Majesty."

"Maybe I will." Lanius hoped he didn't sound too unenthusiastic. He didn't care for the hunt, and went out every now and again only to keep from disappointing Anser. No one wanted to do that. Lanius always shot to miss. He was anything but a good archer. Not so long before, he'd hit a stag altogether without intending to.

"Venison. Boar. Even squirrel." Ortalis sounded enthusiastic enough for himself and Lanius at the same time. Grus' legitimate son liked the meat the hunt brought in. He also liked killing the meat in the hunt. He liked killing *very* much. If he killed animals, he didn't need the thrill of hurting—or killing—people so much.

Of course, Bubulcus was still dead. Lanius' obstreperous servant *had* outrageously insulted Ortalis. People often thought outrageous insults reason enough to kill a man. And it did seem that Ortalis had killed in a fit of fury, not for the sport of it. All the same, he remained far too fond of blood for Lanius' taste.

The woods that served as a royal game preserve were a couple of hours' ride outside the city of Avornis. The hunting party hadn't gone a quarter of that distance before Lanius took a deep breath and said, "By the gods, it's good to get away from the capital for a while."

Anser and Ortalis both nodded. So did the guards and beaters. Anser said, "The clean air would be reason enough to come hunting even without the chase."

"Almost reason enough," Ortalis said.

When they got to the woods, the new leaves uncurling from their buds were a brighter, lighter green than they would be once they'd been out for a while. Lanius pointed to them. "That's the color of spring," he said.

"You're right," Ortalis said. They nodded to each other. In

the palace, they didn't get on well. That wasn't just because of Ortalis' streak of bloodlust, either. Grus' legitimate son wanted to be King of Avornis himself one day, and to have the crown pass to his sons and not Lanius'. At the moment, he had no sons, only a toddler daughter. But who could say how long that would last?

Here in the woods, differences of rank and ambition fell away. Lanius swung down off his horse. He rubbed his hindquarters when he did; he was not a man who made a habit of riding. Anser laughed at him. The arch-hallow loved horses only less than hunting. Even Anser's mockery was good-natured. What would have been infuriating from Ortalis only made Lanius laugh, too, when Grus' bastard did it.

*Why couldn't they have been reversed?* Lanius wondered. *I would never have to worry about a usurpation from Anser. And Ortalis—Ortalis would have made an arch-hallow to set evil-doers trembling in their boots.* Things were as they were, though, not as would have been convenient for him. He knew that only too well. Otherwise, he wouldn't have been a small, oft-captured piece in the great Avornan political game for so much of his life.

Carrying bows and quivers, he and Ortalis and Anser went in among the trees. The beaters spread out to drive game their way. Some of the guards accompanied Anser's raffish crew. Others stayed with the king, the prince, and the prelate. Lanius' boots scuffed through the gray-brown rotting leaves that had fallen the autumn before. Try as he would, he couldn't move quietly. Ortalis was far better at it. As for Anser, he might have been a poacher himself by the way he silently slid along.

A squirrel jeered at them from high in a tree. Ortalis started to reach for an arrow, then checked the motion. "No point to it," he said. "I'd never hit him up there, not shooting through all those branches."

One of the royal guards who'd gone on ahead came pounding back. Anser winced at the racket he made. The guards, however, refused to let Lanius go off without them. If that hurt Anser's hunting, they didn't care. This one said, "There's a nice clearing up ahead."

That made the arch-hallow happier—it didn't take much.

"Lead us to it," he said. "Without too much jingling, if you can."

"I'll do my best," the guard said. And, no doubt, he did. That his best was no good . . . Anser was too kindly to twit him too much.

And the clearing was as good as he'd claimed. Fresh bright grass smiled at the sun. A magpie, all black and white and iridescent purple, hopped on the grass. It flew away squawking when Lanius stuck his head out.

Faintly embarrassed, the king drew back behind a tree trunk. "This does seem a likely spot," he said.

"Well, yes, if you don't frighten away everything within five miles," Ortalis said. Had Anser said the same thing, Lanius would have laughed and forgotten about it. From Ortalis, it annoyed him. Anser might have meant it just as much. He probably would have, as passionate for the hunt as he was. But the words wouldn't have stung coming out of his mouth. Coming out of Ortalis', they did.

What Anser said now was, "Don't worry, Your Highness. The beaters will make sure we don't go home empty-handed. Pity the antlers won't be as fine as they would in the fall."

"I don't care," Ortalis said. "I want the venison." He sounded hungry, all right. Was it for meat? Maybe. Lanius thought it was more likely to be for the kill itself.

A deer bounded into the clearing. "Go ahead, Your Majesty," Anser said. "First arrow of spring."

Awkwardly, Lanius drew his bow, took aim, and let fly. The arrow whistled over the deer's head. That was where he'd aimed it, so he wasn't particularly unhappy. He liked eating venison, too, but he didn't care to be the one who'd killed it.

Killing didn't bother Ortalis. Even as the deer bounded away, he loosed his own shaft. Unlike Lanius, he always took dead aim. He was a good shot, too, also unlike the king. His arrow flew straight and true, and struck the deer in the side.

"A hit!" he cried, and was out of cover and running after the wounded animal. Anser ran after him, bow at the ready. So did Lanius, a little more slowly. "An easy trail!" Ortalis said, laughing with pleasure. Sure enough, the deer's blood marked its path. *Well, it will be over soon,* Lanius thought. *The deer won't suffer long. It won't wander through the woods a cripple.*

There it was, thrashing in some bushes it hadn't had the strength to leap. Ortalis drew a knife that would have done duty for a smallsword. "Careful!" Anser called. "Those hooves are still dangerous." If his half brother heard, he gave no sign. Avoiding the feet that flailed ever more feebly, he cut the deer's throat.

More blood fountained free. "Ahhh!" Ortalis said, almost as if he'd just had a woman. As soon as the deer was dead, or perhaps even a moment before, he flipped it over and began to gut it. Arms red almost to the elbows, he turned and smiled up at Lanius and Anser.

"Good shot," Anser said, and clapped him on the back. Lanius managed a nod that didn't seem too halfhearted. But that avid expression on Ortalis' face as he wielded the knife chilled the King of Avornis. *Yes,* he thought, this *is why he hunts.*

When Grus first got to know Hirundo, his general had been a bright young cavalry captain. King Grus himself had been a bright, reasonably young river-galley skipper. Now his beard was gray and the tendons on the backs of his hands all knobbly and gnarled. *How did I get to be sixty?* he wondered, as any man will with so many years behind him and so few probably ahead.

Hirundo was a few years younger, but only a few. He still had traces, though, of the dash he'd shown all those years ago. "South of the Stura, eh?" he said gaily.

"We've been looking at this for a while now—ever since Ulash's sons started squabbling over the bones of his realm," Grus said.

"Oh, yes. We've been looking at it and thinking about it," Hirundo agreed. "Most of what we've been thinking is, *This doesn't look like such a great idea right now.* And what do you think now, Your Majesty? Do you think Pterocles and the other wizards really can cure the thralls south of the Stura? Do you think they can keep the Menteshe from turning our army—and us—into thralls if we cross the river?"

Before the Menteshe overran the lands south of the Stura,

those lands had belonged to Avornis. The peasants on them had been no different from the ones anywhere else in the kingdom. The descendants of those peasants were different now. Dark sorcery from the Banished One had made them into thralls, only a step or two brighter than the domestic animals they tended. The same cruel fate had befallen the last Avornan army that dared go south of the Stura. Fear that such a disaster could happen again had kept Kings of Avornis from troubling the Menteshe in their homeland for more than two centuries.

The sorcery that made men and women into thralls wasn't perfect. Every so often, a thrall would get out from under the spell and cross the Stura into freedom. But the Banished One sometimes used thralls pretending to have escaped from thralldom to spy on Avornis. That made any runaways hard to trust. The Banished One's magic was so deep, so subtle, that Avornan wizards had an almost impossible time telling a thrall who had truly broken away from it from one serving as the enemy's eyes and ears.

Since the very beginning, Avornan wizards had tried to craft magic to break the spell of thralldom. They'd had very little luck. An escaped thrall could seem free of all traces of the sorcery that enslaved him—until, sometimes years later, he did the Banished One's bidding.

Pterocles thought he'd succeeded where everyone else had failed. He had a hard-won advantage over the wizards who'd come before him. Up in the Chernagor country, a spell from the Banished One had all but slain him. When he recovered—a slow, painful process—he'd understood the Banished One's sorcery from the inside out, as only one who had suffered from it might do.

He had freed one thrall. Otus still lived under guard in the royal palace. No one wanted to take too many chances with him. But, by all appearances, he was a thrall no more. Pterocles could track the Banished One's wizardry deeper than any other sorcerer had ever been able to. By all he could sense, Otus was free.

Grus sighed. "I *think* our wizards can keep us free and free the thralls, yes. That's what we're gambling on, isn't it? When the army crosses the Stura, I'm going with it. I won't ask you or the men to face anything I don't have the nerve to face myself."

Hirundo bowed in his seat. "No one has ever questioned your bravery, Your Majesty. No one would dare to now."

"Ha!" Grus shook his head. "You're too sunny, Hirundo. People always have. They always will. If someone doesn't like you, he'll find reasons not to like you whether they're there or not."

"Maybe," Hirundo said—as much as he would admit.

Laughing, Grus added, "Besides, I have another reason for crossing the Stura this year. I want to get down to Yozgat."

"The Scepter of Mercy?" Hirundo asked.

"That's right." Grus laughed no more. His nod was heavy. "The Scepter of Mercy."

Kings of Avornis had coveted the potent talisman for more than four hundred years. The nomads—and the exiled god— kept it in Yozgat, the strongest citadel they had. If the Avornans ever got it back, it would make a great shield and a great weapon against the Banished One. He had never been able to wield it himself. If he ever found some way to do that, he might storm his way back into the heavens from which he'd been expelled.

"Do you think we can?" Hirundo, for once, sounded altogether serious. No one could take the Scepter of Mercy lightly.

"I don't know. I just don't know," Grus said. "But if not now, when? We have—we hope we have—a spell to cure the thralls. The Menteshe are in disarray from fighting one another. When will we ever have a better chance?"

"If you can bring it off, your name will live forever," Hirundo said.

Grus started to tell him that didn't matter. But it did, and he knew it. All a man could leave behind were his children and his name. Ortalis had always been a disappointment, even if Grus was reluctant to admit it even to himself. As for his name . . . He'd kept the Thervings from lording it over Avornis. He had—or he hoped he had—stopped the Chernagors' piratical raids on his coasts, and he'd kept the Banished One from gaining a foothold in the Chernagor country. He'd also kept Avornan nobles from taking the peasants under their wings—and taking them away from their loyalty to the king and to the kingdom as a whole. The nobles didn't love him for it, but that— since he'd beaten a couple of rebels—wasn't his biggest worry.

If he could bring the Scepter of Mercy back to the capital in triumph . . . Well, if that wasn't enough to get him remembered for a long, long time, nothing ever would be.

He noticed Hirundo watching him. The general smiled, noticing him notice. "You do want it," Hirundo said. "It's as plain as the nose on your face."

Considering how formidable that nose was, it must have been plain indeed. "I can't tell you you're wrong," Grus said. "Ever since the Scepter got stolen, there hasn't been a King of Avornis who didn't want to take it back."

"Yes, but how many of them have had a chance to do it?" Hirundo asked.

"I don't know," Grus answered. "I'm not even sure I have that chance. But I aim to find out."

"One thing, Your Majesty—you can leave Lanius behind to run things here while you go off to war," Hirundo said. "He'll do fine while you're away."

"Yes." King Grus let it go at that. Lanius *had* done fine running things in the city of Avornis while he went on campaign himself. He wasn't sure whether that was good or bad, though. He'd kept Lanius away from power as long as he could. The more the scion of the ancient dynasty held, the less secure Grus' grip on the rest was.

Lanius had never tried to rise against him. If he did . . . Grus didn't know what would happen. Not knowing worried him. He was reaching the end of his prime of life as Lanius entered his. He realized that. He wondered if the other king did, too.

He hoped not.

Lanius washed down his breakfast porridge with a sip of wine, then said, "I'm off to the moncats."

Queen Sosia looked back across the table at him. "Is that where you're going?" she murmured.

Lanius' ears heated. That had nothing to do with the wine. "Yes, that *is* where I'm going," he said. "You're welcome to come along if you care to."

His wife shook her head. "No, thank you—never mind. If I came along, that would be where you went." She took a long pull at her own cup of wine.

"It was where I was going anyway," Lanius said. Sosia didn't answer. The king got up from the table and left in a hurry. Anything he said after that would make things worse, not better. There were times when he told Sosia he was going to visit the moncats and he paid a call on a serving girl instead. It wasn't that he didn't care for the queen. He hadn't expected to when Grus arranged their marriage, but he did. But he was king, even if he was the second of two kings, and he could do more or less as he pleased. Every so often, he pleased to yield to temptation.

Grus was in no position to tell him what a wicked fellow he was. The other king didn't hesitate, either, when he saw a face or a form that struck his fancy. Queen Estrilda had given him as much trouble for it as Sosia gave Lanius.

This time, though, Lanius left the small dining room by his bedchamber in a warm glow of injured innocence. He really had intended to go to the moncats and nowhere else. Well, almost nowhere else—he stopped in the kitchens for some scraps of meat first. "You're going to waste more good food on those thieving, miserable creatures," one of the cooks said, sadly shaking her head.

"They aren't miserable." Lanius couldn't deny that moncats stole, because they did. The cook only sniffed.

When the king got to the moncats' chamber, he opened the door with care. He didn't want them getting out. With their grasping hands and feet and with their agility, they were hard as a demon to catch when they got loose.

Some of the moncats in the room were washing themselves, some sleeping with their tails wrapped around their noses, and some climbing on the framework of boards and branches that did duty for a forest. They stared down at Lanius out of green or yellow eyes.

They were clever animals, clever enough to give him the uneasy feeling they were measuring him with those glances, measuring him and finding him . . . perhaps barely adequate. "Pouncer?" he called. "Are you here, Pouncer, you miserable beast?" He stole the cook's word now that she couldn't hear him do it, though he meant it for reasons different from hers.

He laughed at himself. He was a fairly miserable creature in his own right if he expected Pouncer or any other moncat to come when called. Moncats weren't just like ordinary house cats. Thanks to their hands and sharp wits, they could make bigger pests of themselves than house cats could. But they were every bit as cross-grained as the most ordinary tabby.

Pouncer should have been here. The moncat shouldn't have been able to get out. But it could. Lanius had yet to figure out how it managed the trick. Once, Pouncer had disappeared right before his eyes. He'd stopped watching the moncat for a moment—no more than a moment—and when he looked back, Pouncer wasn't there to be watched anymore. It made the king wonder who was smarter than who.

Moncats crowded around him. They knew he often brought them treats. He doled out a few scraps of meat. A couple of snarling squabbles broke out; moncats had no more in the way of manners than any other animals (or, for that matter, small children) did. As Lanius fed the others, he kept looking around for Pouncer—and finally spotted the male at the top of the climbing apparatus.

Lanius lay down on his back. He thumped his chest with his free hand. Pouncer knew what to do when that happened. The moncat scrambled down and jumped up on top of the king. "That's a good boy," Lanius said, and scratched it under the chin and behind the ears.

Pouncer wasn't a bad-tempered beast, and put up with it. All the same, the moncat practically radiated impatience. *I'm not doing this trick for your sake,* it would have said if it could talk. *Where's my meat?*

"Here, you greedy thing." Lanius held out a piece. Pouncer took it from his hand with a clawed thumb and forefinger. The moncat didn't snatch, but was careful not to hurt the person giving it a reward.

Once Pouncer had the treat, what point was there to staying with Lanius any longer? Away the moncat went, back up on the boards. Lanius stared after it. *I taught you an ordinary little trick,* he thought. *What could someone who really knows how to train animals do?*

# CHAPTER TWO

King Grus swung up into the saddle. General Hirundo, who was already mounted, grinned slyly. "You're getting pretty good at that, Your Majesty," he said.

"Oh, shut up," Grus answered, and Hirundo laughed out loud. The trouble was, the general was right, and Grus knew it. Over the years, he *had* become a pretty decent horseman. He'd never intended to. On a river galley—even on one of the tall-masted ocean-going ships the Avornans were building in imitation of the Chernagor pirates—he knew what he was doing. He'd never planned on riding very much. He'd never planned on becoming King of Avornis, either. That had worked out pretty well, at least so far. As for horsemanship . . . When he shrugged, his gilded mailshirt clinked on his shoulders.

Instead of a stallion, he did ride a good-natured gelding. He'd done that even when he knew he was going to get in a fight. He valued control and obedience more than fire in a horse.

"Are we ready?" he asked.

"If we weren't, would we be doing all this?" Hirundo said reasonably.

"Let's go, then." Grus used the reins and the pressure of his knees to urge his horse into motion. Hirundo's high-spirited charger pranced along beside it.

As they rode out of the stables, mounted imperial lancers formed up around them. The guardsmen wore heavy shirts of mail and rode big, strong horses. Even the horses wore armor that protected their heads and breasts. The lancers' charge was irresistible at close range. The problem was getting the Menteshe, who usually kept but loose order on their ponies, to bunch together long enough to receive a charge.

"Your Majesty!" the guardsmen shouted. Grus waved to them. Under the bar nasals of their conical helmets, a good many of the troopers grinned at him.

He waved again. "Are we going to run the nomads ragged?" he called.

"Yes!" the lancers shouted. Grus waved again. *I hope we are, anyway,* he thought.

The rest of the army he would take south from the city of Avornis waited outside the walls. Before he could go out to it, though, he needed to take care of one loose end. "Where are Pterocles and Otus?" he asked.

"They were in there getting saddled up, too," Hirundo said. "What's taking them so long?"

"Well, if you think I'm a poor excuse for a cavalryman . . ." Grus said. Hirundo threw back his head and laughed. A minute or two later, Pterocles and Otus emerged. Both of them rode mules. Grus had hardly ever known a wizard who trusted himself on horseback, while the freed thrall (Grus *hoped* he was a freed thrall) hadn't had much chance to acquire the equestrian art.

Pterocles dipped his head to Grus. "Your Majesty," he murmured.

"Your Majesty," Otus echoed. He was a brown-haired, open-faced man approaching his middle years. He looked like anybody else, in other words. He sounded like anybody else, too. Oh, he had an accent that said he came from the south, but a lot of Avornans had that kind of accent. He also had a slightly old-fashioned turn of phrase. When thralls spoke at all, they spoke as ordinary Avornans had centuries before. They'd long been cut off from the vital, changing current of the language.

When he was a thrall, Otus might have had as many words as a two-year-old. He might not, too. He'd had to learn to speak as a child would after being freed from the charm that had held him down for so long. He'd learned far faster than a child would have, though. Only tiny traces of how he'd once talked lingered in his speech.

"Are you ready to head down to your homeland?" Grus asked him.

"Yes, Your Majesty," he answered. "I would like to see my woman freed. I would like to see all thralls freed."

"So would I," Grus said. "That's . . . one of the things we're going to try to do. I hope we can." He glanced toward Pterocles. If they couldn't do that, and if they couldn't protect themselves from being made into thralls after they crossed the Stura, they would do better not to go over the river at all.

But Pterocles' magic had said that they would cross it. Not that they should, but that they would. If Grus was going to make the attempt, he wanted to make it on his terms. Pterocles nodded back. He had to know what was in Grus' mind. He seemed confident his sorcery could handle what was required. Grus didn't care whether he was confident. The king cared about whether he was right.

*We'll find out,* Grus thought. "Let's get moving," he said harshly. Flanked by the lancers, he rode toward the capital's southern gate. The streets that led from the palace to the gates were cobbled; most of the ones that ran into them weren't.

A few people came out to watch the king and his retinue go by. Men wore tunics and baggy trousers. Women had on either short tunics and skirts that reached their ankles or long tunics that fell just as far. In past years, Grus had drawn bigger crowds when he went out on campaign. He'd done it every year lately, though, and it didn't impress the jaded city dwellers anymore.

"Beat the lousy Chernagors!" somebody called, and waved a broad-brimmed felt hat.

Grus waved back without batting an eye. He *had* beaten the Chernagors the year before. Some people knew that. Others, like this fellow, hadn't gotten the word. These days, Grus took in stride things that would have infuriated him when he was younger.

The shout did infuriate Otus. "Don't they know what's going on, Your Majesty?" he demanded. "How can they *not* know? They're free. They don't have the Banished One clouding their minds. Why shouldn't they know?"

"They have their lives to lead," Grus answered with a shrug. "They don't care who the enemy is. As long as it's someone far away, that suits them fine. That's all most people want from a king, you know—to make sure enemies stay far away. Nothing else matters nearly as much."

"Except taxes." Hirundo and Pterocles said the same thing at the same time.

But Grus shook his head. "They'll even put up with taxes as long as things stay peaceful. If they get a fight on their doorstep, that's when they start thinking the king is squandering what they give him."

Out through the open gates they rode. The great valves had swung inward. The sun gleamed off the iron that sheathed the heavy timbers. No foreign enemy had ever stormed the city of Avornis. Back when Grus first took the throne, King Dagipert of Thervingia had besieged the Avornan capital. He'd had no better luck than any other invader. These days, King Berto— Dagipert's son—ruled the Thervings. Unlike Dagipert, he cared more for prayer than plunder. Grus hoped he had a long reign, and that he stayed pious. With trouble in the north and south, Avornis needed peace in the east.

Horsemen and foot soldiers were drawn up in neat ranks on the meadow outside the city. Most of the horsemen were archers. Some foot soldiers also carried bows; others shouldered long pikes, to hold enemy soldiers away from the bowmen.

"Grus!" the army shouted as one man. "Hurrah for King Grus! Grus! Grus! Avornis!" The cry came echoing back from the brown stone walls of the city.

Hirundo smiled sidewise at Grus. "You hate hearing that, don't you?"

"Who, me?" Grus answered, deadpan. Hirundo chuckled. The king raised his voice so the soldiers could hear him. "We're going south of the Stura. The Menteshe have had it all their own way down there for too long. Time to show them that land is ours by right. We've beaten them on this side of the river, and we're going to beat them on that one."

"Hurrah for King Grus!" the soldiers shouted again.

Grus pointed south. "We are going to go forward until we

win or until I give the order to retreat. I do not intend to give the order to retreat."

The soldiers cheered again. Guardsmen around him, his general and his wizard and the freed thrall with him, Grus started down toward the Stura.

A dog pranced on its hind legs on a wooden ball. A cat leaped through a hoop. A rooster ran up a ladder and rang a bell at the top. Another dog turned flips on the back of a pony that trotted round and round in circles.

Crex and Pitta clapped their hands. Lanius and Sosia exchanged amused glances. They had to admire the animal trainer's skills, but neither one of them was quite as enchanted as their children.

"How does he make them do those things?" Pitta whispered to Lanius.

"He gives them food they like when they do something he likes," Lanius answered. "Before long, they get the idea."

Pitta shook her head. "It can't be that easy."

And so it wasn't, not in detail. She was bound to be right about that. But Lanius knew he had the broad outlines right. He'd trained Pouncer to come up and sit on his chest that way. It wasn't much of a trick—nothing to compare to what these animals were doing—but the principle couldn't be much different.

When the show ended, the pony lowered its head and extended its right forefoot in a salute. The dogs did the same. The rooster spread its wings while stretching out its leg. The cat . . . yawned. And the trainer, a big-nosed, bushy-mustached man named Collurio, put both hands in front of his chest and bowed very low.

"Well done!" Lanius called. His wife and children echoed him.

Collurio bowed again, not quite so deeply. "I thank you, Your Majesties, Your Highnesses. Always a pleasure to work for such an appreciative audience." He had a showman's voice, a little louder and a little more clearly enunciated than it needed to be. Lanius had also paid him well to perform, but he was much too smooth to bring up such a tiny detail.

He spoke to his assistant, a youth who, except for lacking a mustache, looked a lot like him. The youngster took charge of the animals and led them out of the audience chamber where they'd put on their show. Collurio started to follow. Lanius said, "Wait a moment, if you please."

The animal trainer stopped and turned back. "Of course, Your Majesty. I am at your service." Though he sounded more than a little surprised and curious, the bow he gave the king now was as smooth as any of the others.

Lanius got to his feet. "Walk with me," he said, and Collurio fell in beside him. When a pair of royal guards started to approach, Lanius waved them back out of earshot. They looked at each other, but obeyed. People mostly did obey Lanius . . . as long as Grus was away from the palace.

"Like I say, Your Majesty, I'm at your service. But what sort of service can I do for you?" Yes, Collurio was curious. He also sounded nervous. Lanius didn't suppose he could blame him for that.

"First things first," the king said. "Can you keep secrets? Give me the truth, please. If you say no, I won't be angry—I'll just talk to someone else. But if you say yes and then let your mouth run free, I promise you'll wish you were never born."

"I don't blab, Your Majesty," Collurio said. "And I'm not the sort who gets soused in a wineshop and spills his guts without even knowing he's doing it, either."

Did he mean it? Lanius decided he did. "All right, then. Have you ever tried to train a moncat? Would you like to?"

"I never have," Collurio said slowly. "There aren't many outside the palace." He was right about that. All the moncats in Avornis were descended from the pair a Chernagor ambassador had given to Lanius some years earlier. The king had made presents of a few of them to favored nobles, but only a few. Most he kept himself. Collurio went on, "I would like to, yes, if I get the chance."

"If you want it, I think it's yours," Lanius said. "There's one particular moncat I'd like you to try to teach one particular thing."

Collurio bowed one more time. "I am your servant, Your Majesty. What is it that you want the animal to learn?" But after

Lanius described it, the trainer frowned. "Meaning no disrespect, but that is not one thing. It is a whole series of things. The moncat would have to learn them one at a time, and would also have to learn to do them in the right order. I am not sure whether the creature would be clever enough. I am not sure whether it would be patient enough, either."

Did he mean he wasn't sure whether *he* would be patient enough? Lanius wouldn't have been surprised. The king said, "I want you to do the best you can. If you fail, I will not punish you, though I may try again with someone else. If you succeed, you and yours will never want for anything. I promise you that."

Collurio licked his lips. He was interested—Lanius could see that. But the animal trainer said, "Again, Your Majesty, I mean no disrespect to you, but would King Grus also make me the same promise?"

Even someone as far down the social scale as he was knew that Grus was the one with real power in the palace. "I'm not offended," Lanius said, which was . . . mostly true. Though it wasn't completely true, it needed saying; Collurio looked relieved to hear it. The king continued, "Here, though, I think I can tell you that he would. This is also something in which he is interested. I will write to him and ask, if you like."

"No, Your Majesty, no need for that. I believe you," Collurio said quickly. He'd taken his doubts as far as he could—probably further than most men would have dared. "What you just told me is plenty good enough."

"Then I think we have a bargain." Lanius held out his hand. Collurio clasped it. The trainer's fingers, his palm, and the back of his hand bore an amazing number and variety of scars. Not all the animals he'd dealt with had been docile. Eagerness surging through him, Lanius asked, "Do you want to start now?"

"Might I ask to wait until tomorrow?" Collurio replied. "I would like to tend to my own beasts, if you don't mind."

Lanius realized he'd been too impetuous. He nodded. "Of course. Oh—one other thing." The animal trainer raised a curious eyebrow. Lanius said, "For the kingdom's sake, and also for your own safety, don't talk about what you're doing here, not to anyone, not ever. This is the secret I asked you if you could keep."

"Not talk about training a moncat, for my . . . safety?" Collurio sounded as though he couldn't believe his ears.

"I am not joking," Lanius said.

The trainer's smile and the way he shook his head said he didn't understand but wasn't about to argue. "I'll keep quiet," he said. "My tongue's not a babbling brook. I told you so, and I meant it."

"Good." Lanius nodded again. "That's part of the bargain we just made."

"For a chance to train moncats, I'd keep my mouth shut about all kinds of things," Collurio said. Lanius liked that. Collurio didn't say anything about the chance to work with the king and under the king's eye. Lanius would have been amazed if that weren't in the animal trainer's mind. But he had the sense not to *say* it. Maybe training moncats really was more important to him. Lanius could hope so, anyway.

Impulsively, he stuck out his hand again. Collurio shook it. Lanius said, "I think we're going to get along just fine."

Some of the Nine Rivers were bridged. Ferries and barges took the Avornan army across the rest. River galleys, long and lean and deadly, patrolled upstream and down- at each crossing. With their oars moving in smooth unison, they reminded Grus of so many centipedes striding across the water. They also made him long for the days when captaining one of them was as far as his ambitions ran.

When he said as much to Hirundo, his general laughed at him. "You're only saying that because you've got a sore backside."

"I *don't* have a sore backside," Grus answered. "I've done enough riding by now that I'm hardened to it. But those were simpler days. I didn't have so many things to worry about. I was down on the Stura most of the time, but I hardly ever thought about the Banished One. The Menteshe? Yes—of course. Their lord? No."

"He didn't think about you in those days, either. If you find yourself in the Banished One's thoughts, you've come up in the world," Hirundo said.

Grus laughed. He supposed it *was* funny if you looked at it the right way. Still . . . "I could do without the honor, thanks."

"Could you?" Hirundo was usually the one quick to laugh. As he and the king sat their horses just beyond the riverbank watching the army come off the barges, the general seemed altogether serious. "If the Banished One didn't have you in his mind, would he worry about anyone in Avornis?"

*Lanius,* Grus thought. *And Pterocles.* Like him, they'd received dreams in which the Banished One appeared and spoke. Grus could have done without that honor, too. Never in battle had he known the fear that curdled his innards when he came face-to-face with the Banished One's calm, cold, inhuman beauty, even in a dream. He knew too well he was opposing someone—something—ever so much stronger than he was.

He didn't think Hirundo had ever had one of those horrifying dreams. For whatever reason, the Banished One didn't reckon Hirundo dangerous enough to confront that way. The officer wouldn't have spoken so lightly of the foe if he'd met him like that. No one who'd directly faced the Banished One's power spoke lightly of him.

Swearing sergeants shepherded soldiers back into their places. The army started south again. Peasants working in the fields took one look at the long column coming down the road and fled. Grus had seen that many times before. It always saddened him. The farmers and herdsmen didn't think the Avornan soldiers were invaders. They were afraid of being robbed and plundered just the same.

Here, though, the soldiers didn't have to forage off the countryside to keep themselves fed. At Grus' order, supply dumps awaited the army all the way down to the valley of the Stura. Wheat and barley would give them bread; cattle and sheep, meat; and there was ale and wine to drink. The soldiers had plenty. But the peasants didn't know that, and weren't inclined to take chances.

Low ranges of hills running roughly east and west separated the valleys of the Nine Rivers from one another. The roads that ran straight across the valleys wound and twisted as they went through the hills. They followed the passes that had been there since the gods made the world. Grus' mouth twisted when that thought crossed his mind. The god said to have made the world was Milvago, whose children had cast him out of the heavens and who was now the Banished One.

Had he turned to evil before Olor and Quelea and the rest expelled him? Or had being ousted and sent down to this lesser sphere infuriated and corrupted him, so that he became evil only after coming to earth? Grus had no idea. Only the Banished One and the gods in the heavens knew, and Grus would have bet they told different stories. In the end, how much difference did it make? The Banished One dwelt on earth now and was evil now, and that was all a mere mortal needed to know.

Riding at the head of the column, Grus escaped all the dust the horsemen and soldiers kicked up moving along a dirt road. When he looked back over his shoulder, the cloud the army kicked up obscured most of it.

Then Grus looked ahead, down into the valley of the Stura. The scars from the fire and sword the Menteshe had inflicted on it were still plain to see. Those scars would have been worse yet if the nomads hadn't started fighting among themselves instead of going on with their war against Avornis.

They were bad enough as things were. And they told King Grus everything worth knowing about the Banished One's disposition.

"I have warned you against your plots and schemes." The voice that resounded inside King Lanius' head reminded him of the tolling of a great bronze bell. The face he saw was supremely handsome, even beautiful, yet somehow all the more frightful because of that. The Banished One stared at him out of eyes as fathomless as the depths between the stars. "I have warned you, and you have chosen not to heed. You will pay for your foolishness."

It was a dream. Lanius knew that. He'd had them before. But the dreams the Banished One sent weren't *only* dreams, as people said after they woke up from bad ones. The terror they brought felt no less real than it would have in the waking world, and the memory of it lingered—indeed, grew worse—as the waking world returned. Ordinary bad dreams were nothing like that, for which the king praised the gods in the heavens.

"I would pay worse," Lanius answered, "if I did not do all I could for what I know to be right."

As always, the Banished One's laughter flayed like knives. "You think so, do you? You are wrong, worm of a man-thing. And when the heavens are mine once more, *everyone* will pay! Everyone!" He laughed again, and seemed to reach for the king.

Lanius woke up then, with a horrible start that left him sitting up in bed, his heart pounding like a drum. He breathed a long, slow sigh of relief. The one resemblance the dreams the Banished One sent held to the usual kind was that nothing harmful could really happen in them—or nothing had yet. When the exiled god's hand stretched out toward the king, though . . .

Sosia stirred sleepily. "Are you all right?" she asked, yawning.

"Yes. I'm all right now." Saying it made it feel more true to Lanius. "A bad dream, that's all." He eased himself down flat again.

"Go back to sleep. I'm going to," Sosia said. Within a few minutes, she was breathing softly and heavily once more. Lanius took much longer to drop off. He didn't find sleep so welcoming, not with the Banished One lurking there. He'd never talked with his wife about the dreams the Banished One sent. The only people to whom he'd mentioned them were Grus and Pterocles. They were the only ones he thought likely to understand, for the Banished One sent them dreams, too.

Lanius did finally fall back to sleep. A sunbeam sneaking between the window curtains woke him. When he opened his eyes—normally, sleepily, not with the terrified stare he always had after confronting the Banished One—he found Sosia was already up and about. He got out of bed, used the chamber pot, and pulled off his nightshirt and replaced it with the royal robes. Servants would have swarmed in to dress him if he'd wanted them to. He'd never been able to see much point in that; he was the one who could best tell how his clothes hung on his bony frame.

Halfway through his breakfast porridge, he snapped his fingers in excitement. Collurio was coming to the palace this morning. Lanius wondered what the animal trainer would make of Pouncer—and what the moncat would make of Collurio. The king ate faster. He wanted to finish before Collurio got there.

He did, by a few minutes, which was perfect. But when Collurio came into the palace, he startled Lanius. The animal trainer was far from the confident showman he'd been while presenting his beasts to Lanius and his family the night before. He was pale and subdued, and gulped at the wine a servant brought him. Concerned, Lanius said, "Is something wrong?"

The trainer started. "I'm sorry, Your Majesty. I didn't know it showed. It's nothing, really." His tone and his whole attitude belied the words. "Just . . . a bad dream I had after I got home last night."

"*Did* you?" Lanius said. Collurio nodded. The king urged him aside, out of earshot of the servants. To be safer still, he lowered his voice to something not far from a whisper before asking, "Did you dream of the Banished One?"

Collurio's bloodshot eyes widened. "By the gods—by the gods, indeed—how could you know that, Your Majesty?"

Instead of answering, the king looked around. No one seemed to be paying any special attention to him and Collurio. All the same, he was obscurely glad, or maybe not so obscurely, that Otus was nowhere near the palace. Still in that near-whisper, Lanius said, "How do I know? Because he came to me in the night, too, that's how."

"What—what did he want of you?" The animal trainer's voice shook.

"To warn me. To threaten me, really," Lanius answered. "When you see him, that's what he does. He's come to Grus, too, and to . . . some others." Lanius didn't like calling Grus the king, or even a king. Sometimes, like it or not, he had to, but not here. He didn't know how far he could trust Collurio, either. The trainer didn't need to know the kingdom's chief wizard had seen the Banished One face-to-face in dreams.

Collurio shuddered. "I thought he would do worse than threaten. I thought those hands of his would tear out my liver."

Lanius patted the other man on the back. "I know what you mean. Believe me, I do. But the one thing I can tell you is that he can't hurt you in these dreams. He never has, not in all the years since I saw him for the first time. If Grus were here, he would say the same."

"He can frighten you half to death," Collurio said feelingly.

"Yes, but only halfway there." Lanius hesitated, then went on, "As a matter of fact, I can tell you one other thing, or I think I can. Seeing the Banished One in a dream is a compliment of sorts." By the way the animal trainer shuddered again, it was a compliment he could have done without. Lanius persisted even so. "It is. It means he takes you seriously. It means you worry him. It means he wants to frighten you out of doing whatever you're doing."

"Training a moncat?" Collurio's laugh was raucous. "He must be plumb daft if that worries him."

"Maybe. But then again, maybe not, too," Lanius said. The look Collurio gave him said *he* might have been plumb daft. All the same, Lanius continued, "You never can tell. Come on. You can see the beast for yourself."

By the trainer's expression, he regretted having anything to do with moncats. Lanius wondered if he'd have to look for somebody else. But Collurio gathered himself. "All right, Your Majesty. I'm coming. By Olor's beard, I've earned the right— earned it and paid for it."

"Let's go, then. Shall we stop in the kitchens first for some meat scraps?" Lanius said.

The question made Collurio smile for the first time since he'd set foot in the palace. "You know that much, do you? Yes, let's stop there. The way to get any beast to do what you want is to give it a treat when it does. One step at a time, that's how you work in this business."

He carried the meat scraps in a little earthenware bowl. Lanius led him through the palace's winding corridors to the moncats' chamber. The king hoped Pouncer wouldn't have decided to disappear into the passages between the walls. That would have been annoying, to say the least.

To his relief, the moncat he wanted was there with the others. Collurio stared at all of them with fascination, even after

Lanius pointed out the one he'd be working with. "Here, let me have a scrap," Lanius said. "I've taught him one little trick myself." He lay down on the floor and thumped his chest. Sure enough, Pouncer came running over and scrambled up onto him to claim the treat.

Collurio made as though to bow. "Not bad, Your Majesty. Not bad at all."

Lanius scratched Pouncer behind the ears. The moncat deigned to purr. The king said, "He's also taught himself a trick or two. When he goes into the kitchen, he likes to steal serving spoons. He likes silver best—he has expensive tastes—but he'll take wooden ones, too. Sometimes he'll steal forks, but it's usually spoons."

Now Collurio studied Pouncer like a sculptor eyeing a block of marble and wondering what sort of statue lay hidden within. Here was his raw material. How would he shape it? "Well, Your Majesty," he said, "we'll see what we can do. . . ."

Riding through the valley of the Stura toward the river that marked the border between Avornis and the lands of the Menteshe, Grus was doubly glad the nomads had fallen into civil war. Too much of the damage they'd done here still remained. Too many peasant villages were only crumbling ruins with no one living in them. Here in the south, people planted when the fall rains came and harvested in the springtime, the opposite of the way things worked up by the capital. But too many fields that should have been fat with wheat and barley had gone back to weeds. Too many meadows were untended scrub, and too few cattle and sheep and horses and donkeys grazed on the ones that remained.

When the king remarked on that to Hirundo, the general said, "Now they're doing it to themselves, and it serves 'em right."

"But they're doing it to the thralls, too," Grus said. "If things go the way we hope they will, we're going to have to start thinking of the thralls as Avornans. We can turn them back to Avornans again." *We'd better be able to, anyhow. If we can't, we're in trouble.*

Hirundo raised an eyebrow. His laugh sounded startled. "To

me, they're just thralls. They've always been just thralls. But that's what this is all about, isn't it?"

"That's . . . one of the things this is all about." Grus always had the Scepter of Mercy in his mind, and ever more so as he came farther south and so drew closer to it. But, as he drew closer to it, he also got the feeling talking about it, showing that he was thinking about it, grew more dangerous. He didn't know if that feeling sprang from his imagination alone. Whether it did or not, he didn't care to take the chance.

"By King Olor's strong right hand, it'll be good to hit back at the Menteshe on their own soil," Hirundo said. "We've fought here, inside Avornis, for a cursed long time. All they had to do to get away was make it over the Stura. We never dared go after them. But we owe them a bit, don't we?"

"Just a bit," the king said, his voice dry. Hirundo laughed again, this time sarcastically. How many times had the Menteshe raided southern Avornis in the four centuries and more since the Scepter of Mercy was lost? How much plundering, how much destruction for the sport of it, how many murders, how many rapes were they to blame for? Not even Lanius, clever as he was, could begin to give an accounting of all their atrocities.

The farther the army advanced into the broad valley of the last of the Nine Rivers, the worse the devastation got. Not only villages had fallen to the Menteshe. So had more than one walled city. The nomads didn't have elaborate siege trains, the way the Avornan army did. But if they burned the fields around a city, slaughtered the livestock, and killed the peasants who raised the crops, the townsfolk inside the walls got hungry. Then they had two choices—they could starve or open their gates to the Menteshe and hope for the best.

Sometimes starving turned out to be the better idea.

Otus rode close to King Grus. The former thrall stared at the countryside with wide eyes, as he had ever since leaving the capital. "This land is so rich," he said.

"Here? By the gods, no!" Grus shook his head. "What we saw farther north, that was fine country. This used to be. It will be again, once people finish getting over the latest invasion. But it's nothing special now."

"Even the way it is, it's better than you'll find on the other side of the river." Otus pointed south. "Farmers who care work this land. They do everything they can with it, even when that is not so much. Over there"—he pointed again—"you might as well have so many cattle tilling the soil. Nobody does anything but what he has to. The people—the thralls, I mean—don't see half of what they ought to do."

If things went wrong on the far side of the Stura, the whole army—or however much of it was left alive after the Menteshe got through with it—would probably be made into thralls. It had happened before. A King of Avornis had lived out his days dead of soul in a little peasant hut somewhere between the Stura and Yozgat. After that, no Avornan army had presumed to cross the last river . . . until now.

Was the Banished One laughing and rubbing his hands together, looking forward to another easy triumph? Had everything that had happened over the past few years, including the civil strife among the Menteshe, been nothing but a ruse to lure Grus and the Avornan army down over the Stura? Could the Banished One see that far ahead? Could he move the pieces on the board so precisely? Was Pterocles' thrall-freeing sorcery all part of the ruse?

Grus shook his head. If the exiled god could do all that, there was no hope of resisting him. But if he could do all that, he would have crushed Avornis centuries earlier. Whatever he'd been in the heavens, he had limits in the material world. He could be opposed. He could be beaten. Otherwise, the Chernagors would bow down to him as the Fallen Star, the way the Menteshe did. Grus' campaigns in the north had made sure that wouldn't happen.

Sunlight glinted off water in the distance. A smudge of smoke near the Stura marked the city of Anna. The king knew the town well from his days as a river-galley captain. It hadn't fallen to the nomads, even when things seemed blackest for Avornis. Lying on the broad river, it depended less on nearby fields for food than towns farther from the Stura. And archers and catapults on river galleys had taken their toll on the Menteshe who ventured too close to the bank.

Anna was used to soldiers and sailors. It was always heavily garrisoned. Any king with eyes to see knew the border towns stood as bulwarks against trouble from the south. A great flotilla of river galleys patrolled the Stura now. The river had tributaries that flowed in from the south as well as from the north. They hadn't seen Avornan ships on them for many, many years. Soon they would again.

Along with Hirundo, Grus stood on Anna's riverfront wall, peering south into the land where no Avornan soldiers had willingly set foot for so very long. It looked little different from the country on this side of the Stura. Off in the distance stood a peasant village. It was full of thralls, of course. From this distance, it looked the same as an ordinary Avornan village in spite of what Otus said. No matter how it looked, the difference was there—for now. With luck, it wouldn't be there much longer.

# CHAPTER THREE

King Lanius liked the archives for all kinds of reasons. Where Arch-Hallow Anser took pleasure from hunting deer and wild boar, Lanius enjoyed running facts to earth, and the archives were the best place to do it. The thrill of the chase was every bit as real for him as it was for Anser. Centuries of clerks had stored documents not immediately useful in the archives. Very few of them had used any system beyond throwing the parchments and papers into crates or buckets or barrels or cases or whatever else seemed handy at the moment. Finding any one parchment in particular was an adventure at best, impossible at worst.

Even when Lanius didn't have anything special in mind, he enjoyed the hunt for its own sake. He never knew what he would come across going through documents at random. Tax records could be stuffed next to accounts of controversies in some provincial town's temples or next to the tales of travelers who'd gone to distant lands and written out descriptions of what they saw and did. Until you looked, you couldn't tell.

And the king enjoyed going to the archives for their own sake. When he closed the heavy doors behind him, he closed away the world. Servants hardly ever came and bothered him while he was there. From when he was very young, he'd made it plain to everyone that that was *his* place, and he wasn't to be disturbed.

Sunlight sifted in through windows set in the ceiling that

somehow never came clean. Dust motes danced in those tired sunbeams. If the archives held one thing besides documents, it was dust. The air smelled of it, and of old parchment, and of old wood, and of other things Lanius always recognized but never could have named. It was just the smell of the archives, an indispensable part of the place.

Quiet was also an indispensable part of the place. Those heavy doors muffled the usual noises that filled the palace—rattling and banging and shouting from the kitchens, servants' shrill squabbles in the hallways, carpenters or masons hammering and chiseling as they repaired this or rebuilt that. Peace was where you found it, and Lanius found it there.

Along with peace went privacy, which a king always had trouble getting and keeping. Every once in a while, Lanius would bring a maidservant into the archives. The women often giggled at his choice of a trysting place, but no one was likely to interrupt him there. No one ever had, not when he was in there with company.

This morning, he was there by himself. He knew the document he wanted—a traveler's tale—was in there somewhere. He'd read it once, years before. How many thousands of tales and receipts and records of all sorts had he looked at since? He was a most precise man, but he had no idea. He also had no sure idea where in that mad maze of documents and crates and tables and cases lay the parchment he wanted.

Had it been by the far wall? Or had he found it in that dark corner? Even if he had, had he put it back where he got it? He'd tried to convince his children to do that, with indifferent success. Had he had any better luck with himself?

He shrugged and started to laugh. If he couldn't remember where he'd found that parchment written in old-fashioned Avornan, he couldn't very well blame himself for putting it back in the wrong place, could he?

When he sniffed again, he frowned. Somewhere mixed in with the odors of dust and old parchment was the small, sour stink of mouse droppings. Mice and damp were the worst enemies documents had. Who could guess how much history, how much knowledge, had vanished beneath the ever-gnawing front teeth of mice? Maybe they'd gotten to the traveler's tale he needed. He shivered, though the archives were warm enough. If that tale was gone forever, he would have to trust his memory. It was very good, but he didn't think it was good enough.

Here? No, these were tax registers from his father's reign. He didn't remember his father well; King Mergus had died when he was a little boy. What he remembered was how things changed after Mergus died. He'd gone from being everyone's darling to a lousy bastard the instant Mergus' younger brother, Scolopax, put on the crown. Lanius still bristled at the word. It wasn't *his* fault his mother had been his father's seventh wife, no matter what the priests had to say about it. Avornans were allowed only six, no matter what. To get a son, a legitimate son, Mergus broke the rule. But they *had* wed. If that didn't make him legitimate, what did?

Plenty of people had said nothing did. Over the years, the fuss and feathers about that had died down. Some priests had been forced into exile in the Maze—the swamps and marshes not far from the city of Avornis—on account of it, though, and a few were still there. Others preached in small towns in out-of-the-way parts of the kingdom, and would never be welcome in the capital again.

Lanius went on to another case he thought likely. It held the pay records and action reports from a border war against the Thervings just before his dynasty took the throne—somewhere close to three hundred years ago now. The war seemed to have been a draw. Considering how fierce the Thervings could be, that wasn't bad. One King of Thervingia—Lanius couldn't remember which—had had a luckless Avornan general's skull covered in gold leaf and made into a drinking cup.

Lanius suddenly realized he'd wasted half an hour poking through the action reports. They weren't what he wanted, which didn't mean they weren't interesting. He put them back on their shelf, not without a twinge of regret.

Here? No, these were new. The shipwrights who'd built deep-bellied, tall-masted ships like the ones the Chernagor pirates sailed across the sea had sent King Grus reports on their progress. Grus, a sailor himself, had no doubt appreciated the papers. To Lanius, they might have been written in guttural

Thervingian for all the sense they made. *When Grus comes back to the palace, I'll have to ask him about them,* he thought.

He was squandering more time. He muttered to himself. The trouble was, *everything* in the archives interested him. He had to make himself put aside one set of documents to go on to the next. Sometimes—often—he didn't want to.

The sunbeams slipping through those ever-dusty skylights slid across the jumble of the archives. Lanius found himself blinking in mild astonishment. How had it gotten to be late afternoon? Surely he'd gone in just a little while before. . . . But he hadn't. His belly was growling, and all at once he noticed he desperately needed to piss.

Sosia was going to be angry at him. He hadn't intended to spend the whole day in here. He hardly ever intended to. It just . . . happened. And he still had no idea where that miserable traveler's tale was.

Grus, Hirundo, Pterocles, and Otus all solemnly looked at one another on the walls of Anna. Grus peered across the Stura toward the southern bank. It still didn't look any different from the land on this side of the river. But it was. Oh, yes. It was. No King of Avornis had set foot on the far bank of the Stura for a couple of hundred years. The last king who'd tried invading the lands the Menteshe claimed as their own hadn't come back again.

*That could happen to me,* Grus thought. *That* will *happen to me unless Pterocles' magic really works—and I can't find out for sure whether it works till we cross the river and start trying it on thralls.*

"Well, gentlemen, this is going to be an interesting campaigning season." By the way Hirundo said it, he might have been talking about training exercises on the meadows outside the city of Avornis.

"We can do it." That wasn't Grus—it was Otus. The escaped thrall sounded confident. The trouble was, he would also sound confident if the Banished One still lurked somewhere deep inside his mind. He would want to lead the Avornans on so the Menteshe and his dark master could have their way with them. He continued, "This land should be free. It deserves to be free."

"We'll do our best," Grus said. Suddenly, harshly, he waved to the trumpeters who waited nearby. They raised long brass horns to their lips and blared out a command.

River galleys raced across the Stura. Marines leaped out of them and rushed forward, bows at the ready. No more than a few Menteshe riders had trotted back and forth south of the river. The nomads were—or seemed to be—too caught up in their civil war to care much what the Avornans were up to. Grus hoped they would go right on feeling that way. He hoped so, but he didn't count on it.

Barges followed the river galleys. Riders led horses onto the riverbank, then swung aboard them. They joined the perimeter the marines had formed. Most of the cavalrymen were archers, too. Anyone who tried to fight the Menteshe without plenty of archers would end up in trouble.

The royal guards came next. They were lancers, armored head to foot. The Menteshe couldn't hope to stand against them. But then, the Menteshe seldom stood and fought. They were riders almost by instinct. Grus hoped he could pin them down and make them try to hold their ground. If he could, the royal guards would make them pay. If not . . . He refused to think about *if not*.

Instead of thinking about it, he nodded to the general, the wizard, and the man who'd lived most of his life on the far side of the Stura. "Our turn now," he said.

They descended from the wall. Grus' boots scuffed on the gray-brown stone of the stairs. Out through the river gate he and his comrades went, out onto the piers, and aboard the *Pike*, the river galley that would take them over the Stura. The captain raised an eyebrow to Grus. The king waved back, urging the skipper to go ahead at his own pace.

"Cast off!" the captain shouted. The ropes that held the *Pike* to the quay thudded down onto the ship's deck. As Grus had waved to the captain, so the captain waved to the oarmaster. The oarmaster set the stroke with a small drum. The rowers strained on their benches. The oars dug into the water. The *Pike* began to move, slowly at first, then ever swifter. Soon, very soon, she lived up to her name, gliding over the chop with impressive speed and agility. "She's going to beach," Grus said, bracing himself against the coming jolt. His companions, lubbers all, lurched and almost fell when the pike went aground. Grus had all he could do not to laugh at them. "I told you that would happen."

"You didn't say what it meant, Your Majesty." Otus sounded reproachful.

"Well, now you know," Grus said. "The next time I tell you, you'll be ready." *Or maybe you won't. Making a sailor takes time.*

At the skipper's shouted orders, sailors lowered a gangplank from the river galley's side. It thudded down onto the muddy bank. With a courtier's bow, Hirundo waved for Grus to descend first. The king did. He took the last step from the gangplank to the ground very carefully—he didn't want to stumble or, worse, to fall. That would set the whole army babbling about bad omens.

There. He stood on the southern bank of the Stura, and he stood on his own two feet. No one said anything about omens. He knew everybody who could see him was watching, though. "We've started," he called.

Up at the top of the gangplank, Pterocles and Hirundo argued about who should go next. Each wanted the other to have the honor. At last, with a shrug, the wizard came down by Grus. "Just standing here doesn't feel any different," Pterocles murmured. "I wondered if it would."

It felt no different to Grus, either, but the wizard could sense things the king couldn't. Hirundo descended, and then Otus. The ex-thrall still had no special rank, but everyone who did was convinced of his importance. By the look on his face, he too was trying to tell any difference from what he'd known before. He found only one. "Now I'm here as a whole man," he said. "I hope all the thralls get to see this country the way I do."

Attendants led up horses for Grus and Hirundo, mules for Pterocles and Otus. Sailors sprang out of the *Pike* and shoved the river galley back into its proper element. Grus mounted his gelding. He looked back across the Stura toward Anna. The Avornan town seemed very far away. The barges on the river—

some full of men, others with horses, still others carrying wagons loaded with supplies—were less reassuring than he'd thought they would be.

He looked south again. He'd advanced less than half a mile from Anna's walls. Suddenly, as though he'd gone in the other direction, everything in the Menteshe country seemed much farther away than it had.

Several sessions of sifting through the archives hadn't yielded the traveler's tale Lanius wanted. He refused to let himself get angry or worried. If the mice hadn't gotten it, it had to be in there somewhere. Sooner or later, it would turn up. It wasn't anything he needed right this minute.

He had other things on his mind, too. When Grus left the capital, Lanius turned into the real King of Avornis. All the little things Grus worried about while he was here fell into Lanius' lap now. As he had more than once before, Lanius wished Grus were here to take care of those little things. Grus was not only better at dealing with them but also more conscientious about it. Lanius wanted them to go away so he could get on with things he really cared about.

The treasury minister was a lean, hook-nosed, nearsighted man named Euplectes. Unlike Petrosus, his predecessor, he didn't try to cut the funds that supported Lanius. (Petrosus was in the Maze these days, but not for that—he'd married his daughter to Prince Ortalis. Ambition was a worse crime than keeping a king on short commons; he'd surely had Grus' support in that.)

Peering at Lanius and blinking as though to bring him into better focus, Euplectes said, "I really do believe, Your Majesty, that increasing the hearth tax is necessary. War is an expensive business, and we cannot pull silver from the sky."

"If we increase the tax, how much money will we raise?" Lanius asked. "How many townsmen and peasants will try to evade the increase and cost us silver instead? How many nobles will try to take advantage of unrest and rebel? What will that cost?"

Euplectes did some more blinking—maybe from his bad eyesight, maybe from surprise. "I can give you the first of those with no trouble. Knowing the number of hearths in the kingdom and the size of the increase, the calculation is elementary. The other questions do not have such well-defined answers."

"Suppose you go figure out your best guesses to what those answers would be," Lanius said. "When you have them, bring them back to me, and I'll decide whether the extra money is worth the trouble it costs."

"King Grus will not be pleased if the campaign against the Menteshe encounters difficulties due to lack of funds," Euplectes warned.

Lanius nodded. "I understand that. He won't be pleased about an uprising behind his back, either. How much do you think the chances go up after a tax increase?"

"I will . . . do what I can to try to calculate that, but only the gods truly know the future," Euplectes said.

"I understand that. Do your best. You may go," Lanius said. Euplectes went, shaking his head. Lanius wondered if he'd done the right thing. Agreeing to the tax hike would have been simplest. He didn't want to hinder the war against the nomads. But Avornis had seen too many civil wars since the crown came to him. Now the Menteshe were suffering through such strife, and he wanted them to be the only ones.

He hoped to get away to the archives after seeing Euplectes, but no such luck. He'd forgotten a man who'd appealed to him for a pardon after being convicted of murder. He had to go over the documents both sides had sent up from the provinces. He hadn't ridden south with Grus, but now a man's fate lay in his hands.

He studied the evidence and the convicted man's desperate appeal. Reluctantly, the king shook his head. He didn't believe the man's claim that a one-eared man had fled the house where the victim lived just before he went in. Nobody from the village had seen anyone but him. He'd been standing over the body when someone else walked in. He'd quarreled with the victim over a sheep not long before, too.

*Let the sentence be carried out,* Lanius wrote at the bottom of the appeal. He dripped hot wax on the parchment and stamped it with his sealing ring. He often worried about such cases, but felt confident he'd gotten this one right.

A servant took the appeal with his verdict to the royal post. Before long, Avornis would be rid of one murderer. If only getting rid of all the kingdom's troubles were so simple!

Lanius had just started for the archives when he almost bumped into another servant coming around a corner toward him. "Your Majesty!" the man exclaimed. "Where have you been? The queen has been waiting for you to come to lunch for almost an hour now."

"She has?" Lanius said. The servant nodded. Lanius blinked in mild amazement. Was it that time already? Evidently, and past that time, too. He gathered himself. "Well, take me to her."

He never did make it to the archives that day.

King Grus had seen thrall villages from a distance as he looked from Avornis into the lands the Menteshe held. That did nothing, he discovered, to prepare him for the first thrall village he rode into.

He knew it would be bad even before he rode up what passed for the main street. The breeze came from the south, and brought the stink of the place to his nostrils while he was still some distance away. He coughed and wrinkled his nose, which did no good at all. The muscular stench was the sort that clung to whatever it touched. Avornan villages smelled bad. Any place where people lived for a while smelled bad. This . . . this was far beyond smelling bad. Filth and vileness had accumulated here for a long, long time, and no one had cared—or perhaps even noticed.

"I've never known a battlefield that stank like this, not even three days after the fighting was done," Hirundo said.

Grus wasn't sure the stench was that bad. But the thralls lived with it every day of their lives. How anyone could do that without going mad was beyond the king. He turned to Pterocles. "Now we start to see how good our magic is."

"Yes, Your Majesty." The wizard, usually cheerful, sounded somber. "Now we do."

Ordinary peasants—peasants who were ordinary human beings—would either have run away the minute they saw the Avornans coming near or else would have run toward them, welcoming them as liberators after a long, hard occupation.

The thralls did neither. They didn't seem to care one way or the other. The ones who were out in the fields kept right on working there. The ones in the village went on about their business. Only a handful of them bothered to stop and give the Avornans dull, uninterested stares.

Presumably at the Banished One's impulse, thralls had crossed into Avornis a few years before. Otus was one of them. Grus knew something of the squalid life they led. Seeing them on their own home ground, where they'd lived like this for generation after brutish generation, struck him as doubly appalling.

A fly buzzed around his face. Another one lit on his earlobe, still another on the back of his hand. All around him, other Avornans were swearing and swatting. *This is early springtime,* Grus thought. *How bad do the bugs get later in the year?* A few thralls brushed languidly at themselves. They might have been horses switching their tails in a meadow. More of the luckless wretches in the village didn't even bother. Were their hides dead along with their souls?

Grief etched harsh lines in Otus' face. "I lived like this for years," he said. "The only way you could tell me from my swine was that I walked on two legs, and some of my grunts were words. Now I know better." He held out his hands in appeal to Grus. "We have to free these people, Your Majesty. They could be just like me."

"Avornis could use more people just like you," Grus said. *As long as the Banished One isn't looking out through your eyes,* he added, but only to himself. He wished the doubt weren't there, but it was, and it wouldn't go away. He did his best to keep it out of his voice. "We'll see what we can do to free some of the ones here. Pterocles!"

"Yes, Your Majesty?" the wizard said.

"You'll do one, and I'll want one of the other wizards to do one as well," Grus said. "We have to make sure you aren't the only sorcerer with the knack. If you have to free thralls one at a time, you'll take a while to do it, eh?"

"Er—so I would, Your Majesty." Pterocles sounded as though he wasn't sure whether Grus was joking. Grus wasn't sure, either. Pterocles asked, "Shall I start right now?"

"Tomorrow morning will do," the king answered. "We'll

want to make sure we have a strong cordon around this place. We can't have the Menteshe trying to take it back while you're in the middle of a spell."

"They'd have to be crazy to want it back," Hirundo said. "If I were a nomad, I'd say take it and welcome."

"You might. We can't be sure they will," Grus said. So far, less than a day into their push south of the Stura, the Avornans had seen scattered scouts. Grus hoped the Menteshe were still busy murdering one another. He wanted to make his foothold south of the river as firm as he could before the nomads tried to throw him back.

He slept in a pavilion upwind from the thralls' village. Some of the stink from it reached him even so—or maybe that was the more distant stink of a downwind village. Despite the foul odor, he slept well. The first part of the invasion, and maybe the most dangerous, had gone well. He'd got his army over the river. Now he would see what happened next.

When he woke up, he realized he'd been foolish the night before. Crossing wasn't easy, but it wasn't most dangerous, either. Losing a battle, falling into the hands of the Menteshe— that would be dangerous. He might find out what thralldom was like . . . from the inside.

The first wizard Pterocles had chosen to free a thrall with him was a bald, gray-bearded man named Artamus. Both sorcerers bowed to King Grus. "I'll do my best, Your Majesty," Artamus said. "I'd like to see it really done before I try myself, if you don't mind. I think I know how everything's supposed to go, but you always like to watch before you go and do something yourself."

"Seems reasonable," Grus said. Pterocles nodded.

Royal guards brought two thralls to the king's pavilion—a man with a scar on his forehead and a woman who might have been pretty if she weren't so filthy and disheveled, and if her face weren't an uncaring blank mask. "If I have first choice . . ." Pterocles smiled and nodded to the woman. "What's your name, dear?"

"Vasa." By the way she said it, it hardly mattered.

"Pleased to meet you, Vasa." Pterocles began swinging a bit of crystal on the end of a chain. Vasa's hazel eyes followed it as he went back and forth, back and forth. Grus had watched this once before, when the wizard worked the spell on Otus. The king looked around for the ex-thrall. There he was, standing in the shade of an almond tree, watching intently but keeping his distance.

Pterocles waited, watching Vasa's eyes follow the swinging crystal. When he thought the time was right, he murmured, "You are an empty one, Vasa. Your will is not your own. You have always been empty, your will never your own."

"I am an empty one," she echoed, and her voice indeed sounded empty of everything that made ordinary human voices show the character of the speaker. "My will is not my own. I have always been empty, my will never my own." Even parroting that much was more than a thrall could usually manage.

The crystal kept swinging back and forth. Vasa's eyes kept following it. She might have forgotten everything but its sparkling self. As softly as he'd spoken before, Pterocles asked, "Do you want to find your own will, Vasa? Do you want to be filled with your own self?"

"I want to find my own will. I want to be filled with my own self." By the way Vasa sounded, she couldn't have cared less.

"I can lift the shadow from your spirit and give you light. Do you *want* me to lift the shadow from your spirit and give you light?"

"I want you to lift the shadow from my spirit and give me light." No matter what Vasa said, she still seemed dead inside.

"I will do what I can for you, then," Pterocles said.

"Do what you can for me, then," Vasa said. Back when Pterocles freed Otus, the wizard hadn't expected him to respond there. Now Otus leaned forward intently, eyes staring, fists clenched. What was he thinking? Grus would have given a good deal to know, but he didn't presume to do anything to interrupt Pterocles' wizardry.

Still in a low voice, Pterocles began to chant. The Avornan dialect he used was very old, even older than the one priests used in temple services. Grus could make out a word here and there, but no more. The wizard went on swinging his crystal in its unending arc. Rainbows flashed from it. Before long, there

were more of them than could have sprung from the sun alone.
"Ah," Artamus said softly.

Pterocles made a pass and said, "Let them be assembled," in
Avornan close enough to ordinary for Grus to follow. Those
rainbows began to spin around Vasa's head—faster and faster,
closer and closer. Even the thrall's dull eyes lit at the spectacle.
"Let them come together!" Pterocles said, and Grus could follow that, too.

Again, the rainbows obeyed the wizard's will. Instead of
swirling around Vasa's head, they began swirling through it.
Some of them still seemed to shine even inside her head. Grus
wondered if that might be his imagination, but it was what he
thought he saw. He'd seen—or thought he'd seen—the same
with Otus, too.

Vasa said, "Oh!" The simple exclamation of surprise was the
first thing Grus had heard from her that had any feeling in it.
Her eyes opened so wide, the king could see white all around
her irises. The rainbows faded, but Grus fancied he could still
see some of their light shining out from her face.

She bowed low to Pterocles. "Oh," she said again, and,
"Thank. Thank. Thank." She didn't have many words, but she
knew what she wanted to say. When he raised her up, her face
had tears on it.

So did Otus' as he came up from his place under the tree.
"She is free," he whispered. "Like me, she is free. Gods be
praised for this."

Pterocles nodded to him, and to Grus, and to Artamus. To
the other wizard, he said, "You see."

"Yes, I see, or I hope I do," Artamus answered. "Thank you
for letting me watch you. That was a brilliant piece of sorcery."
He also bowed to Pterocles.

"I've done it before. I knew I could do it now," Pterocles
said, and gestured toward the other thrall. "Let's see you match
it. Then we'll know how brilliant it is."

"I'll do my best," Artamus said. He turned to the thrall,
who'd stood there all through Pterocles' spell, as indifferent to
the marvel as he was to everything else in his miserable life.
Artamus asked, "What is your name, fellow?"

"Lybius," the scarred thrall replied.

Artamus had his own bit of crystal on a silver chain. He began to swing it back and forth, as Pterocles had before him. Lybius' eyes followed the sparkling crystal. Artamus waited for a bit, then began, "You are an empty one, Lybius. . . ."

The spell proceeded as it had for Pterocles. Artamus wasn't as smooth as Grus' chief wizard, but he seemed capable enough. He summoned the rainbows into being and brought them into a glowing, spinning circle around Lybius' head and then into and inside it.

And, as Vasa had—and as Otus had before her—Lybius awoke from thralldom into true humanity. He wept. He squeezed Artamus' hand and babbled what little praise he knew how to give. And Grus slowly nodded to himself. He *did* have a weapon someone besides Pterocles could wield.

Lanius was studying a tax register to make sure all the nobles in the coastal provinces had paid everything they were supposed to. Officials here in the capital had a way of forgetting about those distant lands, and the people who lived in them knew it and took advantage of it whenever they could. But they were Avornans, too, and the kingdom needed their silver no less than anyone else's. Lanius might not have wanted to raise taxes, but he did want to collect everything properly owed.

Prince Ortalis stuck his head into the little room where the king worked. "Do you know where Sosia is?" he asked.

"Not right this minute. I've been here for a couple of hours," Lanius answered.

"What are you working on?" Ortalis asked. When Lanius explained, his brother-in-law made a horrible face. "Why on earth are you wasting your time with that sort of nonsense?"

"I don't think it's nonsense," Lanius said. "We need to see that the laws are carried out, and we need to punish people who break them."

"That's work for a secretary, or at most for a minister," Ortalis said. "A king tells people what to do."

"If I don't already know what they're doing, how can what I tell them make any sense?" Lanius asked reasonably. "And secretaries *do* do most of this. But if I don't do some, how can I know whether they're doing what they're supposed to? If a king lets officials do whatever they want, pretty soon they're the ones telling people what to do, and he isn't."

"You're welcome to it." Ortalis went off down the hall shaking his head.

Grus had tried to get his legitimate son to show some interest in governing Avornis. Lanius knew that. He also knew Grus hadn't had much luck. Ortalis didn't, and wouldn't, care. In a way, that made Lanius happy. Ortalis would have been a more dangerous rival if he'd worried about—or even taken any notice of—the way government actually worked.

Ortalis would also have been a more dangerous rival without the streak of cruelty that ran through so much of what he did. Hunting helped keep it down, which was one reason Lanius would go hunting with him despite caring nothing for the chase. Worse things happened when Ortalis didn't hunt than when he did.

Or was that true? His wife, Princess Limosa, had stripes on her back, and Ortalis had put them there although he hunted. Lanius shook his head. Limosa was a perfect match for Ortalis in a way Lanius hadn't thought possible. She liked getting stripes as much as he liked giving them. The mere idea made Lanius queasy.

Had Petrosus known that about his daughter when he dangled her in front of Ortalis? Lanius had no idea, and he wasn't about to write to the Maze to find out. Which was worse? That Petrosus had known about her, and used her . . . peculiarity to attract Ortalis? Or that he hadn't, but was willing to have Ortalis hurt her as long as it gained him advantage in the court?

"Disgusting either way," Lanius muttered. He knew what Petrosus' . . . peculiarity was—power.

But Petrosus hadn't had the chance to indulge his peculiarity. Grus had made sure of that. As soon as Grus found out who Ortalis' new wife was, into the Maze that treasury minister went. On the whole, Lanius approved of that. Grus had power and liked wielding it, but he'd never been as heartless in his pursuit of it as Petrosus was. *A good thing, too,* Lanius thought. *I'd be dead if he were.*

If only Grus had been as stern with Ortalis as he had with Petrosus. But for a long time he'd had a blind spot about his legitimate son. By the time he couldn't ignore what Ortalis was, it was much too late to change him. Lanius wondered whether Ortalis could have changed if Grus had tried harder earlier. The question was easier to ask than to answer.

Lanius went back to the tax register. As far as he could tell, nobody by the coast was trying to cheat the kingdom. That was how things were supposed to work. Ortalis probably would have asked him why he'd gone to all this trouble just to find out everything was normal. *If I hadn't checked, I wouldn't have known.* Lanius imagined himself explaining that to Ortalis. He also imagined Ortalis laughing in his face.

"Too bad," Lanius said out loud. A servant walking down the corridor gave him a curious look. He'd gotten plenty of those. He looked out at the servant. The man kept walking.

*Hurting things is Ortalis' peculiarity. Knowing things is mine.* A white butterfly flitted about in a flower bed outside the window. As soon as Lanius saw it, he recognized it as a cabbage butterfly. Knowing that would never do him any good, but he did know it, and he was glad he did. As for some of the other things he knew . . . Well, you never could tell.

# CHAPTER FOUR

A scout galloped back toward the Avornan army. His horse's flying hooves kicked up dust at every stride. Like the rest of the Avornan scouts, he rode a small, tireless mount of the sort the Menteshe bred. But he wore a surcoat over chainmail, not the boiled leather soaked in melted wax the nomads favored. And he shouted, "Your Majesty! Your Majesty!" in unaccented Avornan.

"Here I am," Grus called, as though the royal standards weren't enough to let the scout find him.

"They're coming, Your Majesty!" the man said, and pointed southward.

"Now it begins," Hirundo said quietly.

Grus shook his head. "It began when we set out from the city of Avornis—or long before that, depending on how you look at things." He gave his attention back to the scout. "How many of them are there, and how soon will they hit us?"

"Enough to cause trouble," the scout answered—not a precise answer, but one that told the king what he needed to know. The man went on, "You should see their plume of dust in a little while." He patted the side of his horse's neck. The beast was lathered and blowing hard. "I almost killed Blaze here getting to you quick as I could."

"I'm glad you did, and I won't forget it," Grus said. "You've given us the time we need to shake out our battle line. Hirundo, if you'll do the honors . . ."

"Be glad to, Your Majesty," the general replied. He shouted commands to the trumpeters. They raised their horns to their mouths and blared out martial music. Not quite as smoothly as Grus would have liked, the army began to move from column into line of battle.

"Put a good screen of horse archers in front of the heavy cavalry," Grus said. "We don't want the Menteshe to find out we've got the lancers along till they can't get away from them."

Hirundo sent him an amused look. "I thought you asked me to do the honors." In spite of the teasing—which embarrassed Grus—he followed the king's orders.

"You'll want me here with you, Your Majesty?" Pterocles asked.

"Oh, yes." Grus nodded. "We're not on our home ground anymore. This is country where the Banished One has had his own way for a long time. I don't know whether the Menteshe wizards can do anything special here. If they try, though, you're our best hope to stop them."

"You may put too much confidence in me," Pterocles said. "I know these wizards can do one thing—if we lose, if they capture us, they can make us into thralls."

"Yes," Grus said tightly. "If we lose, they won't capture me." He'd made up his mind about that.

Pterocles said, "What I can do, I will do. You have my word."

"Good." Grus made sure his sword was loose in its sheath. The gray in his beard reminded him he wasn't a young man anymore. He'd never been especially eager to trade sword strokes with his foes. He could do it when he had to, and he'd always done it well enough, but it wasn't his notion of sport, the way it was for more than a few men. The older he got, the less enthusiastic a warrior he made, too.

After a while, more horns cried out, this time in warning. Men up ahead of Grus pointed toward the south. Peering through the dust his own soldiers had kicked up, he spied the unmistakable plume that meant another army was on the way.

Soon the Menteshe became visible through their cloud of dust. They were marvelous horsemen. They started riding as soon as they could stay in the saddle, and stayed in the saddle most of their lives. He wished his own cavalry could match them. That the Avornans couldn't was part of what made the nomads so dangerous.

The Menteshe started shooting as soon as they came into range, or even a little before. Avornan scouts sent arrows back. Men on both sides pitched from the saddle; horses fell to the ground. The scouts galloped back toward the main body of soldiers. Whooping, the Menteshe pursued them.

That was exactly what Grus and Hirundo wanted them to do. The king began to wonder just how much he wanted it when an arrow hissed past his ear. If the nomads could cause chaos in his army . . .

They thought they could. Like any soldiers worth their hire, the Menteshe were arrogant. Some of them, surely, had fought Avornans north of the Stura. They must have known their foes weren't cowards. But they must also have taken them for fools or madmen—how many years had it been since Avornans came to fight on this side of the river? Why wouldn't they break up and flee when peppered with arrows?

*We'll show them why,* Grus thought. He waved to Hirundo, who waved to the trumpeters. One of them fell silent in mid-call, choking on his own blood when an arrow pierced his throat. But the rest roared out the command the army had been waiting for. The archers screening the heavy horse drew aside to left and right. Grus and Hirundo both raised their right hands. They both dropped them at the same time. When they did, the horns cried out a new command. The lancers lowered their spears and charged.

Sunlight struck sparks from spearheads as they swung down to horizontal. Hunks of hard earth flew up from under horses' hooves when the chargers thundered ahead. They needed perhaps fifty yards to build up full momentum. They had all the space they needed, and a little more besides.

More than a little more would have been too much. If the Menteshe had had room to turn and flee, they would have done it. They saw nothing shameful in flight, and were past masters at shooting back over their shoulders as they fled. Here, though, they were storming forward themselves.

Grus heard their howls of dismay even above the drumroll of hoofbeats from his heavy horse. That was sweet music in his ears. Beside him, Hirundo's grin was like that of a fox spying an unguarded chicken coop. "By Olor's beard, let's see how they like *that*," the general said.

The Menteshe liked it not at all. They were at their best darting and stinging like wasps. In close combat against bigger men in stouter armor on heavier horses, they were like wasps smashed against a stone. Lances pierced them and lifted them out of the saddle. The Avornans' big warhorses overbore their plains ponies and sent them crashing to earth. Their slashing sabers would not bite on shields or chainmail. Some of their arrows struck home, but more glanced from helms and other ironwork. Down they went in windrows, the heart suddenly ripped from their battle line.

Those who could did flee then, as fast as their horses would carry them. And they did shoot back over their shoulders, and dropped several Avornans who pressed after them too hard. But Grus soon reined in the pursuit. He'd done what he wanted to do in the first encounter—he'd shown the Menteshe that fighting on their own side of the Stura didn't guarantee victory.

"Very neat," he said to Hirundo.

"Could have been worse," the general agreed. "That charge took them by surprise. Doing it once was easy. Twice won't be."

"Yes, that occurred to me, too," Grus said. "But we've got a victory to start with, and that was what we needed. We'll worry about everything else later."

Out on the battlefield, Avornan soldiers plundered the dead—and made sure those they plundered really were dead. Healers and wizards were doing what they could for wounded Avornans. Seeing the wizards at work made Grus look to Pterocles. The sorcerer said, "You *must* have caught the nomads napping with that charge, Your Majesty. They didn't have the chance to try any fancy spells against us."

"I'm not sorry," Grus said. By Pterocles' smile, neither was he. The king snapped his fingers and turned back to Hirundo. "Send out some men to tell our soldiers not to kill every single Menteshe they come across. We'll want to ask questions, and a man with a new mouth doesn't talk so well." He drew a finger across his throat to show what he meant.

"I'll see to it, Your Majesty," Hirundo promised.

"Good," Grus said. "If we can take one of their wizards alive, that will be better yet."

Hirundo looked dubious. "Will it? I think I'd rather find a scorpion in my boot."

"You can step on a scorpion," Grus said. "Our wizards can handle the Menteshe. Or if they can't, we had no business crossing the Stura in the first place."

Hirundo nodded. If he hadn't, Grus would have been more dangerous to him than either a scorpion or a Menteshe wizard. The king looked south. No Avornan army had come anywhere near Yozgat for four hundred years. No Avornan king had touched the Scepter of Mercy for that long or a little longer. What would taking it in his hands be like? He had no idea. Maybe Lanius did. Slowly, Grus shook his head. He didn't believe it, no matter how learned Lanius was. The other king would have read about what wielding the Scepter of Mercy was like, but Grus had the feeling that the difference between reading about it and doing it was as vast as the difference between reading about making love and doing that.

For some things, words were enough. Others required real experience. Grus craved real experience here.

Pouncer stared from Lanius to Collurio. They'd taken the moncat to an unfamiliar room. It didn't care. It yawned, exposing formidable fangs. Lanius started to laugh. "Nice to know we impress the miserable creature, isn't it?"

"Oh, yes," the animal trainer said. "Dogs are easier, no doubt about it. Dogs are eager to please. Cats please themselves. I see this is no ordinary cat, but it's not so very different, eh?"

"No. There are times I wish it were, but it isn't. You're right about that," Lanius said. "But I saw you could train ordinary cats, and I've already trained Pouncer a little."

"It can be done, yes," Collurio said. "It takes longer, though, and it's not so easy. It's not so reliable. A cat does what it wants, not what you want."

"Really? I'd never noticed that," Lanius said.

Collurio gave him an odd look. Then, realizing the king was joking, the trainer smiled. He said, "You can get cats to do what you want. You just have to make sure it's what they want, too. For instance . . ."

Standing there beside him on a sturdy base was a pole as thick as his arm and about as tall as he was. He showed Pouncer a scrap of meat, then ostentatiously put it on the pole's flat top. As the moncat swarmed up the pole, claws digging into the wood, Collurio loudly clapped his hands. Pouncer flinched, but went on climbing. The beast perched at the top of the pole to eat its treat.

Collurio waited till it had finished, then lifted it and set it on the floor again. He produced another bit of meat and put it on top of the pole. As Pouncer climbed, Collurio clapped his hands once more.

"That didn't scare him as much as the first time," Lanius said.

"No, it didn't," Collurio agreed as Pouncer captured the prize and gobbled it up. "After we do it a few more times, it won't frighten him at all. And pretty soon he'll get the idea that when I clap my hands he's supposed to go up the pole, because something good will be waiting for him when he does."

"And he'll go on up even if it's not," Lanius said.

"Yes, he will," the animal trainer said. "You don't want to make him do that too often, though, or he'll get confused. Keep things as simple as you can with beasts." He chuckled. "Come to that, keep things as simple as you can with people, too."

Lanius started to say something pleasant and nearly meaningless. Then he stopped and thought about it for a little while. He set a hand on Collurio's shoulder. "Do you know, that's some of the best advice I ever heard."

"Thank you, Your Majesty." This time, Collurio's chuckle sounded distinctly wry. "It's easy to say. Lots of things are easy to say. Doing it . . . Well, if doing it were easier, then everybody would, don't you think?"

"I'm sure of it," Lanius replied. "And speaking of things that are easy to say but not so easy to do, I haven't found what I was looking for in the archives yet, either."

"I'm sure you will," Collurio said. Lanius wished he were sure he would. The trainer went on, "Meanwhile, we'll do as much as we can without it, that's all."

He didn't fuss. He didn't complain. Lanius admired his attitude. Then the king realized Collurio was getting paid—and getting the prestige of working in the palace—regardless of whether that misplaced document ever turned up. That being so, why should he fuss or complain? Lanius kept things simple, though, by pretending not to notice that. He said, "Very good. Do you want to give Pouncer some more work on this trick?"

"Yes, we can do it a few more times," Collurio answered. "After that, he'll start to fill up. Then he won't care about the signals we give him. You don't want that to happen when you're training an animal, either."

Pouncer went up the pole to get some scraps of meat. He went once on the strength of Collurio's handclap alone. And he climbed it once all by himself, just to see if he could find a treat at the top. Lanius laughed at that. He scratched the moncat behind the ears. "Hello, there. You're a fuzzy optimist, aren't you?" Pouncer gave back a rusty purr.

"He *is* an optimist," Collurio said. "He's a clever optimist, too—you were right about that. He learns very fast. He's quicker to see things and understand things than a dog is, no doubt about it."

"I should hope so." Lanius scratched Pouncer again, or tried to—the moncat snapped at him. The king wasn't especially surprised. He didn't push his luck. Instead, he said, "He's also much more charming than a dog. You can see that for yourself."

"Charming." Collurio eyed the moncat, which remained perched on top of the pole. Pouncer stared right back, as though to say, *Well? Come on, cough up the meat. You think I climbed all the way up here for the fun of it?* Collurio wagged a finger at the beast. "You get treats when we say you get them, not whenever you want them. That's one more thing you have to learn."

Moncats had hands, too. Pouncer pointed back with a clawed forefinger. Even the beast's severe expression mimicked the trainer's. Lanius snorted. "This is a ridiculous creature," he said.

"Yes, Your Majesty." But Collurio kept on eyeing Pouncer. "He knows what he's doing, though, or some of it. He . . . really is quicker than a dog, isn't he?" He acted as though he expected the moncat to answer for itself.

"I've always thought so," Lanius answered. "But you're right that he's more difficult than a dog, too. Moncats . . . are what they are. You can't make them into something they're not."

"Maybe we can persuade this one that he wants to go where we want to take him," Collurio said.

Lanius nodded. "That's what I'm hoping for."

In all his years, in all he'd done, Grus hadn't found a pleasure finer than watching freed thralls begin to discover they were full-fledged human beings after all. Watching children grow up was the only thing he'd ever known that even came close. But children found out what they were, grew into what they were, much more gradually. Thralls were kept artificially childlike— artificially beastlike, really—their whole lives long. Seeing them blossom once taken from the dark shadows of the sorcery that had unnaturally trapped them was like seeing children spring to adulthood all at once.

Seeing them throw off thralldom also reassured the king that Pterocles and the other wizards really did know what they were doing. He'd had faith in Pterocles, much less in the others, who hadn't been tested. Now he'd seen that they could do what Pterocles had said they could. That was a relief.

Watching Otus with the newly reawakened thralls wasn't the least fascinating thing Grus had ever run across, either. He might have been big brother or kindly uncle to them. He knew the road they were on because he'd walked it himself. He was quick to give them a word when they needed one but didn't know what it was, and to show them such things as washing themselves and the filthy rags they wore.

"So many of them have lived this way for so long," he told Grus one evening. "So many of them lived out their whole lives without ever knowing there could be anything better. That's *wrong,* Your Majesty!" He wasn't a very big man or a very tough-looking one, but fury blazed from his eyes—eyes that had been as dull as a cow's till Pterocles lifted the spell of thralldom from them.

"We're doing what we can," Grus answered, munching on flatbread, hard cheese, and onions—campaign food. "Till we had this magic, there wasn't much we could do. If we came south of the Stura without it, we would have ended up as thralls ourselves. More than one Avornan army did. That's why we stopped trying to fight the Menteshe down here."

"I understand your reasons," Otus said. "I can't tell you I like them."

Not many of Grus' subjects would have spoken so freely. Maybe Otus didn't realize how much deference he owed a king. Or maybe he would have behaved this way even if he'd grown up in Avornis and never had his spirit darkened.

He paused to gnaw off a bite of chewy flatbread. "Even the food tastes better now!" he exclaimed. "Being a thrall stood between me and all my senses."

"Maybe this is just better than what you ate while you were a thrall," Grus suggested.

"Oh, that, too," Otus said. "But the days seem brighter. Birdcalls have music in them—they're not just noise. I used to ignore stinks. Now I can't. And when I'm with a woman . . . That's better, too." He sighed. "If we find *my* woman down here . . ."

He had a lady friend back in the palace. The freedom to be a man and not a thrall could make life more complicated, too. Grus didn't tell him so. He'd have to find that out for himself. The king did ask, "Where is the village you came from? If we can, we'll free it."

Otus jumped to his feet so he could bow very low. "You are kinder to me than I deserve, Your Majesty! My village is west of here. I know now that it lies toward the sea. When I was the way I was before, I did not even know there was such a thing as the sea."

"I said we'd free it if we could, remember," Grus warned. "I don't know that we'll have soldiers going over there any time real soon." He doubted the Avornans would—not unless the Menteshe attacked from that direction and made him respond. But he didn't have the heart to crush Otus' hopes.

The ex-thrall nodded. "I understand that, too, Your Majesty. You will do what you need to do before you do what you want to do, yes?"

"Yes," Grus said, glad Otus had taken it so well.

When they set out again the next morning, Grus noticed that the Argolid Mountains to the south reared higher in the sky than they had when he'd first crossed the Stura. The jagged peaks showed more brown and green and less purple haze of distance than they had, too. Long ago, Avornan rule had run almost to their foothills. That was before the Menteshe spilled through the passes and swallowed a third of the kingdom.

Somewhere in those mountains, the Banished One was supposed to have his abode. Did he dwell in the mountains because they were closer to the heavens? Or was that where he'd fallen to earth, somehow leaving him unable to go anywhere else? Maybe the Menteshe knew. No Avornan did.

Before Grus' army had gone very far, it came upon a battlefield where the nomads had fought one another a year or two before. The bones of men and horses lay bleaching in the sun. Not much more than bones remained. As always happened, the winners—whichever side had won—had plundered the bodies of the fallen. Grus spied one skull with an arrow still sticking up from it. No need to wonder how that man had died.

Hirundo said, "The more they kill each other, the fewer left to fight us."

"That thought had crossed my mind, yes," Grus said.

Toward evening, scouts brought a lone Menteshe to the king. "He came up to us with a flag of truce, Your Majesty," one of them said. "He claims he's an ambassador from Prince Sanjar."

"Does he?" Grus eyed the nomad—a swarthy, bearded, hook-nosed man in a leather jacket, breeches, and boots. The Avornan scouts now held whatever weapons he'd carried, most likely one of the deadly Menteshe bows and a saber and dagger for close work. "Go on," Grus told him. "I'm listening."

"I am Qizil son of Qilich, Your Majesty," the Menteshe said in gutturally accented Avornan. "You will know, of course, that Prince Sanjar is the rightful heir and successor to his mighty father, Prince Ulash."

"I've heard that said, yes," Grus replied. Prince Korkut, of course, made exactly the same claim. Korkut was older, Sanjar the son of Ulash's favorite concubine. Neither could bend the knee to the other now, not without putting his own head on the block right afterwards.

"It is the truth," Qizil declared. "Prince Sanjar wishes to join you to help cast out the vile usurper. He will reward you well for your services."

Till Sanjar and Korkut went to war with each other, no Avornan had ever heard any Menteshe talk like that. The nomads always wanted to take, never to give. Now, voice studiously neutral, Grus said, "He will?" Qizil nodded emphatically. The king asked, "What will he give?"

Qizil son of Qilich swept out his arms in a grand, even theatrical, gesture. "Why, whatever your heart desires. Gold? It is yours. Herds of cattle and sheep out to the horizon? They are yours. Fine horses? We have a great plenty. Pretty women? Take them as well, and use them as you would." In a few words, he outlined the nomads' notion of the good life.

"Let him give me the Scepter of Mercy with his own hands," Grus said. "Then I will believe he is serious, not just telling lies to help himself."

Qizil's eyes went very wide. Whatever he'd expected the King of Avornis to ask for, that caught him by surprise. "Your Majesty is joking," he blurted.

"I have never been more serious in my life." Grus meant every word of that. If he could win the Scepter of Mercy by allying himself with Sanjar, he would do it. If he could win it by allying with Korkut, he would do that, too. And if winning it meant standing aloof from both of them, he would do that.

"It is impossible," Qizil said.

Grus folded his arms across his chest. "Then we have no more to say to each other, do we? The scouts will take you out beyond our lines. My compliments to your master, but there will be no alliance."

"You do not understand," Qizil said urgently. "The prince cannot give you what he does not have. The Scepter of Mercy is in Yozgat, and Korkut holds it."

The king had known where the Scepter was, of course. Yozgat still lay far to the south. He hadn't been sure which unloving half brother controlled what had been Ulash's capital. Some of the prisoners he'd taken claimed one did, some the other. But if Sanjar's envoy admitted Korkut held it . . .

"If you aid my master, we can speak of this again after he has triumphed," Qizil suggested.

"No," Grus said. "This is a price he would have to pay in advance. Once he'd won the war, he would surely try to do me out of it."

Qizil made elaborate promises that Sanjar was the very image of honesty. The more he promised, the less Grus believed him. "I'm sorry," the king said at last, which seemed more polite than saying he was bored. "I don't think we have anything to talk about. As I told you, you have a safe-conduct till you're outside of our lines. If things change farther south, maybe Prince Sanjar will talk to me again."

"If things change farther south, the prince will not need to talk to you," Qizil said venomously. "He will drive you from this country like the dog you are."

That sounded more like the Menteshe Grus was familiar with. "I love you, too," he said, and had the small satisfaction of startling Sanjar's emissary again. Qizil sprang up onto his pony's back. He rode away at such a pace, the Avornan scouts had a hard time staying with him. He was so angry, he might have forgotten his weapons.

"Too bad," Hirundo remarked. "That would have made things a lot easier."

"Well, so it would," Grus said. "I had to try. All right—he told me no. Now we go on the way we would have before."

"So Korkut holds Yozgat," Hirundo said musingly. "If he sends someone to you to ask for help against Sanjar . . ."

"Yes, that could be interesting," Grus agreed. "Both of them have sent envoys up to the city of Avornis, so I suppose it could happen. I'll know the right thing to ask if it does, anyhow."

"What will you do if Korkut says he'll send you the Scepter?" Hirundo asked.

*Faint,* was what crossed Grus' mind. "The first thing I'd do is make sure he sent me the real Scepter of Mercy and not a clever counterfeit," he said, and Hirundo nodded. The king went on, "If it was the real Scepter . . . If it was, I do believe I'd take it and go back to Avornis. It means more to me—and to the kingdom—than anything else down here."

"Even freeing the thralls?" Hirundo asked slyly.

Grus looked around. When he didn't see Otus, he nodded. "Even that. If we have the Scepter of Mercy, we can worry about everything else later." *I think we can. I hope we can. How do I know for sure, when no King of Avornis has tried to wield it for all these years?* He blinked when he realized he didn't *know.* What he had to go on was Lanius' certainty. No matter how fine a scholar the other king had proved himself, was that really enough? All at once, Grus wondered.

With a laugh, Hirundo said, "The Banished One wouldn't be very happy if Korkut sent you the Scepter to win his civil war."

He could speak lightly of the Banished One. The exiled god had never appeared in his dreams. He didn't know—literally didn't know—how lucky he was. Grus, who did, said only, "No, he wouldn't." His doubts left him. The Banished One wouldn't worry about losing the Scepter of Mercy if it weren't a weighty weapon against him.

Hirundo stared south. The dust Qizil and the Avornan scouts had kicked up as they rode away still hung in the air. "For now, I guess you're right—the only thing we can do is go on," the general said.

"There's nothing else to do," Grus said.

Lanius had a reputation as a man interested in everything. The reputation held a lot of truth, as he knew better than anyone else. It also came in handy in some unexpected ways. He knew that better than anyone else, too.

Had, say, King Grus poked his nose into one of the little rooms in the palace that held bed linens, any servant who came down the corridor and saw him would have been astonished. Gossip about Grus' odd behavior would have flashed from one end of the palace to the other before an hour went by.

But it wasn't odd for Lanius to go into a room like that. He poked around in the kitchens, and in the archives, and anywhere else that suited his fancy. A servant who saw him opening one of those doors would just shrug and go about his business. It had happened before, plenty of times.

No servants were coming down the corridor now. That did make things simpler. Lanius opened the door to the storeroom, and quietly closed it behind him. He smiled to smell the spicy scent of the cedar shelves on which the linens rested. The cedar was said to help hold moths at bay.

And he smelled another sweet scent—a woman's perfume.

"Why, hello, Your Majesty," Oissa said, as though they'd met there by chance.

"Hello, sweetheart," Lanius said, and took her in his arms. The serving girl was short and round, with curly, light brown hair, big gray eyes, cheeks always rosy even though she didn't seem to use rouge, and a dark beauty mark by the side of her mouth. She tilted her face up for a kiss. Lanius was glad to oblige.

They met when and where they could. The floor of the store-room wasn't the best place for such things, but it was better than a few they'd tried. Lanius didn't think Oissa was in love with him. He didn't think he was in love with her, either. He hadn't made that mistake since his first affair with a maidser-vant. He enjoyed what they did together even so. He tried his best to make sure Oissa did, too; he'd always thought it was better when his partner also took pleasure.

Afterwards, they both dressed quickly. "These to remember the day," Lanius said, and gave her a pair of gold hoops to wear in her ears.

"Thank you, Your Majesty," she said. "You didn't have to do that, though."

"I didn't do it because I had to. I did it because I wanted to," Lanius answered. He thought she meant what she'd said. She wasn't greedy or pushy. He didn't care for people who were. Nothing would make him break off a liaison faster than some-one pushing him for presents.

He coughed once or twice. No, that wasn't quite true. Sosia finding out about an affair could make him break it off in noth-ing flat. He was reasonably, or even more than reasonably, dis-creet, and he tried to pick partners who wouldn't blab. It didn't always work. He didn't like remembering what happened when it didn't.

This dalliance wasn't going anywhere. Even if his wife didn't learn of it, Oissa would find someone she wanted to marry, or else Lanius would tire of her. But it was pleasant. He enjoyed the variety. What point to being a king if he couldn't enjoy himself once in a while?

After a last kiss, he slipped out of the little room. No ser-vants were walking along the corridor. Lanius nodded to him-self. No scandal this time—not even a raised eyebrow.

Had things been different, Grus might have gotten furious at him for being unfaithful to his daughter. But Grus had been known to enjoy himself every once in a while even before he became a king; Arch-Hallow Anser was living proof of that. And he hadn't stopped after he wore a crown. He was hardly one to tell Lanius what to do and what not to.

Lanius hoped everything down in the south was still going well. Grus' letters were encouraging, but they took longer to come back to the city of Avornis than Lanius would have liked. He knew the Avornans were over the Stura and disenchanting thralls. That they'd done so much was reason enough to celebrate. But Lanius wanted them to push on to Yozgat. Like Grus, he cared more about the Scepter of Mercy than anything else.

He could have known more, of course, if he'd campaigned with Grus. He shook his head at the mere idea. The one battlefield he'd seen was plenty to persuade him he never wanted to see another. Listening to vultures and ravens and carrion crows quarreling over corpses, watching them peck at dead men's eyes and tongues and other dainties, smelling the outhouse and butcher's-shop reek, hearing dying men groan and wounded men shriek . . . No, once was enough for a lifetime.

He supposed he ought to be grateful to Grus for going on campaign. The other king had already usurped half—more than half—the throne. He couldn't want anything else. If Lanius had had to send out generals to do his fighting for him, he would always have been as afraid of great victories as of great defeats. A great victory was liable to make a general think he deserved a higher station. Since only one higher station was available, that wouldn't have been good for Lanius. He didn't think many usurpers would have worked out the arrangement Grus had.

While he mused on bad usurpers and worse ones, his feet, almost by themselves, took him to the archives. He went inside eagerly enough. The smile on his face had only so much to do with the hope of finding that missing traveler's tale. As he had with other women before her, he'd brought Oissa here once or twice. It was quiet; it was peaceful; they were unlikely to be disturbed—and they hadn't been, at least not by anyone banging on the door. It was also dusty, here, though, and sneezing at the wrong time had put him off his stride and made Oissa laugh, which put her off hers.

"Business," Lanius reminded himself. The smile didn't want to go away, though. He let it stay. Why not?

Even smiling, he did want to look for that missing tale. What annoyed him most was that he usually had a good memory for where he'd put things. Not this time, though. Most of his pride revolved around his wits. When they let him down, he felt he'd failed in some fundamental fashion. It rarely happened, and was all the more troubling because of that.

"It has to be here," he said. Although true, that didn't help much. No one knew better than he how vast—and how disorganized—the archives were.

He pawed through crates and barrels and plucked documents off shelves. He had to look at each parchment or sheet of paper separately, because things got stored all higgledy-piggledy. A paper from his reign could lie next to or on top of a parchment centuries old. Before long, his smile faded. If he wasn't lucky, he'd be here forever, or half an hour longer.

That less than delightful thought had hardly crossed his mind before he let out a shout of triumph that came echoing back from the ceiling. There it was! He swore under his breath. That crate looked familiar—now. Not so long before, he'd moved it to get at some other documents, and forgotten he'd done it.

Lanius started to take the traveler's tale to a secretary who could make a fair copy. He hadn't gotten to the doorway before he stopped and shook his head. The fewer people who knew anything about what he had in mind, the better. *I'll make the fair copy myself,* he decided. Now he found himself nodding. Yes, that would be better, no doubt about it.

Before long, he would put carpenters and masons to work. But they wouldn't know why they were doing what they were doing. And what they didn't know, nobody could find out from them . . . not even the Banished One.

# CHAPTER FIVE

Grus never got tired of watching Avornan wizards free thralls from the dark mists that had held them all their lives. Part of that was pride at the magic Pterocles had created that he and and other wizards were using. And part of it was simply that the spell of liberation was one of the most beautiful things he'd ever seen. The rainbows arising from the swinging crystal and then spinning around and into a thrall's head were wonderful enough by themselves. The expression on each thrall's face when the mists dissolved, though—that was even better.

"How does it feel to be a mother?" the king asked Pterocles after another successful sorcery.

The wizard frowned. "A mother, Your Majesty?"

"You're giving birth to people, aren't you?" Grus said. "I didn't think a man could. I should be jealous."

"Giving birth to people . . ." Pterocles savored the words. A slow smile spread over his face. "I like that."

"Good. You ought to. How well this would work was my biggest worry when we crossed the Stura," Grus said. "It's gone better than I dared hope. It's gone better than anyone dared hope, I think. What do you suppose the Banished One is thinking right now?"

"I don't know. Please don't ask me to try to find out, either." Pterocles sounded even more earnest than usual. "For me to get inside his mind would be like one of Lanius' moncats trying to understand my sorcery here. The Banished One . . . is what he is. Don't expect a mere mortal to understand him."

"All right." Grus had hoped the wizard might be able to do just that. But he had no trouble seeing Pterocles' point. "Let me ask it in a different way, then—how happy do you think he is?"

"How happy would you have been if the Menteshe had started turning peasants *into* thralls the last time they invaded Avornis?" Pterocles asked in turn.

That had been one of Grus' worst fears. One reason he'd counterattacked so hard and so quickly was to make sure the nomads' wizards didn't get settled enough to do anything of the sort. He muttered to himself. "How will he try to stop us?" he asked.

Now Pterocles just looked at him. "I don't have the faintest idea, Your Majesty. But I expect we'll find out. Don't you?"

Grus didn't answer. That wasn't because he felt any doubts—he didn't. On the contrary; he was so sure Pterocles was right that he didn't think the question needed answering.

He had expected the Banished One to bend every bit of his power toward making sure the Menteshe broke off their civil war and turned all their ferocity against the advancing Avornans. That didn't seem to be happening . . . or maybe the Banished One's puppets had escaped the control of their puppet master for the time being. Small raiding bands struck at Grus' army—struck and, in classic nomad fashion, galloped away again before Grus' less mobile forces could hit back. But those were pinpricks, fleabites. Menteshe prisoners affirmed that the nomads were still using most of their energy to hammer away at one another.

A dispatch rider down from the north let Grus take his mind off the Menteshe for a little while. Among the letters the man brought was a long one from King Lanius. Lanius was conscientious about keeping Grus up to date on what he did in the capital. He probably feared Grus would oust him if he didn't tell him what he was up to—and he might have been right.

That afternoon, Grus frowned to see that Lanius hadn't approved a tax hike. There would probably be a letter—an angry letter—from the treasury minister in this batch, too. *I'll look for it later,* Grus thought, and read on. He ended up disap-

pointed. That wasn't because Lanius didn't justify his reasons
for opposing the increase. He did, in great detail. They even
made a good deal of sense. But the bulk of the letter was an
even more detailed account of how the other king was training
a moncat. If Lanius wanted a hobby, Grus didn't mind. If he
wanted to bore people with it . . . That was a different story.

The king went through the leather dispatch case. He was looking for the inevitable letter from Euplectes, but found one from
the city of Sestus first. Unlike Lanius', it was short and to the
point. Alauda could scarcely write. She scratched out three or
four lines to let him know she and her son, Nivalis, were both
well. Grus smiled—he was glad to have the news. Nivalis was
his son, too, a bastard he'd sired on Alauda a few years before,
while he was driving the Menteshe out of the southern provinces.

He did find the treasury minister's letter then. Reading it
came as something of a relief. Euplectes was indignant about
Lanius' stubbornness, but he wasn't furious. Even if he were
furious, it would only have been a bureaucratic kind of anger.
Compared to the rage of a wife who'd just found out her husband was unfaithful—again—fusses and fumings over tax
rates were easy enough to put up with.

Grus snapped his fingers. Calling the dispatch rider, he
asked, "How was the trip down from the Stura?"

"Not bad, Your Majesty," the fellow answered. "No, not bad
at all, matter of fact. There was one time when I thought a couple of those nomad bastards might take after me, but they spotted a troop of our horsemen and sheered off right smart. Aside
from that, I didn't see a one of 'em all the way down. Didn't
miss 'em, neither."

"I believe you," Grus said. "All right. Thanks. That's good
news."

"You think you can keep the line open all the way down to
this Yozgat place?" the rider asked.

"I don't know," Grus said—that was the question, all right.
"But I aim to try."

Sosia looked at Lanius as though he'd lost his mind. "You're
going to build this . . . this thing off in the country somewhere,
and you're going to spend a lot of your time there? *You?*"

Maybe she thought she was losing *her* mind instead. She certainly didn't seem to believe her ears.

But the King of Avornis only nodded. "That's right."

"Why?" his wife demanded. "Sweet Quelea's mercy, why? If Anser told me that, I'd understand. He'd want it for a hunting villa. Ortalis, too. But *you*?" Again, disbelief filled her voice. "You don't care about hunting. We both know that. You don't care about anything except the archives and. . . ." Her gaze sharpened. Sudden suspicion filled her eyes. "If you think you can put some pretty little thing in this place and go have your fun with her whenever you please, you'd better think again."

"No, no, no." Lanius protested louder than he might have, for that had occurred to him. A little reluctantly, he threw the idea in the dustbin. "Come out whenever you please. Don't tell me you're on the way ahead of time. If you find me with a woman there, do whatever you want. I'll deserve it, and I won't say a word. By the gods, Sosia, I won't. That's not why I'm doing this."

She studied him. "Maybe," she said at last. "You don't usually come right out and lie to me. When you want to hide something, you usually just don't say anything about it at all."

"Well, then," he said, trying not to show how disconcerted he was. She knew him pretty well, all right. He'd spent the past few months not saying anything at all about Oissa, whom Sosia saw several times a day. Seeing her and noticing her were two different things, though.

"Maybe," the queen repeated. "But if you don't want to put a bedwarmer in it, why *do* you want to build something out in the country?"

Lanius didn't say anything about that at all.

Sosia glared. "Next thing you know, you'll tell me it's got to do with the war against the Banished One, and you'll expect me to believe that."

Of itself, Lanius' hand twisted in the gesture that was supposed to keep the Banished One from paying any attention to what was going on. He didn't really believe the gesture did any good, but it couldn't hurt. "Don't talk about such things," he told her. "Just—*don't*. I don't know how much danger it might cause. It might not cause any. On the other hand, it might cause more than you can imagine." He walked over to her and set his hands on her shoulders. "I mean it."

She didn't shake him off. "You do," she agreed wonderingly.

"Yes, I do," he answered, "and I wish I didn't have to tell you even that much." He knew it was his own fault that he did. He'd given her reason to doubt he was faithful. He *wasn't* as faithful as he might have been (he thought of Oissa again, and of the smell of cedar). But this didn't have anything to do with that, and he had to convince her it didn't.

"All right." Sosia still didn't shake him off. Instead, she stepped forward and gave him a quick hug. Then she said, "I'm still going to come out and check on you every so often, and I *won't* tell you when."

"Fine," Lanius said. *Keep thinking it might be a love nest. Then you won't think about what else it might be.* He felt ashamed of himself. If he couldn't tell things to Sosia, to whom could he?

No sooner had he asked himself the question than he found the answer. It wasn't *no one,* either, as he'd thought it would be. He could talk to Grus, to Pterocles, even to Collurio. They all shared one thing—they'd drawn the Banished One's special notice. Lanius would rather have done without the honor, but the choice didn't seem to be his.

Sosia, on the other hand, knew nothing of such nighttime visits. For her, the world was a simpler, safer place. The king wanted to keep it that way for her if he could.

Three days later, he rode out into the country with Collurio, looking for the right place to build. The trainer said, "You're taking a chance, you know."

"Oh, yes." Lanius nodded. "If things go wrong, though, we can start over. We have the time to do this, and we have the time to do it properly. Things aren't moving very fast south of the Stura."

"Should they be?" Collurio asked.

"I can't tell you that. I'm not a general. I never wanted to be a general. There are some things I'm good at, but that isn't one of them," Lanius answered. "But if this whole business were easy, some other King of Avornis would have done it three hundred years ago. You know what we're up against."

The day was fine and bright and sunny. Collurio turned pale all the same. "Yes, Your Majesty. I do know that." He scratched the tip of his big nose. "Who would have thought that teaching an animal tricks would teach *me* such things?"

"You aren't the only one who has it," Lanius said. "Remember that. And remember one more thing—you're the right man for this job *because* you have it." Collurio nodded, but every line of his body said he would rather have been the wrong man. Lanius felt the same way, but the choice wasn't theirs. It lay in the hands of the Banished One—the hands Lanius had seen reaching out for him more than once just before he woke up with pounding heart and staring eyes.

They rode on, bodyguards flanking them but far enough away to let them talk without being overheard. Here and there, farmers worked in vegetable plots and berry patches or tended pigs and chickens. This close to the ever-hungry capital, they raised produce to sell rather than feeding themselves with what they grew. They didn't run away when they saw armored men on horseback, either, the way most peasants did.

Thrushes hopped about, looking for bugs and worms under trees. A squirrel chittered in a treetop. Somewhere not far away, a woodpecker drummed. A rabbit ran through a meadow. Half a heartbeat later, a fox followed like a flash of flame.

"How will you know what you want, Your Majesty?" Collurio asked.

"When I see it, I'll know," Lanius said.

And he did. Willows grew alongside the bank of a stream, their branches dipping down almost to the water. Metallically yammering kingfishers dove after fish. Near the stream, a meadow stretched out away toward a stand of forest off in the distance. No one's cattle or sheep grazed the meadow; the tumbledown ruin of what had been a farmer's hut said nobody had worked the land for a long time. Maybe things weren't perfect, but they were more than good enough.

"Here," Lanius declared. That was the advantage of being a king—when he said *here,* here it would be.

Hirundo bowed to King Grus. "Well, Your Majesty, you were right."

"You say the sweetest things," Grus answered, and the general guffawed. Grus went on, "Here he comes now. Look ferocious."

"*Grr.*" Hirundo bared his teeth. Grus glared at him—that was overacting at its worst. But the Menteshe riding in under a flag of truce was still too far away to notice his mugging. By the time the nomad and the Avornan cavalrymen surrounding him drew near, Hirundo was somber as a pyre builder. Given his usual high spirits, that was overacting, too, but the Menteshe wouldn't recognize it as such.

The fellow swung down off his horse. Two royal guardsmen strode up to him, their boots scuffing up little puffs of gray dust at each step. The Menteshe knew what they had in mind. He surrendered his weapons without any fuss, even a slim knife he carried in *his* boot. When the guardsmen were satisfied, they stepped aside. The Menteshe bowed low to Grus.

"Good day, Your Majesty," he said in fluent Avornan. "I am Falak son of Yinal, and I have the honor to represent Prince Korkut, the son and heir of the great Prince Ulash." He bowed again. He had a proud, hawk-nosed face with broad cheekbones and elegant eyebrows above dark eyes stubbornly unimpressed by anything they chanced to light upon—the King of Avornis very much included.

"Pleased to meet you," Grus said politely. "And what can I do for you on this fine day?" It was, in fact, a beastly hot day. Grus had gotten used to the weather in the city of Avornis and in the cool, misty Chernagor country to the north. Southern spring and approaching summer were reminding him how fierce they could be.

"We have not seen Avornans here for many long years," Falak said. "You would do well to remember what happened to the ones who came before you."

"I remember," Grus replied. "You would do well to remember we can take care of ourselves. So would Korkut. And so would the Banished One." Maybe that last was bravado. No—certainly it was bravado. But if it weren't also what Grus believed, he never would have crossed the Stura in the first place.

One of Falak's elegant eyebrows rose. His eyes widened ever so slightly. He hadn't expected Grus to give back arrogance for arrogance. "You dare speak of the Fallen Star so?" he whispered. "You have, perhaps, more nerve than you know what to do with."

"Perhaps I'll take the chance," Grus said. "I asked you once before—what can I do for you? And for Prince Korkut, I assume?"

He wondered if Falak would try to order him out of the Menteshe country. He intended to say no if Falak did, but it would tell him how confident Korkut was. But Falak did nothing of the sort. Instead, he said, "My master knows you have seen many rebels since you became King of Avornis."

"True," Grus admitted. And not only was it true, it was also shrewd. Korkut showed more wits than Grus had thought he owned.

Falak went on, "Since this is true, you will understand how my master feels when he faces a rebellion against him."

"Oh, I don't know. Quite a few people would say Sanjar has a better claim to Ulash's throne than Korkut does," Grus said.

"Quite a few people are liars and cheats. It is unfortunate, but it is true," Falak said. "I would not want to number the King of Avornis among them."

"You would make a mistake if you did. You might be making your *last* mistake if you did." Hirundo sounded hard as iron, sharp as a spearhead.

Falak son of Yinal bowed to him. "I have done no such thing, Your Excellency." He was a cool customer, all right. Turning back to Grus, he said, "Since you have come into my master's lands with an army behind you, he dares hope you have come to help him defeat the would-be usurper."

Did Korkut really hope that? Grus didn't believe it for a minute. Did the Menteshe hope to use the Avornans against his unloved half brother? That struck the king as a lot more likely. He said, "Sanjar hopes I'll do the same thing against Korkut, you know."

"He would," Falak said scornfully. "He has no chance to defeat my master on his own, and he knows it only too well."

"I'm not so sure about that—and neither is Korkut, or he wouldn't have sent you to me," Grus said. Falak only shrugged, neither admitting nor denying. He knew his business; Grus would have been glad to have a man of his talents on the Avornan side. The king continued, "I have nothing against either prince. But I also have no reason to love either of them."

Falak smiled thinly. "By which you mean you will help the man who gives you the most."

Grus smiled back. "By which I mean exactly that, yes."

"My master will meet any price within his ability," Korkut's emissary said. "Tell me yours, so I may take it to him."

"The Scepter of Mercy."

Falak's face froze. That jolted him no less than it had Sanjar's envoy. He took a deep breath and let it out in a sigh. "That, I am afraid, is not within his ability to give."

"Why not? It's in Yozgat, isn't it? He holds Yozgat, doesn't he? Or has Sanjar taken it away from him in the last few days?"

"Sanjar has done no such thing," Falak said indignantly. "My master *does* hold Yozgat. And the Scepter of Mercy *is* there. I have seen it with my own eyes." Grus was suddenly as jealous as a lovesick youth seeing the girl of his dreams walking with someone else, someone he couldn't stand. Falak either didn't notice or, more likely, affected not to. "My master could not yield it up, though. The Fallen Star—"

"Has nothing to do with it," Grus broke in. "Is your master his own master, or is he not?"

"Prince Korkut owns no man his master. That includes you, Your Majesty," Falak said pointedly.

*So there,* Grus thought. But it wasn't enough of a *so there* to slow him down. "That's nice," he said. "It doesn't answer the question I asked, though. Is he his own master or not? If he is, will he give me the Scepter of Mercy in exchange for help against Sanjar? If he isn't, why am I wasting my time talking to *you?* Let the Banished One send me an envoy if he wants something from me."

Now Falak bared his teeth in what looked like a smile but wasn't. "Be careful what you ask for. You may get it."

Grus pretended less concern than he felt. "Avornis has met his envoys before. The last one came to tell us everyone in the capital would starve to death in the coming winter. You see how true that turned out to be." He remembered the winter the Banished One had sent Avornis. He hadn't been king yet; he'd been down in the south, and it was appalling even there. It had been worse up at the city of Avornis, but the city—and the kingdom—came through. How close it had been . . . He preferred not to think about that, and so he didn't.

Falak bowed. "Say what you will. I see this discussion is pointless. If you and Korkut meet, it will be on the field. And if the Fallen Star does deign to notice your nerve, may you have joy of it." He bowed again, then bounded up into the saddle. He jerked savagely at the reins to turn his horse's head and trotted back toward the south. Hirundo waved to the scouts who'd brought him in. They rode off, too, to return Falak's weapons to him and to escort him out beyond the Avornans' lines.

"As you say, Your Majesty, it was worth asking." Hirundo shrugged. "Too bad he told you no, too."

"Now we have some idea about which of Ulash's sons is more in awe of the Banished One," Grus said. "Sanjar *might* have given up the Scepter if he'd had it. Maybe I should have thrown in with him."

The general shook his head. "I doubt it. If he did hold the Scepter of Mercy, he'd've hung on to it just like Korkut. It's a lot easier to think about giving away something you haven't got." He stared south. The dust their horses kicked up began to swallow Falak and his Avornan escorts.

"I suppose you're right. No, I know you're right," Grus said. "We just have to go on, then. And if the Banished One does send an envoy"—he shuddered—"well, we'll deal with that as best we can, too."


Lanius put smoked salmon and sliced onions and olives on a roll. He slid the silver tray across the table to Ortalis and Limosa. "Here you are," he said. "This will make a fine breakfast." Turning to Sosia, he added, "Pass the pitcher of wine when you're through with it, please."

"Of course," she said, and she did. The pitcher, also silver, was decorated with a relief of Olor in pursuit of a goddess who would become one of his six wives. Since she wasn't overburdened by clothes, she looked as though she had a good chance of escaping him this time.

Ortalis piled salmon and onions high. He went easy on the

olives; he wasn't as fond of them as Lanius was. "Your turn," he said to Limosa.

She usually liked smoked salmon. Today, she put a little on a roll. She looked at it. She added a few sliced olives and then hesitantly reached for a pungent slice of onion. She raised the roll to her mouth, but put it down before she could take a bite. "Please excuse me," she said, and bolted from the table.

"Oh, dear," Lanius said, and then, at the sound of retching a moment later, "Oh, *dear.* How long has she been sick?"

Sosia had another question for her brother—she asked, "When is she going to have the baby?" Lanius kicked himself for not figuring that out on his own.

"Some time this winter," Ortalis answered. "She only realized she was carrying a child a few days ago. We were going to wait until we were surer before we told you—but it looks like there's no more need to wait now. If the gods are kind, they'll send me a son."

Sosia murmured something that had no words in it. Lanius sipped at his wine to make sure Ortalis couldn't see his face till he got it under control. He didn't much want Grus' legitimate son to have a male heir. Ortalis' son would be a rival for Crex. So far, Ortalis hadn't shown much interest in the throne. The kind of power he craved was more personal than political. But he might well want to seize for a son what he didn't care about for himself.

Limosa walked back into the dining room. She looked wan. When she sat down, she reached for her winecup. She sloshed the wine around in her mouth before swallowing it.

"Are you all right?" Lanius asked.

"Better now, anyway," she answered. "I'm afraid I, uh, didn't quite make it to the privy. The servants have a mess to clean up."

"That's what servants are for," Ortalis said with a wave of the hand.

*I'm sure they love you, too,* Lanius thought. He nodded to Limosa. "So—another baby on the way? Congratulations!" He could say that and still hope she would have a girl.

She blushed, ever so slightly; that she'd been so pale made it easier to see. "Thank you, Your Majesty. You're kind to say so." She picked up the roll she'd so hastily abandoned. This time, she did take a bite.

"Will it stay down?" Sosia asked.

"I think so." Limosa's smile was wry. "I'm going to find out, aren't I?" She paused apprehensively, as though listening to her stomach. Then her smile got wider. "Yes, it'll be all right. Everything's fine in there now. I got rid of what was bothering me—until the next time."

"Yes—until the next time," Sosia echoed with womanly sympathy. She knew what Limosa was going through in a way that Lanius couldn't. Morning sickness was nothing he'd ever wanted to learn about at first hand, either.

Even though Limosa said she was feeling better, she didn't finish the roll and the smoked salmon. She excused herself again. This time, Lanius was glad to see, she didn't leave the room at a dead run. The king looked across the table at his brother-in-law. "Be careful with her," he warned.

"What's that supposed to mean?" Ortalis asked, but his eyes said he knew.

Lanius spelled it out anyway. "While she's with child, leave the whip . . . wherever you keep it. Hunt more instead, do whatever else you think you need to do, but don't give her new stripes. This isn't the time for it."

Something hot and unpleasant kindled in Ortalis' eyes. "You mind your business, *Your Majesty,* and I'll mind mine." In his mouth, Lanius' title sounded more like curse than compliment. Grus' legitimate son rose from the table, turned on his heel, and strode out after his wife.

"I wouldn't have told him that," Sosia said.

"Why not? Because Limosa enjoys it as much as he does? That's not reason enough, not when she's going to have a baby," Lanius said. "He's liable to get carried away, and who knows what would happen then?"

His wife shook her head. "No, not because Limosa likes it. Because if she does die . . . then or in childbed, we don't have to worry about any son of Ortalis'. We don't have to worry about him so much, either."

From a political point of view, Sosia made breathtakingly good sense. She had much more of Grus' ruthless pragmatism

than Ortalis did; all he'd gotten was the ruthlessness. Even so, Lanius said, "I don't want Limosa dead. I can't stand her father, gods
know, and your brother—" He broke off before resuming, "Well,
he is what he is, that's all. But Limosa? She's kind of sweet, even
if she . . . likes what she likes. Who would have thought Ortalis
could find such a good match? And having him running wild
again might make things worse, not better."

"Maybe." Sosia didn't sound as though she believed it for a
minute. "You're too soft for your own good, if you care even a
copper for what I think. Who cares about likes? You want Crex
to be king after you, don't you?"

"Of course I do. But—"

"No buts." Now Sosia swept out of the dining room. Lanius
stared after her. One piece of well-meant advice, and he'd managed to clear the room. If that wasn't a record, he didn't know
what would be.


Pterocles pointed to a mound rising from the mostly flat land of
the Menteshe country. Sadly, the wizard said, "Another one.
That's the third or fourth we've seen."

"I know." King Grus sounded none too happy, either.
"They're what cities look like after they die. The rubbish the
people who live there throw out year after year makes the
ground higher than it is anywhere else. And when the walls get
knocked down and the buildings fall to pieces, too . . ."

"This is what's left," Pterocles finished. "I wonder what
happened to the people who used to live here."

"Some of them died," Grus said. "Got killed, I mean. Others? Others are bound to be the ancestors of the thralls you're
freeing. That town's been dead a long time."

As the Avornan army drew nearer, he could see the jagged
remains of walls and buildings crowning the hill and giving it
a silhouette no natural rise would have had. He wondered what
the name of the place had been. If he described where it lay, Lanius could probably tell him. Lanius knew all sorts of things
that didn't matter. Things that did? A different story.

But the Banished One took Lanius seriously. Grus couldn't
let himself forget that. The exiled god wouldn't have threatened
the other king in dreams if he hadn't. He threatened only people

he took very seriously indeed. Hirundo, for instance, had done as much as any man to turn back the Menteshe and to beat the Chernagors, but the Banished One let him sleep undisturbed of nights. Grus scratched his head. He didn't pretend to understand the choices the Banished One made.

Grus laughed. It *was* funny, after a fashion. Had he understood all the choices the Banished One made, he would have been well on the way toward godhood himself. Part of him— the part that wanted to live forever—wished he were. But he knew too well he wasn't. His beard had far more salt than pepper in it these days. He remained healthy enough, but knew he lacked much of the strength and stamina he'd enjoyed when he was half his age. Sooner or later, he would lose what he still kept. He didn't like that—he hated it—but he knew it was true.

He looked toward the dead, abandoned city. Places had lifespans of their own, just as people did. They usually lasted far longer, but the Banished One had watched this town age and wither and die while he went on. He'd probably smiled as he watched, too. The town had been full of Avornans, and had gone to ruin at the hands of the Menteshe. They worshiped the Banished One; why wouldn't he smile to see their triumph?

Unlike people, though, places could come back to life. Grus turned to Hirundo. "Do you know what we ought to do?"

"I've got a list as long as your arm, Your Majesty," the general said. "Most of it is things I need to do day before yesterday. The less important bits, though, I can get away with doing yesterday. So what's yours?"

He sounded as serious as he ever did. Grus explained, finishing, "If we're going to take this land away from the Menteshe, we've got to do something with it for ourselves. If we could bring it back to the way it was before the nomads swept down on it . . ."

"Don't get your hopes up too high," Hirundo said. "Back in the old days, they didn't have to worry about the Menteshe at all. Even if we do drive 'em back, they'll be right over the border, just waiting to pounce when they see the chance. We can't clear them out of this whole country. It's too big, and there are too cursed many of them."

Grus wished he could find some way to contradict that, but he couldn't.

"If things work out the way we want them to, though, people will remember us for as long as Avornis lasts." Grus supposed that kingdoms flourished and then grew old, too, the same way people and towns did. Not wanting to think that might happen to Avornis in years yet to come, he went on, "That's about as close to living forever in this world as we're likely to come."

"There are children," Hirundo pointed out.

"Well, yes. So there are." Grus let it lie there. He was disappointed in his son, and feared he always would be disappointed in Ortalis. His hopes along those lines ran through Sosia and his grandson. He didn't like having more faith in his daughter and her line than in the one he'd always wanted to be his heir.

He also didn't know what Crex would turn out to be like. The boy was still too young to make that plain. The one thing Grus could say was that he didn't seem to be vicious. He wished more than anything that he could say the same about Ortalis. He'd tried to believe Ortalis would outgrow whatever gave him the need to hurt things, tried long after it should have been obvious that his legitimate son's ways were set. He didn't believe it anymore. *I may have been foolish to expect he'll ever have it in him to give. I was foolish. But there's a difference between foolish and blind.*

Did King Olor, looking down from the heavens, have the same sort of thoughts about mankind as a whole? Grus shrugged. He couldn't do anything about that. He didn't look up past the sky. He looked south, toward the mountains where the Banished One lived. The Banished One doubtless had his own thoughts about mankind, too. Grus aimed to prove him wrong.

# CHAPTER SIX

Tinamus the architect looked up in surprise from the sheaf of notes King Lanius had just given him. "These are . . . very detailed, Your Majesty."

"I wanted to have them as exact as I could," Lanius said. "Would you have liked it more if they were vaguer?"

Tinamus didn't answer. All the same, Lanius realized that he would have. The architect wasn't a courtier, and didn't have the courtier's knack for hiding what he thought. His long, thin, rather pale face showed each thought flitting across it. Lanius found that more refreshing than otherwise.

"I'm not just doing this for my amusement, you know," the king said.

"So I gather." Tinamus flipped through the notes. His hands were long and thin and pale, too—clever hands. "Why *are* you doing it, if you don't mind my asking?"

Lanius hesitated. He didn't want to lie to the architect, but he didn't want to tell him the truth, either. At last, he said, "It might be better if you didn't know. It might be safer—not for me, but for you."

"Safer, Your Majesty?" Tinamus' eyebrows jumped in surprise. "Who except maybe another builder could care whether I do this for you? The other builders here in the city of Avornis may be jealous of the commission you pay me, but I don't think any of them would try to knock out my brains with a plumb bob or anything like that."

"Good. I'm glad to hear it. I wouldn't want to believe our architects were wild and unruly men." Lanius smiled at Tinamus, who seemed one of the least unruly men he'd ever met. "Can you do it? Will you do it? Or should I ask one of your ferocious colleagues?"

"It doesn't seem difficult. One of them could probably do it as well as I can." No, Tinamus was no courtier. Anyone used to the ways of the court would have loudly proclaimed he was the only person in the whole world who could possibly handle this job. He wagged a finger at Lanius. "But I tell you this, Your Majesty—any of them will be as curious as I am, and will want to know why you say that what looks like a straightforward piece of work may not be safe."

"Mmp." Lanius wished he could have made a happier noise than that. However much he didn't want to admit it even to himself, Tinamus had a point. If the work was going to endanger him, he had a right to know why. Sighing, Lanius said, "The less you know about why you're doing what you're doing, the less likely you are to have trouble from the Banished One."

Tinamus' eyebrows leaped again. His eyes, gray as granite, opened very wide. "The . . . Banished One, Your Majesty?" He stuck a finger in his right ear, as though to show he didn't believe he'd heard straight.

Lanius only nodded. "That's what I said."

The architect's left hand twisted in the gesture that was supposed to keep the exiled god's glance far away. Lanius used it, too, though he was far from sure it did any good. Tinamus asked, "Why on earth would . . . he care about what I build for you?"

"I won't answer that," Lanius said. "As I told you, the less you know, the better off you'll probably be. Whatever the reason, though, what you're doing may interest him."

"That's the craziest thing I ever heard." Tinamus laughed out loud. "When I tell me wife—" He broke off before Lanius could even open his mouth, and said, "Oh. If this has to do with the Banished One, and if I shouldn't know very much, she should know even less, shouldn't she?"

He was quick. Lanius liked that. He said, "Not telling her

much—or anything—might be a good idea, yes. The fewer people who know and the less they know, the better off they're likely to be."

"What about the stonemasons and bricklayers and carpenters and pick-and-shovel men who work on this? What shall I tell them?" Tinamus asked.

"Tell them whatever you please. Tell them you think the king's gone round the bend," Lanius answered. By the look in the architect's eye, he wasn't far from thinking that. Lanius grinned. "Go ahead. Enjoy yourself. By the gods, I swear I'll never punish you for lèse-majesté."

Tinamus grinned back. "Now that I've got your oath, I ought to go screaming rude things from the housetops."

"Go ahead. I'm sure you'll get people to believe them." Lanius laughed to show he was joking. And so he was—mostly. But some people were still more inclined to believe bad things about him than they would have been for some other king. He'd never quite lived down his father's scandalous seventh marriage and the days when, as a boy, he'd been reckoned a bastard on account of it. The scars he bore because of those days had faded, but they'd never disappeared.

The captain of King Grus' scouts was a tough little man named Strix. Most of the scouts were tough little men. Tough big men did other things in the army. Little men put less weight on their horses than did their larger counterparts. That gave the horses a bit more speed, a bit more endurance, and let them come closer to matching what the Menteshe mounts could do.

Right now, Strix was a tough little man with a worried look on his weathered, sharp-nosed face. He said, "Your Majesty, we've got three scouts missing."

"Missing?" Grus said sharply. "You mean the Menteshe have them?" That would be bad. Grus had trouble imagining anything worse. When the nomads took prisoners, they often made sport of them, and showed a fiendish ingenuity in their amusement. The Banished One would have been proud of them. The Banished One probably *was* proud of them.

But Strix shook his head. "No, or it doesn't seem that way, anyhow. We've followed their trails as best we could, and those trails just—stop. All three of 'em just—stop. No sign of the men. No sign of the horses, either."

No wonder he looked worried. "Sounds like magic," Grus said, and heard the worry in his own voice, too.

"That's what I thought. I sent for a wizard." A sour look on his face, Strix muttered something about a donkey-riding blunderer. Grus couldn't catch all of it, which was probably just as well. After a moment of fuming, the scout captain went on, "He couldn't tell that anything was wrong, not for sure." His expression got more sour still.

"You don't believe that," Grus said.

"Bet your balls I don't," Strix agreed. "People don't disappear for no reason at all. Horses especially don't disappear for no reason at all. Hard to take a horse and stuff it up your—" He broke off, not wanting to offend Grus' delicate ears.

That he thought Grus' ears might be delicate only proved he'd never served on a war galley. "You're right," the king said. "Which wizard was this?"

"A scrawny beggar named Anthreptes," Strix answered with a scornful wave of the hand.

"Oh. Him." Grus said no more than that. He'd brought south the best sorcerers he could. He knew, though, that Anthreptes wasn't one of the best of the best. The man had been able to learn Pterocles' spell for taking the pall from thralls' minds. How much else he'd been able to learn in his career was much less obvious.

"I thought about kicking some sense into his empty head. I thought about it, Your Majesty, but I didn't do it." Strix sounded mournfully proud of his own virtue. He did kick up a puff of dust; no rain had fallen here in the south for quite a while, and no more was likely to until autumn.

"Would you like to find out what a real wizard thinks of this business?" Grus asked.

"That might be nice," Strix said. "It's one of the reasons I came back here, as a matter of fact."

"I'll see to it." Grus shouted for a runner. When one of the young men came up to him, he said, "Fetch Pterocles for me, if you please." The runner bowed and hurried off. He came back with the wizard a few minutes later. Pterocles gave Grus a curious look. The king told Strix, "Tell him what you just told me."

Strix did, though he didn't name the sorcerer with whom he was dissatisfied. After hearing him out, Pterocles said, "I don't much like the sound of that."

"Neither do I. Neither do my men," Strix said. "Don't much fancy the chance of vanishing off the face of the earth."

"Can you work out what's really going on?" Grus asked.

Pterocles shrugged. "I don't know. I can try." That only made Strix look unhappy again. Grus knew Pterocles better than the scout captain did. Unlike a lot of wizards, Pterocles didn't promise before he saw what he was promising. He had fewer broken promises to regret than a lot of wizards had.

Night fell before Pterocles came back. Strix rode in with him. Challenges from sentries warned Grus they were approaching. The king got to his feet. Firelight didn't reach very far or tell very much. He saw the looming shapes of horse and mule, and of the men aboard them, but shadows swallowed their expressions.

"What news?" Grus called.

"Anthreptes is a gods-cursed imbecile. Maybe somebody ought to run the thrall-curing spell on *him,*" Strix said. That wasn't exactly praise for Pterocles, but it came close enough.

With a weary grunt, Pterocles slid down from his mule—it definitely came closer to that than to dismounting in the ordinary sense of the word. The wizard stretched, twisted, and rubbed his backside before saying, "That turned out to be more interesting than I wish it would have."

"Did you figure it out?" Grus asked.

"Finally, yes. Olor's beard, though, I could use something wet," Pterocles said. Grus waved to one of the servants who'd accompanied the royal pavilion south of the Stura. The man brought Pterocles a mug of wine. Pterocles bowed to him as deeply as though he were the king, exclaiming, "Oh, gods be praised!" He drained the mug at one long, blissful pull, then looked around expectantly.

"I *think* our wizard could use another dose of the same medicine," Grus told the servant. Had Pterocles nodded any more eagerly, his head might have fallen off. Grus waited while he gulped the second mug of wine, then said, "All right—you figured it out. What was it?"

"It was a cloaking spell masquerading as a transposition spell."

"Was it?" Grus said. Pterocles nodded again, this time in solemn agreement. Grus went on, "Uh—what exactly does that mean?"

"It means the Menteshe sorcerers wanted us to think they snatched the scouts off to gods know where. They didn't. They didn't." Pterocles blinked, realizing he'd repeated himself. "Oh, I said that already. Oh, I—" He broke off. "What they did do, or the nomads with them, was ambush our men and then hide their bodies—and the dead horses, too—with magic. They counted on that to make us worry."

"They got what they wanted," Strix put in.

"Didn't they?" Grus remembered his own alarm. "I was wondering whether the Menteshe or . . . someone else could snatch people out of our army whenever they wanted to. That wouldn't have been very good."

"Not hardly," Strix agreed.

"That musht—*must*—be what they wanted," Pterocles said. "If we were all running around trying to protect ourselves from an imaginary danger, we wouldn't have worried about the real dangers in this country. And there are, oh, just a few of those."

"Are there? I hadn't noticed," Grus said. Strix laughed raucously. Pterocles giggled. The king eyed him. "I hadn't thought being drunk and disorderly was one of them."

Pterocles bowed and almost fell over. Straightening, he said, "Your Majesty, I am *not* disorderly."

Strix laughed again. So did Grus. He said, "Well, no more than usual, anyway. Why don't you go to bed? In the morning, you can be sober and disorderly." After another imperfectly graceful bow, the wizard lurched out of the firelight and off toward his tent. Grus turned to Strix. "Happier now?"

"A bit." The guard captain followed Pterocles' irregular path with his eyes. "You were right, Your Majesty. He does know what he's doing. Makes that other fellow look even more like an idiot than he did already."

Grus shrugged. "Some men are smarter than others. Some

men are braver than others. Some men are better wizards than others. You can use men who aren't the smartest or the bravest. Wizards who aren't the very best have their uses, too."

Strix chewed on that, then reluctantly nodded. "I suppose so," he said, and then, "I know what *I'd* use him for, by the gods."

Grus had a pretty good idea of that himself. He said, "Well, but once you did, I wouldn't be able to use him for anything anymore." Strix chuckled. He hadn't been joking, though, and neither had the king.

Ortalis seemed to imagine that Lanius had offended him. That offended Lanius. As far as he could see, he'd done nothing but tell his brother-in-law the truth. Whom could the truth offend? Only a fool. So it looked to the younger king, anyhow.

It must have looked different to Ortalis. He stubbornly stayed away from meals with Lanius and Sosia. That meant Limosa stayed away, too. Lanius regretted her absence more than Ortalis', for she was usually better company. When Grus' legitimate son couldn't avoid Lanius—when they passed in a hallway, for instance—he would give as curt a nod as he could get away with and go on with a scowl darkening his face.

Sosia only threw up her hands when Lanius complained. "He's been hard and harsh for as long as I can remember," she said. "You're not telling me anything I don't know. If you want to throw him in a dungeon for lèse-majesté, go ahead. I won't say a word. It might even teach him something." By the way her mouth twisted, she didn't think it would.

Lanius had just promised Tinamus he wouldn't be punished for lèse-majesté no matter what he did. He didn't expect the architect to do anything that deserved punishment, where Ortalis' expression indicted him half a dozen times a day. All the same . . . "The only thing he'd learn in a dungeon was how to hate me forever. Sooner or later, he'll get over this. If nothing else works, Limosa will bring him around."

"Maybe." Sosia's mouth twisted again, as though she'd tasted something sour. She liked Limosa less than Lanius did. To her, Ortalis' wife was more a threat than a person. If Limosa gave Ortalis a son, Ortalis would think the succession passed through him alone. Grus might even think the same thing. Ortalis' opinion didn't matter so much. Grus' mattered overwhelmingly. Sosia went on, "If you want to send Ortalis to the Maze, I won't say a word about that, either."

"I can get away with more and more these days," Lanius said. "Your father's stopped thinking I'll try to overthrow him whenever he turns his back. But if I did that, there would never be peace between us again. No matter what I think, no matter what you think, Ortalis matters to *him*. And . . ." He didn't want to go on or to admit what came next even to himself. But he did. "And if we quarrel with each other, I'll lose, curse it. He's better at such things than I am."

He paused again, hoping his wife would tell him he was wrong. But Sosia only sighed and said, "You're better than you used to be."

He could have directly confronted Ortalis. That was not his way, though. It never had been. He wouldn't have said even as much as he had if he hadn't been worried for the child Limosa carried.

Instead of bearding his brother-in-law, then, he called on Anser in his residence by the grand cathedral. Anser got along with everybody. Maybe he could find a way for Lanius and Ortalis to get along with each other.

A forest of antlers decorated the walls of Anser's study— antlers from stags he'd slain himself. Lanius wondered what Anser's predecessors as arch-hallow would have thought of that. Some of them had been saints, some scholars, some statesmen, even a few scoundrels. The king didn't think any of them had taken his chief pride in his skill with the bow.

Anser wore the arch-hallow's red robe as casually as though it were a greengrocer's tunic and breeches. He took his title more lightly than any of the men who'd gone before him, too. He neither was nor wanted to be a theologian. All he was doing as arch-hallow was making sure the priesthood caused King Grus no trouble. That, Lanius had to admit, he did pretty well.

A smile of what looked like and surely was real pleasure spread over Anser's face when Lanius walked in. "Your Majesty!" he exclaimed. Laughing, he bowed himself almost double. He didn't need to do that; he came as close to being a genuine friend as a king could have. But he didn't do it because he had to. He did it because he felt like it, which made the gesture very different from what it would have been otherwise.

He made Lanius laugh, too, which wasn't always easy. "Good to see you, by the gods," Lanius said.

"Let me fetch you some wine. That'll make it better yet." Anser bustled off. He came back with a jug and two mismatched cups, for all the world like any bachelor who didn't ever bother pretending to be a fussy housekeeper.

Lanius sipped appreciatively. "I tell you," he said, "I'm tempted to take that whole jug and pour it down my throat."

"Go ahead, if you want to. Plenty more where it came from." Anser didn't have a whole lot of use for fighting temptation. He was more apt to yield to it. After a moment, though, he realized Lanius seldom talked that way. He pointed a finger at the king. "Something's on your mind, isn't it?" By the way he said it, he might have feared Lanius was suffering from a dangerous disease.

"Afraid so," the king replied, and poured out the story of his trouble with Ortalis.

"You really do need the rest of the jug, don't you?" Anser said when he was done.

"I don't know that I need it. But I want it." Lanius wondered whether Anser recognized the difference. A glance at all those antlers made him doubt it. Sighing, he went on, "I didn't intend to quarrel with him, but then—"

"It's easy enough to quarrel with Ortalis even when you don't intend to," the arch-hallow finished for him.

That wasn't what Lanius had been about to say, which made it no less true. He said, "All I wanted to do was make sure nothing bad happened to Limosa."

"No matter how much she might enjoy it," Anser murmured.

Lanius had been finishing the cup of wine. He almost choked at that. Anser was in dangerous form this morning. "I was thinking of the baby," Lanius said carefully.

"Well, of course you were," Anser said. That couldn't be anything but polite agreement . . . could it?

Wondering too much would only make matters worse, Lanius decided. He said, "I was hoping you could help persuade

Ortalis I didn't mean to offend him. I was only trying to do his whole family a good turn."

"What's that saying about getting punished for your good deeds and not for your bad ones?" Anser clucked sympathetically. Then he did something more practical—he refilled Lanius' winecup. Lanius drank without hesitation; no, he wouldn't have minded getting drunk by then, not at all. The arch-hallow poured his own mug full again, too. After a sip, he went on, "I'll do what I can, Your Majesty, but I don't know how much that'll be."

"I understand. Believe me, I understand," Lanius said. "When Ortalis gets an idea into his head, he—" He stopped so hard, he almost bit his tongue. What had almost come out of his mouth was *he beats it to death*. It wouldn't have been anything but a figure of speech, but it would have been a disastrous one here.

"Yes, he does, doesn't he?" Anser said. Maybe he was just responding to the pause. Lanius dared hope. The other choice was that Anser knew exactly what he hadn't said, which would be almost as embarrassing as though he'd actually said it. *He can't prove that was what I meant*, Lanius thought. Anser, who didn't need to prove a thing, continued, "I'll try. I said I would, and I will. We don't need this kind of foolishness in the palace when we're fighting the Menteshe, too."

"You've got good sense," Lanius said gratefully.

"A whole fat lot of good it's liable to do me here, too," the arch-hallow replied with a wry grin. Knowing that also showed he had good sense. He added, "You do pretty well that way yourself, Your Majesty. Ortalis, though, once he gets angry, everything else flies out of his head."

Again, he wasn't wrong. Lanius took a long pull at his wine. "I don't expect miracles," he said. "Miracles are for the gods, not for us. Do what you can, and I'll be glad of it no matter what it is."

"Thanks. The family ought to stick together. And we—" Now Anser was the one who broke off in a hurry.

Lanius wondered why. Then, all at once, he didn't. Had Anser swallowed something like, *We bastards ought to stick together, too?* Lanius didn't, wouldn't, think of himself as a bastard, but Anser really was one. Did he ever wonder if he might have been in line for the throne had his birth turned out different? He'd hardly be human if he didn't. But he wasn't—he never had been—a jealous man, which was probably all to the good. Lanius would have been furious at almost anyone who suggested he might not be legitimate. But how could he get angry at Anser, who really wasn't?

"By Olor's prong, we should, shouldn't we?" Lanius said.

If he'd talked about some other part of Olor's anatomy, Anser might not have been sure he'd filled in what the arch-hallow hadn't said. As things were, Anser turned red as a modest maiden hearing her beauty praised for the first time. "I meant no offense, Your Majesty," he mumbled.

"I took none," Lanius said quickly. "And I thank you very much for trying to talk to Ortalis. If he'll listen to anybody, he'll listen to you."

"Yes," Anser said with a nod. "If."

When the Avornan army stopped for the evening south of the Stura, Hirundo always threw out sentries all around it. Whenever he found the chance, he had the men run up a rampart around the encampment, too, made up of whatever timber or stones and rubble they could get their hands on. They sometimes grumbled. Hirundo took no notice of that, not where they could hear.

"I know it's not the strongest defense, and I know it's work nobody likes to do," he said to Grus on an evening when the complaints were louder than usual. "But it's better than nothing, and it'll slow the nomads down, maybe even throw 'em into confusion, if they try hitting us at night."

"You're right. You couldn't be righter," Grus said. "Do you want me to say a few words—or more than a few words—to the soldiers about that?"

Hirundo shook his head. "I think that would make things worse, not better. They're following orders. They just don't like them very much. If you start fussing about it, they're liable to decide they have to have their own way no matter what. That's how mutinies start."

"All right. You know best." Grus thought for a little while, then slowly nodded. "Yes, if I had grumbling sailors to deal with, I'd probably handle them the same way. As long as they don't think you think something's worth pitching a fit about, they won't get too excited themselves."

"That's it exactly," Hirundo agreed. "They need to be worrying about the Menteshe, not about earthworks and such. This should just be part of routine. And it is, pretty much. It's a part they don't care for, that's all."

"All sorts of things down here I don't care for." Grus looked back toward the north. "One of them is that we aren't getting as many wagonloads of supplies as I hoped we would."

Hirundo looked unhappy. The lamplight inside Grus' pavilion deepened the shadows in his wrinkles and made him seem even less pleased than he would have in the daytime. "Miserable nomads have been raiding the wagon trains. They've decided they can make trouble for us that way without meeting our main force face-to-face, strength to strength."

"And they're right, too, curse them," Grus said. Hirundo didn't deny it. Grus hadn't thought he would. The king asked, "What can we do about it?"

"We're doing what we can," Hirundo answered. "We've got solid guard parties going with the wagons. If they were any stronger, we'd start weakening the army here. We've built a line of real strongpoints back to the Stura. All of that only helps so much. The Menteshe get to pick and choose where they'll hit us. That gives them the edge."

Grus drew his sword. The blade gleamed in the buttery light. "I'd like to give them the edge of this, by the gods," he growled.

"We gain. In spite of everything, we gain," Hirundo said. "We've done better down here than I thought we would. Those thrall-freeing spells really work."

"They'd better, by Olor's strong right hand!" Grus said. "I wouldn't have had the nerve to stick my nose across the Stura without them."

Musingly, the general said, "Even if we lose here, we'll still have caused the Menteshe a lot of trouble. With the people who do their work for them able to think for themselves, the nomads won't have it all their own way anymore."

He was right, no doubt about it. Grus scowled even so. "I didn't cross the river to lose. I crossed the river to lay siege to Yozgat, take the Scepter of Mercy away from whichever Menteshe prince happens to be hanging on to it, and to bring it back to the city of Avornis where it belongs."

Hirundo stared south. "I don't know whether we'll be able to get there by the end of this campaigning season. That's a cursed long advance to make in one summer—and a cursed long supply line to protect, too. We're already seeing some of the joys there."

He was right about that, too. His being right made Grus no happier—just the opposite, in fact. "We'll do what we can, that's all," the king said. "And if we don't get everything done that we hoped for . . ." He did some more scowling. "If that's how things work out, then we go back and try again next year. We had to keep going back to the Chernagor country till things finally turned our way. If that happens here . . . then it does, that's all."

"All right," Hirundo said evenly. "I did want to make sure you were thinking about all the possibilities."

"Thank you so very much," Grus said, and Hirundo laughed out loud, for he sounded anything but grateful.

Pouncer swarmed up a stick. When the moncat got to the top, it waited expectantly. Collurio gave it a bit of meat. Then Pouncer jumped to the next stick, which ran horizontally, and hurried along it. Lanius waited at the other end. "Mrowr?" Pouncer said.

The king gave the moncat a treat. Pouncer ate it with the air of someone who'd received no less than his due. Lanius turned to Collurio. "You've taught this foolish beast more in a few weeks than I did in years."

"He's a lot of things, Your Majesty, but he's not a foolish beast," the animal trainer answered. He eyed Pouncer with wary respect. "If these moncats ever learn to shoot dice and hire lawyers, you can start shaving them and docking their tails, because they'll be people just as much as we are."

"Mrowr," Pouncer said again. The moncat's yawn displayed

a mouthful of needle teeth. It also declared that the idea of being a person struck Pouncer as imperfectly delightful.

Laughing, Lanius said, "He's got us to wait on him hand and foot. That must be how he sees it, anyway. And why wouldn't he? What do we do except give him things he likes to eat?"

"He has to perform for them," Collurio said.

"He probably thinks he has us trained, not the other way around. And who's to say he's wrong?" Lanius scratched Pouncer by the side of the jaw. The moncat rewarded him with a scratchy purr.

Collurio gave him a curious look. "Trainers say things like that all the time, Your Majesty. 'Oh, yes, that dog's taught me what I need to know,' they'll say, and then they'll laugh to show they don't really mean it—even when they do. But I've never heard anyone outside the trade talk that way before."

Astonishment spread over his face when Lanius bowed to him. "I thank you. I thank you very much, in fact," the king said. "You just paid me a great compliment."

"Your Majesty?" Now Collurio was frankly floundering.

"I'm nothing but an amateur, a hobbyist, at training animals, but you told me I talk like someone who makes a living at it," Lanius explained. "If that's not a compliment, what is?"

"Oh." Collurio's chuckle had a sharp edge to it. "I see what you're saying. Meaning no offense, but you wouldn't seem so proud of sounding like an animal trainer if you really were one."

"Maybe not, but you never know," Lanius said. "It's honest work. It has to be. The animals are out there on display. Either they'll do what you taught them or they cursed well won't."

"There are always times when they cursed well won't," Collurio said. "Nobody likes times like that, but everybody has 'em. Anybody who tries telling you anything different is a liar. Those are the days when you go home telling your dogs that they don't know a sheep from a wolf and your cats that they belong in rabbit stew."

That puzzled Lanius. "Why would a cat go in rabbit stew?"

This time, Cullurio bowed low to him. "There is a question a king would ask. When you tell your cooks you feel like rabbit stew, you're sure you'll get real rabbit. Anyone else, unless he's caught his bunnies himself—and cooked them himself, too—is liable to wonder whether he's eating roof rabbit instead."

"Roof rab—? Oh!" Lanius had always been fond of a good, spicy rabbit stew. Now he wondered how many times his rabbit would have meowed. Collurio had exaggerated notions about how much a king could influence his cooks. The crew in the kitchens might well laugh behind their hands at the notion of fooling their sovereign. "I don't know that I'm ever going to think about eating rabbit the same way again."

"I'm sorry, Your Majesty," Collurio said.

"Don't be. Having something new to think about is always interesting." Lanius scratched Pouncer again. "You wouldn't care one way or the other, would you? It's all meat, as far as you're concerned."

"Mrowr." To Pouncer, that was the only possible answer.

"Do you think he can learn . . . what I want him to learn?" Lanius asked Collurio. He didn't care to speak too directly. No telling who might be listening, even if no ordinary mortal was in earshot.

The trainer said, "He's clever enough, no doubt of that." Pouncer chose that moment to yawn, which made both men laugh. "Yes, he's clever enough, but he's a cat, all right," Collurio went on. "Whether he cares enough—ah, that's another question." Lanius eyed Pouncer. Could the fate of a kingdom rest on whether a moncat cared enough? He feared it could.

# CHAPTER SEVEN

Another river to cross. Grus looked over to the southern bank, which stood higher than the one he was on. Menteshe horsemen in some numbers trotted back and forth not far from the water. Every now and then, one of them would draw his bow and shoot an arrow at the Avornan army. Grus' archers shot back, but most of their arrows fell in the river. The nomads' bows outranged theirs.

*How many Menteshe am I not seeing?* Grus wondered. He asked Hirundo, "What do you think about making a crossing here?"

The general looked south, too. "If there are a whole lot more Menteshe than the ones we can see, I think I'd rather not."

That came unpleasantly close to echoing Grus' thoughts. Even so, he said, "We can't very well stop where we are."

"I know," Hirundo said unhappily. "If we can keep them busy in front of us and sneak a detachment over the river either upstream or down-, that might do the trick. We try swarming straight across, they'll bloody us."

He wasn't wrong. Grus wished he were. The king said, "If that's nothing but a cavalry screen, the Menteshe will laugh at us for wasting time and effort."

"No doubt," Hirundo agreed. "But if it's not and we crash into their main force headlong, they'll laugh at that, too. They'll spend years laughing at it, as a matter of fact."

"Maybe Pterocles can tell us how many of them there are," Grus said.

"Maybe." Hirundo didn't sound completely convinced.

Since Grus wasn't completely convinced, either, he couldn't blame his general for seeming dubious. He summoned the wizard anyway, and told him what he wanted. Pterocles peered across the river. "I can try, Your Majesty," he said at last. "Numbers are fairly easy to hide sorcerously, though. Have you thought of sneaking a few freed thralls across the river to look around? The nomads aren't likely to pay much attention to them, and they can see how things are and come back."

Grus hadn't thought of any such thing. By the flabbergasted look on Hirundo's face, neither had he. He said, "Maybe you ought to promote him to general, Your Majesty. You can put me out to pasture, and I'll just stand around chewing my cud." He worked his jaw from side to side in uncanny imitation of a cow.

"I don't want to be a general! I'd have to tell other people what to do." Pterocles spoke in obvious and obviously genuine horror.

"Some people would say that's one of the attractions of the job," Grus remarked. By the way the wizard shook his head, he was not one of those people. Grus said, "Well, we will try that."

"Don't waste time before you do," Hirundo said. "Even if there aren't a lot of Menteshe over there now, more and more of them will come up the longer we wait." That also struck Grus as sage advice.

Avornan wizards had lifted the dark sorcery from the men and woman of a village not far from the river. The thralls there were so newly free, they still remained filthy and shaggy. They weren't the same as they had been, though; they were recognizably people, which they hadn't been before. Their eyes had light in them, not the usual bovine dullness.

That worried Grus. Would the Menteshe notice the difference? Thralls clamored to volunteer. Picking and choosing among them was the biggest problem. Not all of them had words enough to do a good job of reporting what they saw. They would soon; as Grus had seen with Otus, they soaked them up even faster than children did. But many of them hadn't yet.

Women were as eager as men to spy on the nomads. Grus hesitated before sending any of them over the river. The Menteshe were in the habit of doing whatever they pleased with women from among the thralls. Male thralls were too sunk in darkness and too terrorized to fight them, and female thralls, ensorceled as they were, hardly seemed to care. But it would be different for someone who was fully awake, fully alive.

"One more time? So what?" one of the women said. "They do us, now we do them, too." She gestured to show what she meant, in case the king hadn't understood her. But he had. And he did send her over the river.

She came back, too. So did both the men Grus sent with her. One of them said, "Not many Menteshe. Like this." He opened and closed his hands a few times. "Not like this." Now he opened and closed them many times. The other man and the woman both nodded.

Grus still had to decide whether he believed them. If the Banished One held some control over them even now, this would be a good time for him to use it. He could badly hurt the Avornans if they ran into more nomads than they expected while crossing the river. He could . . . if he held some control over them even now.

But if he did, then everything the Avornans tried south of the Stura was bound to fail anyhow. Grus refused to believe it. His refusal, of course, might prove one of the last thoughts he ever had while still in possession of his mind and will. He knew as much. He gave the orders anyway.

The Avornans demonstrated downstream from where they'd encamped. A few riders crossed the river. Many soldiers looked as though they were getting ready to cross. The Menteshe galloped west to try to head them off—and most of the Avornans went over the river upstream from their camp. They rolled down on the nomads, scattered them, and drove them off in flight.

Grus gave a golden ring to each of the thralls who'd gone across to spy on the Menteshe. The two men had learned enough by then to bow low in thanks. That woman sent him a smoldering smile. She was awake and fully herself, but she hadn't yet figured out how to hide for politeness' sake what she had in mind.

She was pretty, and shapely, too. Once she was cleaned up, she would turn heads anywhere. All the same, Grus pretended not to notice the way she looked at him. Taking her to bed would be almost as bad, almost as unfair, as bedding a woman who remained a thrall. She needed time to figure out who and what she was. Once she'd done that . . . *Once she's done that, I'll be far away,* Grus thought. *Probably just as well, too, for both of us.*

She didn't try to hide her disappointment, either, or her annoyance. Grus also pretended not to notice those. He had other things on his mind. Maybe the Banished One was biding his time with the thralls. It was either that or the Avornan sorcerers really were taking them out of the exiled god's control. Little by little, Grus began to believe it.

Ortalis came up to Lanius in a palace corridor with an odd expression on his face. Grus' legitimate son seemed to be trying to look friendly, but he wasn't having a whole lot of luck. At least he didn't look as though he wanted to pummel Lanius, the way he had ever since they quarreled.

"Good morning," Lanius said. He'd never given up being polite to Ortalis. As far as he was concerned, the quarrel was all inside his brother-in-law's mind, such as that was.

"Good morning." Ortalis sounded as grudging as he looked. But he went on making an effort, saying, "How are you today?"

"Pretty well, thanks." Lanius pointed out the window. The view showed flowers in the palace garden, bright blue sky, and puffy white clouds drifting along on a lazy breeze. "Nice weather we're having, isn't it?"

"I suppose so." By the way Ortalis said it, he hadn't even thought about the weather until Lanius brought it up. Again, though, he tried to hold up his end of things. "Not too hot. Not too cold. Just right."

It wasn't scintillating conversation, but it was conversation—more than Lanius had had from Ortalis for quite a while. Out in the garden, a sparrow chirped. A jay let out a couple of raucous screeches from a tree not far away. Lanius said, "Good to have all the birds back from the south."

"That's true." Now Ortalis showed some enthusiasm, even if it wasn't of the sort Lanius might have chosen; he said, "Song-birds done up in a stew or baked in a pie with carrots and onions and peas are mighty tasty."

"Well, so they are." Lanius like songbirds in a pie, too. Even if he didn't, he wouldn't have contradicted his brother-in-law just then. He did say, "I like to hear them singing. It's one of the things that tell me spring is here, along with the sweet smells from the flowers."

"Limosa likes flowers, too." Ortalis might have announced that his wife liked Thervingian poetry—to him, it was obvi-ously her eccentricity. "Some of them do have nice colors," he allowed, as though he'd learned a few words of Thervingian himself to humor her.

"Yes, they do." Lanius enjoyed the poppies and roses and bluebells. He eyed Ortalis, wondering as he often did what went on in his brother-in-law's head. He sometimes thought he was better off not knowing. But, if Ortalis was working hard to act civilized, the least he could do himself was keep matching Grus' son. And so he asked once more, "How *are* you today?"

"I'm . . . not too bad." Ortalis hesitated, then went on, "Anser had a few things to say to me."

"Did he?" Lanius worked hard to keep his tone neutral. He didn't want Ortalis to know that had been his idea.

His brother-in-law nodded. "He did. He said he knew why the two of us squabbled. He said the whole palace knew about it. I don't much fancy that."

"Not a whole lot we can do about it now," Lanius said. There would have been a lot less palace gossip if Ortalis' tastes hadn't run to the whip. Telling him so was unlikely to change those tastes, worse luck.

"I suppose not." Ortalis didn't seem convinced. He never believed anything could be his fault, even in a small way. The only exception to that rule that Lanius had ever seen came when his brother-in-law went hunting. If Ortalis missed a shot, he laughed and joked about it the way a miller or a leather worker would have. But he was different in many regards when he went hunting.

"Well . . . any which way, I'm glad you're not angry anymore," Lanius said.

The corners of Ortalis' mouth turned down. Pretty plainly, he *was* still angry. Lanius hadn't really thought he wasn't. But Grus' legitimate son nodded a moment later. "Not worth making a big fuss about," he said. Coming from him, that was the height of graciousness.

Lanius nodded, acknowledging as much. "I don't think it is, either," he said, and held out his hand.

Ortalis clasped it. He squeezed just hard enough to let Lanius know he could have hurt him if he'd squeezed harder. That was Ortalis to the core. Then he cocked his head to one side and studied Lanius. "What are you and the beast trainer doing with that silly animal?"

"Seeing how much he can learn," Lanius answered easily. Whatever else he had in mind was his business, not Ortalis'.

"Seems like you're spending a lot of silver while you're at it," his brother-in-law observed.

Lanius only shrugged. "It's a hobby. Everybody has them." Unlike Ortalis', his didn't involve dealing out pain. Mentioning that just after they'd made up seemed a bad idea, so he didn't. Instead, he went on, "I'm not throwing the money at a lot of loose women. That keeps your sister happy."

Ortalis only shrugged. "I don't lose any sleep over what my sister thinks. I never have, and I don't suppose I ever will." From things Sosia had said, she and Ortalis hadn't gotten along even when they were children. Now, of course, Ortalis had a new reason to resent her—her son might stand in the way of his offspring when it came to the succession.

*I hope Limosa has another girl.* Lanius didn't say that, no matter how strongly he felt it.

Ortalis set a hand on his shoulder. Again, the prince squeezed a little harder than he might have. "Have fun with your hobby," he said, and went on his way.

Lanius had expected he would do more snooping about the moncat. The king would have gone on saying as little as he could if Ortalis had. He might have talked with Grus and Pterocles about what he was up to. If it ever became absolutely necessary, he might have with Collurio.

"With my brother-in-law, my *charming* brother-in-law?" Lanius murmured. Without the least hesitation, he shook his head.

Once upon a time, Trabzun had been the Avornan city of Trapezus. Behind its gray stone wall, it still was a city of sorts, but it wasn't an Avornan city anymore. The tall, thin towers sprouting up in large numbers would never have occurred to a builder from the kingdom Grus ruled.

"They look like asparagus," Grus remarked.

"If you say so, Your Majesty," Hirundo answered. "Me, I think they look like something else myself."

"Something else? Oh." Grus made a face that almost matched Hirundo's leer. "Maybe yours is that skinny. I hope mine's not."

"What you do with it is as important as what you've got," the general declared in lofty tones.

Grus pointed toward Trabzun. "Well? What are we going to do with it? That place can stand a proper siege, and we can't go on without reducing it. The garrison could sally and do horrible things in our rear."

Hirundo could have risen to that, too, but he didn't. He said, "If you expected to get all the way to Yozgat in one campaigning season, you probably expected too much."

"I'd be lying if I said I didn't have my hopes," Grus admitted.

"Nothing wrong with hopes, as long as you don't let them run away with you," Hirundo said.

*Did I let them run away with me when I came south of the Stura in the first place?* Grus wondered. He shook his head. He refused to believe that. And if he had hoped to get all the way to Yozgat (and he had) . . . He'd known he would probably need to be lucky. He had been, up till now.

"Maybe they'll surrender," he said, knowing he would have to be *very* lucky to see that happen.

"It's just like pretty girls—never hurts to ask, but they don't say yes as often as you wish they would," Hirundo answered.

"We won't have as much fun when they do here, either—if they do." In spite of saying that, Grus sent a herald up to the walls of Trabzun. The man shouted out a demand that the city open its gates to the Avornan army. He used both his own language and the guttural tongue of the Menteshe.

Soldiers on the wall shouted insults at him. To leave the rest of the army in no doubt that those were insults, they emptied chamber pots into the ditch in front of the wall. Some of them flung the pots out at the herald. None struck home, but he quickly rode back to the Avornan lines.

"They won't yield, Your Majesty," he reported.

"Oh, yes, they will," Grus said. "They just don't know it yet."

In the previous few years, he'd besieged several Chernagor towns. All of them were stronger than Trabzun seemed to be. This place didn't have the sea covering much of its perimeter. He sent his riders out to close the line around it. All the time, he hoped the Menteshe inside would sally. He would much rather have faced them out in the open than in the advantageous position the walls gave them.

They sat tight, though. Maybe they were hoping for rescuers, or maybe they thought they could outlast the besiegers. Maybe they were right, too. That unappetizing thought made Grus scowl, but he kept at the siege all the same. The Menteshe would surely prove right if he didn't try.

He didn't intend to storm the walls. That would be quick and decisive if it worked—and had about as much chance of working as he did of throwing double sixes back-to-back at dice. You could do it. He'd done it. But you were a fool if you counted on it, because it wasn't very likely.

His men methodically dug a trench around Trabzun. They heaped up the excavated dirt inside the trench to serve as a breastwork to protect them from whatever the Menteshe inside the city might do. Then they dug another trench, this one beyond their encampment. The breastwork on the outer trench faced outward. Any relieving force would have to battle its way through the fieldworks to get at the Avornans.

Even though Grus didn't try to storm Trabzun, he wasn't eager to wait till the defenders starved enough to submit. Summoning Pterocles, he said, "When I was besieging a rebel's castle, the witch who served me as chief sorcerer before you managed to stop up the castle's water supplies, and my foe had to surrender. Can you do the same here?"

*The witch who served me as chief sorcerer.* He sighed. He'd loved Alca for a while. He hadn't loved her well enough to leave Estrilda, though. He sighed again. Nothing seemed sadder than the memory of a love that had fallen to pieces.

Pterocles knew about Alca. He also knew better than to say anything about her, or about the way Grus hadn't mentioned her name. All he did say was, "I don't know, Your Majesty. I can try to find out, if you like."

"Yes, please, if it's not too hard." Grus didn't add, *And it had better not be.* He and Pterocles had worked together long enough to let the wizard understand that without its being said.

"I'll get right at it," Pterocles said. "Seems a pretty straightforward use of the law of similarity. Do we have an arrow that's been shot from the walls of Trabzun? A stone from a catapult would be even better."

"If you want arrows, talk to the surgeons," Grus said. "As for stones, well, I don't think their catapults have done much, but maybe we could provoke them, if that's what you really want."

"If you'd be so kind," Pterocles said. He and Grus had worked long enough to let the king understand that that meant, *You'd cursed well better, if you expect me to work the magic you need.*

Grus concentrated a couple of dozen men beyond bowshot of the walls of Trabzun but within reach of a stone-thrower. They lingered out in the open, not doing very much but seeming fascinated with something on the ground. He wondered how long they'd have to wait for the Menteshe to notice them.

It wasn't long. The nomads were alert to whatever the Avornans did. A stone the size of a man's head hissed through the air. But the Avornan soldiers were alert, too. They scattered. The stone thudded home harmlessly. One of them scooped it up and carried it away. They tried not to offer the Menteshe such a tempting target again.

Pterocles briefly borrowed a hammer from a blacksmith and

knocked chips off the ball of stone the catapult had shot. He mixed them in with the dirt he used to form walls and buildings and round towers that looked like a miniature version of Trabzun's. Catching Grus' eye on him, he nodded. "Yes, Your Majesty, it is a model of the city," he said. "Now it's a model of the city that includes something from the real city. That will make the magic more accurate."

"Good," Grus said, and waited to see what Pterocles would do next.

The wizard held a forked stick over his model, as though he were an ordinary dowser trying to find water for a farmer who wanted to dig a well. But an ordinary dowser would have let his stick rise and fall as it would. Pterocles didn't. He chanted a spell as he worked with it—an insistent charm set, Grus realized, to the tune of a song children sang in the streets of the city of Avornis.

"Here we go," Pterocles murmured, as the tip of the stick dipped, and then dipped again and again and again, pointing now toward one part of the model of Trabzun, now toward another.

"What does that mean?" Grus asked.

After finishing the chant, Pterocles answered, "I'm very sorry, Your Majesty, but I'm afraid it means the town has a great many wells and cisterns and such inside it. We wouldn't be able to close off all of them at once."

"Oh." Grus had been afraid he would say something like that. He'd watched ordinary dowsers at work any number of times. When their sticks dipped, it meant they'd scented water. The same evidently held true here, even if Pterocles, a better wizard than any ordinary dowser, didn't need to walk the whole territory he tested.

"I am sorry," Pterocles repeated.

"I believe you. So am I," Grus said. Sometimes—most of the time, it often seemed—being sorry didn't help. This looked like one of those occasions.

"What do we do now?" the wizard asked.

"What we would have done if the Menteshe hadn't tried to knock my men flat with a catapult ball," Grus replied. "We try to take Trabzun away from them without drying up those wells."

"All right." Pterocles sent the model of the city a reproachful glance, as though he'd expected more from it than it wanted to give him. But then he brightened. "I won't knock this to pieces just yet. Maybe we'll find another way to use it."

"Maybe." Gus did his best to stay polite; it wasn't Pterocles' fault that Trabzun was so well supplied with water. He nodded to the wizard. "You never can tell."

When a cook burst out of the kitchens crying, "Your Majesty! Oh, your Majesty!" it was a good bet Pouncer had done something particularly brazen in there. If the cook wasn't upset about the moncat, then a couple of the meat carvers had probably gone after each other with knives. Given a choice like that, Lanius hoped Pouncer was the one to blame.

The cook rounded a corner and bore down on him like a Chernagor pirate ship with a strong following wind. "Here I am," Lanius said mildly.

"Your Majesty! Your Majesty!" The cook went right on yelling, now in Lanius' face.

"Here I am," the king repeated, not quite as mildly this time. "What do you want?"

"That . . . that . . . that horrible creature of yours!" The cook hadn't gotten any quieter.

"What about that horrible creature of mine?" Lanius knew a certain amount of relief that the trouble did involve Pouncer. At least he wouldn't walk into the kitchens and find somebody dead on the floor. He wasn't relieved by the way the cook kept going on at the top of his lungs. "Tell me what the moncat's done. Try to tell me without making the top of my head fly off."

"Well, Your Majesty, the nasty beast went and stole—" The cook stayed much too loud.

"I said, try to tell me without making the top of my head fly off!" Suddenly, Lanius shouted just as loud. The cook's eyes bugged out of his head in amazement. Lanius dropped his voice to more normal tones and went on, "I said it, and I cursed well meant it, too." He folded his arms across his chest and waited to see whether the man was paying any attention at all.

"I'll try, Your Majesty." Now Lanius could hardly hear the cook at all. That didn't bother him; he didn't mind leaning forward. "It stole a fine silver spoon and a marrow bone, and then it disappeared again. You should have drowned the miserable thing when it was a kitten."

"A marrow bone, too, eh? It must have thought you were rewarding it for being clever enough to steal the spoon," Lanius said.

"Well, then, it's pretty stinking stupid, isn't it?" The cook's voice rose again.

"Easy, there. Easy, I say." Lanius might have been gentling a spooked horse. "Just don't go jumping out of your breeches. You'll probably get the spoon back sooner or later. Pouncer usually takes them someplace where people go. It's not as though some pawnbroker will give the beast a few coins for the silver in it."

"Why does the gods-despised animal steal spoons in the first place?" the cook demanded. He didn't seem much gentled.

"Pouncer is a great many things—willful, obnoxious, annoying, pestilential, mangy. Take your pick," Lanius said. "But one thing that moncat is not is gods-despised. I would stake a great deal on the truth of that."

"Oh, you would, would you?" The cook didn't believe a word of it. "And why wouldn't the gods despise the rotten creature?"

"Because Pouncer just may be the salvation of the kingdom," Lanius replied, and the cook's eyes bugged out of his head all over again. The king continued, "I *am* sorry about the marrow bone. Some soup or stew or gravy won't be all that it might have been. But I suppose you can probably find another."

"This is no joking matter, Your Majesty," the cook protested.

"Good, because I'm not joking," the king said. "The spoon likely will come back. You can come up with a new bone. Do you have any other reasons to shriek in my ear, or was that everything?"

The cook glowered. He scowled. He swelled up like a puffer fish. Lanius stood there waiting. As he'd expected, the cook deflated. "I'm sorry, Your Majesty," he said in a much smaller voice.

"There. That's much better. You see? You *can* talk like a normal human being when you want to. Well done," Lanius said. "And now, what do you expect me to do about my willful, obnoxious, annoying, pestilential—but not, mind you, gods-despised—moncat?" Lanius was proud of himself for remembering all the nasty names he'd called Pouncer.

By the way the cook gaped, the king's memory impressed him, too. He said, "If you can make sure the beast never comes back to the kitchens, that would be nice. If you can get the spoon back, that would be, too." He went out of his way to sound mild.

"I don't think I can stop Pouncer from getting in," Lanius said. "I've tried, and I haven't had much luck. I won't lie to you about anything like that. But I already told you there's a pretty good chance the spoon will turn up."

"All right, Your Majesty. Thank you, Your Majesty." The cook turned around and headed back toward the kitchen, a meeker and more subdued man than the bellowing hysteric who'd come roaring up to Lanius.

The king laughed a little as he made for the archives. Turning excitable people into calm ones wasn't a skill most people thought of when they imagined things a sovereign ought to be able to do. That didn't mean it wasn't valuable, though. Oh, no—far from it.

Lanius hoped he would find Pouncer in the archives with his prize. That would let him bring the spoon back to the kitchens in something approaching triumph. It would also let him feel virtuous for resisting the temptation to wallop the cook over the head with it—unless he yielded to the temptation instead, which offered pleasures of its own.

But there was no sign of the moncat when Lanius got to the archives. He called Pouncer and even lay down on the dusty floor and thumped his chest, the way he did to summon Pouncer for a treat. Pouncer either was too far away to hear or didn't feel like coming. Lanius only shrugged. *So much for neat endings,* he thought, and went back to sorting through documents.

King Grus suspected some generals tried to storm cities for no better reason than that sitting around besieging them was boring. Sitting down outside of Trabzun *was* boring. He wasn't inclined to complain even so. As long as dysentery didn't break out in his army, he thought he could take the city far more cheaply by siege than by storm.

Grus glanced toward the walls of Trabzun. Torches flared every few paces along them. By the flickering torchlight, the king could make out Menteshe archers and a few pikemen. The garrison wanted him to know—or at least to think—it was ready for anything. He let out a wry chuckle.

"How long do you think the siege will last?" Pterocles asked.

"I can't tell you, not within months," Grus said. "Depends on how much food the Menteshe have, on how much they want to starve ordinary people to feed the soldiers, on . . . oh, all sorts of things. It would have been over a lot sooner if you'd been able to shut off their water supply—I'll tell you that."

"I'm sorry, Your Majesty. I *am* sorry," Pterocles said. "I can't help the way the springs and wells are laid out, though. You have to blame the gods for that."

"I wasn't blaming you," Grus assured him. "I can see how you wouldn't be able to do anything about it. But I can wish it were different, though, too." He looked over toward Trabzun again. "I can wish a lot of things were different."

"Your Majesty?" Pterocles made an inquiring noise.

"Oh, nothing . . . nothing," Grus repeated, a little annoyed that he'd shown so much of himself. Pterocles plainly didn't believe him—which seemed only fair, since he wasn't telling the truth. But he didn't want to tell the wizard just how much he wished his one legitimate son had turned out to be a decent, hardworking man instead of . . . what he was. The older Grus got, the more he thought about what would happen after he wasn't here to rule Avornis.

When he first seized the throne, he'd expected Ortalis to succeed him. Lanius could go right on wearing the crown; he was, after all, the last twig of the old, familiar dynasty. If he had a son by Sosia, that boy could be called king, too. But real power would flow through Ortalis and *his* descendants.

That wasn't exactly how things looked anymore, however much Grus wished they still did. Lanius had proved more than

Grus expected, Ortalis less. *If I were to die now . . .* Grus shook his head, shying away from the thought like a horse shying from a buzzing fly. Sooner or later, the fly *would* land. It *would* sting. Sooner or later—*but please, King Olor, not yet.*

Things would only get more complicated if Ortalis had a son. Grus had heard from Lanius that Limosa was expecting another child. He hadn't heard from Ortalis. He couldn't remember whether Ortalis had ever written to him while he was in the field. Maybe a letter of justification or two, to try to put a good light on some palace scrape Ortalis had gotten into. Past that, no.

It didn't necessarily matter. Grus knew that. Being able to write an interesting letter—indeed, being able to write at all— was no prerequisite for kingship. If people would do what you told them to do, and would do it even when you didn't watch over them to make sure they did, you had what you needed to be a king. And if what you told them to do worked most of the time, you had what you needed to be a fairly good king.

"It isn't magic," Grus murmured.

He didn't realize he'd spoken aloud till Pterocles asked, "What isn't?"

"Oh," Grus said. "Being a king, I meant."

"Not the kind of magic I do," the wizard agreed. "But a good king has magic of his own. A good king needs to have people like him and take him seriously at the same time. Plenty of people have one or the other. Having both at once isn't so easy."

That wasn't far from Grus' thought. He said, "I wonder how you get them." He was thinking of Ortalis and Lanius again. There was no doubt people took Lanius seriously. How much they liked him was another question. As for Ortalis . . .

Grus was just as glad when Pterocles broke into his train of thought by saying, "I can't tell you that, Your Majesty. I'm afraid nobody else can, either. Plenty of people besides kings wish they knew the answer there."

"I suppose so." Grus did more than suppose it; he was sure it was true. He looked in the direction of Trabzun once more. "What could we do to make that place fall faster?"

"Undermine the walls?" Pterocles suggested. "I'm no general, but I know besiegers often try that. It must work some of the time."

"It does—some of the time," Grus said. "Times when it does, the men on the other side usually don't know you're doing it until things start falling down on their heads. With all this open country around the town, hiding the digging and getting rid of the dirt without the Menteshe noticing would be a neat trick." His gaze sharpened. "Or do you think you could help bring it off?"

"Maybe." Pterocles made the word long and thoughtful. "It would depend on not letting the Menteshe sorcerers inside Trabzun know I was using a masking spell. Once they realize there's something to see through, they will, and in a hurry."

"Try anyhow," Grus urged. He wouldn't just be sitting and waiting now, and that was—or at least felt—all to the good.

# CHAPTER EIGHT

A bird sang in the gardens around the palace. Lanius wondered what sort of bird it was. Some people could tell one bird from another by the briefest snatch of song. The king wasn't one of them. He knew a hawk from a heron, but not much more, not by note alone.

*I could learn,* he thought. *I could, if I had the time.* But that was a formidable challenge. He already had hobbies—the moncats, the archives, serving girls every now and then. When he was younger, he'd taught himself to draw and paint, but he didn't have the time to stay sharp at that. Being a king swallowed more hours than he wished it did.

The bird went on singing. It didn't care whether he knew what it was. It was singing for the joy of it, or maybe to find a mate—which involved a different kind of joy.

Sosia looked across the breakfast table at Lanius. "I just asked you a question," she said pointedly. "Didn't you hear me?"

"I'm sorry," he said. "I didn't. I'm afraid I was listening to the bird outside."

She gave him the withering glance wives reserve for husbands who aren't all they might be. "I might have known," she said. "How many times have I caught you with your head in the clouds?"

"It wasn't in the clouds," Lanius protested. "Just in the garden."

"Better there than some places," Sosia said. She knew about his occasional hobby, and didn't like it. She also thought it more occasional than it was. She would have liked it even less if she'd known more about it. With exaggerated patience, she repeated herself. "I said, have you been paying attention to the company my brother's been keeping lately?"

Lanius shook his head. "I generally try *not* to pay attention to the company your brother keeps, unless you mean Anser. Wouldn't you say it's more Limosa's worry than mine, anyhow?"

Sosia made an exasperated noise. "Not *that* kind of company." The hooded glance she sent him said she thought he knew too much about *that* kind of company himself. With an obvious effort, she made herself put that thought aside. She went on, "I meant some of the young officers he's been drinking with."

"Ortalis?" Lanius said in surprise. His wife nodded. He took a sip of wine while he thought. "Three things occur to me." He ticked them off on his fingers. "Maybe they're men with pretty sisters—or pretty wives. Maybe they're men who like to hunt. Or maybe, knowing Ortalis, they're men with, ah, peculiar tastes."

"I'd think he's chatted up enough of them to make that last unlikely—although you never can tell." Sosia's mouth twisted in distaste. "The other two? Maybe. There's something else, though—something you're not seeing."

"What?" Lanius asked in real perplexity. He thought he'd thought of everything. He took pride in thinking of as many things as he could.

But Sosia found something he'd missed. "Maybe he's plotting with them."

"Ortalis?" Now Lanius all but squeaked in surprise. "He's done a lot of nasty things, but they're all nasty because he is what he is. They're not nasty because he's after the crown."

"Not yet," his wife said grimly. "But if Limosa has a boy . . . He may care more on account of his children than he does for himself. Plenty of people are like that."

Lanius couldn't tell her she was wrong, for he knew she wasn't. He said, "Well, I'll keep an eye on it." He didn't mean he'd spy on Ortalis himself. He had palace servants he trusted to take care of that for him. "If he's talking with young officers, he can't mean too much by it. He'd be talking with their superiors if he did."

"Maybe," Sosia said again. Again, she didn't sound as though she believed it. "Sometimes, though, if you get the junior officers on your side, they'll bring the senior officers with them."

Once more, Lanius couldn't tell her she was wrong. He said, "You can come up with things like that, because you're as sly as your father." He seldom praised Grus' cleverness, but he knew he couldn't ignore it. "But Ortalis?" He shook his head. "Say what you want about your brother, but nobody's ever accused him of being subtle."

"If he were subtle, I wouldn't know what he was doing, would I?" his wife retorted. "Even if he's not subtle, that doesn't mean he's not dangerous."

"We'll see what's going on, that's all." Lanius could easily imagine Ortalis as dangerous to him in a fit of temper. Imagining his brother-in-law as dangerous in a conspiracy was something else again.

Sosia scowled at him. "You don't believe me. You don't want to believe me. You'd sooner pay attention to the stupid bird that was singing out there."

"I've lived in the palace my whole life," Lanius answered. "I like to think I have some idea when trouble's brewing and when it isn't. Just because I don't agree that Ortalis is doing something particularly bad doesn't mean I'm not paying attention to you."

"You weren't before," Sosia reminded him. "Not very long before, either."

"I am now, though. I have been." Lanius did his best to seem virtuous and innocent. He must have succeeded; his wife stopped nagging him.

Flies buzzed through the Avornan encirclement of Trabzun. Grus ignored them when he could and slapped at them when he couldn't. With all the garbage and sewage accumulating as his army besieged the town, he couldn't be surprised the bugs were bad. If anything, they could have been worse.

Grus made a point of appearing now here, now there, all around the encirclement. He wanted the Menteshe to notice him and to wonder what sort of scheme he was plotting. The only thing he didn't want them to do was come up with the right answer.

Shielded—Grus hoped—by Pterocles' masking spell, sappers dug down toward the walls of Trabzun. The king showed himself to the Menteshe there as often as he did anywhere else. "Shouldn't you stay away from this part of the line, Your Majesty?" Hirundo asked him after one of those appearances.

He shook his head. "I don't think so. If I show myself around four fifths of the circle but not right here, the garrison will start wondering why. If I show myself all the way around, they won't care more about one stretch of the line than any other."

Hirundo thought that over. He overacted thinking it over, in fact; he grunted and stroked his chin and stared up into the sky. At last, reluctantly, he nodded. "You've got a complicated way of looking at the world, haven't you?" he said.

"It's a complicated place," Grus answered. "Making things as simple as you can is good. Making them too simple isn't."

"How do you tell the difference?" The general sounded genuinely curious.

"Well, if you start making a lot of mistakes, you probably think things are simpler than they really are," Grus said.

Hirundo started to say something else. Before he could, a soldier ran toward Grus and him shouting, "Your Majesty! General! Your Majesty!"

"I don't know that I like the sound of that," Hirundo said.

"I do know that I don't like it a bit. Something's gone wrong somewhere." Grus raised his voice and waved to the soldier. "We're here. What is it?"

"Your Majesty, there's a good-sized Menteshe army coming up from the south," the man replied.

"Well, we knew that was liable to happen," Hirundo said.

"So we did," Grus agreed. "We've done what we could to

get ready for it, too. Now we get to see how good a job that was."

"I'd better go out to the outer works and have a look for myself," Hirundo said.

"I'll come, too," the king told him. "If I start joggling your elbow, don't be shy about letting me know."

"Everyone knows how shy and retiring I am, Your Majesty," Hirundo replied. "People have been talking about it for years." He didn't even try to pretend that Grus should take him seriously. He knew better. Grus didn't say anything. He just rolled his eyes and went along with the general.

He made sure trumpeters came with them, too. He didn't *know* what orders Hirundo would give, but he had a pretty good notion. Trumpeters would spread the word far faster than runners could.

The outer works, by now, were head-high, with a rammed-earth step for archers, pikemen, and observers. Grus got up on the step and peered south. Hirundo had gotten up there ahead of him. The approaching army was close enough to let the king see individual riders under the cloud of dust the mass of them kicked up.

"I wonder how serious they are," he said.

"Well, I doubt they came here for a holiday," Hirundo observed.

"Oh, so do I. But whether they make an attack and go away with their honor satisfied or really press it home . . . That makes a lot of difference," Grus said. "What sort of sally the garrison inside Trabzun makes will be interesting, too."

"There's one word for it." Hirundo looked back over his shoulder toward the walls of the besieged city. "I think I'd better order the men into back-to-back. The other *interesting* question—that word again!—is whether we really do have enough men to hold the outer ring and the inner at the same time. Well, we'll find out, won't we?" He sounded lighthearted. If he'd sounded as worried as he felt . . . he probably would have sounded as worried as Grus felt, too.

The king made himself nod. He made himself seem calm while he did it, too. He said, "Yes, that seems to be what needs doing, all right." Hirundo spoke to the trumpeters. They blared

out the command. Other musicians all around the Avornans'
ring took it up.

Swearing soldiers sprinted to their stations. Grus looked
back toward Trabzun, as Hirundo had before him. He didn't see
any sudden burst of activity from the defenders atop it. Of
course, if the Menteshe commander inside the town had any
brains, he wouldn't. The warriors in there would open a gate
and storm out fighting without giving anything away beforehand. Grus knew that perfectly well. He eyed the town anyway.
Not all commanders had brains. That, unfortunately, was just as
true for Avornans as it was for Menteshe.

Something else occurred to him. He did some swearing of
his own, then hurried off to find Pterocles. The wizard, as he'd
expected, stood near the hole in the ground where the miners
worked. "We may need your magic against the nomads outside," Grus said. "Will your masking spell hold up for a while
if you aren't there to keep an eye on it every minute?"

"Nomads outside?" Pterocles peered around in surprise. Up
until that moment, the horn calls and the soldiers running back
and forth had escaped his notice. He sent Grus an accusing
stare. "Something is going on, isn't it?"

"Oh, you might say so," the king answered. Since Pterocles
plainly had no idea what, Grus filled him in with a few sen-
tences, finishing, "*Can* you leave this by itself, or at least to a
junior wizard?"

"Someone will need to keep it going." Pterocles shouted,
and kept shouting until another wizard came up. That took
longer than Grus thought it should have; Pterocles didn't seem
to be the only absentminded sorcerer who'd come south of the
Stura. But Pterocles bowed when the other wizard was in place.
"I am at your service, Your Majesty."

"Come on, then." Grus picked up a shield some foot soldier
had forgotten. He tossed it to Pterocles, who caught it awkwardly. "Here. I expect you'll want this."

By the expression on Pterocles' face, he'd never grabbed
anything he wanted less. But, under Grus' stern eye, he didn't
let go. Grus commandeered a shield for himself a moment later.
Well before they got back to the outer palisade, arrows started

coming down not far away from them. "Oh," Pterocles said in what sounded like real surprise. "Now I understand."

"I'm so glad," Grus said. The look the sorcerer sent him was distinctly wounded. But he yelped like a puppy with a stepped-on tail when an arrow thudded into his shield. It might have gone by harmlessly had he not carried the round, bronze-faced wooden disk. On the other hand, it might not have. Grus gave back a sardonic nod. "You see?"

"Well, now that you mention it, yes," Pterocles replied in an unusually small voice.

Hirundo pointed out toward the Menteshe. "So far, they're just riding around shooting at us. They won't do us much harm that way. We've hit a few of them, too, though their bows shoot farther than ours. But we'll start using the dart-throwers and stone-throwers on 'em any minute. By Olor's mighty fist, they can't outrange those, and I don't think they'll like 'em very much."

He proved a good prophet. The engines began to buck and snap, sending their missiles farther and faster than any arrow could fly. A dart could pin a nomad's leg to his horse, or go right through him and pierce the man behind him. A twenty-pound stone ball would mash a man's head, or a horse's, to red rags. In moving out of range of such weapons, the Menteshe also moved out beyond their own ability to strike at the Avornans.

"If they want to give us trouble, they'll have to close with us." Hirundo sounded somberly satisfied. "Otherwise, they can ride and whoop and holler as much as they please, but they're just a bunch of nuisances."

Before Grus could answer, cries of alarm rose from the inner palisade. "A sally! A sally!" The king caught the news through the general din.

Menteshe were pouring out of the gates of Trabzun and swarming toward the palisade. Their guttural war cries filled the air. "Hold them!" Grus shouted to the men on the inner ring. "Don't let them get over!"

"Now we see how smart they are and how smooth they are. Can they hit us from inside and outside at the same time?"

Hirundo might have been a scholar curious to see what someone else's students knew about his specialty.

Grus admired that detachment without wanting to imitate it. "If they can get over from inside and outside at the same time, we're in trouble," he said.

"There is that," Hirundo agreed. "We just have to make sure they can't, then, don't we?"

"Would be nice," Grus said. Hirundo laughed merrily, as though they were a pair of tradesmen bantering back and forth in front of their shops. And so they were, but at the moment their trade involved bloodshed and slaughter. As though to underscore the point, an arrow thrummed past Grus' head. He jerked up his shield. That would have done him no good at all if the arrow had been a little better aimed.

He trotted toward the inner palisade, drawing his sword as he did. "It's the king!" Avornan soldiers called to one another. "The king is coming to help us!"

Grus laughed almost as hard as Hirundo had a moment earlier. He would fight if he had to. He hadn't been a bad swordsman when he was half his present age. He still knew what to do with a blade. His body, though, was less willing—no, less able—to do it than it had been thirty years before.

Pikemen, archers, and swordsmen were holding back the garrison of Trabzun. The ditch in front of the palisade also helped. Some of the Menteshe leaped down into it and then tried to scramble up over the palisade and into the Avornans' ring around their city. Most of them got shot or stabbed before they even came close to the top.

Grus had always thought that the Avornans knew more about attacking works than the nomads did. The Menteshe hadn't proved good at taking walled towns in southern Avornis during their last invasion. They'd destroyed crops around them and tried to starve them into submission. The few times they'd tried to storm them, they'd failed, and paid heavily for their failure.

Here, though, they knew what to do about the ditch—or some of them did. They threw brush hurdles into it and ran across those before the Avornans could set them on fire. Then they started trying to boost one another over the palisade. They had a much better chance of managing that from the hurdles than they did from the bottom of the ditch.

Now they could strike back at the Avornans. One of Grus' men fell, his face a gory mask from the sword stroke that had laid him low. A Menteshe scrambled over the palisade and inside. Several Avornans rushed at him. He went down before any other nomads could join him.

Even so, shouts from all around the inner ring warned that this wasn't the only place where the Menteshe were using those bound piles of brush to span the ditch. More cries rose from behind Grus. That could only mean the horsemen outside the ring were trying to break in, too. He wondered whether they'd also brought brushwood with them. *I'll find out,* he thought.

Meanwhile, more Menteshe made it over the inner palisade. Knots of cursing, shouting men battled one another. A nomad broke out of the nearest knot and rushed at Grus.

The nomad cut at his head. He blocked the blow. Sparks flew as iron belled off iron. The Menteshe slashed again. He had no style, but what seemed like endless youth and vigor. That might suffice, and Grus knew it.

Then another Avornan ran at the nomad. The Menteshe's face twisted in anger and fear. He didn't fancy facing two at once. He had no choice, though. Figuring—no doubt accurately—the young soldier was more dangerous than the frost-bearded king, he gave more of his attention to the new foe.

He likely would have beaten Grus without much trouble had they faced each other with no interference from other fighters. But he couldn't fend off the king with only a third or a quarter of his aim focused on him. Grus' sword went home below the nomad's right arm, a spot the fellow's boiled-leather corselet didn't protect. The Menteshe howled like a wolf. The pain of the wound distracted him, and the other Avornan's sword bit into his neck. He swayed, blood spurting from the wound, and then crumpled.

"We make a good team, Your Majesty," the Avornan soldier said.

"So we do," Grus replied. "Tell me your name."

"I'm called Esacus, Your Majesty."

"Esacus," Grus repeated, fixing the name in his mind. "Well, Esacus, you'll have a reward when all this is done."

"Thank you very much, but I didn't do it for that," the soldier said.

"Which makes you more deserving, not less," Grus told him. Esacus scratched his head, plainly not understanding. That proved he'd never had anything to do with the royal court. People there were apt to act much more heroic if they thought the king's eye was on them than they might have otherwise.

"You stay back, Your Majesty," Esacus called as more Menteshe made it over the palisade. Shouting, "Avornis!" the soldier rushed into the fight.

Grus did stay back. He knew good advice when he heard it. The Menteshe couldn't get enough men within the Avornan ring at the same time to give the defenders too much trouble.

The nomads were also trying to break into the palisaded ring from the outside. Despite the barrage of arrows they rained on the defenders, they weren't having much luck. They must have hoped that barrage would break the Avornans, which would give them the chance they needed to force an entry. Unlike the Menteshe inside Trabzun, the relief force hadn't brought any hurdles or other ways to cross the ditch and come to grips with Grus' men at close quarters.

They were brave. Like anything else, bravery didn't matter so much without the talent that would have supported it. If anything, it made the nomads take heavier losses than they would have with less courage. They kept on attacking even when the attacks couldn't succeed—and they paid for it.

At last, they had taken as much as they could take. They gave up trying to force their way into the ring. A few at a time, they began to ride off. Some lingered to keep on shooting at the Avornans from beyond the range where Grus' archers could respond. Then a stone flung from an engine knocked a chieftain out of the saddle—and knocked over his horse, too. After that, the nomads seemed to decide they'd had enough. The men who'd lingered rode away after their comrades.

Grus ordered some of the Avornans from the outer works to go to the aid of the men who were fighting off the much more stubborn attack on the inner ones. When the Menteshe trying to break out of Trabzun saw that the Avornans battling them were being reinforced, they sullenly drew back into the city—those who could, at any rate.

Later, the king realized he should have tried to force an entry then. The Menteshe were in disarray, and the gates had to stay open for a while to let them back within the walls. But the nomads, though they hadn't won, had fought well—well enough to rock the Avornans back on their heels. Grus did not issue the order. Neither did Hirundo. No one pursued the Menteshe as they retreated.

What Grus did do as the fighting eased was let out a long sigh of relief and stab his sword into the soil to clean the blood off the blade. He sent runners out to find Hirundo and bring him back. The general nodded as he came up. "Well, Your Majesty, we got through that one," he said.

"I was thinking the same thing." Grus spotted Pterocles and waved to him. "Is the mine still masked from the Menteshe? I hope none of them stumbled down the hole when they broke in. And I hope the wizard you set there didn't run away from his post when that happened."

"I'll go find out," Pterocles said, which was exactly what Grus wanted to hear from him. The wizard hurried away.

"We can always start the undermining again somewhere else if things did get buggered up," Hirundo said.

"I know. But we would have wasted a lot of time and a lot of work," the king replied. "And if the Menteshe know we're trying to dig under the wall, they'll countermine to keep us away." He snapped his fingers. "Which reminds me—we have to bring in the hurdles the nomads used to cross the inner ditch."

"I should hope so. If we don't, they're liable to sneak out at night and see if they can slit our throats while we're sleeping," Hirundo said.

"Well, yes, that, too," Grus said. Hirundo gave him a puzzled look. He explained what he had in mind.

Hirundo heard him out and then bowed. "That's very nice, Your Majesty. Very fitting, you might say. I'll give the orders right away." As Pterocles had a few minutes earlier, he bustled off to tend to what needed doing.

The wizard returned at a trot, the smile on Pterocles' face

telling Grus what he needed to know even before the wizard said, "All's very well, Your Majesty. No trouble came too close to Calidris, and he kept the spell going all through the fight. The Menteshe in Trabzun don't know what we're up to."

"Ah." Grus smiled, too. His was a more wolfish expression than the one the wizard wore. "Then that work will go on. How much longer till we're under Trabzun's walls? Do you happen to know?"

Pterocles shook his head. "I spoke to the sorcerer, not to the minemaster."

"Too bad," Grus said. "We'll go on till we finish, that's all." He looked south, toward Yozgat. "Yes, we'll go on till we finish."

King Lanius looked up toward the skylight set into the roof above the royal archives. Dusty sunbeams filtered down to where he sat. No one had ever been able to get those skylights clean. Lanius suspected much of the dirt was on the inside of the glass, and thereby inaccessible. The only way to be rid of it would be to take out the panes and replace them with clean ones.

A faint skittering noise came from somewhere in the bowels of the archives. Lanius sighed. He knew mice got in here. The only thing he didn't know was how many precious parchments they'd chewed up before he ever got the chance to see them.

Grus had written that he was besieging Trabzun, formerly Trapezus. Avornis hadn't owned the city for centuries. Even so, the archives held papers and parchments about the city and what it had been like in bygone days—tax records, reports on the state of the walls, appeals to lawsuits that had gone all the way to the city of Avornis. Lanius had run into them from time to time when he was looking for other things, sometimes when he was looking for nothing in particular.

He'd run into them, yes, but he hadn't thought anything about it. Why should he have? The Kingdom of Avornis had lost more than a few cities in the Menteshe invasions. Quite a few of them, these days, were only ruins. The one that really impinged on Avornan consciousness was Yozgat, and that more because it held the Scepter of Mercy than for any other reason.

Lanius shook his head. The road to Yozgat ran through Trabzun, and he had to think about Trabzun now.

Dust rose in choking clouds when the king pulled a crate off a shelf. Coughing, he carried the crate to a table. He thought he remembered finding papers from Trabzun—or rather, from Trapezus—in it. As he pulled out documents and started reading them, he happened to look down at himself. His tunic, though old, had been clean when he put it on. Now dust and dirt streaked and spotted it. He tried to brush off some of the dust with his hands, and raised a small cloud around himself without getting the tunic much cleaner.

The king began to wonder whether he knew what *he* was talking about. The crate didn't seem to have any of the documents he was looking for. Were they really somewhere else? Was he misremembering? He'd done that when he was looking for papers from Yozgat. Once could happen to anybody. Twice? Didn't twice suggest his memory wasn't as good as he thought it was? For a man who prided himself on his wits—not least because he didn't have a whole lot of other things on which to pride himself—that was a disheartening notion.

"Ha!" he exclaimed as he got near the bottom of the crate. There they were! He'd buried them under other documents that had seemed more interesting the last time he went through them.

Tax registers from Trapezus wouldn't do Grus any good. The people who'd dutifully paid those taxes (or not so dutifully tried to evade them) were hundreds of years dead. Their descendants, if they had any, were probably thralls. But . . .

"Ha!" Lanius said again, and plucked a parchment from the crate. Here was a map of Trapezus long ago, showing which of those taxpayers—recalcitrant or otherwise—owned which properties in the city. Again, those property owners were ashes for a very long time. Many of the buildings were bound to have fallen down between then and now. Odds were, though, that the streets still ran as they had in those far-off days, which meant Grus might find the map worth having.

Lanius sighed once more. Part of him still resented working for the man who'd stolen half his throne and far more than half his power. But he couldn't deny, however much he wanted to, that Grus had done a good job with that power. If, say, Ortalis had been the usurper . . . Lanius shook his head. No, he didn't want to think about that.

Below the map lay a report from an officer in Trapezus on the walls, and on repairs that had been made after an earthquake. Lanius decided to send that along, too. Maybe there had been more earthquakes since, but it might prove useful.

He was sure Grus would be interested in some of the things he'd found out about Yozgat. He would tell his father-in-law about those when Grus got back to the city of Avornis. He didn't want to put them in writing. They would have to travel a long way south of the Stura before they got to Grus. Lanius knew Menteshe raiders bedeviled the route by which supplies and letters went down to the Avornan army. If he went into too much detail and the dispatch happened to be captured—that wouldn't be good at all.

And it could end up a lot worse than merely no good at all. A captured dispatch from one King of Avornis to the other might end up in the Banished One's hands. That would do for a catastrophe until a more emphatic word came along. If the Banished One suspected any of what Lanius had in mind, all his carefully laid plans would fall to pieces then and there.

He heard another skittering noise and looked up, hoping it was Pouncer. But no moncat came out hoping for a treat. *Just another mouse,* he thought. He'd tried setting traps in the archives, traps that would smash any mouse taking the bait. The next dead mouse he saw in any of them would be the first. He had almost smashed his own foot in one; only a hasty backward leap saved him. After that, he took out the traps.

Thinking of that fiasco made him start to laugh. What if he'd forgotten one and left it here? How long would it be before some other king—or perhaps some scholar—prowled through the archives the way he liked to do? A hundred years from now, or two hundred, would the man who went through the archives have any idea the trap that had smashed his foot was set by a King of Avornis? Lanius didn't see how he could.

Sosia gave him a peculiar look when he told her about the thought later that day. "You find the oddest things to worry about," she said.

"I wasn't worried. I just thought it was . . . interesting," Lanius said.

"Interesting!" His wife snorted. "Who in the world could care about what happens a hundred years from now?"

*The Banished One could,* Lanius thought. But he didn't want to be compared to the exiled god, and the Banished One wasn't in the world willingly. There was another answer he could give her, though. "I do. The dynasty reaches back further than that. I'd like to see it reach forward further than that, too." He pointed a finger at her. "Wouldn't you? You're part of the dynasty yourself, you know."

Sosia looked surprised. Then she nodded. "You're right. I am," she said, wonder in her voice.

Lanius knew why she looked surprised and sounded wondering. She thought of herself as part of Grus' family. Grus had wed her to Lanius not least so she could keep an eye on him. She would back him against Ortalis—he was sure of that. Nobody liked Ortalis, though (*except Limosa,* Lanius thought uneasily). But would Sosia back him against Grus?

That was the wrong question. The right question was, would it matter if she did? Lanius feared it wouldn't. A good thing, then, that he and Grus both aimed at Yozgat and not at each other.

# CHAPTER NINE

Much of the dirt dug out of the tunnel approaching Trabzun went to strengthen the inner and outer fieldworks surrounding the town. That was Hirundo's idea, and King Grus liked it very much. It gave the Avornans somewhere inconspicuous to conceal the spoil from the mine. As the amount of dirt dug out grew greater and greater, that became ever more important.

After being beaten back once, the Menteshe outside Trabzun did not return for another attack on the besiegers. That relieved Grus, and also rather surprised him. One evening, he remarked, "I hope they've gone back to fighting their civil war again."

"That would be nice," Hirundo agreed. He fanned himself with the palm of his hand. "I'll tell you something else that would be nice—it would be nice if it got cooler around here."

"So it would," Grus said. The air was still and breathless. Things farther than a few hundred yards away shimmered in a heat haze. A drop of sweat tickled as it trickled through his beard. A bird called. Even the noise seemed flat and dispirited—or maybe that was Grus' imagination, as overheated as everything else that had to do with Trabzun. He went on, "Don't expect anything different, though, not till summer finally decides to let up."

"Oh, I don't. I've seen what the weather's like around here." Hirundo swatted at a bug that landed on his bare arm. He killed it, and wiped his hand on his tunic. "Knowing it doesn't mean I have to like it."

"No, I suppose not. I don't much like it myself." Grus snapped his fingers. "Did I tell you? No, of course I didn't, because it just happened today. I got a plan of the streets inside Trabzun."

"*Did* you, by the gods?" The general beamed. "That's good news. Where did you get it from? Did Pterocles pull a new spell out of his belt pouch?"

Grus shook his head. "No. He was just as surprised as you are. I got it from Lanius. He found it in the archives back at the palace."

Hirundo laughed so loud, several soldiers stared at him. "He's all the way back there, and we're here, and he knows more about this stinking place than we do? That's funny, is what that is." He paused. "That plan will be older than dirt, if he pulled it out of the archives. D'you think it's still good?"

"Funny you should ask. He warned me about that. He said he didn't know what the buildings were like in there, but the way the streets ran shouldn't have changed much."

"That does make sense," Hirundo allowed. "His Majesty thought of everything, didn't he?"

"So it seems. He has a way of doing that." Grus heard the edge in his own voice. He'd been happy to have Lanius excavate the archives. If the other king played with things from long-ago and far-off days, he wouldn't worry about other things—like power for himself, for instance. But Lanius, not for the first time, had found a way to make the past matter here and now. And if he could do that, then he wasn't so disconnected from the real world after all, was he? *As though I need more things to worry about,* Grus thought.

"He certainly does. He's a clever fellow, King Lanius is." Hirundo, by contrast, sounded enthusiastic. And why not? He would keep on being a general no matter who gave him his orders. Not only that, he'd never shown the least interest in the throne himself. That alone would have been plenty to keep him a general regardless of who wore the crown. Capable soldiers without undue ambition were worth their weight in gold.

"I'll have my secretaries copy out the street plan so our officers can use it when they break into Trabzun," Grus said. "No matter how old it is, it'll come in handy."

"Fair enough," Hirundo said. "The timing was good. The way these things usually work, we would have gotten it two days after we fired the mine."

"I know, I know." Grus nodded, and then asked, "How much longer before the diggers get under the wall?"

"Another few days," the general answered. "The engineers have some way of figuring out when they're in the right place, or maybe it's the wizards who know. I don't worry my head about that kind of thing too much. I suppose it's a little more complicated than unrolling a ball of string till you've gone far enough."

"Probably. Most of the time, things do turn out more complicated than you wish they would. If they were easy all the time, just about everybody could do just about anything. I suppose that's why people in songs and stories can do whatever they want so easily—if you're listening to that kind of thing, you think you can do anything."

Hirundo gave him a wide-eyed, innocent stare. "You mean I can't, Your Majesty?" He looked as though he were about to break into tears.

Grus laughed. "With you, nothing would surprise me."

"Me? What about you?" Hirundo pointed at him. "Am I the fellow who made Dagipert of Thervingia leave us alone? Am I the fellow who taught the Chernagors respect? Am I the fellow who took an Avornan army south of the Stura for the first time in gods only know how many years?" He paused. "Well, I suppose King Lanius would know how many years, too."

"Yes, I suppose he would." Grus was sure the other king would know not just the year but to the hour. That was Lanius' way. And if he talked about Lanius, he didn't have to talk about himself.

But his general wouldn't let him get away with modesty. "What do you aim to do when you grab the Scepter of Mercy?" Hirundo asked.

*Bash you over the head with it,* was the first thing that came to Grus' mind. Hirundo was a cheerful soul who didn't worry about things as much as he should. "Don't talk about that, please," Grus said. "I may not be the only one listening."

"What? There's nobody else around. Oh." Another pause from the general. "You mean the Banished One? This for the Banished One." Hirundo snapped his fingers.

He'd never had the exiled god come to him in dreams. He'd never started up in bed after one of those dreams, heart pounding, eyes staring, cold sweat and gooseflesh all over his body. He didn't know how lucky he was. "For my sake if not your own, please—please!—don't mention him again," Grus said carefully.

"Sure, Your Majesty." Hirundo was nothing if not agreeable. "How come, though?"

"Because he really might be listening," Grus answered, and let it go at that. Most of the time, a man learned only by experience. Hirundo had no experience. Grus wished *he* didn't, either.

A mug flew past Lanius' head and shattered against the wall behind him. "You—You slimy *thing,* you!" Sosia shouted, and looked for something else to throw.

"Oh, dear," Lanius said unhappily. He knew what sparked fury like that in his wife. Knowing, he tried to pretend he didn't. "What's wrong, dear?"

"You are, that's what. You're wrong if you think you can bed any cute little chit of a serving girl and have me sit still for it. Not even Queen Quelea would put up with the trouble you give me." Sosia scaled the tray the mug had sat on at him. He sidestepped more nimbly than he'd thought he could. The tray slammed into the wall with a noise like a thunderclap.

No servants came running to see what the trouble was. When the servants heard shouts and bangs like that, they already had a good idea what the trouble was. They were likely to interfere only if they saw blood dribbling out under the doorway to the royal bedchamber.

Sosia went on, "Well, you won't be bedding Oissa again, by the gods! I sent her packing—you can bet on that."

"Oh, dear," Lanius said again. He'd have to find out where Sosia had sent Oissa. Was she still in the city of Avornis, or had

Sosia exiled her to the provinces? The provinces, probably; the queen didn't do those things by halves. Wherever she was, Lanius knew he would have to find a quiet way to make sure she stayed comfortable. That was only fair. He was, in his own way, scrupulous about such things.

"What have you got to say for yourself?" Sosia snarled. " 'Oh, dear' doesn't do the job, believe you me it doesn't."

She wouldn't believe him if he called Oissa a liar. The next best thing was to plead for mercy. He tried that, spreading his hands placatingly and saying, "I'm sorry."

She laughed in his face. "How many times have you told me that? How many times have I believed it? How many times have I been a fool? The only thing you're sorry about is that I found out again."

"I *am* sorry," Lanius insisted. "I don't want to make you unhappy." That was true. He also noticed Sosia was careful not to say she'd never let him into her bed again. If she said that, what was to keep him from going out and looking for another serving woman? If the King of Avornis looked, he wouldn't have to look very far, either. They both knew that.

"If you don't want to make me unhappy, why do you do things like this?" Sosia demanded. "You don't fall in love with them, not anymore."

"I only did that once," Lanius said. Sosia rolled her eyes. Lanius' cheeks heated. No matter how embarrassing, what he'd said was true. Only his first affair had turned into what he thought was love.

"Why?" Sosia asked once more.

That had but one possible answer, the obvious one: *Because it's fun.* The trouble with that answer was equally obvious— Sosia wouldn't want to hear it. That being so, Lanius looked around for something else. "I don't know," he said at last. "I just do."

"You certainly do," his wife agreed bitterly. "You can't resist a pretty face, can you?" *Face* wasn't exactly the word she meant.

Lanius felt himself flush again. "I am sorry," he repeated.

She went right on glaring at him. "That doesn't mean you don't want to keep on doing it. It only means you don't want

me to find out about it. Pretty soon, there'll be banished serving girls in every country town in the kingdom."

"How can I make it up to you?" Lanius said.

"You could start by not dropping your drawers whenever
you walk into a linen closet," Sosia snapped. That was more
precise information than he'd thought she would have. Somebody had been spying on him.

"I'll . . . do my best," Lanius said—a promise that was not
a promise.

Sosia knew perfectly well that it wasn't a promise, too. She
looked no happier. "If you were somebody ordinary, I could
walk away from you and try my luck somewhere else. But I
can't even do that, can I?"

"No," Lanius said, thinking, *And neither can I.* He compen-
sated for it by sporting with the maidservants. If Sosia tried
turning the tables on him that way, the scandal would be enormous. It probably wasn't fair, which didn't mean it wasn't true.
He sighed once more. "We are what we are, and one of the
things we are is, uh, left with each other." He'd almost said
*stuck with each other,* which was true but less polite.

His wife sent him yet another furious glance. This one said
she had no trouble reading between the lines. She looked
around. He thought it was for something else to throw. He got
ready to duck. Instead, she burst into tears and stormed out of
the bedchamber. She slammed the door behind her—one more
punctuation mark on the quarrel.

"Is . . . Is everything all right, Your Majesty?" a servant
asked him when he too left the bedchamber.

"These things happen," Lanius answered vaguely. That he
and Sosia had fought would be all over the palace by now. Before long, all the intimate details of the fight would be blown
so out of proportion that the two people who actually knew the
truth would never recognize them. Such things were all too familiar to the king. They'd happened before; they would happen
again. *What a depressing idea,* he thought.

King Grus stood by the entrance to the mine the Avornan soldiers had dug under the walls of Trabzun. A last couple of men
came out of the shaft. They'd filled the end of it with wood and

brush—the hurdles the Menteshe had used to bridge the ditch in front of the palisade were now playing a new role—and then drenched all that with oil. An oil-soaked rope led from the entrance to the mass of waiting fuel.

A captain handed Grus a lighted torch. "Would you care to do the honors, Your Majesty?" the man asked.

"I'd be delighted," Grus replied, matching courtesy with courtesy. He stooped and touched the flame to the rope. It caught at once. Fire snaked down it and out of sight. Grus asked, "How long will we have to wait?"

"Shouldn't be long," the captain said. "If smoke doesn't start pouring out of the hole pretty soon, something's gone wrong in there." The corners of his mouth turned down. "In that case, somebody has to go down in there and start things up again."

"Who?" Grus asked. That struck him as an unenviable job, especially if the break was very close to the brush and wood that would become a conflagration as soon as flames reached them.

"Who?" the captain echoed. "Me." No wonder he looked unhappy.

Pterocles stood close by. He and the other wizards had been maintaining the masking spell ever since the digging started. Now he asked, "Your Majesty, may I lift the spell when the smoke bursts forth?"

"That depends. Can the Menteshe work any kind of magic to foil the mine in the time between when they see the smoke and things start falling down?" *If things do start falling down,* the king thought; mining was an imperfect art.

"I can't imagine how," Pterocles answered.

"Then go ahead," Grus said.

He waited. So did the captain, apprehensively. So did Pterocles, who looked pleased he was about to be relieved of a burden. Just when Grus began to wonder whether something *had* gone wrong, thick black smoke began billowing from the hole. Coughing, Grus stepped upwind of it. So did the captain, his face now wreathed in smiles. Pterocles had had sense enough to stay upwind from the beginning.

Grus wondered how long the fire would take to consume the

supports that had kept the mine from collapsing under the weight of earth and stone above it. He started to ask the officer, then held his tongue. He would find out as soon as anyone did.

Avornan soldiers waited near the shaft. When the moment came—if it came—wooden gangplanks would take them over the ditch and let them charge to the attack. On the wall, Menteshe pointed out toward the rapidly swelling column of smoke. The motions were tiny in the distance, but Grus saw them distinctly. What did the defenders think? Were they hoping something had gone wrong within the Avornan lines? Or did they realize the very stones on which they stood were liable to come tumbling down at any moment?

The question had hardly occurred to Grus before the stones under the feet of the Menteshe must have begun to tremble and shake. The defenders began to run this way and that. Thin and attenuated, their shouts of alarm came to the king's ears. And then those shouts were lost in a great rumbling roar as a long stretch of Trabzun's wall crumbled into ruin. The ground beneath Grus' feet also shook, as though from an earthquake.

But the gods sent earthquakes. This collapse was man-made. Grus and Pterocles and the captain who hadn't had to go down into the mine all whooped and clapped their hands. They pounded one another on the back and embraced like a band of brothers.

A great cloud of dust rose from the shattered wall. Smoke rose, too, as rents in the ground exposed the fire down below. How many men lay crushed and maimed among the tumbled blocks of stone?

*They are the enemy,* Grus reminded himself. *They stand between us and the Scepter of Mercy, between us and a crushing defeat for the Banished One.* A Menteshe who caught him would have cut his throat right away—or else cut his throat after torturing him first. He knew that full well. The men who reverenced the Banished One had chosen evil. Grus knew that, too. But they were still men, and he flinched a little, imagining their suffering.

Horns bellowed within the Avornan lines. Like long tongues, the gangplanks stuck out over the ditch. Soldiers ran across them. Cheering, the men rushed toward the downfallen length of wall. They scrambled over and through the rubble and into Trabzun.

Not all the city's defenders had perished, of course. Most of the wall and most of the garrison remained intact. But then, most of a man remained intact after a spear pierced his chest. He was likely to die even so. And Trabzun, with its defenses breached, was likely to fall.

Menteshe from the undamaged stretches of the wall rushed to try to push back the Avornans. Seeing that, more Avornans went forward all around the city. Now scaling ladders could thud into place against the walls. Now soldiers could rush up them to gain the battlements. Some of the ladders went over. With the defenders so distracted, though, more of them stayed in place. Avornans atop the wall waved banners so the besiegers could see they'd won their lodgements.

Everywhere in Trabzun, Avornans who could speak a little of the Menteshe language shouted, "Surrender! We take prisoners!" Scrawny defenders, their hands in the air and dismay naked on their faces, began stumbling out of the city, herded along by Avornans.

When Trabzun's main gate swung open, Grus whooped again. He thumped Pterocles almost hard enough to knock him flat. "It's ours!" he shouted. "Trabzun is ours!"

"Uh, yes, Your Majesty. So it is." The wizard straightened up. "A good thing, too. If they'd thrown us back, you probably would have murdered me."

"Don't tempt me." Grus sounded as though he was joking, which he was. Pterocles flinched even so. Grus felt ashamed of himself. If a king felt like murdering someone, he could. Who would punish him? Avornis had known its share of bloody-handed tyrants. He didn't care to be remembered as another one. Setting a hand—gently—on Pterocles' shoulder, he said, "I'm sorry."

A king might murder with impunity. Apologizing looked to be something else again. Pterocles stared at him as though he'd said something in some exotic tongue. "I didn't mean anything by it, Your Majesty," the wizard said. *He* might have been the one at fault.

"I don't think either of us did." Grus laughed at himself; he'd just reduced their conversation to meaninglessness.

His guards weren't laughing when he decided to go into Trabzun late that afternoon. Only spatters of fighting were left in the city by then, but they didn't like it anyhow. "Too many places for enemy soldiers to hide," one of them said. "We won't have the place cleaned out for days. If one of those buggers lets fly with a bow . . ."

"That's what you people are for, isn't it?" Grus asked mildly.

"Yes, Your Majesty, but there's such a thing as taking chances when you don't have to," the royal guardsman insisted. Grus muttered to himself. The man had a better point than he cared to admit.

Grus finally entered Trabzun two days later. The guards were still unhappy, and so was he. He supposed that made for a reasonable compromise. He went in through the main gate, not over the tumbled masonry the mine had brought down.

Most of the people left in the city were desperately thin. By then, the Avornans had taken the men from the garrison out of Trabzun. They had been in reasonably good shape. They'd kept most of the food for themselves, leaving the civilians—especially the women and children—just enough to sustain life.

"Will you feed us?" a man called in Avornan. By his hazel eyes and light brown hair, he was descended from the folk who'd lived here when Trabzun was Avornan Trapezus. By his hollow cheeks and broomstick forearms, he needed feeding.

"We'll do everything we can," Grus said. It wasn't quite a promise, as he was uncomfortably aware. He had plenty to keep his soldiers fed. His soldiers and the folk of Trabzun? He wasn't so sure.

A woman even skinnier than the man who'd called held a baby in her arms. The baby's belly stuck out, not because it was plump but on account of starvation. Grus had seen children like that in districts where the crops failed and famine set in. The baby, too listless even to wail, stared at him with dull eyes.

Grus shouted for a quartermaster. When the officer came up to him, he said, "Find out how much the granaries here hold. Feed these people with it. They're going to start dying soon."

"Yes, Your Majesty." The man sketched a salute and hurried away.

*So much to do,* Grus thought. Getting the fallen part of the wall into defensible shape would keep his engineers busy. He'd have to garrison Trabzun if he didn't want to lose it as soon as he moved on. The Menteshe would try to take it back. He didn't intend to let them. How much *was* in the granaries? Enough to feed the locals and his army, too? That would be good. It would mean he wouldn't have to bring so much down from the north. How much farther could he push on in this campaigning season? Could he hold everything his army had taken?

Behind all those questions—every one of them important—lay another, one that seemed to shrink them into insignificance. What would the Banished One do now that the Kingdom of Avornis had succeeded south of the Stura for the first time in centuries? What would he do? What *could* he do?

The king stared south. *We'll find out,* he thought, and hoped learning the answer wouldn't prove too expensive.

Ceremony dictated that the king and queen of Avornis should eat together. Lanius and Sosia bent ceremony as far as they could. He didn't mind her company—he never had—but she wanted nothing to do with him. She couldn't get all of what she wanted, though. Sometimes, as at supper one evening, they found themselves at the same table.

Sosia looked daggers at him. By the way she eyed the knife beside her plate, she might have been thinking of using it as a dagger. "How are you today?" he asked, doing his best to pretend everything was fine.

"I *was* all right," she said pointedly, and sent him another poisonous stare.

"I had a letter from your father this afternoon," Lanius said.

"Did you?" A little interest stirred in Sosia's voice. That could be important. Of course, she wasn't altogether happy with Grus, either, for he had as much trouble staying faithful to her mother as Lanius did to her. Grudgingly, she asked, "What did he say?"

Before Lanius could answer, the servants brought in the meal—roast mutton with cabbage and parsnips. The spicy scent of crushed mint leaves rose from the mutton. Some sort of cheese sauce covered the parsnips. The cabbage was what it was. A servant splashed sweet red wine into Lanius' goblet, and into Sosia's. At the king's gesture, the servants withdrew.

Lanius raised his silver goblet to Sosia. "Your health," he said.

"What did the letter say?" she asked again, instead of pledging him in return.

Biting his lip, he answered, "Trabzun has fallen." Even good news fell flat when delivered to such a hostile audience.

"Well, good, I suppose," Sosia said. "Does he tell you whether he's found a new lady friend down there, too?"

"Oh, no," Lanius replied. "Do you have to make this as hard as you can?"

"Why not? You did. It was plenty hard with Oissa, wasn't it?"

Air hissed out between Lanius' teeth. That hit below the belt. "You can't say I've ignored you," he said, which was true enough.

True or not, it didn't help. "Oh, good. I got your leftovers," Sosia said sardonically.

"That . . . isn't how it worked." Lanius said no more than that. Explaining that Oissa had gotten Sosia's leftovers would also have been true. He hadn't made love with the serving girl when he thought Sosia would soon expect him to make love with *her.* Somehow, he doubted his wife would appreciate the details of how he'd managed his affair.

He was right to be dubious, too. Even the one sentence proved too much. "Huzzah for you," she told him. "You must be very proud of yourself."

Lanius had a bite of mutton in his mouth. He knew that. All the same, it tasted uncommonly like crow. "You're not making this easy, you know," he said.

"Should I? Should I smile and say, 'Oh, yes, dear, sleep with all the pretty women you want. I don't mind'? Should I say that?" Tears ran down Sosia's face. "I don't see how, because I *do* mind. I've done everything I know how to do to make you happy. I bore your son, by the gods. And this is the thanks I get?" She left the table very suddenly.

Lanius finished supper by himself. Yes, it definitely tasted of crow. Even the wine tasted of crow, which was probably an all-time first. He declined dessert. The servant who'd proposed it gave him a reproachful look. "The kitchens worked hard on the tarts, Your Majesty," he said.

The king didn't want to think what Sosia would have done with that line. Not least to keep from thinking about it, he said, "I hope the cooks enjoy them, then."

That was an uncommon bounty. "Are you sure, Your Majesty?" the servant asked. The king nodded.

After the servant left, Lanius walked out into the garden. A nightjar called plaintively. He'd heard the night birds many times. He didn't think he'd ever seen them.

Something fluttered past his face. That wasn't a nightjar—it was a bat, skittering wildly through the air. He looked up into the sky. The stars spilled across the darkness like tiny jewels on velvet. How many of them there were! And yet, as he'd seen when he spent a night in the woods with Anser and Ortalis, more stars shone than he could see from the city of Avornis. Smoke from uncounted hearths and lamps and candles smudged the sky over the capital. The glare from all those candles and lamps and other open flames also robbed the heavens of some of their luster.

Lanius sighed. Sosia wouldn't have mocked him for wondering about bats and nightjars and stars, but she wouldn't have understood, either. She didn't have that sort of curiosity herself, or the one that drove him to poke through the archives. But she was better with people than he would be if he lived a hundred years.

He sighed again. He knew he would have to patch things up with her. Jewelry might help, if it wasn't too obviously a bribe. That had done some good before. Staying away from serving girls would be bound to help, too. It would, if he could. Could he? One more sigh burst from him. He doubted it. He couldn't spend all his time in the archives—not alone in the archives, anyhow.

Grus looked back over his shoulder, in the direction of Trabzun. His soldiers stood on the walls there now. The Menteshe who hadn't died in the fall of the city were on their way up to Avornis now. Their labor would do something to repair all the harm they'd worked in their invasion of his kingdom—not enough, not nearly enough, but something.

Sweat rivered down Grus' face. He felt as though he were being steamed inside his mailshirt. He swigged from a jar of water mixed with wine. Standing orders were for soldiers to drink as much as they could hold. Some of them ignored standing orders, as some soldiers ignored standing orders of any kind. Telling who ignored orders here was easy. The miscreants were the ones who toppled from the saddle with heatstroke. Several men had died. Grus would have thought that might give the others a hint. But men went right on not drinking enough and collapsing because they didn't.

Hirundo brought his horse up alongside Grus'. "How much farther do you plan on going this campaigning season, Your Majesty?" the general asked.

"I'd like to go to Yozgat," the king answered.

"I'd like a lot of things I'm not going to get. I'd like to lose twenty years, for instance," Hirundo said. "I didn't ask what you'd like. I asked what you planned. You're one of the people who know the difference—or I hope you are."

"I hope so, too," Grus said. "I really had hoped to get there before the season ended. But you're right—it won't happen. We ought to take what we can get and do our best to see that the Menteshe don't take it back."

"Sounds good to me." By the relief in Hirundo's voice, it sounded very good to him. "I did want to make sure you weren't getting carried away."

"Tempting, but no." Grus sounded dry enough to make Hirundo laugh. He went on, "I'm not falling in love for the first time, you know. I've gone along this kind of road before. I won't let a pretty face fool me."

That got another chuckle from the general. "Fine. In that case, how does stopping at the next river line sound?"

"Terrible," Grus answered, and Hirundo's face fell. The king continued, "But we'll do it anyhow. I know how thin we're stretched. I know how much work we still have to do behind the line, too. Gods only know how many thralls still need freeing. And we have more forts to set up—otherwise the Menteshe will start nipping in to chew up our supply wagons. We have a thousand other things to take care of besides those, I know, but they're the most important. Or am I missing something?"

"I don't think so, Your Majesty," Hirundo said. "You might ask Pterocles what he thinks, though."

"I'll do that," Grus promised.

*But I won't do it just yet,* he thought. He had accomplished more south of the Stura than any Avornan king since the loss of the Scepter of Mercy. By that standard, the campaign was an outstanding success. He hadn't done as much as he'd hoped he would. Did that make it a failure?

With some hesitation, he shook his head. It just meant he would need longer to get what he wanted. So he told himself, anyhow.

Looking south, he swore softly. Prince Korkut would have the coming winter to try to figure out what to do when the war resumed come spring. So would Prince Sanjar. They would also have the winter to try to figure out what to do about each other.

And the Banished One would have the winter to work out his next moves against Avornis. Grus liked giving him a breathing space even less than he liked giving one to the Menteshe princes. But going too far too fast would be worse . . . he supposed.

# CHAPTER TEN

King Lanius relished getting away from the city of Avornis. If he wasn't in the palace with Sosia, she couldn't quarrel with him. Things were going well in the countryside. Lanius still suspected that Tinamus thought he was crazy. That didn't matter. What did matter was whether the architect and the swarm of stonecutters and bricklayers and carpenters and other artisans at his command could create what Lanius wanted. By all appearances, they could.

Watching their work grow gave the king an unusual sense of accomplishment. Here was something real rising at his command. So many of a ruler's monuments were intangible—laws, decrees, orders. Not here. Not now. This he could reach out and touch. His son could come here and see for himself what Lanius had been up to.

And Crex, seeing for himself, would probably decide Lanius was crazy, too.

The air was full of the rich greenness of growing things. Had the breeze blown from the other direction, it would have carried the smoke and stinks of the artisans' encampment, an odor much more like those usual in the city of Avornis.

Some of the workmen washed in the stream that ran by the encampment. Some of them splashed one another to fight the late-summer heat or just to have a good time. They whooped and hollered as they played. Lanius sighed. The foolishness looked like fun, but it wasn't the sort of fun in which a king could indulge. All he could do was watch and be wistful.

"Here comes Tinamus, Your Majesty," the guard said.

"Well, good," Lanius said. "I was going to want to talk to him today."

Tinamus bowed to the king. "Good morning, Your Majesty," he said. "Everything here seems to be going very well. No builder could ask for a more generous client. The only thing I wish is . . ." His voice trailed away.

"Yes?" Lanius knew what Tinamus wanted. Grus would have been able to make that *yes* so intimidating, Tinamus never would have had the nerve to come out and say it. Grus was made of fabric coarser than Lanius, and really was as tough as he sounded. Lanius wasn't particularly tough, and couldn't sound as though he were.

Proof of that was his utter failure to intimidate Tinamus. The architect went right on with what he'd been at the point of saying. "What I wish, Your Majesty, is that I had some notion of what all this is *for.*"

If Lanius couldn't sound severe, maybe he could look that way. His eyebrows came down. He pursed his lips and frowned. If his father had made a face like that, anyone who saw it would have quaked in his boots. By all accounts, King Mergus had been as tough as a boot. Lanius still didn't seem to impress Tinamus very much. He said, "We've been over this ground before. The less you know, the better off you are."

"So you've said." Tinamus looked as unhappy as he sounded. "You understand that drives me wild, I'm sure. If you tell a baker to make you one thin slice of cake, don't you think he'll wonder why?"

"If I paid a baker what I'm paying you, he wouldn't have any business asking questions," Lanius answered.

"Well, maybe not," the builder said. "But a baker's slice of cake would be gone in a hurry. What I'm doing here could last for the next five hundred years. People will look at it and say, '*This* is how Tinamus wasted his time?' "

"You're not wasting your time. Whatever else you're doing, you're not doing that," Lanius assured him.

"What *am* I doing, then?"

"Do you really want to know?" Lanius asked. Tinamus nodded eagerly. The king smiled and said, "You're building a fancy run for one of my moncats."

Tinamus gave him a stiff bow. "If you'll excuse me, Your Majesty, I'll go away now. Perhaps one day you'll be serious, or you'll decide that I am." He bowed again and stalked off.

Lanius looked after him, then quietly started to laugh. Sometimes the worst thing you could do to someone was to tell him the exact and literal truth. Unless the King missed his guess, Tinamus wouldn't come troubling him with more questions for a long, long time—which was exactly what he'd had in mind.

Grus looked at the river with something less than delight. It was narrow and shallow, not really the sort of barrier between his men and the Menteshe that he'd had in mind. Mud by the riverside sent up a nasty smell as it dried in the sun. "I wonder how much farther we'll have to go to find a real stream."

Hirundo took a more optimistic view of things than he did. "Oh, it won't be so bad, Your Majesty."

"No? Why not? I could piss across this miserable thing." Grus exaggerated, but not to any enormous degree.

Hirundo didn't lose his smile. "Yes, you could—now. But the Menteshe aren't going to try to hit us now. We've rocked them back on their heels. They'll need some time to regroup. If Korkut and Sanjar do decide to join forces against us, they'll need to do some dickering so one of them doesn't murder the other one anyhow. And pretty soon the fall rains will start. This is an ugly little excuse for a river now, but I think it'll fill out nicely once the rains get going."

He might have been talking about a girl on the edge of womanhood. Grus eyed the valley through which the stream ran. He had at least as much experience gauging such things as his general did. More than a little reluctantly, he nodded. "Well, you're probably right about that."

"Then let's stop here if we're going to stop," Hirundo said. "Otherwise, you may decide not to stop at all."

Grus didn't want to stop. He wanted to push on to Yozgat. Knowing it was impractical didn't make him want it any less.

*Are your eyes bigger than your stomach? They'd better not be,* he told himself sternly. "All right," he said. "We'll garrison this line, and we'll head home."

"Thank you, Your Majesty," Hirundo said. "This is the right thing to do. The Banished One would thank you for going on."

Would he? That was the question—or one of the questions, anyhow. The Banished One had tormented Avornis through the Menteshe for centuries. The nomads remained men, though, with wills of their own; they weren't thralls. And now they were a weapon that had broken in the Banished One's hands. Since Prince Ulash's death, his sons had cared more for fighting each other to lay hold of his throne than for raiding north of the Stura. And Korkut and Sanjar had kept right on going after each other despite the Avornan thrust south of the river.

If they kept on like that, they would have no principality left to rule even after one of them finally won their civil war. Neither prince seemed to care. Beating a brother was more important to both of them than turning back an invader. Grus would have scorned them more if he hadn't known a good many Avornans who thought the same way.

In the Argolid Mountains south of Yozgat, where he'd dwelled since being cast down from the heavens, the Banished One had to be beside himself with fury. What dreams was he sending to Ulash's unloving children? Having been on the receiving end of more of those dreams than he cared to remember, Grus almost pitied Korkut and Sanjar. No one, not even a Menteshe prince, deserved that kind of attention.

The king looked south again. Haze and clouds hid the mountains for now. If the exiled god couldn't use the Menteshe as he'd been accustomed to doing in days gone by, how could he strike at Avornis?

Weather was one obvious weapon. The Banished One had afflicted Avornis with at least one dreadful winter in the recent past. He'd tried to make the capital starve—tried and failed. Probably because he'd failed, he'd hesitated to use that ploy since. But it still remained not only possible but dangerous, deadly dangerous. No ordinary wizard could do much with the weather, either for good or for ill; it was beyond a mere man's strength. Such restrictions meant little to the Banished One, who was neither ordinary wizard nor mere mortal.

Lanius had done a good job of laying in extra stocks of grain before that harsh winter came down. Grus thought it would be wise to do the same thing again. Suppose the Banished One didn't choose to repeat himself. What else might he do?

Feeling his own imagination failing, Grus looked around for Pterocles. When he didn't see the sorcerer close by, he sent horsemen out to hunt him down. Before long, Pterocles rode up on his mule. "What can I do for you, Your Majesty?" he asked.

"Come aside with me a little ways." The king rode off until no one could hear what he and the wizard had to say to each other. Pterocles followed. The royal guards stationed themselves to ensure that no one approached the two of them. Grus said, "If you were the Banished One, what would you do to Avornis now?"

"Why ask me?" Pterocles said, his indignation at least partly genuine.

"Because whatever he does, it will probably be through magic," Grus replied. "Who here knows more about magic than you? The answer had better be *nobody,* or I'm putting my trust in the wrong man."

The wizard's shrug was altogether fatalistic. "I can't tell you anything about that, Your Majesty. All I can tell you is, the Banished One has noticed some of what I've done, and he's decided he doesn't like me." He spread his hands, palms up. "That's really about all. Believe me, he knows more about me than I do about him."

Grus looked south again. Reluctantly, he found himself nodding. He had also felt the futility of trying to outguess a being far older, far wiser, and far stronger than himself. "All right." He explained his own reasoning, such as it was, and went on, "So I was trying to figure out what he might do if he didn't decide to give us another hard winter, or maybe what he might do on top of another hard winter."

"Ah. I see. Well, that makes more sense than asking what I would do if I were the Banished One." Pterocles' voice was tart. "Put that way . . ." He didn't look south. He looked up to the heavens, his eyes far away. Was he asking the gods for guidance, or was he just making his own calculations, as a man will? Grus couldn't tell and didn't want to ask. At last, the wizard came out of his reverie. "Hunger. Disease. Fire. Fear," he said. "Those are the weapons he has, it seems to me. Which one will he use? How will he use it? Will he use more than one?" He shrugged. "I don't know. I have no way of knowing. Before too long, I expect we'll find out."

Grus expected the same thing. Hunger? Hunger went hand in hand with bad weather. Anyone to whom the Banished One had appeared in a dream learned more than he ever wanted to know about fear. Disease? Fire? Now the king was the one who nodded. Yes, those were surely possible. "What can you do against him? What can any of our wizards do against him?"

"What can I—what can we—do?" For a man who was cheerful most of the time, Pterocles smiled a peculiarly bleak smile now. "Why, the best I can, of course, Your Majesty."

"I see." Grus almost asked the wizard how good he thought that best would be. But part of him feared Pterocles didn't know. Another part feared Pterocles *did* know, and would tell him. With a heavy sigh, he said, "Well, we'll do what we can to hold on here, and then we'll go home, and then . . . then we'll see what happens next."

"That's right, Your Majesty," Pterocles said with another of those bleak smiles. "Then we'll see what happens next."

Ortalis didn't say anything to Lanius about the king's latest quarrel with Sosia. Lanius hadn't really thought he would, but was glad to be proved right. Ortalis never had gotten along very well with his sister; he made no bones about that. Then again, Ortalis never had gotten along very well with anybody.

A moment after that thought crossed the king's mind, he shook his head. Ortalis and Anser managed to stay on good terms, not least because sunny Anser stayed on good terms with everyone. And Ortalis seemed genuinely devoted to Limosa— and she to him.

He eyed Limosa's swelling belly with the same anxious pride most new fathers showed. He had more reasons for pride than most prospective fathers did, too. "I hope it's a boy," he told Lanius one day when they met in a corridor. "I want a son of my own."

"I know," Lanius said, as politely as he could. Ortalis had never figured out much about politics. If he had a son, it would complicate the succession. It would endanger the place Lanius' son Crex held now. The smartest thing he could have done was keep his mouth shut about what he wanted when he was talking to Lanius. Ortalis seldom did the smartest thing.

Ortalis probably wasn't thinking about the succession right this minute, for he asked, "Do you have your boy crawling around in the archives with you? I know that's your favorite sport. I can't see why, but I know it is."

"Crex . . . hasn't shown much interest in it yet," Lanius answered. That his son hadn't was a grief to him. He kept telling himself that there was time, that Crex might yet see how important and how fascinating state papers could be. He kept telling himself, yes, but he had a harder and harder time making himself believe it.

Ortalis laughed. Why shouldn't he? It wasn't his worry. Lanius came close to hating him in that moment. Then Ortalis said, "Maybe he'd rather get out to the woods and see what he could do with a bow in his hands."

"He's still a little young for that, I think," Lanius said, and went on his way before his brother-in-law could find some other way to make him feel bad. Ortalis had jabbed at exactly what Lanius feared most—that Crex might sooner have a good time than gain the knowledge he needed to make a proper ruler. Lanius wondered what he could do about that. He wasn't sure he could do anything—another grief, one that wouldn't go away.

A royal guardsman tramping stolidly up the corridor sketched a salute as the king walked by. His mailshirt jingled. He smelled of leather and stale sweat. Lanius stopped and looked after him, a thoughtful expression on his face.

*If I order the guards to seize Ortalis and take him to the Maze—and Limosa with him—will they obey?* The king plucked at his beard. These days, he was the effective ruler of Avornis, or at least of the city of Avornis, when Grus went out on campaign. Most of what he did, though, was as close to what

Grus would have done as he could come. That was how Grus
had let him accrue bits of power little by little—Lanius had
made sure that what he was given wouldn't be threatening.

Grus would not send his legitimate son to the Maze, not for
complicating the succession. After all, Ortalis' son would be as
much Grus' grandson as Crex was. If Lanius banished Ortalis,
would Grus let it stand? Lanius sighed. He didn't think so. And
he didn't think he had a prayer of resisting or defeating Grus,
especially not when his father-in-law would be coming back
from the first successful Avornan campaign south of the Stura
in centuries.

"Too bad," Lanius murmured. "Too bad, too bad, too bad."

He wondered what Sosia thought. If she believed he could
get away with it . . . He shook his head. He couldn't trust her
judgment in this. She was biased, too. But—another interesting problem—which way was she biased? Against Ortalis, for
threatening Crex's succession? Or against Lanius himself, for
his choice of amusements? He still thought the former, but the
latter was a long way from impossible, and he knew it. He
would have to decide for himself.

And he did. He decided he couldn't take the chance of getting rid of Ortalis like that. Chances were, he wouldn't get
away with it. He would have to hope Limosa had another girl.
Plenty of people did, he thought optimistically.

As King Grus rode north toward the Stura, he had one of the
few experiences that made him really and truly glad he'd taken
his share—or, as Lanius no doubt would have seen it, more
than his share—of the Avornan crown. Again and again, freed
thralls came running up to him. "King Olor bless you!" they
would shout. "Queen Quelea bless you! All the gods bless
you!"

Guardsmen kept the thralls from coming too close. You
never could tell, not till too late. One of them was liable not to
be a freed thrall at all, but a thrall still guided and controlled by
the Banished One. An assassin was as easy to hide among others who looked and acted just like him (or, perhaps even more
dangerous, just like her) as a poisoned needle in a haystack.

Grus understood that. He didn't argue with it. It left him sad even so. Doing his best to smile, he said to Hirundo, "I was never so popular up in Avornis proper."

"Well, maybe not," the general allowed. "But you never did so much for the proper Avornans as you have for these people."

Slowly, Grus nodded. He thought he'd made a pretty good King of Avornis. He didn't think even Lanius could argue with that, though the other King of Avornis might—would—look down his nose while grudgingly admitting Grus hadn't been so very bad. Grus had done his best to keep the peasants out of the rapacious nobles' grasp. He'd won enough civil wars against the nobles to persuade them that rebellion was a bad idea. He'd held the Thervings at bay. He'd beaten back the Chernagor pirates. And he'd fought the Menteshe to something that was, at the moment, better than a draw.

But even though he'd done all that, he hadn't given the proper Avornans their souls again. He couldn't have. They already had them. The thralls, now . . . The thralls and their ancestors had gone on for centuries with something missing from their spirits—most of what separated men from beasts. Thanks to Grus (and to Pterocles; he didn't aim to steal the wizard's credit), they had that part of themselves back again. They had it, and they knew they had it, and they were grateful.

"Don't let it worry you," Hirundo told him. "Give them some time to get used to it and they'll be as selfish as anybody else."

Grus made a horrible face. "I'll remember you in my nightmares," he said. He was laughing, but quickly sobered. His nightmares featured not Hirundo but the Banished One. And if Hirundo was right—well, so what? One of his goals in coming over the Stura was to turn the thralls into normal human beings. And one thing normal human beings did was sometimes act like ungrateful wretches. He couldn't complain if that happened here.

One evening not long before he'd go back over the river, Otus approached him as he sat eating supper outside his pavilion. Guards hung by the first freed thrall, but unobtrusively. They didn't really believe Otus remained under the spell of the Banished One, but they were still guards.

But Grus also didn't think the Banished One was looking

out through Otus' eyes right this minute. He recognized the expression on the thrall's face—that of a man who wanted something. Unlike the thralls south of the Stura, Otus had been free for a while, and he seemed very much a normal man.

"Hello," Grus said. "What can I do for you today?"

Otus bowed. He'd learned court ceremonial—no doubt the first thrall who ever had. "Your Majesty, they have freed the village with my woman in it."

"Have they?" Grus said. "That's good news." It was very good news, since he hadn't expected his men to go so far west. The Menteshe had proved weaker than he'd thought.

"I—think so, yes." Otus sounded distinctly nervous.

*He's not worrying about the Menteshe,* Grus realized. "You had a woman in that village, didn't you?" the king said, and then the light dawned. "And you also have a woman back in the city of Avornis, eh?" He started to laugh, not that Otus was likely to find it funny. He understood those difficulties only too well. So did Lanius, come to that. And now the ex-thrall?

Otus nodded. Yes, he looked distinctly nervous, too. "What am I going to do, Your Majesty? What *can* I do?"

"You can choose one of them, or you can choose the other one, or you can hope they won't gang up on you if you try to keep them both," Grus answered. "These are the choices a free man has to make."

"Sometimes this business is not so easy," Otus observed.

"No, sometimes it isn't," Grus said. "Have you seen your woman here now that she's had the spell lifted?"

"No, not yet."

"Go do that first. You can't decide anything—not so it makes sense—till you know where you stand with her. Maybe she isn't the person you thought she'd be. Maybe whatever you saw in her when you were both thralls, it won't be there anymore. If it's not, that will tell you what you need to do. And if it is, well, bring her along up into the north if you want to. The choice is yours."

"You are a wise man, Your Majesty," Otus said humbly.

Grus laughed out loud. "Ask my wife about me and women and you'll get a different story, I promise. If I were wise in such things, I would have gotten into a lot less trouble than I have."

"But you give good advice."

"Giving good advice is easy." Grus laughed again, at himself. "What's hard is taking good advice, by Olor's beard." Otus didn't look as though he believed the king. If that didn't prove how inexperienced he was, Grus couldn't imagine what would.

The freed thrall rode off the next morning. Grus sent a squad of horsemen with him; he didn't want Otus gallivanting over the countryside by himself. Being the first freed thrall might still make him special. Grus didn't want Menteshe raiders grabbing him and taking him away so the Banished One could find out exactly how he'd been freed.

After Otus rode away, Grus forgot about him for a little while. Part of the Avornan army would stay behind in the south to protect the land they'd won this campaigning season. Getting the rest back across the Stura was a large, complicated job. Coping with it, and especially coping with the absence of some barges that should have been there, kept the king busy for several days.

Once the army had crossed, Grus let everyone rest in Anna for a while before pressing on up to the capital. He and Hirundo were making sure everything was going smoothly when Otus walked up to them. With him was a dark, quiet-looking woman. Otus' face lit up whenever he looked at her. He said, "Your Majesty, this is Fulca. My woman." Pride filled his voice.

"I'm pleased to meet you, Fulca," Grus said gravely. "I'm glad you're free."

"Glad to be free." Like any newly liberated thrall, she spoke hesitantly. She hadn't needed many words when she lay under that dark magic. She pointed to Otus. "He knows you? Knows king? Really? Truly?"

"Really. Truly," Grus assured her.

"I told you so," Otus said. By that alone, he and Fulca might have been married for a long time.

She sniffed in response. "Tell all sorts of things. Tell is easy. Tell true? No, tell true not so easy. Even free, not so easy."

Grus was no prophet, no soothsayer. But he would have bet anything he owned that Otus' serving girl in the palace was going to end up disappointed. Fulca had a spark Otus plainly responded to. And that was the way she was now, with the veils of thralldom newly lifted. How she'd be once she really learned to speak, really learned to think . . . How would she be? She'd be formidable, that was how. Grus beamed at Otus. "You did the right thing, deciding to go over there."

Otus beamed back. Grus had let Fulca think coming for her was Otus' idea. A white lie wouldn't hurt here, the king judged. Otus still needed some practice at being a man. *As who does not?* Grus thought. *As who does not, by the gods?*

Lanius had often ridden out of the city of Avornis to greet Grus and a returning army. More often then not, he'd been annoyed and resentful at having to help aggrandize the other king. Today, though, he rode out and waited for the army without the least bit of resentment. Considering who—considering what—Grus' principal foe had been, how could he do anything else?

"I want to see the soldiers, Father," Crex said from a pony beside Lanius.

"Soldiers!" Pitta added. Lanius wasn't at all sure she cared about them, but she wasn't going to let her brother get away with anything.

"They'll be here soon," Lanius promised. "Be patient, both of you."

They looked at him as though the word did not belong to the Avornan language. As far as they were concerned, it didn't.

Anser was also there to greet the returning army. Even dressed in the arch-hallow's red robe, he looked as though he would rather be hunting. Sosia and Estrilda had made the journey as well. Grus' daughter and wife talked quietly with each other. Lanius suspected he was lucky he could not hear what they were saying.

Ortalis and Limosa had stayed back at the royal palace. Limosa could use her pregnancy as an excuse for not getting on horseback. Ortalis? Ortalis rarely showed any interest in Grus' campaigns—or in doing anything that would please his father. In a way, that was a relief to Lanius. In another way, he thought it was too bad.

Scouts rode past, saluting Lanius and the rest of the royal family and the arch-hallow—who was also part of the royal family, even if he was on the wrong side of the blanket. More horsemen trotted by. Then Grus came into sight, guardsmen in front of him and behind him, Hirundo on his right, Pterocles on his left. The leading guardsmen reined in. So did Grus, when he was directly in front of Lanius. He inclined his head. "Your Majesty."

"Your Majesty," Lanius echoed. He hated giving Grus the royal title. He did it as seldom as he could. Grus seldom tried to force it from him. Here, though, he didn't see what choice he had. If he insulted Grus by refraining in front of the army, which was the other king's instrument . . . No good would come of that.

Still speaking formally, Grus went on, "We have taken the arms of Avornis beyond the Stura River. We have defeated the Menteshe in battle. We have taken the city of· Trabzun, with many smaller towns. We have freed thralls beyond counting from the evil magic of the Banished One."

Lanius had wondered if he would dare name the exiled god, and admired his nerve for doing so. Lanius also heard the pride under Grus' formality. Like Grus or not, the other king had earned the right to be proud. No King of Avornis since the loss of the Scepter of Mercy could say what he had just said.

"It is well. It is very well," Lanius replied. "All of Avornis rejoices in what you and your men have done."

"I thank you, Your Majesty," Grus said.

"I thank *you,* Your Majesty," Lanius said. If he was going to give Grus his due, best to give with both hands. He went on, "The kingdom and the city of Avornis have remained at peace behind you." After Grus' vaunting claims, that one seemed small, but it was the most Lanius could offer.

Grus could have mocked him for it. He could have, but he didn't. "That is the best news you could give me, Your Majesty," he said. "May I never hear anything less." Along with Hirundo and Pterocles and the guardsmen, he took his place with Lanius and the other members of the royal family.

Greeting Grus was hard enough for Lanius. Reviewing the soldiers who rode and marched into the capital was harder, in a different way; Lanius had to fight to keep boredom from overwhelming him. One thing court life trained him in, though—

not showing what he thought. The men who saluted and received his answering salutes had no idea that he would rather have been almost anywhere else.

At last, there were no more soldiers. Lanius let out a silent sigh of relief. Grus still seemed fresh and resilient. "Shall we go into the city, Your Majesty?" he said.

"Yes, let's." Lanius' voice showed only polite acquiescence, not the quivering eagerness he really felt.

As he and Grus had watched soldiers go by—endlessly— so the people of the capital lined up to watch the royal family and high functionaries return to the palace. Lanius didn't care to have so many people he didn't know staring at him. That was one reason he went out into the city of Avornis only rarely. Being the center of all eyes didn't seem to bother Grus. Hirundo, for his part, reveled in it. He smiled and waved and, whenever he saw a pretty girl, blew kisses.

Under cover of the shouts from the people, Lanius said, "The spell to free the thralls works as it should, then?"

"So it would seem." Grus nodded, partly to Lanius and partly, Lanius thought, to himself. "Yes—so it would seem. Pterocles and the other wizards did a fine job."

"Very glad to hear it," Lanius said. "Next campaigning season, then, you'll . . . move farther south?" He didn't want to speak of Yozgat, much less of the Scepter of Mercy.

"That's what I have in mind, yes," Grus answered. "I think we'll also have to see what, ah, happens this winter, though."

*What the Banished One does,* Lanius translated. "What do you think will happen?" he asked.

"I don't know," Grus said. "That's what I told you—we'll just have to see."

# CHAPTER ELEVEN

Every time a cloud rolled across the sky, Grus worried. Every time rain fell, he frowned. Every time a funeral procession wound through the city of Avornis taking a body to its pyre, he bit his lip. Every time a fire broke out, he grimaced. Every time anything went on, he jumped more nervously than one of Lanius' moncats.

The other king noticed. That told Grus how nervous he must have been, for Lanius failed to notice a good many things. "What *is* troubling you?" Lanius asked. "You should be happy. If you're not happy now, seeing what you did south of the Stura, when will you be?"

"It's because of what I did south of the Stura that I'm not so happy now," Grus answered. Lanius looked baffled. Grus glanced around. You never could tell when a servant might be listening—or when someone else might be listening through a servant's ears. "Where can we talk without being overheard?"

"Why, the archives, of course," Lanius said.

Grus laughed, more in surprise than for any other reason. The archives weren't *of course* to him; he could count on the fingers of one hand the times he'd gone into them since becoming king. But that didn't mean Lanius was wrong. "Let's go, then."

Men bowed and women dropped curtsies as the two kings walked through the palace. Grus nodded back. So did Lanius, when he happened to see them—which was about half the time. The younger king chatted about this and that till he closed the heavy doors to the archives behind himself and Grus. Then his attention sharpened. "Well?" he asked.

Before answering, Grus looked up at the smeared skylights. The piles and crates of documents, the dusty sunshine, the musty smell . . . Yes, this was a place that suited Lanius. The other king *belonged* here, the way Grus *belonged* on the deck of a river galley. This was where Lanius would be at his best. Grus repeated, "Because of what I did south of the Stura." He went on, "Now I have to wonder what the Banished One will do on account of it."

"Ah." Lanius might be vague when it came to people, but not to something like that. "Do you think we'll have another one of those unnatural winters? Shall we start laying in extra grain again?"

"It wouldn't be a bad idea," Grus replied. "Or he might do something different. A pestilence, maybe. Maybe something else. No way to tell what, not until it happens. But *something*."

He waited to see what Lanius thought. Yes, the other king might be blind to a lot of the human drama that went on around him, but he was nobody's fool. He said, "I think you're likely to be right. And I wish I could tell you that you were likely to be wrong."

"So do I," Grus said.

"What does Pterocles think of this?" Lanius asked.

"That I'm likely to be right," Grus answered.

"Anything more? Does he have some better notion of what the Banished One might try?"

"He was the one who thought of a plague," Grus said. "Past that, no." He waved an arm, encompassing the archives in a single gesture. "Can you tell me more, Your Majesty? You know things nobody else does."

"I doubt that. But here, sometimes, I can find things other people have trouble finding," Lanius said. "And if I can't find them here, sometimes I can find them in the archives under the cathedral." Even here, where no one else could possibly be spying, he warily looked around before mouthing a single word: "Milvago."

Grus had known he would name that name. So the Banished

One had been called before he was cast down from the heavens. He had fathered the gods who later ousted him. He had been the mightiest god in the heavens—until he wasn't anymore. If he ever found a way to *use* the Scepter of Mercy instead of just holding it . . . In that case, Avornis wouldn't have to worry about anything as trivial as an ice-filled winter that lasted into spring or a pestilence.

Sighing, Grus said, "Well, see what you can learn. I'll do the same, and so will Pterocles. And we'll find out what happens. That's liable to teach us more than we can learn any other way."

Lanius looked unhappy, almost unhappy enough to tempt Grus into a smile. The other king wasn't much for learning by experience. He wanted to find answers written down somewhere. That handbook on kingship he'd written for Prince Crex . . . Grus had glanced at it. It held a lot of information—and a lot of good advice, too. But so what? So much of the advice was only good if you had the experience to understand it . . . in which case you probably didn't need it.

A scratching noise came from somewhere deep within the archives. Grus started in alarm. Maybe that was a mouse or a rat—if this place wasn't a paradise for mice, he'd never seen one that was. But maybe it was something else. Maybe it was the Banished One somehow spying on him and Lanius across all these miles. Grus didn't know if that was possible. Better, though, with the Banished One, to take no chances.

Then, to his amazement, Lanius started to laugh. Grus realized the other king recognized the noise, whatever it was. "I think you'd better tell me what's going on," Grus said carefully.

"I'll do more than that," Lanius replied. "I'll show you." He amazed Grus again by lying down on his back on one of the less dusty stretches of floor. Then he started thumping on his chest as though he were beating a drum. Grus wondered if he'd lost his mind.

But he hadn't. A moncat came strolling up and climbed onto his chest. Lanius had a scrap of meat handy, and gave it to the animal. Grus gaped. He said, "Now I've seen everything."

"Oh, this is nothing special. Pouncer gets in here every once in a while, and into other places where I need meat to lure him out." Lanius sounded elaborately casual. "So I usually carry a few scraps with me. I have to remember to get fresh ones pretty often. Otherwise, he doesn't want them."

"I see," Grus said. "I meant to ask you about some of the things you've been spending money on. I've heard about an animal trainer, an architect, and quite a few workmen. What haven't I heard about?"

"Why I'm doing it," Lanius answered, stroking Pouncer behind the ears. The moncat purred loudly.

"All right. Why?"

Lanius went on petting and scratching the moncat as he talked. The longer Grus listened, the more astonished he got. At last, the other king finished by asking, "What do you think?"

"What do I think?" Grus echoed. Lanius had told him a little of this the winter before, but only a little. Now that he'd heard it all, he thought he'd *really* heard it all. He said, "I think it's crazy, that's what. What could anybody who heard something like this think?"

"Now I'll tell you something you don't know," Lanius said. "Not long after we started this, the Banished One sent Collurio a dream."

Grus had to take that seriously. The Banished One sent dreams only to those who worried him. Some of the enemies who'd struck him heavy blows never saw him in their sleep. Hirundo was one of those, and had no idea how lucky he was. Grus whistled softly, trying to take this in. "He sent dreams . . . to an animal trainer?"

"By Olor's beard, Your Majesty, he did." Lanius might have been taking an oath. His use of the royal title impressed Grus much more than his calling on the current king of the gods.

Grus said, "He didn't send one to the builder, though?"

"Not yet, at any rate," the other king said. "The builder knows less of what's going on than the trainer does. He would also be easier to replace than the trainer. That all makes him less essential and less dangerous."

"You've thought this through, haven't you?" Grus laughed at himself. Of course Lanius had thought it through; that was what Lanius did best. Grus aimed a forefinger at the other king as though it were an arrow. "You can't tell me the builder is less expensive than the trainer, by the gods. Oh, you can, but I won't believe you."

"I won't even try. You'd know I was lying. Here, wait—I'll stop lying." He got up off the floor, still holding Pouncer. Grus made a horrible face. Lanius continued, "Even if he is more expensive, we need him. Will you tell me I'm wrong about that?"

"I'll tell you that you *could* be wrong," Grus said. Lanius considered that in his usual grave fashion, then slowly nodded. But Grus felt he had to add, "You could be right, too. We'll find out. I hope we'll find out. In the meantime . . . In the meantime, you'd better go on."

The harvest was good. Rain didn't fall at the wrong time. Wheat and barley poured into the city of Avornis by riverboat and, from nearby farms, by wagon. The granaries filled—if not to overflowing, then very full indeed. Watching the golden flood mount, Lanius grew confident the capital could ride out even the worst of winters. Reports that came in from the rest of Avornis said no one was likely to starve this year.

As more and more grain arrived, Lanius began to doubt the Banished One would use weather as a weapon against Avornis. The king didn't doubt the exiled god would use something. What Grus had said made altogether too much sense for Lanius to doubt it. At some point, the Banished One would have to strike back against Avornis. Not striking back would be confessing weakness. Whatever else he was, he was not weak. His chosen weapons, the Menteshe, were for the moment of less use to him than he would have wanted. But he surely had others—had them or could devise them.

Lanius knew what he would do if he were in those southern mountains, all alone and furious. He summoned Pterocles. The wizard bowed low before him. "How may I serve you, Your Majesty?"

"I fear you may be serving all of Avornis before long, not just me," the king answered. "What do you know of plagues begun and spread by sorcery?"

The corners of Pterocles' mouth turned down. The lines that ran up from the corners of his mouth to beside his nose got deeper. Sorrow and worry filled his eyes. "I was afraid you would ask me that."

"How can you be so sure of—?" Lanius broke off and pointed an accusing forefinger at the wizard. "You've been studying."

"Ever since I got back to the capital," Pterocles agreed. "I only wish there were more to study. This sort of thing is a lot like weatherworking—it's too big for a mortal wizard to bring off, which means not many people have had much to say about it."

"What do they say? The ones who speak at all, I mean," Lanius said.

"That only a wizard without a heart would even think of trying one of those spells," Pterocles said. "The trouble is, that fits the Banished One too well. They also say that the sicknesses behave like natural ones once they're loose. If a wizard or a doctor can come up with a way to cure them or to keep them from killing, that will work as well as it would against an ordinary illness."

"If," Lanius said heavily. Pterocles nodded. The two of them shared an unhappy look. The trouble with the optimistic-sounding news the wizard had given was simple—plenty of natural illnesses had no known cure. Many people went to physicians only as a last resort, when they were desperately ill and nothing the doctor did to them was likely to make things worse.

"Maybe he'll do something else," Pterocles said. "Maybe it will be the weather. Maybe he can find some way to make the Menteshe stop fighting among themselves. Maybe . . . maybe almost anything, Your Majesty."

He sounded like a man whistling past a still-smoking pyre. Lanius understood sounding that way, for it was also the way he felt. "And maybe he'll send a plague, too," the king said. "It would be about the best thing he could do, wouldn't it?"

"Not as far as we're concerned, by the gods!" Pterocles exclaimed. Then he got what Lanius was driving at. "Yes, I think from his way of looking at things a plague might be the best he could do. I see one thing that might help us, though."

"Oh? What?" Lanius asked. "It's one more than I see, I'll tell you that."

"Winter *is* coming," Pterocles said. "People don't travel as much in the wintertime. Even if a plague starts, it won't spread as fast as it would if it got going during the summer."

"That will give us something to look forward to when the weather warms up, won't it?" Lanius said.

The wizard winced. "I wish you hadn't put it quite like that."

Thinking about it, Lanius also wished he hadn't said it like that. "Do the best you can, that's all. And if I come across anything in the archives that has to do with plagues, I'll pass it on to you."

Anser and Ortalis would have laughed at him. Sosia would have rolled her eyes at the time he wasted in the archives (she would have done more than that if she'd known how he occasionally spent time there). Grus would have rolled his eyes, too, though he knew Lanius often found things worth knowing as he poked around. Pterocles nodded eagerly. "Thank you, Your Majesty. I appreciate that, believe me. You never can tell what might turn up."

"No, you never can." Some of the things Lanius had learned in the archives—both royal and ecclesiastical—he wished he never would have found. The name *Milvago* went through his mind again. This time, he didn't say it aloud. Somehow, it seemed all too potent just the same.

Pterocles bowed to him once more. "I'm glad you and King Grus are alert to the possibilities," he said. "That's bound to help when . . . whatever happens, happens."

Lanius wasn't so sure. Suppose the plague killed both kings in the space of a few days. Then Crex would take the crown, assuming he lived—and assuming Ortalis didn't try to steal it. Ortalis would be regent if he wasn't king.

Lanius had been a little boy when his father died and King Mergus' younger brother, Scolopax, succeeded him. Scolopax had ruled briefly and badly. Lanius didn't see Ortalis doing any better. The king shivered. With luck—and, he hoped, with the aid of the gods still in the heavens—it wouldn't come to anything like that.

He hoped Olor and Quelea and the rest of the gods in the heavens were paying attention to what was going on in the material world. They often seemed to give it as little notice as they could get away with. Would they have cast the Banished One down here if they'd taken seriously the material world and what happened in it? Lanius didn't think so.

The king wished Avornis boasted an arch-hallow who held his seat because of his holiness, not because he happened to be the other king's bastard. Like everybody else, Lanius liked Anser. Even Ortalis, in whom the milk of human kindness had long since curdled, liked Anser. Even Estrilda, who should have despised him as the living symbol of her husband's betrayal, liked Anser. However likable he was, though, he found deer more dear than Queen Quelea, and King Olor more boring than boar.

But then again, maybe it wouldn't matter one bit. If the gods in the heavens were so nearly indifferent to what went on in the material world, how much would they care whether the arch-hallow was a refined and subtle theologian or a crackerjack archer? Maybe less than Lanius hoped they did.

And in that case . . .

"In that case," the King of Avornis muttered, "it's up to Grus and me and Pterocles and Collurio and Tinamus and Otus and Hirundo and—" He broke off. He could have gone on naming names for quite a while. On the other hand, he could have stopped after the ones to whom the Banished Ones had sent dreams. They might have been enough by themselves.

Or maybe no one and nothing would be enough. How could anyone do more than hope when confronting an exiled god? Sometimes even holding on to hope seemed hard as holding up the weight of the world on his shoulders.

When he stood up, he was a little surprised, or maybe more than a little, to find he labored under no literally crushing burden. He walked slowly down the corridor that would take him to the kitchens if he followed it all the way. He didn't really intend to; he wasn't really going anywhere at all. He was just ambling along, thinking about what might happen, what he could do, what would be possible if things went the way he wanted, and what he would have to do if they didn't.

Servants bowed and curtsied. Lanius noticed them just enough to bow in return. But when Limosa started to drop him a curtsy, he came back to the real world with a snap. "Don't bother," he said quickly. "You might not be able to get up again if you do."

Her belly seemed to bulge more every day now. The baby was still a couple of months away, which meant that belly would be even bigger by the time it was born. She carried a chunk of raisin loaf in one hand.

"I'll be all right," she said. "I'm just getting to where all I want is for this to be over. Pretty soon, it will be."

"I remember Sosia saying the same thing," Lanius said.

"I feel like I'm carrying around a great big melon, except melons don't kick," Ortalis' wife said, setting the hand without the raisin loaf just above her navel.

She was another likable one. Lanius cordially loathed her father, and wasn't a bit sorry when Grus sent Petrosus to the Maze. She was wed to a man who'd alarmed the king for as long as he'd known him. She carried a baby that could throw the succession into turmoil. All the same, Lanius didn't dislike her. He worried about her, but that wasn't the same thing.

"Everything will be fine," Lanius said.

Limosa nodded. "Oh, I think so, too. It's not a lot of fun when it finally happens, but it does usually turn out all right. If it didn't, there wouldn't be any more people after a while. And when it is over"—her face softened—"you've got a baby. Babies are fun."

Babies were a lot more fun if someone else did the cleaning up after them. Limosa took that for granted. Since Lanius did, too, he didn't call her on it. He only smiled and nodded and said, "I remember."

"Crex and Pitta are getting big now," Limosa said. "You and Sosia ought to have another baby yourselves."

Since Lanius wasn't currently welcome in Sosia's bed, prospects for a new royal prince or princess lay nowhere in the immediate future. If Limosa didn't already know that, Lanius didn't feel like explaining it to her. He just said, "Maybe one of these days."

"It would be nice," Limosa said. If she worried about the succession, or about a son of hers threatening Crex's place, she didn't show it. Maybe that was good acting on her part. Petrosus had surely grafted her onto Lanius' family in the hope that a grandson of his would wear the crown. But even Lanius had trouble believing she attached enormous importance to it.

"So it would," he said. She wasn't wrong—he'd enjoyed Crex and Pitta very much when they were small.

"May I ask you something, Your Majesty?" she said.

"You can always ask. Whether I answer depends on what the question is," Lanius replied.

Limosa nodded. "Of course. All I want to know, though, is what you're doing out in the country. Why do you want to build what sounds like a slice of a city?"

She wasn't the only one wondering about that. Even Tinamus, the architect responsible for it, wondered. Wondering was harmless. Knowing? Knowing was all too likely to be anything but. With what Lanius hoped was a harmless smile, he said, "It's a hobby, that's all. Why does Ortalis like to go hunting?"

For some tiny fraction of a heartbeat, alarm spread over Limosa's face. She knew the answer to that question, then. It was something on the order of, *He hunts animals so he doesn't hunt people.* Lanius started to apologize; he hadn't meant to embarrass her. But maybe what he'd said wasn't so bad after all. She didn't press him about what he was building anymore.

Instead, she murmured, "Hobbies," made as though to curtsy again without actually doing it, and went on up the corridor.

Lanius shook his head. If things didn't work out the way he hoped, plenty of people would be unhappy with him for wasting so much time and money. For now, though, he didn't have to worry about that. Even Grus agreed what he was doing was worth a try. As soon as the building was finished, he and Collurio could get down to some serious work there. In the meantime . . .

In the meantime, shrieks erupted from the kitchens. Maybe that meant one of the cooks had stuck a knife in another. Such things happened every once in a while. More like, though . . .

"Your Majesty! Your Majesty!" A cook came running toward Lanius, waving her arms in the air. "Oh, there you are, Your Majesty! Come quick! It's that horrible creature of yours, Your Majesty! It's stolen a big silver spoon!"

"Sooner or later, we'll get it back," the king said. "Pouncer hardly ever loses them."

"Miserable thieving animal." None of the cooks had a good word to say for moncats. "Nothing but vermin. We ought to set traps."

"You will do no such thing." Most of the time, Lanius was among the mildest of men. When he wanted to, though, he could sound every inch a monarch. The cook blinked, hardly believing her ears. He went on, "You *will* not. Do you understand me?"

The cook turned pale as milk. "We won't do it, Your Majesty. Queen Quelea's sweet mercy on me, I was only joking."

"All right, then." Lanius knew he'd hit too hard. But she'd alarmed him. He asked, "Is the moncat still in the kitchens, or did it run off?"

"It went up the wall like it was a big, furry fly, and then in through some crack or other. It's gone." The cook regained a little spirit. "And so is that stinking spoon." She sounded as indignant as though she'd bought it herself.

"Maybe I can lure it back. Let's go see, shall we?" Lanius said. "A few scraps might do the trick."

Warmth from the fires and ovens surrounded him when he walked into the kitchens. So did the savory smells of roasting meat and baking bread. A pastry cook was drizzling honey over some fruit tarts. The cooks, men and women, sassed one another in a lively slang enriched by more obscenity and profanity than any this side of the royal army.

The old crack near the ceiling had been sealed up. The cook pointed to another likely one. The king clambered up on a ladder, a lamp in one hand, some scraps of beef cut from a joint in the other. That left no hands free in case he slipped. He resolved not to slip. *This is very undignified,* he thought, but only after it was far too late to do anything about it.

He held the lamp up to the crack, hoping to see Pouncer's eyes glowing yellow somewhere not far away. No such luck. All he could make out was a spiderweb with the pale spider that had made it squatting near the edge. The spider ran away when his breath shook the web. He climbed down the ladder and shook his head. "He's gone."

"Well, it's not like that's a big surprise," the cook said, but then, recalling to whom she was talking, she added, "Thank you for trying, Your Majesty."

"It's all right," Lanius said. "Sooner or later, the spoon will show up. Pouncer doesn't keep them."

She nodded. The cooks did know that. The moncat had lost a couple, but only a couple. Things could have been worse. As it was, Pouncer's thieving gave the kitchens something to complain about. Everyone needed something to complain about. It was as much fun as . . . stealing spoons.

The past few years, Grus had spent every summer in the field. Coming back to the city of Avornis—coming back to the rest of the royal family—always took adjusting. This fall, it seemed to take more than usual. Estrilda greeted him with, "Any new mistresses I should know about?"

"No," he answered at once. He would have said the same thing had the answer been yes. He fought battles in the summertime; he didn't want to fight more of them after he got back to the palace.

His wife greeted his declaration with something less than a ringing endorsement, inquiring, "Any mistresses I *shouldn't* know about?"

"None of those, either," he told her. She sniffed. Here, though, he was at least technically truthful. The last mistress he'd had that Estrilda shouldn't have known about—and didn't—was Alauda, a widow he'd met during the Menteshe invasion of Avornis' southern provinces. Estrilda also shouldn't have known—and didn't know—about Grus' bastard boy named Nivalis. Grus made sure his son and the boy's mother lacked for nothing money could buy. He'd never seen Nivalis. He wanted to, one of these days.

Estrilda looked at him. "Why not?" she asked him, something approaching true curiosity in her voice. "Are you really getting old?"

"There are times when I think so," Grus admitted. There were times when he was sure of it. He didn't feel like admitting that, even to himself. He went on, "Besides—thrall women? They're only a short step up from the barnyard animals."

*As though that would stop you.* It hovered in the air, but Estrilda didn't say it. She did say, "What about after they've had the spell lifted?"

She wouldn't let it alone. Grus didn't suppose he should have been surprised. He'd given her plenty of reasons to doubt him—more reasons than she knew, in fact. But he wasn't lying when he said, "They still have a lot of growing up to do after that happens."

"Really?" Estrilda's voice was as chilly as any winter sent by the Banished One. "I saw the woman Otus brought back from south of the Stura. She looked all grown up to me."

"Fulca will grow up faster than a little girl would," Grus said. "Otus certainly did. But talk to her. You'll see what I mean."

Estrilda still didn't seem happy. In fact, she seemed determined not to be happy. She said, "What about when you go back next year? The women who were thralls will be all grown up by then."

"I hope they will," Grus said. Estrilda sent him a sharp look. He explained, "If they aren't, something will have gone wrong. Either we won't have truly freed them or the Menteshe will have found a way to enslave them again."

His wife looked as though she wanted to challenge that, too, but she couldn't figure out how. "Well, all right," she said reluctantly. "You really did beat back the Banished One, didn't you?"

Grus shook his head. "No. We beat back the Menteshe. They're still fighting among themselves, and that made it harder for the Banished One to do anything to us. I'm afraid we're not out of the woods yet, though." He told her why not.

"Oh," she said, and then, "Queen Quelea in her mercy grant that he can't do anything so wicked."

"May it be so," Grus said, doubting it would be. What had the gods in the heavens done to stop the Banished One since exiling him to the material world? Some people said they'd given Avornis the Scepter of Mercy. If that was true, though, why had they let the Banished One and his minions hold it for so many centuries? Grus had no answer for that, and didn't think anyone else did, either.

Changing the subject, Grus asked, "When did Ortalis start keeping company with these junior guard officers?"

"This past spring," Estrilda answered. "He goes hunting with them sometimes, when he's not with . . . the arch-hallow." She couldn't help reminding Grus that Anser was his bastard.

"Hunting," Grus said with relief. "That's all right, then." He wasn't going to worry about his son as long as Ortalis had some reasonable cause to hang around with the guardsmen. Ortalis had never shown himself to be very interested in politics.

"Limosa will have her baby before long," Estrilda remarked.

That wasn't quite a change of subject, though Grus wished it were. He said, "Maybe she'll have another girl. That will leave things the way they are."

"So it will." His wife looked at him. "What if she has a boy instead?"

"What if she does?" Grus answered. "It makes life more complicated, that's what. Crex isn't just connected to us. He's part of the old dynasty, too. Limosa's son wouldn't be."

"Will Ortalis care?" Estrilda asked.

"Not by the way he's been talking, from what I hear," Grus said.

Estrilda studied him some more. "Will *you* care?"

"Him having a son would make things . . . untidy," Grus said. "I don't like untidy things." He didn't want to come right out and say that he preferred the succession to pass through Lanius to Crex, not through Ortalis to his son. He wasn't sure Estrilda agreed with him.

"I can't say that I blame you," Estrilda said now. "We had a pretty good idea of how things would go. Now it could be all up in the air again." She sent Grus another sour stare. "All the gods in the heavens be praised that Anser doesn't care about the throne. That's only luck, you know."

She wasn't wrong there, either. Grus thought about Nivalis in a way he hadn't before. If he himself lived another fifteen or twenty years—far from certain, but also not impossible—his bastard little boy would grow to be a young man. What would Nivalis think about his place in life? Would he think about what might have been his if he'd been born on the right side of the blanket? Would he think it might be his any which way?

"He's a good fellow, Anser," was all the king said, and even Estrilda couldn't disagree with that.

Again not really changing the subject at all, she repeated, "Maybe Limosa will have another girl."

"Here's hoping." There. Grus had said it. He didn't want his only legitimate son to have a son of his own. If that wasn't sad, what was? He couldn't think of anything to match it. A moment later, though, he found something, for the mother of his only legitimate son nodded agreement.

Not only did she nod—she also said, "I wish Lanius and Sosia would have another baby—with luck, another boy. So many things can happen, even when children aren't in line for the throne."

That was also true. Grus said, "They've seemed . . . not too happy with each other lately, from what I've heard."

His wife glared at him. "You know the reason why, too, or you'd better. He seduces serving girls, or lets them seduce him. It amounts to the same thing either way. And you're a fine one to tell him to stop being unfaithful to our daughter, you are, when you can't keep it in your drawers."

Since Grus couldn't deny that as a general working rule, he did his best to deny it in this particular case, saying, "Well, if you're worrying about what goes on south of the Stura, you can cursed well worry about something else. I already told you, nothing's going on down there—nothing like that, anyway."

"Oh, such thrilling news!" If Estrilda had used a different tone of voice, Grus might have thought she meant it. As things were, her sarcasm only stung the more.

# CHAPTER TWELVE

The last time Limosa had a baby, there'd been a small scandal when all the rumors about lash marks and scars on her back proved true. By now, that was old news. When she disrobed for the midwife this time, no one would get—too—excited about it.

Lanius had other things to worry about this time around, chiefly whether she would have a boy or a girl. Ortalis had the same worry, even if his hopes and the king's ran in opposite directions.

It had just started to snow when Limosa's bag of waters broke. That was a sure sign of labor beginning in earnest, and servants hotfooted it from the palace to bring back the midwife. Lanius listened to Ortalis burble and babble for a little while, then excused himself and got as far away from his brother-in-law as he could.

He started to head for the archives, but changed his mind. He'd needed years to teach the servants not to bother him there. Someone would have to come with news of Limosa's baby. Better not to be with the moncats, either. And he also couldn't go to his own bedchamber, because Sosia was there. She still didn't appreciate his company.

That left . . . what? He ended up in one of the palace's several small dining rooms. Instead of eating, he caught up on correspondence. He felt virtuous. He also rapidly grew bored. This was the part of governing that Grus did better than he did.

Someone opened the door and stuck his head into the room. "Oh," Grus said. "Sorry to bother you, Your Majesty. I was just looking for a quiet place where I could get a little work done until Limosa has her baby, however long that takes."

Laughing, Lanius answered, "That's exactly what I'm doing here."

"Oh," Grus said again, and then, "Mind if I join you?"

"Not a bit," Lanius told him. "And if you want to write some letters for me along with your own, I don't mind that, either. I was just thinking you're better at this part of being a king than I am."

"Well, I don't know about that," Grus said. "When something interests you, you get better at it than I ever could. When it doesn't, you don't bother with it so much, that's all."

Lanius thought about that. He didn't need long to decide Grus was right. "I should do better," he said.

"Probably," Grus said. "Everybody has some things he should do better—and if you don't believe me, you can ask either one of our wives."

"Ha!" Lanius said. "We don't need to ask them—they come right out and tell us."

"Wives do that sometimes. Husbands do it to wives, too, I expect." Grus sat down across the table from Lanius. He dumped a disorderly pile of letters and blank leaves of parchment on the table in front of him, pulled the stopper from a burnt-clay bottle of ink, dipped a goose quill, and began to write. The pile stayed disorderly. Lanius was much neater about the way he worked. But Grus dipped his pen and wrote, dipped his pen and wrote, dipped his pen. . . . He wasn't neat, but he got the job done, turning out letter after letter.

"I'm jealous," Lanius remarked.

The other king only shrugged. "It's nothing very special," he said. "Most of the time, the simplest answer will do. Yes, no, tell me more, whatever the local official decided also seems right to me. It's only on the odd things that you really have to slow down and think." He passed a letter across to Lanius. "Will you read this to me, please? My sight hasn't lengthened too badly, but I have trouble when somebody writes as small as this."

Lanius read it. It was an appeal of a conviction for theft. "Thanks," Grus said. He wrote a few lines, set the letter aside, and went on to the next.

"What did you tell him?" Lanius asked.

"What would you have told him?" Grus asked in return.

"It doesn't seem likely that the victim and the captain and the city governor are all in league against the appellant," Lanius said. "They would have to be for him to be innocent, seems to me."

"Seems the same way to me," Grus replied. "So I told him no. Not worth wasting a lot of time on it."

"I suppose not." Lanius had come up with the same answer as his father-in-law. He would have fussed much more over the letter, though. He wanted things to sound good. Grus just wanted to make sure no one could misunderstand what he meant. Lanius had rarely seen him fail to live up to that standard.

After a while, Grus stopped writing. He looked at Lanius and said, "I wonder how much longer it will be."

"No way to know," Lanius answered, having not the slightest doubt about what Grus meant. "Babies come when they feel like coming, not when you tell them to."

"I'm not going to say you're wrong. I can't very well when you're right, can I?" The other king inked his pen, started another letter, and then stopped once more. "Here's something you haven't heard from me. If you tell anybody I said it, I'll call you a liar to your face. Have you got that?"

By the way he said it, Lanius knew he was liable to do worse than call him a liar. "I won't blab. I *don't* blab."

"Well, that's true, too—you don't." Grus leaned forward and dropped his voice to something not much above a whisper. "I hope it's a girl."

"Do you?" Lanius hoped he didn't squeak in surprise. Grus solemnly nodded. "Even though Ortalis is your legitimate son?" Lanius asked. Grus nodded again. Lanius couldn't believe he was telling anything but the truth. He also couldn't help asking, "Why?"

"It makes things simpler," Grus told him. "When you get as old as I am, you decide simpler is better most of the time."

His answer wasn't as simple as it might have been. Lanius had no doubt the other king knew as much. Had Grus been pleased with Ortalis, had he thought his legitimate son would make a good successor, he would have done whatever he needed to do to make sure the crown went to him and his descendants. If anyone—Lanius included—stood in his way, that would have been too bad for the person who proved an obstacle.

As things were, though . . . "Thank you," Lanius said quietly, though he knew Grus' choice wasn't so much praise for him as a judgment on Ortalis.

"Don't worry about it," Grus said. "You're not the boy I shoved aside to take the throne anymore. Don't think I haven't noticed. I don't believe you'll ever make much of a warrior—I don't see you taking the field and driving everybody before you. But except for that, you make a good king."

Lanius didn't see himself as much of a warrior, either. Fighting wasn't something he was or wanted to be good at. He nodded to Grus all the same. "You haven't made a bad king yourself." He wasn't sure he'd ever admitted even that much to the man who'd stolen more than half his throne.

Grus gave him a seated bow. "Thank you, Your Majesty."

"You're welcome, Your Majesty," Lanius responded, every bit as seriously.

Grus seemed to be casting about for something else to say. Whatever it was, he didn't find it. Instead, he went back to the letter that he'd stopped halfway through. He finished it and went on to the next. Lanius started writing again, too. He still couldn't match his father-in-law for speed.

An hour later, or maybe two, shouts in the corridor outside made them both look up from their work. Someone knocked on the door to the dining room. "Come in," the two kings said together.

"Your Majesty!" a servant said excitedly. He paused, blinked, and tried again. "Uh, Your Majesties, I mean. I have great news, Your Majesties! Princess Limosa has had a baby boy!"

Grus had to reward the servant who brought him word of Ortalis' son. He had to pretend it *was* good news. Things in the palace would have been even worse if he hadn't.

Ortalis gave money to every servant he saw. He kissed all the women, including those old enough to be his mother. He slapped all the men on the back. He didn't walk down the palace hallways. He danced instead.

"Marinus!" he said to anyone who would listen. "We'll call the baby Marinus!"

It wasn't a name from Grus' side of the family. Maybe it was connected to Petrosus'—or maybe Ortalis and Limosa had just decided they liked it. Grus didn't feel like asking. He said, "Congratulations," to his legitimate son, and hoped his face wasn't too wooden while he did it. Evidently not, for Ortalis only grinned at him. Seeing Ortalis grin felt almost as strange as congratulating him. Ortalis' face frequently wore a frown or a scowl or a sneer. A grin? Grus wondered where those usually sour features found room for one.

Lanius did somewhat better, saying, "I hope Limosa is well?"

"Oh, yes." Ortalis stopped cutting capers long enough to nod. "The midwife said she came through it as well as a woman can."

"Good," Lanius said.

"Wonderful," Grus agreed, thinking nothing of the sort. But then, that wasn't fair. Say what you would of Petrosus, Limosa was an inoffensive creature. Her worst failing up until now had been the unfortunate taste for pain that made her such a good match for Ortalis. But bearing an inconvenient boy came close to being an unforgivable sin.

Did she realize as much? If she did, she had the sense to hide the knowledge. Naïveté, here, worked to her advantage. Ortalis understood what she'd done, all right. He started dancing again, dancing and singing, "I have an heir! Thank you, King Olor! I have an heir!"

Lanius showed none of what he was thinking. Grus admired that, and hoped his own features were under something close to as much control. He wouldn't have bet on it, though. And then something occurred to him that actually let him smile. *He's calling on King Olor. He isn't calling on the Banished One.*

That he should think such a thing about his own son . . . He shrugged. Yes, it was sad. But Ortalis had given him plenty of reason to worry about whose side he was on. Seeing and hearing such a worry come to nothing wasn't the worst thing in the world.

Grus studied his joyful legitimate son. Just because Ortalis didn't shout the Banished One's praises didn't mean he saw eye to eye with Grus and Lanius. The way he was carrying on showed he didn't, at least as far as the succession went. He could do the Banished One's work without acknowledging the exiled god as his overlord. He might work more effectively in the Banished One's behalf if he didn't acknowledge him. Few men got out of bed thinking, *I'm going to do something evil today.* Many more thought, *I'm going to do something good,* not seeing that what they reckoned good was anything but in the eyes of most of their fellows.

Prince Vasilko of Nishevatz, up in the Chernagor country, had been like that when he rose against his unloving and unlovable father. He saw all the things Vsevolod was doing, and didn't care where he looked for help to overthrown him. If men who backed the Banished One would help him overthrow Vsevolod, so much the better. And if they—and the exiled god—gained ever greater power in Nishevatz and then in the rest of the Chernagor city-states . . . well, Prince Vasilko hadn't worried about that. He'd gotten what he wanted, and nothing else mattered nearly so much to him.

Overthrowing him and others whom the Banished One had seduced had cost Avornis years of fighting. It also cost Grus the chance to take advantage of the civil war among the Menteshe for all that time. (Of course, the civil war down in the south cost the Banished One the chance to take advantage of Avornis' being busy in the north. Things evened out—except when they didn't.)

Would Ortalis lean toward the Banished One if he saw that as the only way to get what he wanted? Grus eyed his son again. He'd had that worry before, had it and dismissed it from his mind. Should he have? He didn't know. And asking Ortalis what he'd do would only put ideas in his mind—ideas that might not have already been there. Grus sighed. Nothing was as simple as he wished it were.

Ortalis, for his part, was glancing at Lanius. He didn't proclaim that Marinus was the rightful heir not just to him but also to the Kingdom of Avornis. If he had, he would have had trouble on his hands right away. But did the gloating look in his eyes say what Grus thought it did? He couldn't see what else it was likely to mean.

What Ortalis did say was, "It's a good thing the kingdom has another prince." He didn't say Lanius should father more children. If he had, Lanius couldn't have been too unhappy. As things were, Ortalis made it sound as though Prince Crex was liable to be in perilous health. If he was, Ortalis was all too likely to be the one who made his health perilous.

"Maybe it is," Lanius replied, in tones that couldn't mean anything but, *You must be out of your mind.*

"Can we see the baby?" Grus asked. That seemed harmless enough.

"If the midwife lets you." Ortalis rolled his eyes. Grus had all he could do not to laugh out loud. Ortalis and Limosa were no doubt using Netta, the midwife who'd also come when Sosia was brought to bed. She was the best in the city of Avornis. She was also probably the toughest woman Grus had ever met. She took no nonsense from anybody. Even Ortalis had figured that out. If he could, anybody and everybody could.

Sosia had given birth in a special palace room reserved for queens. Limosa, only a princess, had had to do it in her own bedchamber. *They'll need new bedclothes in there,* Grus thought. Ortalis knocked before presuming to go inside. He waited till he heard a gruff, "Come in," too—only then did he open the door.

He came out with Marinus in his arms. Like any newborn, his son could have looked better. Marinus' head seemed misshapen, almost conical, and was much too big for his body. His face looked smashed. His eyes were squeezed shut. He was redder than he should have had any business being. Netta had put a bandage over the stump of the cord that had connected him to his mother.

"Isn't he handsome?" Ortalis said, proving all new fathers are blind.

"Congratulations." Grus held out his hand not to his son but to his new grandson. Marinus' tiny hand brushed against his forefinger. The baby clung to the finger with a grip of sudden and startling strength. Grus laughed himself then. He'd seen that with other newborns. It faded after a little while.

Ortalis looked down at the tiny shape in his arms. "A boy. A son. An heir," he said softly. Grus would have been happier if he'd left out the last two words.

Gossip about Limosa's back and the scars on it had quieted down in the palace. It revived even before the midwife left. Naturally, a couple of servants had been in there with Ortalis' wife and Netta. They blabbed about everything they'd seen. By the way the news sounded to Lanius, they blabbed about quite a bit they'd made up, too. He didn't think a person could have as many scars as they said Limosa did and go on living.

Naturally, the servants paid no attention to his opinion. The scandals of their superiors were more interesting and more entertaining than the possibility that a couple of their own number were talking through their hats. He'd seen that before. It didn't bother him. It was part of palace life.

That evening, Sosia said, "You can sleep in the bedchamber—if you feel like it." Her voice held an odd note of challenge. She'd made it plain he wasn't welcome there ever since she found out about Oissa.

"I'm glad to," Lanius answered. He paused. "Are you sure?" His wife nodded. She didn't hesitate before she did it. He found himself nodding, too. "All right."

When he came to bed, she was already under the covers. That didn't surprise him; the night was chilly, and braziers did only so much to fight the cold. "Good night," he said, and blew out the lamp on his night table. That was all he did—she'd invited him to sleep in the bed, not to sleep with her. But when she slid toward him, as though for a good-night kiss, he almost automatically reached out to take her in his arms. He jerked back in surprise when his hands found soft, bare flesh.

Sosia laughed a brittle laugh. "It's all right," she said. "You can go on—if you feel like it." The challenge rang stronger now.

"Why?" he asked. "What made you change your mind?"

"Two things," Sosia answered. "If you don't do it with me,

you will do it with somebody else. Even if you *do* do it with me, you may do it with somebody else—but you may not, too." She clicked her tongue between her teeth; that might have been too bald even for her. After a moment, she went on, "And we really ought to have more than one son—especially now."

She wasn't wrong. Marriages for reasons of state sometimes held love. Theirs had, on and off. Whether love was there or not, though, duty always was. Not getting out from under the covers, Lanius wriggled free of his nightshirt. "I'm glad to," he said as he embraced her.

He wasn't even lying. He'd never stopped enjoying what the two of them did together, not through all his other liaisons. He didn't think she understood that or believed it, but it was true.

Now he took special care to please her, kissing and caressing her breasts and her belly for a long time before sliding down to the joining of her legs. If she was angry enough at him, of course, nothing he did would bring her pleasure. But she sighed and murmured and opened her legs wider. He went on until she gasped and quivered. Then he poised himself above her and took his own pleasure.

When they lay side by side again, she asked him, "Was that as good for you as it was for me?"

"Yes, I think so," Lanius said, adding, "I hope it was good for you."

"It was, and you know it was," Sosia said, which was true. After a moment, she went on, "If it was good for you, why do you want to look anywhere else?"

"I don't know," he answered, and muffled his words with a yawn. Sosia made a small, exasperated noise. Pretending he didn't hear it, he got up, used the chamber pot, and then lay down again. Before long, he was breathing deeply and regularly. Men had a reputation for rolling over and going to sleep afterwards.

But, reputation or not, Lanius wasn't asleep. He lay there on his side, not moving much. Sosia muttered again, more softly this time. Then *she* started breathing deeply and regularly. Maybe she was pretending, as he was. He didn't think so, though. He thought she really had dropped off.

*Why do you want to look anywhere else?* He knew the answer, regardless of whether he felt like giving it to Sosia, which he didn't. He knew it wouldn't make sense to her, and would only make her angry. *Because I knew everything you were going to do before you did it.* The serving girls he bedded weren't that much prettier than his wife, if at all. They weren't that much better in bed, if at all. But they could surprise him. He liked that.

He did love Sosia, as much as he could in their arranged marriage. Would he have chosen her if he could have picked from all the girls in the kingdom? He had no idea. For one thing, the idea of marrying for love and only for love was an absurdity. Most of him accepted that. The part that slept with maidservants didn't.

His deep, regular breathing became shallower and less regular for a moment. No doubt he had as much trouble surprising Sosia as she did surprising him. She'd threatened to take a lover now and again. He hadn't believed her or taken her seriously. He didn't think she was looking for variety, as he was.

Revenge? That might be a different story. He knew too well that it might.

But she could no more keep it a secret in the crowded world of the palace than he could. Servants always talked. It might take a while, but it always happened. He'd never heard anything that made him think she was doing anything of the sort.

A good thing, too. She was angry at him. He would have been much more angry at her. Maybe that wouldn't have been fair. He didn't care. It was how he would have felt.

Another child? He smiled and yawned, this time genuinely. Another child wouldn't be so bad, especially if it was a boy. He yawned again. If he had another son, what would he name him? He fell asleep before he found a name he liked.

Grus kept a wary eye on Ortalis. If his son was going to show signs of plotting, having Marinus to plot for might start him off. But he seemed no more than a new father happy at the birth of a son. *Maybe I misjudged him,* Grus thought. *Or maybe he's just sneakier than I figured.*

Every day that went by without word of trouble from the south, without word of pestilence or other natural disaster that might not be so natural, felt like a triumph to the king. He dared hope the Banished One was so weakened by everything that had gone wrong for him lately, he couldn't hit back at Avornis the way he would have a few years earlier. Grus didn't really believe that, but he dared hope. Hope marked progress, too.

He didn't need long to realize that Lanius and Sosia had reconciled. Neither his son-in-law nor his daughter said much about it, but their manner with each other spoke louder than words could have. Grus suspected Marinus' arrival had a good deal to do with that, but whatever the reason, he hoped it lasted. And so it would—till Lanius found another serving girl attractive and Sosia found out about it. Grus didn't know what he could do about that. Seeing trouble ahead didn't always mean seeing any way to stop it.

Grus had had that thought down south of the Stura, when Otus plucked his woman from a village of freed thralls and decided to bring her up to the city of Avornis. The king had nothing against Fulca, who seemed nice enough and very capable. He also had nothing against Calypte, with whom Otus had taken up while Fulca remained a thrall. And Otus himself was solid as the day was long. But when one of his women found out about the other one . . .

When that happened, it proved as hard on Otus as it would have on anyone else whose two women suddenly discovered neither of them was his one woman. A lot of men, in a mess like that, would have lost both of them. Otus didn't. While Calypte departed in a crockery-throwing huff, Fulca stuck by him. But she was furious, too.

"What was I supposed to do, Your Majesty?" Otus asked plaintively after the dishes stopped flying. "Was I supposed to act like a dead man while I was far away from Fulca and I thought I would never see her again? Once I'd found she'd been freed and found her, was I supposed to pretend I'd never known her?"

"I suppose not, and I suppose not." Grus answered each question in turn. "But I didn't think you would be able to keep both of them once they found out about each other. Things don't usually work that way."

"Why not?" Otus said. "They should."

"Well, suppose Calypte had taken another lover while you were south of the Stura with me," Grus said. "Would she have been able to keep two men?"

"I don't think so!" Otus sounded indignant.

"There, then. Do you see?" Grus said. Otus didn't, or didn't want to. Few men wanted to when the shoe was on the other foot. Grus set a hand on the ex-thrall's shoulder. "Be thankful Fulca is sticking by you. You don't have to start over from the beginning."

"Even she wants to knock me over the head with something," Otus said. "Shouldn't she be glad I came looking for her and took her out of the village?"

"Oh, I think she is," Grus said. Otus hadn't told her anything about his other woman when he took her out of the village. She'd thought—not unreasonably, as far as Grus could see—she was his only woman, and that he had no others. No wonder she was none too happy to discover she was wrong. "If the two of you really love each other, you'll figure out how to patch things up." *And if you don't patch them up, it wouldn't be the first time things fell apart.* Grus kept quiet about that. Otus wouldn't appreciate it.

"I don't know what to do," Otus said sorrowfully.

A lot of that sorrow was no more than self-pity. Grus knew as much. Even so, he soberly answered, "Congratulations."

Otus stared at him. Grus hadn't expected anything else. "Congratulations, Your Majesty?" the ex-thrall echoed. "I don't understand."

"Not knowing what to do, not being sure, needing to figure things out for yourself—all this is part of what being a free man is all about," Grus explained. "You wouldn't have said anything like that when you were a thrall, would you?"

"No, I don't suppose I would." Otus shook his head. "No, of course I wouldn't. I knew everything I needed to know then. It wasn't much, by the gods, but I knew it." He spoke with a certain somber pride.

"That's about what I thought," Grus told him. "You have more things to know and to try to figure out now that you're on your own. Not all of it's going to be easy. It won't be much fun some of the time, especially when you get yourself into a mess like the one you're in now. But this is part of what being free is all about. You're free to make an idiot of yourself, too. People do it every day."

"Freedom to get in trouble, I think I could do without," Otus said.

"I don't know how you're going to separate it from any other kind," Grus said. "You've done a good job of getting the hang of being your own person. You didn't have years and years to learn how, the way ordinary people do. You had to start doing it right away after Pterocles lifted the spell of thralldom from you. Now Fulca has to do the same thing, and do it just as fast as you did—maybe faster. Remember, it won't always be easy for her, either."

"I suppose not," Otus said, and then, "Thank you, Your Majesty."

"For what?" Grus said. "I don't have any real answers for you. I've landed in this exact same trouble myself, and more than once." *So has Lanius,* he thought. *It's something that happens, all right.*

"For listening to me," the freed thrall said with a rueful smile. "Just for listening to me. That was something neither of my women wanted to do."

"Oh. Well, you're welcome." Grus fought hard to hide a smile. "Between you and me, when a man's women find out about each other—or when a woman's men find out about each other, which happens, too—they aren't usually in a listening mood."

"Yes, I'd noticed that." By the way Otus said it, it was for him some strange natural phenomenon, like the fogs that afflicted the Chernagor country or the tides that swept the sea in and back along Avornis' coastline.

"Good luck," Grus told him. "Part of what makes being free, being a whole man, worthwhile is that it isn't simple. You may not always believe that, or want to believe it, but it's true."

Otus went on his way scratching his head. Grus hoped he would work things out with Fulca, for her sake as much as for his. She didn't know enough yet to have an easy time as a free woman. If she had to, though, Grus suspected she would get along. Just how much would Avornis gain from the suddenly released talents of so many thralls? More than a little—he was sure of that.

At the midwife's suggestion, Limosa had nursed Marinus for the first few days after he was born. Lanius remembered Netta giving Sosia the same advice after she bore Crex and Pitta. She'd said babies whose mothers did that ended up healthier. That had persuaded Sosia, and it persuaded Limosa, too.

After those first few days, Limosa let her own milk dry up and brought in a wet nurse. With Sosia as grumpy as she was, Lanius wondered how she would react to a woman who often bared her breasts in the palace. That turned out not to be an issue. The wet nurse Limosa hired was almost as wide as she was tall, and had eyes set too close together, a big nose, and a mean mouth. Maybe Limosa was taking no chances with Ortalis, too.

Not long after Marinus' birth, the winter turned nasty. Three blizzards roared through the city of Avornis one after another, snarling the streets, piling roofs high with snow, and making Lanius wonder whether the Banished One had decided to use the weather as a weapon after all. As the city began to dig out, several people were found frozen to death in their homes and shops. That happened after almost every bad storm, but it worried the king all the same.

And then the sun came out. It got warm enough to melt a lot of the snow—not quite springlike, but close enough. Here and there, a few prematurely hopeful shoots of grass sprouted between cobblestones.

Lanius laughed at himself. Plucking one of those little green shoots outside the palace, he held it under Grus' nose. "This probably *won't* be a winter like that dreadful one," he said.

He must have held the shoot too close to Grus' nose, for the other king's eyes crossed as he looked at it. "I'd say you're right," Grus answered. "Of course, there's still some winter left. Other thing is, just because he's not sending snow and ice at us doesn't mean he won't do *something*."

"And here I wanted to be happy and cheerful," Lanius said. "How am I supposed to manage that when you keep spouting common sense at me?"

"I'm sorry, Your Majesty." Grus bowed almost double; he might have been a clumsy servant who'd dropped a pitcher of wine and splashed Lanius' robe. "I'll try not to let it happen again."

"A likely story," Lanius said, laughing. "You can't help being sensible any more than I can, and you know it."

"Well, maybe not," Grus said. "Between us, we make a pretty fair pair—now that each of us knows he can trust the other one with his back turned."

That had taken a while for Lanius. After Grus took more than his share of the crown, Lanius had feared the other king would dispose of him and rule on his own. Odds were Grus was strong enough and well enough liked to have gotten away with it. But it hadn't happened. For his part, Grus had taken even longer to learn to trust Lanius. Grus had kept him nothing but a figurehead for years. Little by little, though, when Grus went on campaign, Lanius began handling things in—and from— the capital.

"Here we are, getting along . . . well enough." Try as Lanius would, he couldn't make his agreement any warmer than that. Wanting to lighten things with a joke, he added, "And all we have to worry about is the Banished One."

Grus laughed—not the sort of laugh that says something is really funny, but more the kind that comes out when the choice is between laughter and a sob. The other king said, "I'm not worried about that. After all, you've got things all figured out, don't you? As soon as we get to Yozgat, the Scepter of Mercy falls into our hands." He laughed again.

"I wish things would be that simple," Lanius replied. "Still, though, there's no denying that some of the things we've both done have made the Banished One sit up and take notice."

He waited to see if Grus would try to deny that, or would try to deny him any credit for it. The other king didn't. He just said, "To tell you the truth, Your Majesty, I could do without the honor."

"So could I," Lanius said. "I've come awake in my bed too many times with the memory of . . . him staring at me." Grus nodded. As anyone who'd known them could testify, dreams from the Banished One seemed more vivid, more real, and certainly more memorable, than most things in the waking world. Lanius went on, "If he didn't worry about us, about what we're doing, he wouldn't trouble us so. That is an honor of a kind."

"Of a kind," Grus agreed. "Or we tell ourselves it is, anyhow. We don't know much about the Banished One for certain. Maybe he doesn't send dreams to some other people because he can't, not because he doesn't think they're important."

"Maybe." Lanius was usually polite. But he didn't believe it. If someone worried the Banished One in any real way, the exiled god threatened that person. Who the victim was—king or witch or animal trainer—didn't seem to matter.

Before they could take the argument any further—if that was what Grus had in mind—someone in the palace started calling, "Your Majesty! Your Majesty!"

Lanius and Grus looked at each other. They both smiled. Lanius said, "I don't know which one of us he wants, but I think he's going to get both of us."

They went toward the noise until a servant coming out from it ran into them and led them back to a weather-beaten courier who smelled powerfully of horse. Bowing, the man said, "Sorry it took me so long to come up from the south, Your Majesty—I mean, Your Majesties—but the weather's been beastly until a couple of days ago." He took a waxed-leather message tube off his belt and thrust it at the two kings—at both of them, but not quite at either one of them.

They both started to reach for it. At the last instant, Lanius deferred to Grus—things coming out of the south were the older man's province, and he'd earned the right to know of them first. With a nod and a murmur of thanks, Grus took the waterproofed tube and worked off the lid. He pulled out the letter inside, unrolled it, and began to read. His face got longer and longer.

"What is it?" Lanius asked. "Something's gone wrong—I can tell. Where? How bad is it?"

"Down south of the Stura," Grus told him. "And it's not good. Thralls and freed thralls . . . they're dying like flies."

# CHAPTER THIRTEEN

Like almost every wizard Grus had ever known, Pterocles normally rode a donkey or a mule. He was on horseback now, on horseback and apprehensive at how high off the ground he perched and how fast he was going. The king showed him no mercy. "By Olor's beard, we need to get there as fast as we can," Grus growled.

Pterocles sent him a piteous stare. "What good will I be to you if I fall off and break my neck long before we get near the Stura?"

"Oh, nonsense," Grus said, or perhaps something stronger than that. He waved at the snowdrifts to either side of the road. "If you fall off, you'll go into the snow here, see? It's nice and soft—just like your head."

"Thank you so much, Your Majesty," the wizard said stiffly.

"Any time." Grus couldn't have been less sympathetic. He jabbed a thumb at his own chest. "Look at me, why don't you? I didn't know what to do on a horse for years—I was a river-galley captain, remember? But I managed. I'm still not what you'd call pretty on horseback, but even Hirundo hardly bothers teasing me anymore, because I got the job done." He did some more glowering. "I get the job done—*and so will you.*"

"You're a cruel, hard man." Pterocles sounded like a convict who'd been denied clemency.

Grus bowed in the saddle. "At your service." He paused, then shook his head. "I may be a hard man, but I hope I'm not cruel." He pointed south. "There's the cruel one, killing off people because he thinks he can get some good out of it."

Pterocles chewed on that for a little while. Grus waited to see whether he would keep arguing. The king wouldn't have minded much if he did; it gave them both something to do as they rode along. A troop of guards rode in front of them and another in back of them to make sure no Menteshe raiders sneaked north over the border and struck at them, but the soldiers were all business. And so, for the moment, was Pterocles. Grus decided he'd won his point.

The snow would get thicker as they rode through the low, rolling hills separating one of the valleys of the Nine Rivers from the next. Then, when they came down out of herding country and into better farmland once more, the weather would warm up a little. Bare dirt would show through here and there, more and more of it with each valley farther south. Even in most years with bad blizzards up in the city of Avornis, the valley of the Stura saw more rain than snow. What things would be like south of the Stura . . . Grus shrugged. For hundreds of years, no Avornan had personally known what things were like south of the Stura. Now his countrymen were getting the chance to find out.

This proved a year like most years. Grus cursed when snow gave way to rain. Up until then, he and the unhappy Pterocles and their escorts—about whose opinions no one had asked—made fine time. The road was frozen hard, and there wasn't even the usual summer annoyance of dust rising in choking clouds. But the horses had to slow down slogging their way through mud.

Every so often, Pterocles—and Grus—had to dismount to get their beasts through the worst stretches. Mud was no respecter of rank or of person. A king riding through it got as filthy as a farmer or a wandering tinker.

Afterwards, though, a king could do more about it than a farmer or a tinker. When Grus and Pterocles got to Cumanus, the city governor whisked them to his residence. He had a big copper tub, which his servants filled with hot water. First Grus and then Pterocles soaked away the dirt and the chill of the road. A blazing fire in the room with the tub kept Grus comfortable as he sat wrapped in a thick robe of soft wool. He sipped warm wine as he sat with Pterocles, who seemed ready to stay in the tub until he either grew fins or came out wrinkled as a prune.

"How much do you think you'll be able to do against this plague or curse or whatever it is?" he asked, not for the first time.

Not for the first time, Pterocles shrugged. This time, though, the motion threatened to send waves slopping over the edge of the tub and out onto the slate floor. The wizard had warm wine, too, the cup resting on a stool within easy reach. He took a sip before answering, "Your Majesty, I'll do the best I can. Until I know more, how can I say more?"

That was reasonable. Grus was usually a reasonable man, one who craved reasonable answers. Even Lanius had said so, and he was reasonable to a fault. Tonight, though, despite not being soaked and shivering anymore, Grus craved reassurance more than reason. He said, "You have to find a cure, you know. Everything will unravel if you don't. It's already started hitting soldiers along with the thralls." That unwelcome bit of news had come to him only a couple of days before; he'd intercepted it on its way north to the capital.

"Yes, Your Majesty." Now Pterocles sounded patient.

Grus was in no mood for patience, either. "What happens if—no, what happens *when*—it spreads to this side of the river?"

"We do the best we can, Your Majesty," Pterocles said again, patient still. "Maybe you shouldn't have come south yourself."

The same thing had occurred to Grus. He'd been fighting the Banished One for years, so he'd naturally assumed that fighting the pestilence required him to be here in person. Would the Banished One mind killing him by disease instead of more directly? Not a bit—the king was sure of that. He was also sure of some other things. "If the plague crosses the Stura, it will get all the way to the city of Avornis," he said. "Or am I wrong?"

"I wish you were," Pterocles said.

"In that case, it doesn't make any difference," Grus said. "If it can get me down here, it can get me up there, too. And if it gets me a little sooner down here than it would up there—well, so what?"

He might have fought an ordinary outbreak of disease by ordering that no one south of the Stura should cross to the north side of the river. That might have slowed things down. For a plague in which he suspected the Banished One played a part . . . well, what was the point? The exiled god could make sure a diseased thrall came over the river, or might waft the illness across it some other way.

And, even if Grus had given the order, it would have come too late. Less than an hour after Pterocles finally came out of the tub, a messenger ran up to the city governor's residence shouting that two soldiers and a merchant by the waterfront had come down sick.

People who heard the news gasped in horror. Some of them seemed ready to disappear as fast as they could. When people heard a pestilence was loose, they often did that—and they often brought it with them and spread it places where it wouldn't have gone if they hadn't. That was one more reason Grus couldn't have hoped to hold the disease on the southern side of the Stura.

He and Pterocles looked at each other. "Well, now we get the chance to find out what we're up against," Grus said, hoping he sounded more cheerful than he felt.

"So we do." Pterocles frowned. "You don't have to do this, you know, Your Majesty. No one will call you a coward if you don't."

"A coward?" Grus stared and then started to laugh. "I wasn't worried about that. No, my thinking went in the other direction—if the Banished One wants me to come down with this disease, he'll find a way to make me catch it. I don't expect I can escape it just by staying away from the first few people we find who've come down with it."

"Oh." Pterocles kept frowning, but the expression took on a slightly different shape. "Well, when you put it like that, you're probably right. I wish I could tell you that you were wrong, but you're probably right."

"Come on, then," the king told him. "We're only wasting time here."

The waterfront at Cumanus was a busy place, full of barges and boats that went up and down the river, and lately even more full of those that crossed the river and brought the Avornans on the far side whatever they chanced to need. It smelled of horses and wool and olive oil and spilled wine and puke and the cheap floral scents the barmaids and doxies splashed on themselves to draw customers and fight the other odors. Dogs scratched through rubbish. So did derelicts. Someone sang a syrupy love song and accompanied himself on the mandolin; the music floated out through the shutters of a second-story window.

Normally, the dockside was where you could also hear the most inspired cursing in the kingdom. Riverboat men, long-shoremen, the taverners and the wenches who served them, and the merchants who tried to diddle them were all folk of passion and vivid imagination. Back when Grus was a river-galley captain, he'd had to try to hold his own in such company, and it hadn't been easy.

Now, though, the wharves and the warehouses and whore-houses and inns and shops close by were, apart from that love song, quieter than they had any business being, quieter than the king had ever heard them. The few voices that did come to his ear were high and shrill and frightened. He was frightened, too, though he tried not to show it.

The messenger who'd brought them down from the city governor's castle pointed to a tavern. "They're in there," he said, "in a back room." He showed no interest in going into the place himself.

"Thanks." No, Grus wasn't falling over with eagerness to go inside, either. But this was what he'd come for. He dug into the pouch on his belt and handed the messenger a couple of pieces of silver. The man made them disappear—and then made him-self disappear.

Pterocles went into the tavern first, as though being a sor-cerer guaranteed him more protection than it did Grus. Grus knew that wasn't necessarily so, and Pterocles no doubt knew the same thing. The king followed close behind. The front room of the tavern, the room where people did their drinking, was empty. By all appearances, it had emptied in a hurry. Some stools were pushed back from tables. Others lay overturned on the rammed-earth floor. A lot of the cups of wine and ale on the tables were half full, several quite full. Some of them had been knocked over, too. Wine spilled across tabletops like blood, but smelled sweeter. A goose had been roasting over the fire in the hearth. It was one sadly burnt bird now.

Grus pointed. "There's the door to the back room." It stood open. By the signs, someone must have led or dragged the sick people in there and then departed along with or just behind everybody else. *That's bound to help spread whatever this is, too,* Grus through morosely.

Again, Pterocles went in ahead of him. Again, Grus didn't let the wizard lead by much. "Well, what have we got?" the king inquired.

He needed a moment to adjust to the gloom in the back room. A little light came in through the open door, a little more through a small window set high in one wall. Stout iron bars made sure no one could climb in through that window. The taverner stored jars of wine and barrels of ale and salty crackers and smoked fish and pickled cucumbers and olives in brine and all the rest of his stock back there. The three men who'd been taken sick lay in the narrow space between a row of earthenware jars and another of barrels.

Pterocles and Grus had just enough room to kneel beside them. Two were unconscious, barely breathing. The third, a soldier, twisted and muttered to himself in some dream of delirium. Pterocles set a hand on his forehead, then quickly jerked it back. "Fever?" Grus asked. There, he didn't want to imitate the wizard.

"High fever," Pterocles answered, and wiped his palm on his breeches. Grus wasn't sure he even knew he was doing it. He went on, "He's burning up. And the rest—well, you can see for yourself."

"Yes," Grus said, and said no more. Blisters branded all three sufferers' faces and hands, and no doubt the parts of them that clothing concealed as well. Some of those blisters were still closed; others had broken open and were weeping a thick, yellowish fluid. Grus had to nerve himself to ask, "Have you ever seen the like? Have you ever heard of the like?"

"No, Your Majesty, I'm afraid I haven't," Pterocles answered. "I'm not a physician, mind you. Maybe one of the healers here will be able to give this . . . illness a name."

"How much good will that do, even if someone can?" Grus asked.

"I don't know," Pterocles said. "Healers and wizards go after disease in different ways. We see if magic can do anything against it. They try to treat it without sorcery. Sometimes we do better, sometimes they do, and sometimes nobody has much luck."

That struck Grus as honest, if less encouraging than he would have liked. One of the sick men let out a soft sigh and stopped breathing. A moment later, a latrine stench filled the tavern's back room. His bowels had opened, as they usually did when men died.

Grus said, "The other thing is, no physician in his right mind is going to want to come anywhere near this place."

"I think you're wrong about that, Your Majesty," Pterocles said. "Healers deal with sickness all the time—more than wizards do, as a matter of fact. They won't let it faze them here."

"No, eh? It fazes *me*," Grus said. "Can you tell anything about what this is and what to do about it?"

"About what it is? It's bad. It kills people," Pterocles said. "I don't need to be a wizard to know that, do I? About what to do about it? Not yet. I'll have to do more tests, cast more spells. . . ."

"How long will it take?" Grus asked. "I don't think we've got very long."

There were times when Pterocles got so caught up in sorcerous theory that he lost sight of the real world, the world in which that theory had to operate. That would have irked Grus even more than it did if he hadn't been such a good wizard. Now, though, he understood exactly what his sovereign was telling him. Looking up at Grus, he said, "I don't, either."

*Left behind again,* Lanius thought, not that he'd ever been eager to travel very far from the city of Avornis. He saw the progress of the plague through a series of dispatches. He'd watched the campaign south of the Stura the same way, and the campaign against the Chernagors before that.

There was a difference this time, though. When couriers came with news of the war south of the Stura, Lanius hadn't worried that they'd brought the war with them. Whenever a letter came up now, he wondered if the man carrying it would get sick two days later. He also wondered if he himself—and the other people in the palace—would get sick two days later.

He did what he could to help. He was neither wizard nor physician, though he knew a little about both crafts. If he was anything besides a king, he was a scholar. He knew how to find out about things he didn't already know. Maybe plagues like this one had gone through Avornis in years gone by. If the archives held records of a similar illness, they might also hold records of what the healers and wizards of days gone by had done about it.

On the other hand, they might hold records that showed the healers and wizards of days gone by hadn't been able to do anything about the illness. But if that were true, wouldn't the pestilence have killed off everyone in the kingdom?

Trying to find out gave him a new excuse to poke around in the archives. As he usually did before going there, he put on an old tunic and a pair of breeches that had seen better days. He forgot every once in a while, and had to put up with sarcastic remarks from the washerwomen. He supposed he didn't *have* to put up with them. If something dreadful happened to the first servant who complained, the second one would think twice, or maybe more than twice. His father might have done something like that; by all accounts, King Mergus hadn't put up with nonsense from anybody. But Lanius conspicuously lacked a taste for other people's blood. He shrugged and went on to the archives in his shabby old clothes.

He opened the door to the archives, then closed it behind him. As soon as he breathed in, the odor of dust and old paper and parchment and wood shelves and—very faintly—mouse droppings made him smile. It told him this was *his* place, the place where he belonged. The dusty, watery sunbeams sifting down from the skylights said the same thing.

In an open space near the center of the big room, where the light was as good as it ever got, he had a table nobody else in the palace wanted, a stool, a bottle of ink, some pens, and paper for scribbling notes. He'd done a lot of writing when he was putting together that book on how to be a king for his son. The next interest Crex showed in it would be the first. The boy was still young. So Lanius told himself. *He* would have been interested in a book like that at Crex's age, but even he knew he'd made an unusual boy. Crex was much more nearly normal. Most of the time, Lanius thought that was a good thing. Every once in a while, he wondered.

Where to look for evidence of plague? Lanius guessed he would find it around the time when the Menteshe swarmed out of the south, took away that part of the Kingdom of Avornis, and carried off the Scepter of Mercy. A pestilence in Avornis would have helped those who served the Banished One. The exiled god would surely have been clever enough to realize as much, too.

Lanius nodded to himself. That was one question answered. The next one, at least as important, was, where in the archives would those documents be hiding? Would they be here at all, for that matter? Those had been chaotic times. Not everything got written down. What did get written down didn't always get stored.

He had to try. He knew where a lot of papers and parchments from those times were. He didn't recall seeing any records of an unusual pestilence in those documents, but he'd never gone looking for records like that, either. So many things had gone wrong for Avornis in those days, he might not have noticed a plague. In more peaceable, more stable times it would have seemed something noteworthy. Here? Here it would have been just one of those things.

Reports of battles lost. Reports of towns taken by the enemy, towns abandoned by the Avornans. Reports of peasants butchered, of herds run off, of crops burned. The report of the loss of the Scepter of Mercy—that was one long cry of anguish all by itself. The archaic language only made it sound more pathetic.

Plague? He didn't see any report of plague, or nothing out of the ordinary. Disease would break out every now and then. Sometimes it got into the records, sometimes it didn't.

For a moment, he thought he was on to something. Avornans

in the south reported a horrible new malady, one that . . . As he read more, he shook his head. This wasn't what he was after. He realized what they were seeing—they were seeing thralls for the first time. They didn't quite understand what the Menteshe wizards had done to peasants down there. Even if they had understood, how much difference would it have made? No one had been able to do anything about thralldom until Pterocles came along.

Lanius went on searching. Every once in a while, his instincts—and the archives—let him down badly. Grus, of course, didn't know what he was doing here. He wouldn't have to be too embarrassed if he didn't come up with anything. But the other king had come to know him and know the way he thought alarmingly well over the years. Grus understood that whenever something unusual came up, Lanius' first reaction was to go into the archives and see what other kings had done when something like it happened in distant days.

That was only sensible, at least to Lanius. Sometimes he found things interesting enough to make Grus agree with him, or at least keep quiet about disagreeing. Whenever he came up empty, he heard Grus laughing at him—or, at least, he imagined he did.

He discovered it was too dark to go on working when he couldn't read the documents he was sorting through anymore. He looked up toward the skylights and discovered no light to speak of was coming through them. As though a spell were wearing off, he realized he was hungry and thirsty and desperately needed to ease himself.

He almost tripped three or four times going to the door. *Yes, walking around in the dark will do that,* he told himself, feeling foolish. He made it out with a sigh of relief, and hurried to the nearest garderobe with another. Feeling better, he walked back to the royal quarters.

Sosia was already eating supper. The servants scrambled to get some for Lanius. "Why didn't you wait?" he asked. "Why didn't someone call me?"

She set down the lamb shank she'd been gnawing. "You are joking, aren't you?" she said. "You know it's worth anyone's life to try to pry you out of the archives. If you hadn't come out until *tomorrow* night, we would have started worrying."

Lanius laughed. Then he realized she'd meant it. He wanted to laugh again, this time at himself. Somehow, though, he knew his wife would not find it funny. In a small voice, he asked, "Am I really as bad as that?"

"Maybe not quite," Sosia answered. "Maybe we would have started worrying tomorrow afternoon."

This time, Lanius choked off the laugh before it passed his lips. He waited for the servants to bring him a lamb shank and buttered parsnips and bread of his own.

Sosia toyed with a piece of honey cake topped with chopped walnuts so she could stay at the table while he ate. She asked, "Did you find what you were looking for?"

"No," Lanius said around a mouthful of parsnips. "I found the documents from what I think is the right time, but I haven't come across any that talk about a pestilence. Maybe I haven't uncovered them yet, or maybe I need to be looking earlier or later."

"Maybe you should try the temple archives," Sosia said. "When people take sick, they ask priests to pray for them. They think they have a better chance with priests than with doctors or wizards, and a lot of the time they're right."

Lanius got up, hurried around the table, and kissed her. The honey swirled through the cake made her lips sticky and sweet. Right then, he would have kissed her if she'd been gnawing cloves of garlic. "The very thing!" he exclaimed. "I'll do it first thing in the morning. I wish old Ixoreus were still alive. He would know exactly where to look." But the ancient archivist had died several years earlier. His successor wasn't fit to stand in his shadow. Lanius would have to do his own searching. Maybe he would come up with something, though.

Sosia smiled at him. "Some wives get kissed for telling their husbands what big, strong, handsome fellows they are. *I* get kissed for telling you which dusty old papers to go burrowing through."

"Are you complaining?" Lanius asked.

"Oh, no," she answered quickly. She might have reflected that, if he wasn't kissing her for whatever reason, he was all too likely to be kissing a serving girl instead.

After Lanius finished his supper, they went back to the bed-chamber together. Maybe he was still in a good mood because of her suggestion. Maybe the extra cup or two of wine he'd drunk had something to do with things, too. Whatever the reason, their lovemaking had none of the wariness, none of the tension, it had often seen of late—when they'd been making love with each other at all.

She did him an uncommonly large favor at the end, though he never knew it. She didn't say anything like, *Why can't it be like this all the time?* She let him go to sleep with a smile on his face, and she went to sleep with one on hers, too.

Accompanied by royal guardsmen, the king walked over to the great cathedral the next morning. The guards weren't likely to do him much good with what really worried him—if the plague came to the city of Avornis, chainmail and spears and swords wouldn't hold it away. When Lanius went inside, he found Anser not far from the altar. He didn't think Anser had been praying. He thought Grus' bastard son had been playing a little catch with a green-robed priest. The young cleric hastily tucked away what Lanius was almost sure was a ball.

"Hello, Your Majesty," Anser said cheerfully. Whatever he'd been doing, it didn't embarrass him. "Always good to see you. Do you need me for something, or are you going to dive into the archives?"

*He knows me, too,* Lanius thought with a certain wry amusement. "It's the archives, I'm afraid, unless you're up on what was going on south of the Stura four hundred years ago."

"That's when we lost the Scepter of Mercy, isn't it?" Anser said.

Lanius nodded. He wouldn't have expected the arch-hallow to know even so much. "It is," he said, and hoped he didn't sound too surprised. "I'm trying to find out if there were any plagues around that time."

"Oh," Anser said, and nodded. Word of the outbreak among the thralls hadn't spread widely, but it had gotten to him.

The ecclesiastical archives resided in a series of descending subbasements under the great cathedral. Most of the time, the papers and parchments dwelt in darkness. When someone went down to search among them, he took a lamp with him and lit torches that waited for fire.

Torchlight was even less satisfactory to read by than the dusty sunlight that illuminated the royal archives. Lanius wondered how anyone ever found anything here, though he'd done it himself. To be fair, these archives were better organized than the ones in the palace, which, as far as the king could see, weren't organized at all. The king suspected that was the late Ixoreus' doing. The royal archives hadn't had such a conscientious keeper for centuries, if ever.

Here were records of prayers for the salvation of the kingdom, prayers for the safe return of the Scepter of Mercy, prayers for . . . Lanius bent closer and began to read more attentively. He started scribbling notes.

"Something, Your Majesty?" a guard asked. The soldiers had insisted on accompanying him down into the quiet dark, though he wasn't likely to be assailed by anything more ferocious than a termite here.

"Something, yes," Lanius answered abstractedly. He scribbled faster. If he bent too low over the manuscript, his shadow kept him from reading it. If he didn't, he had a hard time making sense of the faded, old-fashioned script.

In the end, he got what he wanted, or hoped he did. When he stood up and stretched, the guard said, "Up now?" He sounded eager, and explained why. "Feels . . . peculiar down here with all the dark pressing on you."

"Really?" Lanius shrugged. "It doesn't bother me. I didn't even notice, in fact."

"Lucky you," the guard said with a shudder.

"Maybe so," the king replied. "Yes, maybe so."

As the pestilence spread in Cumanus, Grus wondered more and more whether coming to the town by the Stura had been a good idea. He shook his head. That wasn't true—or rather, that wasn't half of what he wondered these days. He wondered exactly how big an idiot he'd been.

Fleeing back to the city of Avornis wouldn't help him, either. By now, the disease was established to the north of him. He wasn't sure it had gotten back to the capital, but he knew it was loose in some of the towns through which he would have to go. And so he stayed in Cumanus, and so he worried.

He stayed healthy. So did Pterocles. If the wizard escaped the disease, it was either good luck or a strong constitution, for he immersed himself in learning all he could about it. That meant studying people who came down with it, trying to cure them, touching them, poking them, prodding them—doing everything he could to catch it except petitioning the Banished One.

Pterocles worked closely with the handful of wizards and witches in Cumanus. A couple of them caught the disease. A witch promptly died. Her body went on an enormous pyre with those of others who'd perished of the pestilence. The yellow-robed high hallow asked Grus to thrust a torch into the pyre. Since the high-ranking priest was there to pray for those who had died, the king didn't see how he could refuse.

The wood of the pyre had been well soaked in oil. When Grus lit it, the blast of heat and flame made him retreat in a hurry. A great column of black smoke rose into the gray sky.

"May their souls find repose," the yellow-robed prelate said solemnly.

"May it be so," Grus agreed. Setting the pyre alight made him remember the time some years back when he'd brought a torch up to the pile of wood on which his father lay. Some men would have mentioned that to the priest for the sake of his sympathy. Grus kept it to himself. To his way of thinking, it was no one's business but his own.

"Thank you, Your Majesty," said a gray-haired woman in somber black—she had a husband or a child or perhaps a brother or sister burning on the pyre. "Thank you for showing you care."

That touched him. He asked, "Are you well?" He had to raise his voice to make himself heard through the roar and crackle of the flames.

"I think so," she answered, and then shrugged. "And if I'm not, they'll burn me, too, and I'll have company in the world to come." She bobbed her head to him and limped away.

Pterocles hadn't come to the ceremony. He was working with still-living victims of the plague, trying to come up with magic that would counter the torment from which they suffered. The next luck he found would be the first.

"I've tried all the usual spells," he told Grus that evening, his voice clotted with frustration. "I've tried all the variants I can come up with. None of them does any good that I can see. The physicians are trying everything they know, too. They aren't having much luck, either. If you catch this, you get better or else you die. That's about the size of it."

A lot of people *were* dying. Grus tried not to think of the stink of the pyre. He had as much luck as anyone usually does when trying not to think of something. He said, "Did you try any spells that made people worse instead of better?"

"Plenty of them," Pterocles answered. "You can be sure I only tried those once."

"Do they have anything in common?" Grus asked. "If they do, and if you take whatever that is out of them, is what's left worth anything?"

The wizard frowned. "That's an interesting way of looking at things. I don't know. I suppose I could find out." He paused. Enthusiasm built slowly in him. After what he'd been through, anything except exhaustion built slowly in him. "I suppose I *should* find out," he said after another little while. "Thank you, Your Majesty. That's something, anyway."

"I have no idea whether it is or not," Grus said. "I throw it out for whatever you think it's worth. I'm no sorcerer, and I don't pretend to be one—a good thing, too, or some poor fools would be in trouble for depending on my magic."

"You may not be a wizard, but you can think straight," Pterocles said. "And don't think you'll get away with telling me that isn't so."

"I wasn't sure thinking straight mattered for wizards," Grus said. "The way it looks to ordinary people, the crookeder you go at things, the better."

"Oh, no, Your Majesty. There are rules," Pterocles said firmly. Then he paused again, paused and sighed. "There are rules for ordinary sorcerers, anyway, for wizards and witches. Whether the Banished One has any rules . . . Well, people have been asking themselves that for a lot of years."

"You so relieve my mind," Grus said, and wished that were truth instead of irony.

# CHAPTER FOURTEEN

anius had a large map of the Kingdom of Avornis brought to his bedchamber. He pinned it to the wall despite Sosia's squawks. In most years, the map inhabited the treasury minister's office, and was used to show which cities and provinces had paid their taxes and which had revenues still outstanding.

This year's revenues had all come in. Lanius used the map for a different and grimmer purpose—to chart the plague's advance through Avornis. It spread along the routes he would have expected. It came up from the Stura toward the city of Avornis along the roads couriers and merchants most often used. When it took sidetracks, it traveled more slowly. Large stretches of the kingdom well away from the main routes stayed happily unaffected. They probably didn't even know a new pestilence was on the loose. Anyone who brought the word might bring the sickness, too.

The disease was going to get to the capital. Lanius could see that. He said nothing to Sosia about it. Odds were she could figure it out for herself. If she couldn't, he didn't want to worry her.

One day, she said, "Ortalis and Limosa have taken their children out to the countryside. Do you think we should do the same?"

She could see, then. And so could her brother—or, perhaps more likely, his wife. Lanius only shrugged. "I don't know. I don't think anyone can know right now. Maybe this will follow them. Maybe it will get there ahead of them. We have no way of knowing."

Sosia sent him a sour look. "You aren't much help."

"I'm sorry," he said, though he was more annoyed than sorry. "I have no good answers for you, or even for myself."

"You're talking about the heir to the throne," Sosia said. "If anything happens to Crex, it passes through Ortalis to Marinus."

That appealed to Lanius no more than it did to Sosia. He wanted to point out that they were trying to have another child, but realized she wouldn't heed that. They might not succeed. If they did, it might be a girl. If it was a boy, it might not live long. So many things could go wrong.

What he did say was, "If you send the children away and they get sick, you'll blame whoever told you to send them. The same if they stay. My own view is that it won't matter much one way or the other, so do whichever you please. I swear by Olor's raised right hand that I won't blame you no matter what happens." He raised his own hand, as though taking an oath.

"You're no help at all!" Sosia said angrily. "These are your children we're talking about, you know."

"I do know that. I'm not likely to forget it," Lanius said with a touch of anger of his own. "I also know I can't foretell the future. If you want to know which would be better, or whether either one will make any difference, you'd do better asking a wizard than me."

To his surprise, Sosia smiled and nodded and kissed him. "That's a *good* idea," she said. But then her face fell. "I wish Pterocles weren't down in the south. I wouldn't like to trust a spell like that to anyone else. It would be like putting Crex and Pitta in some stranger's hands."

She exaggerated, but not by too much. Lanius said, "Write to him, then. Tell him what you want. He'll find a way to work the magic and let you know what it tells him—if it tells him anything."

"I don't like to wait. . . ." Sosia said.

Lanius laughed. That made her angry in a new way. Quickly,

he said, "Now you're being silly. How can waiting matter when there's no disease here? Write your letter. Send it."

He mollified her again. He wished he could have calmed his own worries as easily. Yes, Sosia could write to Pterocles. And Pterocles would cast his spell and write back. And who was chiefly responsible for spreading the pestilence? Couriers coming up from the south. Maybe the one who carried the wizard's answer would also carry the plague. Could the sorcery take that into account?

"What is it now?" Sosia asked. She pointed a finger at him. "And don't tell me it's nothing, either. I know better. I saw something on your face."

He shrugged and tried to minimize it. "The disease is down in the south. I hope Pterocles and your father are well." That wasn't exactly what he'd worried about, but it came close enough to be plausible.

"Queen Quelea watch over both of them!" Sosia exclaimed. She didn't ask him any more questions, for which he was duly grateful.

These days, couriers came south to Cumanus only reluctantly. King Grus had trouble blaming them. He offered extra pay to the men who did ride into danger. Some remained reluctant. Grus forced no one to this duty, and punished no one who refused it. The couriers who would not undertake it could still serve Avornis in other ways, ways less dangerous to them.

One of the riders who did brave the journey brought Grus a letter from Lanius. The older king wondered what the younger had to say. Only one way to find out—he broke the seal on the letter. Sometimes chatty court gossip filled Lanius' letters. Sometimes it was the doings of the animal trainer the other king had hired. And sometimes Lanius would go on about things he'd fished out of the archives. *Those* letters could be interesting or anything but.

This was one of *those* letters. Grus saw as much at a glance. He went through it, thankful that Lanius wrote in a large, round hand. The other king was considerate enough to remember that he needed to read things from farther away than he had when he was younger.

By the time Grus got through the first half of the parchment, his face bore a thoughtful frown. He sent a servant to bring Pterocles to his room in the city governor's palace. When the wizard got there, his face wore a frown, too—an unhappy one. "You interrupted a spell, Your Majesty," he said irritably.

"I'm sorry," Grus said, "but I'm not *very* sorry, if you know what I mean. Here. Tell me what you make of this." He held out the letter he'd just gotten from Lanius.

Pterocles took it with poor grace. He was about Lanius' age himself—maybe even younger—and had no trouble reading it at the normal distance. He hadn't gone far before the frown disappeared from his face. A little later, one of his eyebrows rose. He raced through the rest of the letter. "I suppose, up in the heavens, Olor's beard collects all kinds of crumbs and scraps," he said.

Grus gave him a quizzical look. "I'm sure you're going somewhere with that, but I can't for the life of me imagine where."

"I am, Your Majesty," Pterocles assured him. "The god can't even comb out what gets stuck in there, because things that touch him turn holy themselves. And so nothing ever gets thrown away or discarded. If it's in his beard, it's in there for good."

"Queen Quelea has even more mercy than I thought," Grus said.

Pterocles ignored that sally. "Our archives are just like Olor's beard," he said. "If something gets in there, it's in there for good. And every once in a while we can fish something out, dust it off, and maybe—just maybe—use it again."

"This does sound like the same illness to you, then?" Grus said. "It did to me. Maybe the Banished One got lazy."

Pterocles stared, blinked, and started to laugh. "I can just imagine him going through his keep down there in the mountains. 'Mm,' he'd say. 'I had pretty good luck with this plague a few hundred years ago. They won't remember it, those miserable mayfly mortals. Why don't I haul it out again and see how they like it?'"

Grus laughed, too, in tones somewhere between admiration and horror. Pterocles had caught the Banished One's way of thinking almost blasphemously well. The exiled god often mocked men for their short lives when he came to them in dreams. He might well believe a disease not seen for centuries was forgotten. And so it would have been, but for Lanius.

"I didn't read the whole letter," the king said. "What did they do about the pestilence, all those years ago? What *could* they do about it? Anything? Or do we know what's biting us without being able to bite back?"

"He's passed on the spell the wizards were using then," Pterocles answered. "Whoever thought of it had nerve. It uses the law of similarity in a way I wouldn't try unless I was desperate." His laugh was grim. "Of course, if I watched people dying all around me, I expect I'd get desperate pretty fast."

"Can you use it? Can other wizards use it? Will it work again?" Grus asked.

"I can use it. So can others. It's not hard to cast—I can see that at a glance," Pterocles said. "It's not hard to cast like that, anyway. You don't have to be a senior sorcerer to be able to get the incantation right. But it's going to be wearing on the wizards who use it. And you don't want to make a mistake about which direction the spell runs in. You'd be very unhappy if you did, and so would your patients." He explained what he meant, and showed Grus the end of the letter to give him more detail.

The king read that part. He had no sorcerous talent to speak of, and no sorcerous knowledge, either, except the bits and pieces he'd picked up from talking with Pterocles and other wizards and witches over the years. He wasn't sure he would understand, but he had no trouble at all. The problem was nothing if not obvious.

"Well," he said, "you don't want to do *that,* do you?"

"Now that you mention it," Pterocles said, "no."

If the plague came to the city of Avornis, Lanius realized he was one of the people likeliest to catch it. Couriers seemed intimately involved in spreading it, and couriers from infected parts of the kingdom kept bringing word of its progress up to the capital. And to whom were they bringing that word? Why, to him. He was the king, the man who most needed to know what was going on elsewhere in Avornis.

That meant other people in the palace were also among the likeliest to come down sick. And it meant—or might mean— he'd been wrong about what he told Sosia. Maybe getting Crex and Pitta away from the city for a while was a good idea after all. He waited for Pterocles' letter. When it came back from the south, it said, *Getting them away from the capital will not hurt, and may do some good.* Lanius wished the wizard would have said something stronger than that, but it was plenty to persuade him—and Sosia, too.

He wondered if he'd made a mistake waiting for Pterocles' response. If the children had gotten out of the city sooner . . . Three days after Crex and Pitta left the palace, Sosia came up to him with a worried look on her face. "Mother's not feeling well," she said.

"What's wrong?" Lanius hoped dread didn't clog his throat too much. People had any number of ways of falling sick. Queen Estrilda wasn't a young woman. If she didn't feel well, that didn't necessarily mean anything. So he told himself, grasping at straws like a harness maker or a farmer. In some ways, all men *were* very much alike.

"She has a fever," Sosia answered. "She says the light hurts her eyes, and she has some . . . some bumps on her face."

"Bumps," Lanius echoed tonelessly. His wife nodded. He knew—and Sosia obviously did, too—the pestilence showed itself with fever and with blisters. Not quite apropos of nothing, he said, "I wish Pterocles weren't down in the south."

"I said that before," Sosia replied—a handful of words with a world of worry in them.

Lanius had been so proud of himself when he sent Grus his letter along with Sosia's. He'd uncovered what might be a cure for the plague, and wasn't that wonderful? Wasn't *he* wonderful for being so clever?

Now he would have to test that cure, if it was a cure, on someone who mattered to him very much—and who mattered even more to his wife, and to the other king, and possibly even to his brother-in-law. He sighed and said, "I'd better send for Aedon." Aedon was the leading wizard in the city of Avornis after Pterocles—a long way after Pterocles, unfortunately.

A servant went hotfooting it out of the palace to bring him

back. He came within the hour. He was closer to Grus' age than to Lanius'—a stately man with a neat gray beard and with the pink skin and mild smile of a kindly grandfather. "How may I serve you, Your Majesty?" he asked.

"The plague is in the city," Lanius said bluntly. "You will have heard of it?"

"Yes," Aedon admitted. "But how do you know this to be the case?"

"Queen Estrilda has it," the king replied, more bluntly still.

Aedon licked his lips. "What . . . do you wish me to do?" He couldn't have sounded more wary if he were an actor on a stage. If he tried to save King Grus' wife and failed, his head might answer for it. He said, "You do understand, I trust, that I have no experience in facing this disease."

"I do understand that," Lanius said. While waiting for Aedon, he'd gone to the archives and gotten the document on which he'd based his letter to Grus. "This seems to be the same plague as the one the Banished One used against us about the time the Scepter of Mercy was lost. Here is what the sorcerers of that time did against it."

Like Grus, Aedon held things out at arm's length to read them. No one had found a magical cure for lengthening sight. By the time the wizard finished reading, his skin was less pink than it had been. He licked his lips again. "You wish me to attempt this untested sorcery on Her Majesty?"

"It's not untested. It just hasn't been used for a while," Lanius said, proving technical truth could live in the same sentence with enormous understatement.

"If I understand the spell correctly, we will need one other, ah, participant besides the queen and me," Aedon said.

Lanius nodded. "I read it the same way." He pointed to himself. "I will be the other one."

Now the wizard went from wary to horrified. "Oh, no, Your Majesty! Use a servant or someone else who will not be missed if something goes awry."

"No," Lanius said. "This is my responsibility. I found it. I was the one who thought it would work—and I still think so. I have . . . the courage of my convictions, you might say." He'd been on a battlefield once, and never wielded a sword in anger.

*This may be the first really brave thing I've ever tried to do in my life,* he thought. *I'm old to start, but I hope I can do it right.*

He waited, trying to look as kingly as he could. Grus would have had no trouble getting the wizard to obey *him*—Lanius was resentfully sure of that. Aedon went right on grimacing, but at last he nodded. "Let it be as you say, Your Majesty. But please do me the courtesy of showing in writing that you have given me this order. I do not wish to be blamed if something goes wrong."

"I suppose that's fair," Lanius said, remembering the sorcerer would be trying a spell he'd never used before. Remembering that sent a chill through him. *Am I brave or just foolhardy?* Before long, he'd find out. He called to a servant for parchment and pen and ink, and also for sealing wax. He wrote rapidly, then used the royal signet ring. "Here," he told Aedon. "Does this satisfy you?"

After reading the pledge to hold him harmless, Aedon nodded. "It does. I thank you, Your Majesty." He tucked the document into his belt pouch, no doubt ready to pull it out if things failed to go the way he wanted. "And now, if you would be so kind, take me to Her Majesty."

Actually, a serving woman led both Lanius and Aedon to Queen Estrilda. Lanius fought back a wince when he saw his mother-in-law. Estrilda had gotten worse since Sosia told him she was sick. Grus' wife seemed only half aware of who he was, and either didn't care or didn't understand who the wizard was. The blisters described in both Grus' dispatches and the ancient ecclesiastical document were plain on her face and hands.

When Aedon gently touched her forehead, he flinched. "She is very warm, Your Majesty," he said. "Very warm indeed." *If she dies, you can't blame me.* He didn't shout that, but he might as well have.

"Then you'd better not waste any time, had you?" Lanius said.

That wasn't what the wizard had wanted to hear. He said, "I also note that this spell involves a most unusual and uncertain application of the law of similarity."

"All right. You've noted it. Now get on with it." When Lanius wanted to get something done, he started sounding brisk and brusque like Grus. One of these days before too long, he would have to think about what that meant. At the moment, he had more urgent things to worry about.

Even with the pledge, Aedon seemed on the point of balking. After a longing look back toward the door, though, he seemed to realize he would take his reputation with him if he walked out through it.

He took a deep breath, gathered himself, and managed a dignified bow for Lanius. "Very well, Your Majesty, and may King Olor and Queen Quelea and the rest of the gods in the heavens watch over my attempt," he said.

"Since the pestilence comes from the Banished One, I hope they will," the king replied. Aedon looked startled, as if that hadn't occurred to him. Maybe it hadn't. A lot of things had happened to the wizard all at once.

He carried a stool over by the side of the bed and set the text of the spell on it. Lanius, who was a little shortsighted, wouldn't have wanted to try to read it from there, but Aedon seemed to have no trouble. For once, his lengthening sight worked for him, not against. "Please give me your hand, Your Majesty," he said, and took Lanius' right hand in his own left.

Then he took Queen Estrilda's left hand in his right. Since the wizard had neither hand free for passes, the spell necessarily depended on the verbal element. Lanius hoped Aedon would be able to handle that. Avornan had changed some in the centuries since it was written down. Words that had rhymed then didn't anymore, while some that hadn't did now. If Aedon performed in a play and made a mistake on the stage, that would be embarrassing. It would be much worse than embarrassing if he made a mistake now—for him, for Lanius, and for Estrilda.

As soon as he started to read, Lanius let out a silent sigh of relief. He didn't know Aedon well, or know where the wizard had learned to cope with the old-fashioned language. But learn he had. It fell trippingly from his tongue, and Lanius felt the power build with each word that passed his lips.

The king was no sorcerer, but he had tried to learn something about conjuration, as he'd tried to learn something about everything. He knew what Aedon meant when he called this magic a strange use of the law of similarity. It treated the sick person and the well one as similar in everything save the sickness, and sought to transfer the well person's health to the victim. If the wizard got a couple of things backwards, it would work the other way, and send the plague to the well person—and probably to the wizard, too. Other things could also go amiss. Lanius had more than enough imagination to see several.

On Aedon went. He fought his way through a particularly intricate part of the spell. As soon as he did, his confidence seemed to rise. After that, he read more quickly. He almost stumbled once, but caught himself at a warning squeeze from Lanius. With a grateful glance toward the king, he saved the fluff and hurried toward the end.

Lanius watched his mother-in-law. He didn't know what to expect, even if the magic worked. Would she suddenly be better? Or would it be as though a fever broke, so that, while still ill, she was no longer in danger? He hoped for the one while expecting the other.

What Aedon and he got was something more or less in the middle. He could see the blisters shrink back into themselves on Estrilda's face. They had almost disappeared when the wizard finished the spell. Estrilda let out a long, long sigh as Aedon let go of her hand and Lanius'. "Better," she whispered. "Much better. I thought I was on fire, and now I'm not."

She wasn't her former self yet, either. She was plainly still weak from the pestilence. How long would that last? Lanius had no way of knowing. All he did know was that she was on the right track again. That counted for more than anything else. He nodded—he almost bowed—to Aedon. "Thank you. That was well done. Your fee will match your skill and your courage."

Aedon did bow to him, deeply, from the waist. "Speak to me not of my courage, Your Majesty, which is as nothing when measured against your own. And as for skill . . . You caught me when I was about to go badly astray. Everyone says you are a learned man, but I did not look for you to correct me in my own field, and to be right." He bowed once more.

What exactly did he mean by that? Had he looked for Lanius

to try jogging his elbow, and to be wrong when he did? That was how it sounded. Lanius thought about anger, but set it aside. What point to it? Any expert would feel the same about amateurs.

Then Lanius stopped worrying about such small, such trivial, things. The spell he'd found—the spell Avornan wizards had found all those centuries before—worked. If it worked in the city of Avornis, it would work down by the Stura, too. And it would work on the far side of the river. The folk who had been thralls would suffer no more—no more than they already had, anyhow. And the war against the Menteshe and the Banished One would go on.

Smoke from a funeral pyre darkened the sky above Cumanus. The stench of burning wood and oil and dead flesh never left the city; it stayed in Grus' nostrils day and night. And yet things were getting better, here and in the land south of the Stura where the Banished One first unleashed the pestilence.

Grus didn't see Pterocles very much lately. The wizard was busy from before dawn until after nightfall every day. He ran himself ragged curing plague victims himself and teaching others how to do it. Grus had no idea when he slept, or if he did. The king knew the wizard ate erratically. Grus had servants send him food wherever he was. If not for that, Pterocles might not have eaten at all.

When Pterocles fell asleep in the middle of explaining to half a dozen wizards from towns along the Stura how the spell worked, Grus had him carried back to the city governor's palace and put to bed with guards in front of his door not to keep other people out but to keep him in until he'd had at least one good rest. The wizard complained, loudly and angrily. Then he slept from one midafternoon to the next.

He woke insisting he hadn't closed his eyes at all, and at first refused to believe he'd slept the sun around. Then, when he woke a little more and his wits began to work, he realized he wouldn't be so hungry or have such a desperate need to piss if he hadn't lost a day. He ate enough for two, almost filled a chamber pot, and declared himself ready to charge back into the routine that had caused his collapse.

"No," Grus told him. "Wait. Spend a little time relaxing, if you please."

"But I can't!" Pterocles said. "People are dying. If I don't cure, if I don't train other wizards—"

"Wait," Grus repeated. "If you kill yourself, you can't help anybody. And you were right on the edge of doing that. Go ahead and tell me I'm wrong. Make me believe it." He folded his arms across his chest and stared a challenge at Pterocles.

The younger man took a deep breath. Then he laughed, let it out again, and spread his hands. "I wish I could, Your Majesty, but I fear I can't."

"All right, then," Grus said. "You've done more than any three men could be expected to. And you've got more than three men doing your work now, because of everybody you've taught. We're getting the upper hand on this cursed thing."

"We should be doing more." But that was Pterocles' last protest, and a fading one at that. The wizard shook his head and ran his fingers through his hair, which hadn't been combed, let alone washed, in some time. "We owe this one to King Lanius."

"Well, so we do," Grus said. "Fine—we owe it to him. I like to think he owes us one or two, too."

"It's a good spell. It's a very good spell," Pterocles said. "And it's a novel approach to the problem. I never would have thought of it myself."

"Really?" Grus hoped he kept his tone neutral. He did his best. But he didn't like to think there were many sorcerous matters that wouldn't have occurred to his best wizard.

Pterocles understood what he meant, even if he didn't say it. With a wry smile, the sorcerer answered, "Afraid so, Your Majesty. Magic is a big field. Nobody can know all the blades of grass—and the flowers, and the weeds—in it." That smile vanished like snow in springtime. "Nobody who's a mere man, I should say. About anyone else, I reserve judgment."

"No doubt you're smart to do it, too." Grus started to look south toward the Argolid Mountains—toward the Banished One's lair. He started to, but then deliberately checked the motion. "Now if only he would reserve judgment on us."

"I'm afraid that's too much to hope for," Pterocles said.

"So am I," Grus answered. "And if you'd left off everything

but the first two words, that would have been just as true, wouldn't it?"

"Oh, yes," the wizard said, and then, as though that didn't put his meaning across strongly enough, he repeated it with a different emphasis. "*Oh,* yes. Anyone who isn't afraid of the Banished One doesn't know anything about him."

"Right." Grus let it lie there. Had he been the Banished One—a truly terrifying thought—he would have done things differently. The freed thralls could only be an annoyance to him, never a real danger. Danger lay in the Avornan army and in the farmers north of the Stura who kept it fed. Grus would have struck there. But freeing the thralls might have pricked the Banished One's vanity. And so he had struck at and avenged himself upon that which annoyed him, and concerned himself much less with everything else. The folk who really threatened his longtime dominion over the lands south of the Stura did not suffer in proportion to their menace.

Pterocles poured some wine into his cup from a silver pitcher. "So here's to King Lanius. He was our memory this time. Without him, the pestilence probably would have gone through the whole kingdom, and gods only know how many would have died."

Grus filled his winecup, too. "To Lanius," he agreed. Both men raised their cups and drank the toast. Grus had the feeling Pterocles might have put his finger on the Banished One's plan. The exiled god, with his contempt for mankind, wouldn't have expected the Avornans to be able to stop the disease. That showed his arrogance, but perhaps less in the way of bad planning than Grus had thought.

Drinking to Lanius as a real salute, not to the other king's place as a member of the longtime ruling dynasty, bothered Grus less than it would have a few years earlier. The two kings had come up with a working arrangement that probably didn't altogether satisfy either one—Grus knew it didn't altogether satisfy him—but that both men could live with. Lanius wasn't afraid anymore that Grus would murder him if he got out of line. And Grus didn't worry that he would find himself outlawed and the gates of the capital closed against him when he came back from a campaign. He still wished he could campaign and stay in the city of Avornis at the same time. Maybe the gods could be in two places at once, but mere men couldn't.

And since he couldn't, having Lanius there in his place worked . . . pretty well.

Lanius rode out from the city of Avornis with Collurio and with a troop of royal bodyguards. The soldiers fanned out to give the king and the animal trainer room to talk without being overheard. By now, they'd seen Collurio in the palace often enough and for long enough to be used to him and to be fairly confident he harbored no evil designs against Lanius.

Collurio laughed in some embarrassment. "It's a funny thing, Your Majesty," he said. "I train beasts for a living, but I fear I'm not much of a horseman. I never have been."

"Well, I'm not, either, so don't let it worry you," Lanius said.

"But it's different. You're the king. You have other things to worry about," Collurio said. "I spend all my time with animals. I should be able to ride better than a farmer bringing a couple of baskets of turnips to town."

"Why can't you, then?" Lanius asked. As usual, his attitude was down-to-earth. Before you could solve a problem, you had to figure out what it was.

And Collurio had the answer for him. "Because I don't get on horseback more than a couple of times a year. Why should I, when I live in the capital? All my kin are there. All my work is there, or near enough. I don't need to leave the city very often, and it's not such a big place that I need to ride to get where I'm going. I just walk, the way most people do. If you ride a lot inside the city, you're doing it for swank, not because you need to. Ordinary folks haven't got the time or the silver to waste on swank."

"No, I suppose not." Lanius hoped he didn't sound too vague. The only ordinary people with whom he had any acquaintance were the palace guardsmen—who had to know how to ride—and the servants inside the palace. And what the servants did when they weren't actually working was a closed book to him.

"It is nice getting away every once in a while, isn't it?" Collurio said, looking around at the countryside with the fascination of a man who didn't see it very often. "Everything smells so fresh." Everyone who got outside the walls said that. Lanius had said it himself, more times than he could count. In a lower voice, Collurio went on, "And I'm not sorry to get out with that cursed disease loose in the city, either."

"No." Lanius let it go at that. The animal trainer didn't know, or need to know, the disease was nothing ordinary, but came from the Banished One. Sicknesses of the more usual sort were only too common in the city of Avornis. With so many people packed so close together, sickness spread all too easily.

Collurio didn't notice how Lanius had said as little as he could. "Looks like the wizards and the healers have figured out what to do about it, anyhow."

"It does, doesn't it? I hope they have." Again, Lanius didn't say much. He didn't want people exclaiming that he was the one who'd found the spell that let the wizards stop the pestilence in its tracks. For one thing, word of that might get back to the Banished One, which wouldn't—couldn't—be good. For another, he never had much cared to have people exclaiming about him for any reason. He did what he did, and he did it as well as he could, and what point to getting excited about it?

They rode up a low swell of ground—nothing grand enough to be called a hill. When they got to the top, Collurio pointed ahead. "What's that? It's one of the funniest-looking things I've ever seen."

"Glad you like it," Lanius said. Collurio looked at him as though pretty sure he was joking—pretty sure, yes, but not completely. The king added, "That's where we're going."

"Why are we going there?" the animal trainer asked. "How long has that place been here? Why didn't I ever hear about it?" He was full of questions, and comments, too. "I'd think I would have. I'd think anybody would have. It's peculiar enough, by the gods. It looks like somebody cut a slice out of a city and set it down right there."

"Somebody did." Lanius tapped his own chest with the first two fingers of his left hand. "I'm the somebody, as a matter of fact."

"All right, Your Majesty." Collurio might have been humoring a lunatic who didn't seem violent . . . at the moment. "I hope you'll tell me *why* you built a slice of city out in the middle of the country."

Lanius smiled. "Not quite yet, if you don't mind too much. I'd like you to look it over first."

"Whatever you please, Your Majesty," Collurio said. Again, Lanius had no trouble recognizing his tone—he sounded like a man who had taken another man's pay and realized he had to take the other man's eccentricities along with the silver. Since that was exactly how things were, Lanius didn't contradict him.

They rode up to the structure Tinamus and his workmen had built the summer before. A few workmen were still there, to make sure things didn't come to grief. Most of them, though, had gone back to the city of Avornis.

The two men got down off their horses. Accompanied by royal guardsmen, they went into the slice of the city—Lanius thought Collurio's description apt—through a door in one of the walls forming the sides of the slice. Collurio craned his neck, eyeing everything closely. Lanius had told him to look things over, and he was taking the king at his word.

After they'd walked along for a while, Collurio said, "It isn't a slice of the city of Avornis. I thought it would be. But I know the capital pretty well, even if I don't know much else. There's no place in it that would look like this." He spoke with complete confidence.

And Lanius nodded. "You're right—it isn't the city of Avornis. It's not even close to the city of Avornis."

"I figured that out." Collurio sounded proud of himself now—and he'd earned the right. Then he asked the question Lanius had been waiting for. "If it's not the capital, where is it? It's *somewhere*. It's bound to be. You wouldn't make up something this detailed."

"Oh, you never can tell." Before answering, really answering, Lanius waved the royal guardsmen back out of earshot. They went, their chainmail jingling. One of them tapped a finger against the side of his head, thinking Lanius wasn't watching him. The king said one word to the animal trainer.

Collurio's eyes widened. "That means—"

"It does, doesn't it?" Lanius said with a smile.

# CHAPTER FIFTEEN

King Grus looked back toward Cumanus from the south bank of the Stura. The town looked smaller and more distant than it should have. The river wasn't *that* wide. But there was the sense that it separated two different worlds. There was also the sense that Grus didn't belong in the one he'd just entered.

He said as much to Pterocles, who'd crossed the Stura with him. When he finished, he asked, "Am I making that up? Is it coming out of my head because I know too much about what's happened to Avornans down here? Or is it something real?"

"I can't say for sure, Your Majesty," the wizard replied. "All I can tell you for sure is that I feel it, too, for whatever that may be worth. Maybe it's my nerves. Maybe it's nerves for both of us. Or maybe . . . someone's hand still lies heavy on the land in spite of everything we've done."

"That could be," Grus said, and let it go right there. He noticed that Pterocles shied away from saying the Banished One's name here in the country the exiled god had dominated for so long. Hirundo was the one who didn't worry about such things. Hirundo didn't have as many reasons to worry about the Banished One as Grus and Pterocles—and Lanius—did. Having seen the Banished One in the night, the two kings and the wizard were members of a club whose dominant feature was that all the people who belonged to it wished they didn't.

A royal guardsman brought up Grus' gelding. Another, with

a perfectly straight face, led up Pterocles' mule—Grus wasn't forcing him up onto horseback now. The king mounted. So did Pterocles. A troop of guardsmen surrounded them. Grus said not a word about it. Menteshe raiding parties could easily break into lands from which the Avornans had driven them the year before. The nomads might not rule all this country anymore, but they could still cause trouble here. The king was glad to have solid protection around him.

Toward the close of day, the armed party rode into one of the first villages of thralls Grus had ever entered. It was different now from what it had been a year before. Most of the stink and most of the filth were gone. What was left was about what he would have found riding into a peasant village on the north bank of the Stura.

The people were different, too. They *were* people now, and acted like it. Instead of with bovine stares, they greeted Grus with shouts of, "Your Majesty! The gods bless Your Majesty!" They were, if not spotlessly clean, no dirtier than any other peasants would have been. They wore ordinary clothes, not filthy remnants of rags.

They were different in another way, too. A large number of houses in the village stood empty. The plague had hit hard here. From everything Grus had been able to learn, it had hit hard everywhere south of the Stura. That spoke more clearly than anything else Grus had found concerning how the Banished One felt about losing control of the thralls.

"Congratulations," the king told Pterocles. "If not for your spell, none of this would have happened."

Pterocles nodded soberly. "I'm glad I was able to take some of what I went through up in the Chernagor country and use it against . . . the one who put me through it." Again, he left the Banished One unnamed.

"Yes," Grus said. "That's something I understand, sure enough. Most of the time, from all I've seen, revenge costs more than it's worth. Every once in a while . . ."

"That's right, Your Majesty. Every once in a while . . ." The wizard's expression was, for him, uncommonly fierce. But that didn't last long. He looked farther south. The towering Argolid Mountains were still far away, but he—and Grus—could make out their shadowed purple bulk low on the horizon. All at once, something in Pterocles' face went from hunter to hunted. "Of course, we haven't won anything yet. For all we know, we're nothing but fleas waiting for the dog to notice he's got an itch and start scratching."

"There's a cheerful thought!" Grus exclaimed. "And such a jolly way of putting it, too." Pterocles inclined his head as regally as if he were the king. Grus looked toward the mountains, too—and toward Yozgat, which also lay in that direction. Still naming no names, he went on, "Well, if I'm a flea and he's a dog, I aim to bite him someplace where he'll notice me."

"Good, Your Majesty," Pterocles said. "Bite hard."

Lanius studied his slice of city. He drummed the fingers of his right hand against his thigh as he worried. "Last summer, when the architect asked me why I was having him build this, I told him I was making a fancy run for my moncat," he said.

Collurio scratched his nose. "What did he think of that, Your Majesty?"

"That I was out of my mind, I expect," the king answered. "Or that I was mocking him. Or maybe both at once."

The animal trainer laughed. "And there you were, just telling the truth. What better way to put a spike in somebody's wheel?"

"Yes, I remember thinking the same thing at the time," Lanius said. "But I'm more worried than I was that Pouncer's going to be able to get away."

"I don't see what else you could have done," Collurio said. "The insides of the side walls—that sounds funny, doesn't it?—and the front and back are too high for him to jump to the top, and the tile that lines them is glazed too smooth for his claws to get a grip. What can he do? He can't fly, even if it sometimes seems like he's able to."

"I'm not so worried about him flying," Lanius said. "I'm worried about him thinking, and I'm worried about him getting into trouble." His fingers drummed his thigh again. "He's awfully good at getting into trouble. Moncats are troublesome beasts, and he's a troublesome moncat."

"Uh, Your Majesty . . ." Collurio hesitated.

"Go ahead," Lanius said. "I'm not Pouncer. I don't bite."

"No, indeed, Your Majesty. You've been very kind to me," Collurio said hastily. "I just wanted to say—even if Pouncer should run off, there are other beasts back at the palace. I don't want you to take that wrong, now. I'm not saying it just so you'd go on giving me money. I'm grateful for your bounty— don't get me wrong—but I made a living before, and I can go right on doing it."

"I understand that," Lanius said. "If we have to, we'll do as you say and try another moncat. But I pray to the gods in the heavens we won't have to. Pouncer has . . . advantages."

"We've been working with him and not with the others. If we had to train a different moncat, it would cost us some time," Collurio said. "Other than that, I don't see anything all *that* special about him."

"He has a habit of stealing from the kitchens," Lanius said. "That could turn out to matter quite a bit."

"I can't imagine why," the trainer said with what would have been a distinct sniff if he weren't talking to a king.

Lanius didn't enlighten him. The king usually liked telling other people what he knew—would he have written a book called *How to Be a King* for Crex if he hadn't? But Tinamus didn't know why he'd built this slice of city, and Collurio had only guesses about why he'd be running Pouncer through it. As far as Lanius was concerned, the less they knew, the better. What they didn't know, they couldn't talk about. They couldn't write it down, either. And even if the Banished One took them in his terrible hands and *squeezed* them, they couldn't tell him what he would assuredly want to know.

That probably wouldn't do them any good if the Banished One *did* lay hold of them. No, it wouldn't do them any good, but it might do the Kingdom of Avornis a great deal.

Collurio asked, "Your Majesty, this has something to do with that, uh, frightening dream I had after I said I'd train your moncat, doesn't it?"

Lanius glared at him in annoyed admiration. *Here I keep trying to save you from more danger than you'd know what to do with, and how do you pay me back? You add two and two and get four. Why couldn't you come up with five, or even three?*

"I'm going to do you a favor," the king said. "I'm going to pretend I didn't hear a word you said."

He wondered whether Collurio would get angry. A lot of men would have. Lanius knew he would have himself; he always wanted to know what was going on. He always had; he was sure he always would. But Collurio only scratched his nose again with a tooth- and claw-scarred hand and nodded thoughtfully. "All right, Your Majesty. That tells me what I need to hear."

"Does it?" Lanius said tonelessly. The less informative he wanted to be, the more informative he seemed to be. *Maybe I should have started out telling lies right from the beginning. Too late now, though.*

"Don't worry. I told you when I got into this that I don't blab," Collurio said. "I meant it. And if there's a reason Pouncer is the best moncat because he steals from the kitchens—well, then there is, that's all." Now the animal trainer scratched his head, not his nose. "What difference it makes that an animal will steal food when it gets the chance is beyond me, though. Any other moncat in the kitchens would do the same thing."

"You may be right," Lanius said, which, as a polite response, ranked right up there with *how interesting.* You could say it in reply to almost anything, it sounded accommodating, and it didn't mean a thing.

No matter how shrewd Collurio was, he didn't notice the emptiness of the answer this time. "I'm sure of it, Your Majesty," he said. "When you're talking about things like that, they're all alike."

"I suppose so." Lanius looked up to the sky above the slice of city that had risen out of nothing. "I don't suppose there's any way the moncat could get out or anything could get in at him."

"I don't see how," the trainer said. "You'd need wings. Besides, Pouncer is fast and smart and tough. Anything that did try to catch him might be biting off more than it could chew."

"Wings . . ." Lanius looked up into the sky again. He saw nothing with wings except a yellow butterfly. Pouncer would have tried to catch that, not the other way around. It put a thought in the king's mind, though. He nodded to Collurio. "Thanks. I'll have to make sure we have some more archers around here."

"Your Majesty?" Collurio gave him the same *This is one of the strangest people I've ever tried to deal with* look Lanius had seen on Tinamus' face.

"Wings," Lanius said again. Collurio looked unenlightened. Lanius had expected nothing different. "Don't worry about it," he told the animal trainer. "You see that they let me wander around loose and everything. That's because they're pretty much convinced I'm harmless. I haven't had a really bad spell in—oh, days now."

"Days," Collurio echoed. He seemed in something of a daze himself. "Why would anything with wings want to go after Pouncer? He'd be a handful even for something the size of an eagle."

"Well, I don't know that anything would. But I don't know that anything wouldn't, either," Lanius said, which seemed to go a long way toward persuading Collurio that he had no business wandering around loose. The king went on, "The fewer chances I take, the happier everyone's likely to end up. Everyone on our side, I should say."

"Our side?" Collurio's gaze sharpened. "This *does* have to do with that dreadful dream the Ban—"

"Don't say the name," Lanius broke in. "I don't know that it makes any difference, but I don't know that it doesn't, either. So don't say it, not while you're here. Better safe than sorry, eh?"

"I would do—or not do—whatever I have to so I don't *ever* have another one of those dreams again," Collurio said earnestly.

"I understand that. I not only understand, I agree with you," Lanius said. "I don't know if this will help, but I know it can't hurt. In the meantime, shall we walk through here? I want to show you just what you'll be teaching Pouncer to do. . . ."

The Menteshe called the river where Grus had stopped his advance the autumn before the Zabat. Hundreds of years earlier, it must have had a proper Avornan name. King Grus had no idea what that was, though. Lanius might have been able to pull it out of the archives, but Grus had no intention of asking him to. If Grus talked about the Zabat, people knew what he meant. That was all that mattered, as far as he was concerned.

It was a much wider river than it had been the last time he looked at it. Hirundo saw him eyeing it and said, "You see, Your Majesty?"

"Well, what if I do?" Grus said gruffly. Hirundo only laughed at him. The king went on, "All right—we didn't have much trouble from Menteshe raiders coming up out of the south. We had a pestilence instead. Between you and me, I'm not sure we got the best of the bargain."

"Since you put it that way, neither am I," Hirundo said. "But it won't be long before we're ready to go see what's on the other side."

At the moment, three or four Menteshe horsemen were on the other side of the Zabat. They weren't doing anything but watching; they wanted to see what the Avornans were up to. Grus had his army do as much as it could out of sight of the nomads on the southern bank of the river. He hoped that would help.

And he knew what lay well on the other side of the Zabat— Yozgat. *This year,* he thought. *This year we get there.* He could feel the hunger in his belly. Was that the Scepter of Mercy calling—or was it the Banished One, trying to lure him to destruction? How could he know? All he could do was go on. The other choice was giving up and heading home, and that would be unbearable.

As though thinking along with him, Hirundo said, "One good thing—Korkut and Sanjar are still at war with each other. From what our men down here heard, they fought a big battle over the winter. Korkut's still holding Yozgat, though, and that's what counts as far as we're concerned."

"Yes." Grus let it go at that. If he didn't let it go, he would show how hungry he was. Hirundo already knew, of course, but Grus didn't want to be too open, not here in the south where the Banished One had so many eyes and ears.

A man came toward the king. Grus' guardsmen got between

him and this fellow who had to be a freed thrall. "I mean no harm," the man protested.

"Then you'll understand why we take no chances," a guard answered.

The man thought about that, shrugged, and finally nodded. "Smash 'em up!" he called to Grus. "Smash 'em all up, those horse-riding pigs!" He probably hadn't been free very long—otherwise he would have come up with something juicier to call the Menteshe.

Grus appreciated the sentiment even if it could have been expressed more forcefully. "That's what I intend to do," he said. "Tell your friends. Tell everybody you know." He wasn't keeping that a secret. The Menteshe had to know he was coming. When and how and exactly where—those were different questions.

"I'll do it," the man said. "By the . . . gods in the heavens, I'll do it." Grus caught the brief hesitation. He knew what it meant. The local had almost sworn by the Fallen Star, the name the Menteshe gave the Banished One. If a thrall had any reason to think of a supernatural power, he thought of the Banished One, not the gods. But things were changing here.

*And if we lose, they'll change back again, too,* Grus reminded himself. Things had gone well so far. That didn't mean they would keep on going well. One way to make sure they didn't was to assume they would.

"We need to talk," the king told his general. "We need to figure out where we're going once we cross the river, and where the Menteshe are likely to try to stop us."

"If we're not going to Yozgat, Your Majesty, somebody's been talking to you while I wasn't looking," Hirundo said. Grus sent him a severe look. Hirundo ignored it with the fortitude of a man who'd known worse—and he had.

"How are we going to get there?" the king said, as patiently as he could. "What will we run into on the way?"

"Menteshe?" Hirundo suggested. When Grus looked severe again, the general spread his hands in affable innocence. "You said so yourself."

"Well, so I did," Grus answered with a sigh. "But where? How many? And what are they likely to try against us?"

"We need to talk about that." Hirundo sounded altogether serious. Grus didn't pick up a rock and hit him over the head with it. That proved only one thing—years on the throne had given him much more tolerance than he'd ever imagined.

Lanius nodded to Collurio. "Put him through his paces."

"That's what I'm going to do, Your Majesty," the animal trainer replied. They stood on the outer wall of the city slice Lanius had built out in the country. It was twenty-five or thirty feet high; Lanius could see for a long way. Above the stand of trees to the south was a smudge on the sky that marked where the city of Avornis lay.

Collurio waved to his son, who'd come out to help him. The younger man was on the ground out beyond a dry ditch. The youth picked up a pole about as thick as his thumb. He swung it up and over the ditch until the end of it came to rest on top of the wall not far from Lanius and Collurio.

Then Collurio's son—his name was Crinitus—opened a door to a wooden cage by the base of the pole. Out came Pouncer. The moncat saw the pole and swarmed up it, holding on with all four clawed hands. No ordinary cat with ordinary feet could have done it. For the moncat, it was as easy and normal as walking along a palace corridor would have been for Lanius.

Once at the top, Pouncer looked expectantly at the king and the trainer. Collurio gave the moncat a piece of meat. Lanius said, "This isn't so good. Nobody will be around—nobody who would give Pouncer anything, anyway."

"We'll take care of it, Your Majesty," Collurio answered easily.

He did, too. The next time Pouncer did the trick, the trainer and Lanius stood well away from that stretch of the wall. They'd left a reward behind, though. The moncat ate it and then looked around as though considering what to do next.

Collurio smiled when he saw that. "He knows he'll get something he wants if he does what we want him to do. He *knows*. You were right, Your Majesty. These are very clever animals."

"Is he clever enough, though?" Lanius said.

"Clever enough for what?" Collurio asked.

"For what you need to teach him," the king answered.

Collurio let out an exasperated breath. "I wish you would tell me more, Your Majesty."

For his part, Lanius wished he'd never told the trainer which city this was a slice of. "Do you? Do you really?" the king said. "Do you want more visits in the night from . . . ?" He did not name the name.

"This truly does have to do with that?" Collurio asked once more.

"It truly does," Lanius agreed with a sigh. "Do you think . . . he would have visited you if it didn't? He is like the law in one way—he does not concern himself with trifles."

Shuddering, Collurio said, "In that case, I wish he wouldn't concern himself with me. I was happy to be a small man, bothering no one and bothered by no one."

"We all wish he wouldn't concern himself with us. We were all happier when he didn't," Lanius said gravely. "But wishes here have as much to do with what is as they usually do."

"Yes, Your Majesty." Collurio sounded no more delighted with the world. "I still sometimes wish I never stuck my big nose into this business." He gave the organ in question a mournful tweak.

He and Crinitus and the king worked with Pouncer until the moncat got tired or bored or full. Then they put Pouncer in the cage and took it back to the enclosure where the moncat stayed when it wasn't working. Pouncer climbed up the poles they had in there, found a perch to its liking, and fell asleep.

A few minutes later, a royal guardsman came up to Lanius and said, "Excuse me, Your Majesty, but Her Majesty the Queen has just arrived."

"*Has* she?" One of Lanius' eyebrows rose. He'd invited Sosia to come out and look this place over. He hadn't expected her to take him up on it, but here she was. He hadn't started fooling around with any maidservants; no frightened washerwoman hid under the bed not overburdened with clothing. Sosia could prod and poke as much as she pleased. She wouldn't find anything to complain about here.

She barely greeted Lanius. She prowled through all the tents around the slice of city, then pointed to it. "Let me have a look in there, if you please."

"All right," Lanius said. He had nothing female lurking inside.

He walked her through it. Her expression got odder and odder the farther she went. "This really is what you said it was, isn't it?" she said as the tour neared an end.

"Nothing else," Lanius answered.

"But—what good is it?" the queen asked. "You've built something enormous for Pouncer to run around in. Couldn't you have found something else to do with all that silver?"

"You sound like your father," Lanius said, and Sosia made a face at him. He went on, "Actually, your father knows what I'm doing here. He knows and he doesn't mind."

"If he knows, then he knows more than I do," Sosia said. "What *are* you doing here that's important enough to impress my father?"

"Staying out of his way and not causing trouble for anyone." Lanius did his best to sound annoyed as he said that. Grus would have been happy to keep him on a shelf doing nothing, or nothing worthwhile. Only the urgencies of what the other king had set himself to do had let Lanius gain a little—and just a little—freedom of action of his own.

The answer almost satisfied Sosia. When she said, "There has to be more to it than that," she didn't sound as though she believed it herself. "What a funny place this is," she added, as much to herself as to him.

"It's—not the city," Lanius said. "By the gods, I'm a city man, but even I like to get away once in a while. There isn't smoke in the air all the time here. I think that's part of the reason Anser likes to hunt. I'm—not all that fond of hunting, but I like it here myself."

His wife's nod was slow and hesitant, as though she found herself yielding a point she hadn't expected to. "I can see why," she said.

"I brought a good cook along, too," Lanius said. "And the food couldn't be any fresher. It doesn't have to travel into the capital. It's right here."

Supper proved that. The lamb they ate came from a farm

only a few hundred yards away. The meat was so tender, it almost fell off the bone. The wine was a local vintage, too. Lanius had to admit he'd drunk better. But the finest wines came from special regions scattered across the kingdom, and this didn't happen to be one of them. The stuff wasn't dreadful. It just wasn't of the best.

If you drank enough of it, you stopped noticing it wasn't of the best. Sosia looked around the inside of the pavilion. "You kept your promise," she said.

"I told you I would," Lanius answered.

She waved that aside, as though of no account. "You've told me all kinds of things," she said. "Some of them are true. Some of them—" She stopped and shook her head. "I didn't come here to quarrel with you—as long as I didn't find you in bed with a milkmaid, anyhow."

"No milkmaids," Lanius said solemnly.

"I don't see any, anyhow," his wife said, which was not quite a ringing endorsement. But she shook her head again, this time apparently at herself. "You deserve a reward for keeping your word."

"A reward?" Lanius blinked. "What sort of reward?"

She looked at him sidelong. "What would you like?"

The cot in which he slept was crowded for two, but proved not too crowded. The reward left them both sweaty. "If we could give something like this to all the people in Avornis who do something good, we'd see a lot more done," Lanius said.

Sosia poked him in the ribs. He jerked; she'd hit a ticklish spot. Trying to keep her voice severe, she said, "This isn't something the kingdom supplies. And besides, what would you give to women?"

"Men?" he suggested. She poked him again. But she didn't ask him anything more about why he'd brought Pouncer out here. As far as he was concerned, that was part of her reward for him, too.

"Over the river!" Grus said triumphantly.

"Did you have any doubts?" Hirundo asked him. "If you did, maybe we shouldn't have started this campaign at all."

"Well, it's nice to know we can still fool the Menteshe, anyhow," Grus said. He'd used a familiar ploy to cross the Zabat—feinting a crossing at one place to draw the nomads there, then crossing somewhere else and hitting them from behind. A jug of wine sat on the folding table in his pavilion. He poured his cup full and added, "Now we get to find out how they can fool us."

"They didn't have much luck last year." Hirundo never lacked for confidence.

Grus had drunk enough wine to make him melancholy. "They made us lay siege to Trabzun. They didn't let us get all the way to Yozgat, the way I hoped they would." Looking back on things, that had probably been wild-eyed optimism on his part before he set out from the city of Avornis, but still. . . .

"We'll get there," Hirundo said—confidently.

Menteshe horsemen shadowed the Avornan army when it started moving south the next day. Grus wondered whether they belonged to Korkut's faction or Sanjar's. He also wondered how much difference it made. If he penetrated deep enough into the Menteshe country, wouldn't the nomads abandon their feuds and band together to attack his men? *They didn't last year,* he thought, trying his best to be as hopeful as Hirundo.

The air was warm and moist—*sultry* was the word that came to Grus' mind. He nodded to himself. That seemed right, even if it wasn't a word he got to use very often. He hadn't gone far south of the Zabat before he saw trees that put him in mind of outsized feather dusters. Their trunks were long, bare columns, some straight, others gracefully curved. Leaves spread out fanlike only from the top.

Hirundo and Pterocles stared at the curious growths along with the king. "Aren't those the most peculiar things you ever set eyes on?" Pterocles said.

"Not when we're riding with you," Hirundo told him, and the wizard sent the general a wounded look.

"I know what they are," Grus said suddenly, and Pterocles and Hirundo both turned toward him. "They're palm trees!" he declared. "They have to be."

"They don't *have* to be anything," Pterocles said, which was bound to be true. He eyed the strange trees. "They don't have to be anything, no, but I'd say they're more likely to be palm trees than anything else."

"What good are they?" Hirundo asked.

Grus wished Lanius were riding with them. The other king would have known what palm trees were good for if anybody did. Maybe they were nothing but overgrown ornaments. But then Pterocles said, "You get dates from them, don't you?"

"Personally?" Hirundo said. "No."

"I think he's right," Grus said. "I've heard of date palms, though I don't know if that's what these are."

"When we start freeing thralls, they'll be able to tell us," Pterocles said. "They'll probably think we're a pack of fools for needing to ask, but they'll tell us. Do you feel like being laughed at by men three steps above idiot?"

Before Hirundo could say anything, Grus coughed warningly. Hirundo kept his mouth shut. Grus felt as though the gods had doled out a miracle, if only a small one.

And then a scout came back shouting frantically for his attention. "Your Majesty! Your Majesty!"

"I'm here," Grus called. "What do you need?"

"Your Majesty, there's an ambassador from the Banished One behind me."

"From . . . the Banished One, you say?" Grus got the words out through lips suddenly numb with alarm.

"That's right, Your Majesty." The scout nodded. He didn't sound particularly afraid. Why should he? Any envoy from the Banished One wasn't *his* worry—not unless the whole army went down to ruin, anyway. "Will you see him, or shall we send him off with his tail between his legs?"

"I'll see him," Grus answered after no more than a heartbeat's hesitation. Avornis was at war with the Banished One and those who worshiped him, yes. But that didn't mean the forms were forgotten. It didn't mean insulting the exiled god in any small way wasn't dangerous, either.

The Banished One's envoy rode up to Grus a few minutes later. He gave his name as Tutush son of Budak. "I speak for the Fallen Star, and he speaks through me," he declared, and sounded proud that that was so.

Grus could imagine no greater horror. He asked, "How do I know that you speak the truth?"

Tutush looked at him—looked through him, really. "You will have dreamt of my master," he said.

Beside Grus, Pterocles inhaled sharply. The king had better self-control, but only barely. He no longer doubted Tutush. "Say on," he told the Menteshe. The words were harsh in his mouth.

"Hear the Fallen Star, then. Hear him and obey." Tutush looked almost as arrogant as he sounded. He had a hawk's proud face, with a scimitar of a nose and a slash of a mouth almost hidden by mustache and graying black beard. "The Fallen Star orders you from his lands. Go now, go in peace, and he will suffer you to leave unharmed." The envoy spoke fluent, slightly old-fashioned Avornan. "Should you flout his will, though, you shall have only yourself to blame for your destruction."

"I'll take the chance," Grus replied. "The way it looks to me, the Banished One wants to scare me into leaving when he and his puppets haven't been strong enough to make me leave. He knows where I'm going, and he knows why. I'm bound for Yozgat, and for the Scepter of Mercy. If Prince Korkut gives it to me, I *will* go home—or if Prince Sanjar does, for that matter." Maybe he could make the Banished One suspect Ulash's warring sons.

Or maybe not. Tutush threw back his head and laughed uproariously, as if Grus had just made some rich joke. "Fool! Do you think holding the Scepter of Mercy will make you happy? Even if you should touch it—which you never will—you would remain nothing but a puny mortal man, soon doomed to die and be forgotten."

Grus only shrugged. "I'll take the chance," he said again. "I'm not doing this for me—I'm doing it for Avornis, and for those who come after me."

Tutush laughed again, even more woundingly this time. "He who comes after you will never wield it—never, do you hear me? So says the Fallen Star, and he speaks the truth. So he says; so he swears. He would swear by the accursed so-called gods in the heavens that he speaks truth here."

"He can swear whatever he pleases, and take whatever oaths he pleases. That does not mean I would believe him, not when he is the fount from which all lies spring." Grus tried to hide how startled he was. Had the Banished One *ever* sworn an oath like that? The king doubted it.

"This being so, you see that it makes no sense for you to do anything but give up your vain and foolish adventure," Tutush said, as though the king had not spoken. "If you go on, you will only bring ruin to your kingdom, your army, and yourself. Go back, then, and enjoy what the Fallen Star permits you to retain as your own."

The exiled god's implacable arrogance came through in every one of his envoy's words. It chilled Grus, but also angered him. "I'll take my chances," he said one more time. "And whoever comes after me will have to take his chances with the Scepter of Mercy. I don't intend to worry about that. I want him to have the chance to take his chances."

"Do you presume to reject my master's mercy?" Tutush sounded as though he couldn't believe his ears.

"I don't think your master knows the meaning of the word," Grus replied. "He can't use the Scepter, after all. The only thing he can do is keep it away from people who can use it—and that does include the Kings of Avornis."

"You will live to regret this," Tutush said angrily. "But you may not live long."

"So tell me," Grus said, "who is the Banished One's favorite in the civil war?"

Tutush knew. Grus could see as much. And the ambassador started to answer. He started to, but he didn't finish. Grus had hoped to catch him by surprise and learn something important, something he could have used against both Menteshe princes. But all Tutush said was, "You'll find out—if you live so long. Good day." He rode off. Grus thought the day was better because he was gone.

# CHAPTER SIXTEEN

L anius was not sorry to come back to the city of Avornis, even though he'd enjoyed himself out in the country. Collurio and Pouncer stayed a while longer, working on what the moncat had to learn. The trainer seemed perfectly happy to remain. He'd gotten friendly with a washerwoman and his son had gotten friendly with her daughter, a neat arrangement that satisfied everyone except, perhaps, Collurio's wife.

As for the king, he was glad to return to the archives and the other moncats—even if they were neither as clever nor as exasperating as Pouncer. Returning to Sosia and his own children was pleasant, too, though he took longer to realize it. He did have the sense not to tell anyone, especially his own wife, that he took longer to realize it.

He also returned to a good deal of the petty business that surrounded a king, which for him was much less pleasant. He wished Grus were around to take care of it, but Grus, beginning a new campaign in the Menteshe country, had more urgent things to worry about. Appeals from lawsuits and from criminal cases did not appeal to Lanius. He had to take care of them, though; that was one of the things a king was for.

A report came in from a seaside province of a series of robberies and rapes and one murder committed by a man missing his left ear. Lanius remembered the luckless fellow the year before who'd claimed a one-eared man had done the killing for which he was blamed. Lanius hadn't taken that appeal any more seriously than the others who'd reviewed it, and the man was dead now.

"I'm afraid I made a mistake," the king said to Sosia at supper that evening.

"You?" His wife raised an eyebrow. "I don't remember the last time you said that—and sounded like you meant it." He winced. He'd called several of his affairs with serving girls mistakes. Somehow, that hadn't convinced Sosia. She went on, "What happened this time?"

He explained, finishing, "A man is dead on account of me." He felt as though he were Ortalis at the hunt—except Ortalis enjoyed killing.

"It sounds like you did make a mistake," Sosia agreed, which made him feel no better. But then she said, "I don't see how you can blame yourself for it. I wouldn't have believed a story about a one-eared man, either. And you're sorry now, aren't you?"

"I certainly am!" Lanius said. "I don't want someone dying who shouldn't have. That's not what a king's supposed to do."

"Too late to worry about it now," Sosia said. "It can happen once in a while, that's all. As long as you're not laughing about it, I think you're all right. You do try hard to make sure you don't make mistakes very often—gods know that's so. And I think you do pretty well at it. So remember you were wrong, yes, but don't have nightmares about it."

Lanius' nightmares were of a different sort, and from a different source. But he nodded his thanks at Sosia's brisk, practical advice. "You sound a lot like your father—do you know that?" he said.

"Do I?" Sosia thought about it. Then she nodded, too. "Well, maybe I do, some. Is that such a surprise? He raised me—when he wasn't out on one of the Nine Rivers, anyhow." Her mouth twisted. Lanius thought he knew why, and didn't ask to find out if he was right. One of the things Grus had done while he was out on one of the Nine Rivers was father her bastard half brother, the current Arch-Hallow of Avornis.

What Lanius did say was, "I meant it as a compliment. Your father is a shrewd man. Nobody would say anything else." Not even he could say anything else, and he was the man whose crown Grus had . . . not stolen, since he still wore it, but brushed aside.

"Do you think he can bring the Scepter of Mercy back from the south?" Sosia asked.

That surprised Lanius; she seldom asked about affairs of state. "I hope he can," the king said after a brief pause. "He has a better chance than any other King of Avornis since we lost the Scepter all those years ago. I'm doing everything I can to help him."

"You haven't been in the archives so much lately," Sosia said. "You've been fooling around with your moncats instead. You can't tell me *they've* got anything to do with getting the Scepter of Mercy back." By her tone, she was as sure of that as she was that he couldn't give her any sort of good explanation for his fooling around with maidservants.

If he tried to tell her anything different, he'd just end up with an argument on his hands. He didn't want any arguments. Getting away from the palace had meant getting away from them. Even when Sosia came to check on him, they hadn't quarreled. He hadn't given her anything to quarrel about. He just shrugged and said, "I enjoy seeing what Pouncer can learn."

"Well . . ." Sosia paused. Lanius waited for her to say something rude about how useless or how foolish that was, but she didn't. When she resumed, what came out was a grudging, "It's better than some hobbies you could have, I suppose."

*Better than seducing serving girls,* she doubtless meant. And she had a point. Training Pouncer was certainly more challenging than pursuing maidservants, many of whom hardly required seducing. Going after the serving girls, though, was more fun. Lanius kept that opinion to himself.

Even keeping it to himself didn't help. Sosia wagged a finger at him and said, "I know what you're thinking, you wicked wretch." She tried to sound angry and severe, and—almost—succeeded.

"You can't prove a thing." Lanius tried to sound naïve and innocent. He—almost—succeeded, too. They both started laughing. It was the first time they'd ever done that when they were talking about his going after other women. He hoped it meant Sosia wasn't angry at him anymore. That was probably too much to expect, though. Maybe she wasn't *very* angry. . . .

Grus never got tired of watching wizards free thralls. The beauty of the spell drew him. The rainbows that swirled around the heads of men and women lost to themselves, lost in darkness, would have been enough by themselves to attract his eye. But the look on the thralls' faces when the darkness fell away like a discarded cloak and they were thralls no more—that, to him, eclipsed even the rainbows.

The Avornan wizards he'd taken south of the Stura never seemed to tire of casting the liberation spell, either. Even the bumblers and the bunglers among them came away smiling when they succeeded—and constant practice meant even they got the spell down pat and succeeded almost all the time.

"They're so grateful, Your Majesty," one of the wizards said after a woman who would have been pretty were she cleaned and combed kissed him as soon as she came fully into herself.

"I've seen that, yes," Grus said. By the smoky looks the woman sent the sorcerer, she would have been glad to go on from kisses. Grus didn't think taking advantage of women who didn't yet fully know their own minds was sporting. He suspected not all the Avornan wizards and soldiers were so scrupulous. They were men (and most of them were much younger than he was), they were a long way from home, and they had . . . admirers. He hoped not too much trouble would spring from that.

"I know me!" the newly freed thrall exclaimed. She pointed to her well-rounded chest. "I know *me*!" She kissed the wizard again. "Thank, thank, thank!" Like most of her kind, she didn't have a lot of words, but she made the most of the ones she did have—and she would soon start picking up wagonloads of new ones.

"You're welcome, sweetheart," the wizard murmured. The glance he sent Grus said he wished the king were busy doing something, anything, else. Maybe he didn't care how grimy the girl was.

Grus hadn't issued any orders about fraternizing with freed

thralls. He saw no point to giving orders he couldn't enforce. That being so, he took himself elsewhere.

The village was the same sort of tumbledown ruin as all the other thralls' villages he'd seen on this side of the Stura. Some of the houses looked as though they hadn't been repaired since the days before the Menteshe took this land away from Avornis. Some of them looked as though their roofs hadn't been thatched since those days. That had to be an exaggeration . . . Grus supposed.

Scrawny chickens scuttled through the narrow, filth-clogged streets. An even scrawnier dog yapped around a corner from Grus. Ordinary Avornan peasants would have hanged themselves for shame over the way livestock here was treated—not because ordinary peasants particularly loved their animals (they didn't) but because treating the beasts so badly meant they yielded less than they would have with a little more effort turned their way.

As Grus got upwind of the village, he shook his head. That wasn't right. It wouldn't have taken more effort to do right by the animals—indeed, to do right by the whole village. It would have taken a little more *attention.* By the nature of what the dark sorcery did to thralls, though, attention was the last thing they could give.

Royal guardsmen bowed to Grus as he came up. Pterocles and Otus were talking outside the wizard's tent, which had gone up next to the bigger and grander royal pavilion. Pterocles waved to Grus. The king waved back and ambled over. The breeze chose that moment to shift, blowing the stink from the village over the encampment. Grus made a face. "How does anybody stand living with a stench like that?" he asked.

"Your Majesty, I didn't even notice it when I was a thrall," Otus said. "It was just part of the air I breathed."

"A nasty part," Grus said.

Otus nodded gravely. "I think so, too—now. In those days, I didn't think about it any more than a dog thinks about rough ground under its feet."

Grus remembered the dog he'd heard in the village. With all the bad smells, the poor beast had to be in torment—or else, thinking about the way some dogs liked to roll in filth, it was having the time of its life.

Pterocles said, "Otus has asked me to teach him his letters. I'm glad to do it."

"I'm sure you would be," Grus said, and then turned toward the freed thrall. "Why do you want to learn them? Most men born free can't read and write, you know." There had been Kings of Avornis who needed to use a stencil to sign their names to decrees. Not all of them were bad kings, either.

"Fulca is a long way away now," Otus said. "We can't talk anymore. If I am going to say anything to her, I have to say it with words I write down. Someone back at the palace will read them to her. She will say what she wants to answer, and someone will write it down."

*He* didn't want to dictate a letter. That gave Grus an idea. "Maybe Fulca will learn her letters, too," he said.

Otus looked startled. Then he nodded, a nod that was almost a bow. "You're right, Your Majesty. Maybe she will. Learning things is good. I've seen that ever since I found out I could."

"I'm glad," Grus said. "I hope all the thralls will be like you and turn into ordinary people as soon as they can."

"So do I," Otus said. "The other king told me learning as much as I could was the most important thing I could do."

"Did he?" Grus said. Otus solemnly nodded. Grus hid a smile. Lanius was a born scholar, so of course he thought that way. Grus wasn't sure Lanius was wrong, but he wouldn't have put it as strongly as the other king had.

"Freeing *all* the thralls will take a lot of wizardry," Pterocles said. "We haven't come close to doing it, not yet. We won't for quite a while, either, even if we win all the fights."

He was bound to be right about that, and he was wise to be cautious. What he said wasn't what Grus wanted to hear; the king wished everything were going smoothly, and that all the thralls would be free by day after tomorrow at the latest.

What he got two days later wasn't the freeing of all the thralls south of the Stura. Scouts came galloping back to the army from the south and southeast, shouting, "The Menteshe! The Menteshe are coming!"

"Well, well," Hirundo said. "Maybe this is what we get for telling the Banished One's ambassador where to head in."

"Maybe it is," Grus said. "But I'd rather fight the nomads out in the open than have them stand siege in Yozgat."

"A point," Hirundo agreed. He shouted to the trumpeters. Horn calls blared out. The Avornans started shifting from columns into line of battle. Hirundo and Grus both shouted for them to hurry. If the Menteshe were moving forward as aggressively as that, the army needed to be ready when they got there. An attack before the Avornans were fully deployed was only too likely to turn into a disaster.

Hirundo also shouted for the engineers to get the stone- and dart-throwing engines into place as fast as they could. Grus echoed that cry, too. The engines could do what Avornan archery couldn't—they could outrange the nomads' fearsome horn-backed bows. If the Menteshe wanted to make the fight nothing but an archery duel, they would pay for it.

"Are these Korkut's men, or are they Sanjar's?" Grus asked a scout.

"I'm sorry, Your Majesty," the man answered. "They just look like a bunch of howling barbarians to me."

Grus laughed in spite of himself. "Well, by the gods in the heavens, we'll give them something to howl about, won't we?"

More scouts began falling back on the main body of the army. Some of them were wounded, and either lurched in the saddle or rode behind men who hadn't been hurt. Some, no doubt, wouldn't make it back at all.

Hirundo pointed ahead. "Here come the Menteshe."

"There are enough of them, aren't there?" Grus said.

"Too many, if anybody wants to know what I think," the general replied.

The plainsmen shouted something, but Grus couldn't make out what it was. He shrugged. They were unlikely to be welcoming him to the lands south of the Zabat. He did some shouting of his own. He and Hirundo both noted a hillock on their left flank, and posted a sizable detachment of archers and lancers there. That would make a good anchor for the left wing. On the right, the ground was far less generous. To make sure the Avornans didn't get outflanked there, Hirundo sent over a large fraction of the catapults. The great darts and flying stones would—with luck—keep the Menteshe from getting too adventurous over there.

"Nicely done," Grus said. "If they have to come straight at us, it's our kind of fight."

"That's what I'm hoping for, Your Majesty," the general agreed. "The only thing wrong with the scheme is, the cursed Menteshe are liable to have hopes of their own." He clucked in indignation that the nomads should presume to do anything so impolite.

Grus looked around to the royal guardsmen, who waited behind a screen of archers and other men more lightly armed and armored. If the Menteshe tried to smash through the Avornan center, they would get the same sort of unpleasant greeting as they had the last time they fought a large battle against Grus' army. Grus wondered whether any of the Menteshe commanders here had fought his men the summer before. That was something he wished he knew. It would have made a difference in his own dispositions.

Arrows began to fly. The first ones fell short, as happened in almost every battle Grus had ever seen. Men got more excited than they should have. They thought the enemy was closer than he really was, or thought they were stronger than they really were. Those wasted arrows mattered little. Soon enough, the shafts would bite.

And, soon enough, they *did* bite. Hit horses screamed. So did wounded men. Others crumpled to the ground without so much as a last sigh, dead before they struck it. In a way, they were the lucky ones. A quick death without pain was hardly more common on the battlefield than it was in the humdrum world of everyday life.

Hirundo bawled orders, shifting men to the right to cover what looked like building trouble there. The trumpeters' horn calls sent those orders winging even farther than his battle-trained voice could have. One of the trumpeters took an arrow in the arm even as he blared out a call. The music drowned in a horrible false note. Then the man lowered the horn and let out an honest shriek.

No sooner had Hirundo swung men to cover the perceived

threat than he discovered that these Menteshe generals, whoever they were, had more imagination than the leaders he'd faced the year before. The perceived threat turned out not to be the real one. After luring Avornan reinforcements to the right, the nomads struck hard at the left, about halfway between the Avornan force on the hillock and the center.

For a moment, Hirundo and Grus seemed to be struggling to find out who could curse more foully. Grus had hoped his royal guardsman would hurtle forward and smash the nomads, as they'd done before. Now, with Hirundo sending the heavily armed and armored riders back and to the left, the king hoped the guardsmen could keep the Menteshe from smashing *his* army.

"Grus!" the guardsmen shouted as they spurred their horses forward. "Hurrah for King Grus!" That was flattering. The king would have liked it better had they not used his name for a war cry in such desperate straits.

The Menteshe poured a fierce volley of arrows into the guardsmen. Some of the Avornans fell from their horses with a clatter. Some of the horses went down, too. But armor for men and mounts proved its worth. The Menteshe didn't break the guardsmen's charge, as they'd plainly thought they would.

Because they didn't break it, they had to try to withstand it. Their ponies and the wax-boiled leather they used in place of chainmail were not up to opposing lancers on big, heavy horses. They fought bravely. Grus didn't think he'd ever seen the nomads fail to fight bravely; they would have been much less dangerous if they hadn't been brave. Brave or not, though, they couldn't keep the guardsmen from breaking the momentum of their advance.

When Grus saw that the Menteshe had stalled, he dared breathe again. With the nomads in his own army's rear, he'd feared his force would come unraveled like a poorly woven cloak. He began to think past mere survival. Pointing toward the hillock on the left, he said, "I wish we could get a messenger over there. If they hit the nomads from behind now . . ."

"I know," the general answered. "I'll try if you like, but I don't think anybody can get through the Menteshe."

Grus gauged the ground and grimaced. He feared Hirundo

was right. He didn't want to send a man—or, more likely, several men—to death with no hope of success. But the battle hung in the balance. Part of being a king was doing things that needed doing, no matter how unpleasant they were. "I think you'd better—" he began.

He never finished giving the order. As they had not long before, he and Hirundo both cried out together. This time, though, they whooped with delight instead of shouting in anger and dismay. The officer in charge of the Avornans on the hill charged into the rear of the Menteshe without orders from anybody. Seeing what he ought to do, he went and did it.

He could hardly have timed the move better. The nomads had just discovered that they couldn't go forward anymore. Now they had enemy soldiers coming at them from behind, as they'd hoped to come at the Avornans. Thrown into confusion, they started streaming away toward the south. They were brave, yes, but they had never been much for taking a beating to no purpose.

"Push them!" Grus yelled. "Punish them! Make them sorry they ever tried to fight us! By the gods, they'd better be!"

The Avornans did what they could. It was less than Grus had hoped for, though not less than he'd expected. The Menteshe could flee faster than his men could pursue. They wore less armor to weigh them down. And they did not have to worry about keeping good order as they galloped away. The Avornans did, lest the nomads re-form and counterattack. A lot of the Menteshe, then, managed to escape.

"We beat them," Hirundo said. "We drove them back." He allowed himself a long, loud sigh of relief.

"We should have done more." But Grus could not make himself sound too disappointed. They *had* won. They *had* driven the Menteshe back. "For a while there, I wasn't sure we were going to keep our heads above water." That was putting it mildly.

"Me, too, Your Majesty." Hirundo sighed again, this time theatrically. "When they broke through there . . . They had a better general than anyone we've seen in charge of them before. And, I'm afraid, the general we had could have done a better job." He made a wry face.

"I'd be angrier at you if the nomads hadn't fooled me, too," Grus said.

Hirundo shook a finger at him—a fussy, foolish sort of thing to see on a battlefield. "Aren't you paying me to be smarter than you are?"

"I suppose I am," Grus admitted. "But we both got by with being stupid this time." He paused. "We'll want prisoners, too, quite a few of them. I need to know who was in charge of the Menteshe, and who fought for him."

"He was formidable, whoever he was," Hirundo said.

Grus hadn't been thinking about the enemy general just then, though Hirundo was right. He'd been wondering about the overlord that general served. Had Sanjar's men attacked him? Had Korkut's? Or had their warriors joined forces, perhaps under the banner of the Banished One?

Avornan soldiers brought Menteshe prisoners before him. Some of the captives spoke Avornan. He used an interpreter to talk to the others. One by one, he asked them, "Which overlord do you follow?"

Some of them said, "Korkut." Some said, "The Fallen Star." And some said, "Sanjar." That helped him very little.

He tried a different question, asking, "Which overlord commanded your army?"

Most of the Menteshe answered, "Bori-Bars," which gave him the name of their general.

Then Grus asked, "Which prince does Bori-Bars serve?" Some of the nomads gave Sanjar's name, others Korkut's. Grus scratched his head. He didn't see how one general could serve both princes. For that matter, neither did the Menteshe. They shouted angrily at one another. Grus summoned Pterocles, wondering whether the wizard could get to the bottom of it.

Pterocles looked at the prisoners. He listened to them. He cocked his head to one side, intently studying them. He muttered under his breath. "I think I am going to have to try a spell," he said. "This is . . . interesting."

"Glad to intrigue you," Grus said.

The spell the wizard used reminded Grus a little of the one he employed to free the thralls. It involved a clear crystal swinging on the end of a silver chain and flashes of light. These weren't rainbow flashes, though; they were sparks of clear green light, the color of freshly sprouted grass in bright spring sunshine. The Menteshe smiled as the sparks swirled around them.

Pterocles wasn't smiling; his face wore a mask of intense concentration. After he had used the spell on three or four nomads, he turned to Grus and said, "It's very interesting."

"What is?" Grus asked, as he was surely meant to do.

"It's something less than thralldom and something more than nothing," the wizard replied. "It makes the Menteshe . . . believe whatever they're told, you might say. They all heard that this Bori-Bars was against us and for their prince, and they didn't worry about who the prince might be. They all just followed Bori-Bars and made this attack on us."

Grus whistled tunelessly between his teeth. "Sounds like something the Banished One could deliver, doesn't it?"

"Well, I can't see anyone else who benefits more from it," Pterocles said.

"Neither can I," Grus said. "Is there a counterspell?"

"Maybe there is. I would have to work it out, though," Pterocles replied. "We may not need one. You saw how these nomads started going at each other like a kettle of crabs when they realized they weren't one big happy army after all. What do you want to bet the same thing is happening in their camps right now?"

"That would be nice." Grus had a vivid mental image of civil war breaking out anew among the Menteshe. He hoped it was a true image. But then, a moment later, it flickered and blew out. "If the Banished One wants to use this spell of his again, he can bring them together for another attack, can't he?"

Pterocles looked thoughtful. "That's a good question, Your Majesty. I haven't got a good answer for you. My guess would be that the spell wouldn't work so well a second time; people would remember what had happened before. If he wanted to do it again, he might have to find warriors who hadn't already been enchanted once. But I can't prove any of that, not until I see the magic in action again. It's only my feeling about how things are likely to work."

"All right. What you say seems reasonable to me—but I

don't know how much that has to do with the way magic works," Grus said. "So the Menteshe may well come together against us in big armies again, regardless of whether Sanjar and Korkut kiss and make up."

"That's the way it looks to me," Pterocles said. "It's happened once. I don't see why it can't happen again."

"Neither do I," Grus said. "By Olor's beard, though, I wish I did." If the Menteshe kept throwing everything they had at his men . . . *We'll just have to beat all of them, that's all. Then maybe they won't be able to keep us out of Yozgat.*

Lanius waited anxiously for letters from the south. Grus' accounts of what went on were bald but, as far as Lanius could tell, generally accurate. One of these years, some yet unborn king with a taste for history would find Grus' letters in the archives and waste a lot of enjoyable time reconstructing his campaigns.

Grus usually wrote a letter every few days. He didn't have a precise pattern; even if he had, the vagaries of the courier system would have disrupted it. Lanius had learned not to worry when a week or ten days went by without word from the other king. All it meant was that a courier had been delayed, or perhaps that the Menteshe had waylaid one.

When two and a half weeks passed, though, he began to get anxious. He wasn't the only one around the palace who did, either. Sosia and Estrilda both snapped for what seemed no reason at all. Even Ortalis wondered aloud what was going on.

Perhaps the most anxious person in the palace was Fulca. "What will happen if something goes wrong down there?" she asked Lanius. "Will they turn poor Otus back into a thrall?"

She had lived almost her whole life as a thrall, and had only a few months of freedom behind her. But she knew what freedom was worth—probably knew better than those who had never been without it.

And her fear made Lanius remember the disasters that had overtaken other Avornan armies in years gone by when they tried to campaign south of the Stura. "I hope not," was all he could tell her.

"It would be terrible if they did!" Fulca exclaimed. "Terrible!"

"You're right. It would," Lanius agreed gravely. "And it would be terrible for the whole kingdom, not just for Otus."

"Oh!" Fulca filled the word with more surprise than most people could pack into it. "I hadn't even thought of that."

If someone normal since birth had said such a thing, Lanius would have laughed at her, and not in a kind way, either. He forgave Fulca more readily; she had an excuse for worrying first about what concerned her most intimately. "The world is a bigger place than you know," he said, as he might have to a child.

Fulca nodded seriously, in a way no child would have. "Yes, Your Majesty. It looks that way."

Now—was the world big enough to include a courier bringing a new dispatch from Grus? For the next couple of days, it did not seem as though it was. The more time that went by, the more Lanius worried. When a courier *did* come up out of the south, the king all but tackled him. "Is all well with the army?" he demanded.

The courier only shrugged and handed him the message tube he carried. "This will tell you better than I can, Your Majesty," he replied. "I don't know what it says. I just rode the last stage of the journey."

"Oh." By contrast with Fulca, Lanius filled the little word with self-reproach. "Yes, of course."

He opened the tube, drew out the letter, and broke the seal. It was, he saw, Grus', which showed a river-galley prow; at least the other king still lived. He unrolled the parchment and began to read. He didn't know he'd made a sound until the courier asked, "Is everything all right?"

"Yes—better than all right, in fact," the king said. "A victory—a big victory."

"Ah. That's good news." The man's grin held more than a little relief. Stories often spoke of kings who punished messengers bearing bad news. Lanius had never found anything in the archives that said any of those stories were true, but that didn't stop people—and especially couriers—from believing them. A king *could* punish a courier for bad news; no doubt of that.

Lanius hoped he wasn't the sort of king who would, but how was a courier supposed to be sure of that?

Stories also spoke of kings who rewarded messengers bearing good news. Lanius fumbled in the pouch he wore on his belt. Kings didn't need to spend money very often, so he wasn't sure what he had in there. His fingers closed on a coin. He drew it out. It was a copper. That wouldn't do. He sneaked it back into the pouch and tried again. The next coin he found felt smoother between his thumb and forefinger, which seemed promising. When he pulled it out, it proved to be a goldpiece. That was what he wanted. With a certain amount of relief in his own smile, he handed it to the courier. "This for what the letter holds."

"Thank you very much, Your Majesty!" The man bowed himself almost double. Was he really as delighted as he looked? If he was, Lanius had given him too much. The king shrugged—he couldn't take it back now and substitute half as much in silver.

The courier bowed again and hurried away. Maybe he feared the king would try to get back some of what he had given. Lanius read through Grus' letter again. *The Menteshe have seen once more that they cannot stand against us,* the other king wrote. *If all goes as we hope and as it now appears, the way to Yozgat lies open.*

Lanius' eyes went back over that last clause, not because he hadn't understood it but because he liked it so much. *The way to Yozgat lies open.* Every Avornan ruler for centuries had dreamed of writing a sentence like that. Now Grus, about the least legitimate ruler Avornis had seen since the loss of the Scepter (with the possible exception of the jumped-up brigand who'd founded Lanius' dynasty), had actually done it.

And what would happen if the Avornan army reached the walls of Yozgat? *Why, then,* Lanius thought, *I'll write Grus and . . .*

"What have you got there?" asked someone behind the king.

He jumped and turned. There stood Ortalis, a grin on his face because he'd startled Lanius. "It's a letter from your father," Lanius said.

"Oh." Ortalis' grin disappeared. "Well, what does he say?"

"He's beaten the Menteshe south of the Zabat River, where he stopped last fall," Lanius answered. "He's beaten them, and the way to Yozgat lies open." Yes, he *did* like the sound of that.

"Good, I suppose." Ortalis sounded much less impressed. Lanius wondered why, but not for long. The only thing Grus could do to make Ortalis happy was drop dead.

When Grus first took the crown, Lanius had felt the same way, though his reasons were more personal than political. Not anymore. Now . . . Now things between him and Grus were— not so bad. The two of them were going in the same direction, anyhow. He didn't waste time trying to explain that to Ortalis, who wasn't. He said, "It's an important victory," and let it go at that.

# CHAPTER SEVENTEEN

Grus munched on dates candied in honey. He couldn't decide if they were the most delicious things he'd ever
eaten or just the most cloying. Hirundo and Pterocles
both licked honey and sticky bits of date from their fingers.
Grus hesitated only a moment before imitating them. He didn't
know what local manners said about eating dates, but he did
know his fingers were sticking together.

"We ought to import these," Pterocles said—he evidently
liked them.

"Now maybe we will," Grus answered.

"Have to think up a fancier name than 'dates,' " Hirundo
said. "Have to think up a name that really makes people want
to go out and spend their silver. How about something like
'sugarfruit'?"

"How about 'winefruit'?" Pterocles said. "They do make
wine from them."

"Have you tasted it?" Grus made a face. "It's thick and it's
sweet and it's nasty."

"I didn't mind it that much," the wizard said. "I don't think
it's up to what we make from grapes, but it's not bad." His
sweet tooth had to be stronger than Grus'.

"And even if date wine is the foulest stuff this side of mule
piss, who cares?" Hirundo said cheerfully. "Nobody north of
the Stura's going to know. A lot of the time, what things seem
like is more important than what they really are."

"I don't know about that," Grus said.

"Any wizard will tell you it's true," Pterocles said. "Illusion, appearance, belief . . . They're the things that matter. How can you say for sure what's real, anyhow?"

"Hrmm," Grus said—a discontented rumble down deep in his throat. The flickering lamplight and the smell of hot olive oil from the lamps inside his pavilion were real. So was the buzz of the mosquitoes that got in despite the netting in front of the flap. So were the pressure on his backside from the stool where he perched and the ache in his thighs from another day in the saddle. He ate another date and spat out the seed. The taste was real, too, and so was the way the honey coated the inside of his mouth.

But then Hirundo said, "A lot of spells are nothing but illusion, aren't they?"

"Not quite nothing but," Pterocles answered, "but illusion's no small part of them. A lot of spells make illusions turn real."

"How can you say for sure what's real?" Grus enjoyed throwing Pterocles' words back at him. He enjoyed it even more when the wizard turned red and spluttered and didn't answer.

"I'll tell you what I want to be real," Hirundo said. "I want one more good victory against the Menteshe to be real before we get to Yozgat. If we beat them again—do a proper job of beating them, I mean—they won't be so hot to come breathing down our necks."

"Do you want to provoke them into attacking us, then?" Grus asked. "Can we set an ambush for them?"

"I'd love to try," Hirundo said. "I'll laugh if we can bring it off, too. It's what the cursed nomads always try on us. By the gods, paying them back in their own coin would be sweet."

"Yes, by the gods. By the gods in the heavens," Grus said. They hadn't been invoked much in these parts lately. "Not by . . ." He let that hang. Hirundo nodded. He understood what Grus wasn't saying. Grus went on, "Let's look for a chance to do that and see how it goes."

"No guarantees," Hirundo said. "A lot will depend on the terrain and the weather and how we bump into the nomads or they bump into us."

"I understand. It's always that way," Grus said, and the general nodded again. Grus wished Hirundo hadn't mentioned the weather. So far this campaigning season, it had been good. Hirundo reminded him it didn't have to stay that way.

He worried about summertime rain. That could turn the roads to porridge and slow the Avornans to a crawl. Summer rain this far south wasn't just unseasonable; it would be the next thing to miraculous. Of course, that didn't necessarily stop the Banished One.

Rain, though, wasn't what the army met a few days later. A hot wind blew out of the south, a hot wind full of clouds of dust and sand. The grit got into Grus' eyes. He tied a scarf over his mouth and nose to keep from swallowing and breathing so much of it. That helped, but less than he wished it would have.

All through the army, men were doing the same thing. Some of them tried to tie cloths over the animals' mouths and nostrils too. The horses and mules didn't like that. Neither did the oxen drawing the supply wagons.

Grus thought about asking Pterocles whether the sandstorm was natural or came from the Banished One. He shrugged, coughing as he did so. What was the point? Natural or not, the army had to go through it. Pterocles couldn't do anything about the weather.

It went on and on and on. Swirling dust blotted the sun from the sky. From blue, the dome overhead went an ugly grayish yellow. Hirundo finally had to order the army to halt. "I'm sorry, Your Majesty," he shouted above the howl of the wind, "but I don't have any idea which way south is anymore."

"Neither do I," Grus admitted. "I just hope this dust isn't going to bury us."

"You're full of cheerful ideas, aren't you?" Hirundo said.

"Cheerful?" Grus echoed. "Yes, of course." He rubbed at his eyes, not that it did much good.

The storm was still roaring when the sun set. It got darker but not a lot. The soldiers did what they could for themselves and their animals, settling down to make the best night of it they could. Grus would have liked to get inside his pavilion, but he wasn't sure it would stay up in the gale. He swaddled himself in a blanket and hoped for the best. When he fell asleep, he surprised himself.

He woke up some time in the middle of the night. He needed a moment to figure out why. Something was missing—the wind wasn't ravening like a hungry wild thing. "Gods be praised," he muttered, even if he doubted they'd had anything to do with it. He yawned, rolled over, and went back to sleep.

Light the color of blood and molten gold pried his eyelids open. If this wasn't the most spectacular sunrise he'd ever seen, he had no idea which one from years gone by would top it. And the brighter it grew, the stranger grew the landscape it showed. Dust and grit lay over everything, smoothing outlines and dulling colors. The world might have been reduced to yellow-gray.

When he got to his feet, dust spilled off him and made a little cloud around him. Soldiers were stirring, and stirring up the dust. Grus coughed. He spat—and spat brown. He felt as though he were covered with bugs. He might have been, but suspected it was grit and dust instead.

Hirundo uncocooned himself from his blanket and looked around. Even though he'd been entirely wrapped up, his face and beard were the same yellow-gray that filled the rest of the landscape. Seeing that, Grus suspected he was also the color of dirt—almost the color of a corpse.

As Grus had, Hirundo spat. He looked revolted when his spittle too proved brown. "Well," he said in tones of forced—and false—gaiety, "*that* was fun."

"Wasn't it just?" Grus said. "A little more, and it would have swallowed us up."

"Not the way I plan to go." Hirundo coughed again. Dust spurted from his nostrils when he did.

"And how *do* you plan to go?" Grus inquired. The inside of his mouth tasted like dirt. He swigged from the canteen of watered wine he wore on his belt, then spat again. Even after that, his mouth still felt gritty.

"Me?" Hirundo grinned. "I intend to be murdered by an outraged husband at the age of a hundred and three. It will be a great scandal, I promise." He sounded as though he looked forward to it.

"There are worse ways to go," Grus said. "I'll help spread the gossip after it happens, I promise."

"Oh, who'd listen to you?" Hirundo said scornfully. "You'd be nothing but an old man."

They both laughed. Part of the laughter was relief. They'd brushed up against disaster with the sandstorm, and they both knew it. Grus stared south. The haze and dust still floating in the air hid the Argolid Mountains. Was the Banished One pleased with what he'd just accomplished, or was he disappointed he hadn't managed more? He still might manage more, of course (Grus assumed the storm was his, for it seemed too nasty to have been natural). He might send more wind and dust and sand. Or . . .

"We'll need scouts out," Grus said. "The Menteshe may try to pay us an early morning visit."

"So they may," Hirundo agreed. "Don't worry, Your Majesty. I'll take care of it."

By then, lots of Avornans were coughing and spitting and rubbing their eyes and cursing the storm and putting more dust in the air every time they moved. When scouts trotted off to take their positions all around the army, their horses kicked up more dust still. "How will we see the Menteshe even if they're there?" Grus wondered.

"I don't know." Hirundo didn't sound worried. "We'll see them the same way they see us, I expect."

"The same way . . . ? Oh," Grus said. Any nomads close enough to attack would also have been close enough to get caught in the storm themselves.

Still more dust surrounded the soldiers as they began to move. They went right on grumbling and coughing and wheezing. Grus wondered what the storm had done to the crops growing around here. True, grain came up in the winter in these parts, to take advantage of what rain fell. But vines and olives and almonds grew through the summertime. Could they ripen the way they should if they were covered in dust? Could livestock find enough to eat if sand and dust buried grass? He didn't know. Before long, he would start finding out.

Pterocles had a similar thought. Steering his mule up close

to Grus' horse, the wizard said, "I wonder what the thralls make of all this."

"Probably about what their cattle do," Grus answered. "You're talking about the ones that hadn't been freed?"

"Well, yes," Pterocles said. "The others are just . . . people."

"Just people," Grus repeated. It wasn't that Pterocles was wrong. It was, in fact, that he was right, and that being right was so important. "Who would have thought a couple of years ago that we would have freed thralls by the thousands? You've done something marvelous, you and all the other wizards."

"Thank you, Your Majesty," Pterocles said. "Up in the Chernagor country, the Banished One tried his best to make sure I never got the chance to do anything ever again. What I've done here—what we've done here—is the best way I know to pay him back."

"It's good, all right," Grus agreed. "But I can think of one thing better still." He looked south toward Yozgat as he spoke.

Surrounded by beaters and royal guardsmen, Lanius and Arch-Hallow Anser rode to the hunt. Lanius said, "I hope everything is all right with Ortalis. I worry when he doesn't feel like hunting."

"I think it's just us he doesn't feel like hunting with today," Anser said. "He went out with some friends of his own the other day."

"Did he? I didn't know that," Lanius said. The idea that Ortalis might have friends faintly bemused him. "Who were they? Do you know?"

"Not exactly," Anser replied. "I can't name names, if that's what you mean. Guard officers—nobody too important, though."

"Isn't that interesting," Lanius said, which was normally polite and neutral and nothing more. It was still polite and neutral, but it also *was* interesting. Maybe a fondness for hunting explained why Ortalis congregated with some guard officers and not others.

Then Anser said, "I didn't even know some of them liked to hunt."

Lanius scratched his head. In that case, he *didn't* know what

Ortalis' choice of companions meant. Did that make it more interesting, or less? One more thing the king didn't know. It gave him something to think about.

A bird somewhere up in an oak tree screeched. "That's a jay," Lanius said.

"So it is," Anser agreed. "You wouldn't have known what it was before we started hunting."

"I've learned quite a bit," Lanius said, which was also true and polite.

It turned out not to be polite enough. Chuckling, Anser said, "Some of the things you've learned, you probably wish you hadn't. But that's all right—Ortalis isn't with us today."

If even Anser joked about his half brother . . . "What must the servants think?" Lanius said.

"Servants never think anything good about you." If Ortalis had said that, he would have sounded angry—but then, Ortalis often sounded angry. Anser just thought it was funny. He went on, "You know what they say—nobody's a hero to his own servants."

"No, I suppose not." *What do the servants think of me?* Lanius wondered.

He knew he was fairly mild, fairly easygoing. Grus was stricter; by what some of the servants who'd been around the palace forever said, his own father had been much stricter. But what did they really think of the way he spent so much time in the archives and with his animals? Even more to the point, what did they really think of the way he took mistresses from among their ranks? What did they say about him behind his back?

*Well, he's nice to them, mostly. He doesn't hurt them, the way Ortalis would. That's something, anyhow. And when he gets tired of them or his wife finds out, he doesn't leave 'em flat. He could be worse, I expect.*

The king heard an imaginary servant inside his own head so vividly, he turned to see if a real one were in earshot. Of course he didn't see anyone of the sort, so he felt foolish. But his best guess about the servants' gossip had seemed impressively real. He didn't think he was very far wrong, anyway. *He could be worse.* Servants could say worse things.

Anser had been chasing the same game, but down a different track. "Do you want the help complaining that you never bring any meat back to the palace, Your Majesty?" he said with a sly smile. "If you don't, maybe you ought to learn to shoot a little straighter."

Did the people in the palace, and especially the people in the kitchens, complain or laugh because Lanius came home empty-handed so often? That hadn't occurred to him, either, but odds were they did. "Oh, well," he said. "If I have to be an archer to lead Avornis, the kingdom is in trouble."

The king and the arch-hallow teased each other until they got to the woods. Lanius would have been happy to go on joking there, but Anser took hunting much more seriously than he took his ecclesiastical post. He wore the red robe because Grus wanted him to, but he went after deer because *he* wanted to.

Silent as usual, the beaters vanished among the oaks and beeches. Anser headed for the edge of a familiar clearing. Lanius followed. He would have to do some shooting before too long, and, as usual, he didn't look forward to it. *You can condemn a man to death and then go off and eat supper without a second thought. Why can't you shoot a stag?*

*The stag hasn't done anything wrong. And I don't have to kill the man myself,* he thought. Were those reasons enough? Evidently.

"Are you going to try to hit something this time, Your Majesty?" Anser asked, his voice quiet and amused.

Lanius felt almost as embarrassed as he had when Sosia first found out about his affairs with serving girls. "How long have you known?" the king asked.

"Quite a while now," Anser told him. "Nobody could be quite as bad a shot as you are unless he did it on purpose. It just isn't possible. How *did* you kill that one stag?"

"I didn't mean to." Confession felt oddly liberating to Lanius. "He—ran into my arrow, I guess you'd say."

"Why do you come out if you don't want to shoot anything?" the arch-hallow inquired.

"Must be the company I keep," Lanius replied.

Anser looked sharply at him, suspecting irony. Finding none, he said, "You don't need to do that, Your Majesty. I'd still like you if you didn't."

"Thank you." Lanius meant it from the bottom of his heart. "But haven't you ever gone out of the way for a friend?"

"I don't know that I've ever gone *that* far out of the way," Anser said thoughtfully. "You don't ask me to go pawing through the archives with you."

"It's different," said Lanius, who would not have wanted Grus' bastard—or anyone else except maybe the late Ixoreus, who'd loved them as much as he did—pawing through the archives with him. "You wouldn't have a good time in the archives because you don't care what's in them. I can enjoy the woods whether I shoot anything or not. It's nice out here. It's just dusty in the archives."

The arch-hallow laughed. "All right, Your Majesty. I'll take your word for it—and I won't tell Ortalis, either. Do you want to bother shooting at all?"

After a moment's thought, Lanius nodded. "Yes, I think I'd better. Otherwise the guards and the beaters would talk, and that wouldn't be so good. You can go on giving me a hard time when I miss, too."

"All right. I will." Anser laughed again. Then, genuine curiosity in his voice, he asked, "How bad a shot are you really?"

"I don't know," Lanius answered. "I'm not very good, but I'm not as bad as I pretend to be, either. It's not something I need to know how to do, you know."

"No, I suppose not. Things stay in one place in the archives, don't they? You don't have to put arrows in them to make them hold still."

Remembering how some of the documents he'd looked for hadn't stayed where he thought they belonged, Lanius wondered about that. But he said, "I suppose not." The documents hadn't gone wandering. His attention had.

A stag bounded into the clearing. "Your shot, Your Majesty," Anser sang out, as though they hadn't been talking about Lanius' fraudulent hunting. The king nocked an arrow and let fly. The arrow—what a surprise!—went wide. The stag dashed off. "Oh, too bad, Your Majesty!" Anser exclaimed. He was a good actor.

"You shoot first the next time." Lanius did his best to seem disappointed. "Maybe you'll have better luck."

"Maybe I will. I can hope so, anyhow." Anser sounded amused.

He killed a stag about an hour later, and butchered it as it lay on the ground. He did a good, careful job, but showed none of the relish for it that raised Lanius' hackles when Ortalis had a knife in his hand. One of the beaters started a small fire. Anser roasted and ate the mountain oysters himself, but shared the liver, kidneys, sweetbreads, and heart with Lanius and the beaters and guardsmen.

Lanius couldn't deny that very fresh meat cooked over open flames was, in its way, better than most of what the cooks made. These slices needed only a little salt to bring out their full flavor. A lot of the palace dishes were spicy enough to make someone's eyes water. Partly that was because spices were expensive, and so suited to a king's table. And partly it was because those spices helped disguise the taste of meat that was starting to go off.

And then there was a crashing in the woods, and a loud, deep grunt, and a shout of, "Boar! Boar!"

The hunters all leaped to their feet and grabbed for their weapons. Wild boar were the most dangerous beasts in the woods. Their tushes could gut a man as easily as a knife gutted a deer. Some of the guards had boar spears, with a crosspiece on the shaft to keep a boar from running up it and savaging the spearman despite being wounded.

More yells said the beaters were trying to head off the boar and keep it away from Lanius and Anser. But the crashing came closer with terrifying speed. The boar sounded like an angry common pig when it squealed, or what a common pig would have sounded like if it were much larger and fiercer than it really was.

And then, fast as a stone flung from a catapult, the boar was upon them. An arrow stood in its shoulder, but seemed only to enrage it. Its little eyes were red as blood. Its head swung until it aimed straight at Lanius. Then it charged.

Two guards managed to spring between the boar and the king. One of the men went down. The boar lowered its head and slashed at him with its tushes. The other guardsman drove his spear home and hung on for dear life. The boar screamed and kept trying to break free.

Anser put an arrow into it, then another and another. Lanius nocked a shaft and let fly, too. This time, he wasn't trying to miss. Anything to make that bellowing, sharp-toothed horror lie down and never move again!

Blood ran from the boar's mouth. The flow choked its bellows. Slowly, struggling to the end, it yielded to death.

"Olor's beard!" Anser exclaimed. "That was more exciting than I really wanted."

"I should say so," Lanius agreed shakily. "Why would anyone want to hunt a monster like that?" He turned to the guardsman the boar had savaged. He wasn't sure he wanted to look at what the animal had done to the man, but the guard was sitting up and getting to his feet. "Are you all right?" Lanius asked in amazement.

"A little trampled, Your Majesty, but not too bad," the guardsman answered. "The mailshirt kept him from opening me up."

"Let's see your beaters say that about the leather they wear," Lanius told Anser.

"They can't," the arch-hallow admitted. "I'm glad the guardsmen managed to slow that beast down. The miserable thing was coming right at you."

Lanius had noticed that, too. "Yes, it was, wasn't it?" he said, as calmly as he could. Was the Banished One able to take over a boar's mind the way he could take over a thrall's mind? Had he used this boar as a weapon against someone who was giving him trouble? *Or is my imagination running away with me?* Lanius wondered. He doubted he would ever know.

*I hope I'm giving the Banished One trouble, anyhow*, he thought, and wondered if he would ever know the answer to that.


"Another river to cross," Grus said, staring across a stream shrunken in the summer drought. A few Menteshe rode back and forth on the other side, not far from the southern bank. Right now, the river wasn't anywhere close to a bowshot wide. The nomads stayed out of range of Avornan archers.

Hirundo looked across the river, too. "Now the question is, how many of those bastards *aren't* we seeing? How many of them are waiting somewhere not too far away to hit us when we cross?"

Grus shaded his eyes with the palm of his hand. "Doesn't look like country where you could hide anything much bigger than a dragonfly." Several of them danced in the air above the river. They had blue bodies so bright they almost glowed and wings of a dusky brown. Grus didn't remember seeing any like them farther north.

The general nodded. "No, it doesn't," he agreed. "But how much aren't we seeing? Do they have wizards hiding a forest— and a swarm of Menteshe inside it?"

"Good question," Grus said, and shouted for Pterocles.

"You need something, Your Majesty?" the wizard asked.

"Who, me?" The king shook his head. "No, I was just yelling because I like to hear myself make noise." Pterocles blinked, not sure what to make of such royal irony. Grus went on, "Are the Menteshe on the far side of the river using magic to hide an ambush?"

"Ah. Now that's an intriguing question, isn't it?" Pterocles said. "I'll see if I can find out." Before, he hadn't seemed to care one way or the other what lay on the far side of the river. Now he looked over there with fresh interest. "Where would be the best place for them to hide their men, if they're doing that?"

"Hirundo?" Grus said. He had his own ideas, but the general knew—or was supposed to know—more about such things than he did.

Hirundo stroked his neatly trimmed salt-and-pepper beard. "Well, I can't say for certain, mind," he warned, and Grus and Pterocles both nodded. Hirundo pointed east. "If I were in charge of the Menteshe, that's where I'd put them. They can strike at our flank from a position like that, do us a lot of harm."

"Why not the other flank?" Pterocles pointed west.

"Well, they could," Hirundo said, "but that's not how I'd do it. The ground is better the other way. They'd be coming down-hill at us—do you see?—not trying to climb. It makes a dif-ference."

"I suppose it would." Pterocles plainly didn't see how.

Patient as a father teaching his son to swim, Hirundo said, "You want to have the ground with you if you can. Either mounted or on foot, a charge uphill is harder than the other kind. Arrows don't go as far when you're shooting them up a slope, either."

"Oh." Pterocles nodded, perhaps in wisdom. "All right."

Grus, who agreed with his general, set a hand on the wizard's shoulder. "Every trade has its tricks and its secrets. Hirundo and I wouldn't have any idea what to do if we needed to cast a spell, but we've tried to learn a thing or two about soldiering."

"All right," Pterocles said again. "I'll take your word for it, then, and I'll stick to things I know a little something about myself." He took from his belt pouch an amulet made from a brown, shiny stone pierced and penetrated by a duller, darker one. "Chalcedony and emery," the wizard explained. "Together, they are proof against all manner of fantastical illusions."

"Good," Grus said. "But don't use them yet." Pterocles, who had clutched the amulet and was about to start a spell, stopped in surprise. The king went on, "If you find there are trees there and the Menteshe are lurking in among them, or something like that, you ought to be able to make them sorry they ever decided to try to attack us."

"I can try," Pterocles said doubtfully.

Hirundo snapped his fingers. "What about that spell you used against the Chernagor ships that were trying to bring grain into Nishevatz? You know—the one where you set them on fire when they were still out on the ocean. If they're hiding in a forest or an olive grove, say, you could roast 'em easy as you please."

"If roasting them were as easy as you make it sound, I wouldn't have any trouble—that's true enough." Now Pterocles' voice was tart. He rummaged some more in his belt pouch, and finally pulled out a clear disk of rock crystal thicker at the center than the edges. "I can try that spell, anyhow," he said. "One thing's sure—the sun is stronger here than it was up in the Chernagor country. I'll need some greenery—with luck, some twigs torn from trees—to work the spell if I turn out to need it."

Grus sent some of his guardsmen off. They came back with olive branches, twigs from almond trees, and fragrant orange and lemon boughs. No doubt the thralls who watched them would be puzzled—if puzzlement could soak into the sorry wits of thralls. When Pterocles had the greenery piled in front of his feet, Grus said, "Now, if you please."

"Certainly, Your Majesty." The wizard had a knack for being most exasperating when he was most polite. He gave a bow that struck Grus as more sardonic than sincere, then clutched the amulet in his left hand and looked east and south. He pointed in that direction with his right forefinger. Grus wished he hadn't; any watching Menteshe would get a good idea of what he was doing. But maybe there was no help for it. The king kept quiet.

Pterocles began a chant that started softly but grew louder and more insistent as it went on. Grus peered in the direction of the wizard's outthrust forefinger. He waited to see if the landscape would change. If it did, he would deal with whatever the nomads were hiding. If it didn't . . . well, better safe than sorry.

He and Hirundo and Pterocles all exclaimed at the same time. The sere, dun, dry landscape on the far side of the river wavered and rippled, as though it were being seen through running water. And then, quite suddenly, an almond grove that hadn't been there—or hadn't seemed to be there—appeared out of nowhere. Menteshe horsemen—Grus couldn't see how many—waited in the shade of the trees. There were plenty to cause his army trouble; he was sure of that.

He got only a brief glimpse of the grove before it vanished again. A woman whose skirt was flipped up by the wind might have yanked it down again that fast, leaving him with only a memory of her legs. Sometimes a memory would do, though. "Use your spell now," the king told Pterocles. "They know you've gotten through theirs."

"I'm already doing it," the wizard said. And, sure enough, he was separating almond twigs out of the greenery the guardsmen had set at his feet. "I hope the Menteshe don't have a counterspell handy. The Chernagors never did figure out what to do about this one, but the nomads have more worry about fire than the northerners did, because they live in a hot, dry country. Well, we'll see before long."

He held the crystal disk perhaps a palm's breadth above the bits from the almond branches. A bright spot of sunlight—it almost seemed a miniature sun—sprang into being on a twig. Grus wondered what magic lay in the crystal to make it do such a thing. Whatever the cause, that bright spot of sunlight seemed hot as a miniature sun, too. Smoke rose from the twig. A moment later, it burst into flame.

Pterocles chanted and pointed, sending his fire where he wanted it to go. For some little while, nothing—or nothing visible—happened. Then the illusion on the far side of the river wavered again, wavered and winked out. Pterocles wasn't attacking it now, not directly. But the Menteshe sorcerers abandoned it because they had other things that needed their power more.

Smoke streamed up into the sky. The leafy tops of the almond trees were on fire. Even from that distance, Grus could hear the nomads' horses screaming in terror and panic. The Menteshe had no chance to keep their mounts under control, not with flames above their heads and burning leaves and branches falling down on them. The horses galloped off in all directions, carrying their riders with them.

Grus nudged Hirundo. "Get our men across the river now, before the nomads can pull themselves together."

"Right." The general started shouting orders.

Pterocles looked as happy as a six-year-old with a brand-new wooden sword. "They haven't got a counterspell for that one, either," he said, grinning widely. "I always did think it was a pretty piece of magic, and it's done some good things for us."

"I should say so." Grus remembered tall-masted Chernagor ships catching fire out in the Northern Sea, where he could have reached them in no other way than through magic. He looked at the burning trees. Now he had another memory to go with that one. He slapped Pterocles on the back. "Nicely done."

"I'll have to thank Hirundo when he's done yelling his head off," Pterocles said. "That might not have occurred to me if he hadn't suggested it."

"It seems to be working pretty well," Grus said. "Hard on the almonds, but nothing we can do about that."

Avornan soldiers formed a perimeter on the far bank of the river. A few Menteshe rode toward them, but only a few—not nearly enough to keep them from making the crossing. And, at Hirundo's orders, the Avornans had brought some stone- and dart-throwers over the river with them. The missiles they flung discouraged the nomads from getting too close. Before long, even the handful of Menteshe who'd tried to oppose Grus' army wheeled their horses and trotted away.

"We took care of that," Pterocles said.

"They aren't gone for good," Grus said. "They'll try to give us trouble somewhere else. But they won't give us trouble here, and that's what I was worried about." He grinned at the wizard. "Thank you."

"My pleasure, Your Majesty, and I mean every word of that," Pterocles answered. "Every time we set another thrall village free, I'm getting some of my own back against . . ." He did not say the name, but looked south. Grus nodded, understanding whom he meant. Pterocles went on, "Every time I do something like this, I'm getting some back, too."

"All of Avornis owes . . . him a lot," Grus said. "If this campaign goes the way we hope, we'll get to pay a lot of it back. We'll have . . . something he's kept for a long time."

If they got to Yozgat, if they got the Scepter of Mercy—what then? Grus didn't know, but oh, how he wanted to find out!

# CHAPTER EIGHTEEN

Y es, I'm going out to the country again," Lanius said.
Sosia's expression was dubious, to say the least. "You
can't tell me you enjoy it there," she said. "You can't, I
mean, unless you've got someone there waiting for you."

"I do," he said, and her eyes flashed furiously. He held up a
hand to hold back the lightning. "It's not a woman. You saw that
the last time you were there. You can come again, whenever you
please. Don't tell me ahead of time. I'm not worried about that.
But I've got Collurio and Crinitus out there, and Pouncer, too."

"That miserable moncat," his wife said. "The way you talk
about it, it might as well be a person."

"One of these days, maybe, all Avornis will be talking about
it," Lanius said.

"What makes you think all Avornis isn't talking about it already?" Sosia paused to spoon up some breakfast porridge and
sip from her cup of wine. "I know what Avornis is saying, too.
'Why is the king spending so much money and wasting so
much time on a dumb beast?' People can understand mistresses. But the moncat?" She shook her head.

"Pouncer is a beast, but he's a long way from dumb. People
will see that, too," Lanius said. He started to say even more, but
held his tongue at the last moment. The Banished One had
never stalked Sosia's dreams. He wouldn't have talked about
Pouncer with Anser or Hirundo, either. Grus and Pterocles . . .
understood.

Sosia didn't. "Well, go on, then. I can't stop you, but I don't like it, either."

"It has nothing to do with you," Lanius said, and he wasn't lying. "It's business of state, that's what it is."

His wife sniffed. "Tell me another one. I wonder what a bricklayer or a candlemaker says when he wants to get away from his wife for a while."

Lanius exhaled in exasperation. "Do you want to come with me? You can, if you care to."

"No." Sosia made a face. "*I* don't care for the country at all. I like it right where I am. You always liked it here, too. Is it any surprise I wonder what you're up to when you start doing things you don't usually do?"

She might have been a constable keeping track of a sneak thief's habits. Lanius thought that was unfair. He never took anything that wasn't freely given. Whether he took something Sosia didn't want him to have was a different question, one he didn't care to examine so closely.

He did ride out to the country a few days later. While he was interested in what Pouncer had learned, riding out to see the moncat was not his idea of fun. Some people enjoyed horseback riding for its own sake. Lanius found that almost as strange—and almost as perverse—as Limosa's taste for the lash. He'd become a good enough rider to stay in the saddle if his horse didn't get too frisky, and he rode placid geldings to try to make sure that didn't happen. He could do it, but he did it without enjoyment.

There was something he had in common with Grus. The other king wasn't a natural equestrian, either; Hirundo, who was, never tired of teasing him. But Grus did well enough not merely to ride but to fight on horseback. Grus might not—did not, in fact—have a lot of education, but he'd proved competent in any number of ways.

A hawk wheeled overhead in the blue. Somewhere in the fields of ripening grain scurried the rabbits and mice on which it lived. Lanius couldn't see them or smell them, but the hawk could. As often as not, peasants shot at hawks or netted them because they sometimes stole chickens and ducks. Lanius thought they did more good than harm, and by a wide margin, too.

He wondered if a royal edict would keep peasants from killing them. As far as he knew, no king had ever issued a decree like that. In the back of his mind, he heard Grus saying, *Don't make a law if you can't enforce it. People won't obey it, and they won't respect the other laws so much, either.*

That was probably true, however little he cared for it. And he knew he could not force people to obey a law protecting hawks. He sighed. Good ideas often broke to pieces when they ran up against brute fact.

The road was dusty. The only time roads weren't dusty was when they were muddy, which made them worse. How much would cobblestoning all the kingdom's main roads cost, how long would it take, and how many men would it need? *Too much, too long, and too many*—the answer formed almost as fast as the question.

Collurio and his son didn't know the king was coming. The animal trainer greeted him with a bow and the words, "By the gods, Your Majesty, you were right."

"Was I?" Lanius always liked hearing that. "Uh, about what?"

"About hawks, Your Majesty," Collurio replied. "The soldiers have shot three of them that tried to swoop down on the moncat."

"*Have* they?" Lanius said, surprised in spite of his precautions.

Collurio nodded. "They sure have. One eagle—biggest bird I've ever seen, I think—one fish-hawk, and one ordinary hawk. Others were circling around, too, but they didn't do anything more than circle. It was almost like they knew to stay away from the archers' bows."

"*Was* it?" Lanius said, and Collurio nodded again. The king plucked at his rather unkempt beard. "Isn't that interesting?" He remembered the hawk he'd seen floating in the air earlier in the day. Maybe it hadn't been thinking about mice and rabbits. Maybe it had been thinking of moncats instead. And maybe the Banished One had been doing its thinking for it.

Grus looked down into the well. The stench wafting up from the shaft told him what the Menteshe had done, but he wanted to see for himself. Sure enough, the cut-up carcasses of a couple of sheep, or possibly goats, bobbed in the water.

Hirundo looked down the shaft, too. "Well, we won't get any use out of that one," he said matter-of-factly.

"They've poisoned quite a few of them," Grus said. "It's getting to be a nuisance." It was getting to be more than a nuisance, but he tried to admit as little as he could, even to himself.

"Where there's one well, odds are we can dig another one close by," Hirundo said.

"Yes, that's true, but whenever we have to stop and dig, it takes time," the king answered. "I worry about every day we don't spend pushing on toward Yozgat. You can only stretch a campaigning season so far."

"If we can get supplies down from the north, we'll do all right," Hirundo said. "We *could* stay through the winter if we had to. No blizzards to worry about here, not like in the Chernagor country or even in Avornis."

"No, I suppose not." Grus looked south just the same. If the Banished One wanted to badly enough, could he bring a snowstorm screaming down on an army besieging Yozgat? Grus didn't know, and hoped he wouldn't have to find out the hard way. He brought his thoughts back to more immediate worries. "Do we have enough water to keep moving?"

"For now, yes," Hirundo answered. "If we don't come across any in the next couple of days, then we have a problem. But I'm not going to fret about that. Something will turn up. It usually does."

"I hope so." Grus envied the general's easy optimism. Hirundo had been saying things like that his whole life long, and he'd been right most of the time. If he happened to be wrong here, that would be more than a problem. It would be a disaster. The king pounded a fist against his thigh. "This country is a lot drier than Avornis."

"We've managed to get this far." Yes, Hirundo had no trouble staying cheerful. "Yozgat's just over the next rise—oh, not really, but close enough. Don't worry, Your Majesty. We'll do all right."

"Maybe we will," said Grus, who certainly wanted to believe it. "This is liable to be hard on the thralls, though. Everything lately has been hard on those poor people—war across their fields, the plague during the winter, and now this."

"Not everything," Hirundo said. "They're free—the ones who are left are free, anyhow. And I'll tell you something else, Your Majesty. I'll bet the freed ones will know of more wells and such than the Menteshe do. If we run into what looks like trouble, asking them is likely to do us more good than anything else."

"Mm, I'd say that's a pretty good bet," Grus agreed after a little thought. "And it's something the Banished One and the Menteshe are liable to miss. Who pays attention to thralls unless he has to?"

"We do," Hirundo answered.

Grus nodded, wondering whether that was a weakness the enemy could exploit or a strength that might help Avornis win this struggle. He had no idea—it would all depend on how things played out. And caring about the thralls also might turn out not to matter one way or the other.

The army did move forward, and found more poisoned wells in its path. Men and animals started getting thirsty. Most streams were either dry or tiny trickles in the summer heat. Grus sent wizards ahead with the scouts, to bring freedom to some thralls and try out Hirundo's notion.

It worked even better than the general might have guessed. The thralls found wells and streams and even a pond the Menteshe had missed. The army got enough water to keep going—not a lot of water, but enough. And the thralls, even with the darkness freshly lifted from their spirits, were not just willing but eager to do all they could for the Avornans. The Menteshe had been hard on them and hard on their ancestors for hundreds of years. How much of that oppression did they really understand? Enough to know which side they were on; that was clear.

"Well, you were right," Grus told his general as they encamped for the night.

Hirundo bowed. "Thank you kindly, Your Majesty. One of the reasons people want to do things for you is that you say things like that. Plenty would just take the credit, whether it belonged to them or not."

"I've known officers like that—who hasn't? Nothing's ever their fault, either," Grus said. Hirundo nodded. The king continued, "If you have a choice, you'd rather lean on the other kind. I do try to remember that myself."

Hirundo bowed again. He didn't say anything. His silence was part of the price Grus paid for being king. If he had spoken, Grus was sure he would have said something like, *Most people would forget all about that as soon as they got a crown on their head.* It was probably—no, certainly—true, but it wasn't the sort of thing you told a sovereign, even an easygoing one.

The Menteshe didn't need long to realize something had gone wrong. Seeing the Avornans moving forward, seeing their animals healthy and not on their last legs, told the nomads Grus' army had found water one way or another. But the nomads didn't turn any special savagery against the thralls. It was as though they couldn't imagine those near-beasts doing anything for good or ill—doing anything at all, except what beasts did.

Instead, with a fury that seemed to Grus not far from despair, the Menteshe struck at the Avornan army. As always, they hit hard. Volleys of arrows stung Grus' force. Wounded men and wounded horses screamed. The Avornans wavered. If the nomads had kept pelting them with arrows from long range, they might have broken.

What saved the Avornans were the siege engines rattling along in the baggage train. Those could hit the Menteshe where Avornan archery couldn't. And, as always, each of the flying stone balls and stout darts did far more damage than a mere arrow could have. The Menteshe abruptly seemed to lose patience with the long-range duel. Shouting curses in their own language, they charged.

In charging, they threw away the advantage they'd enjoyed. They'd had the better of the missile duel even if they didn't like stones flying their way. At close quarters, the Avornans, who wore heavier armor and rode sturdier horses, had the edge.

The Menteshe didn't need long to realize they'd made a mistake. By the time they did, though, it was too late. They were already entangled with the Avornans. Getting out of trouble proved harder than getting into it, which was usually true. The Avornan lancers and archers and spear-carrying foot soldiers made the Menteshe sorry they hadn't stayed farther away.

And when the nomads did finally break free, they were too battered and too disorganized to go back to the strategy that had worked well for them before. They were also too closely pursued. They rode off toward the south. Grus didn't push the pursuit hard. That would have let his men get shaken out into loose order, where they would be vulnerable to the nomads. He wanted to play to his own countrymen's strengths as long as he could.

Watching the Menteshe retreat, Hirundo said, "That will give them something to think about."

"I hope so," Grus said. "They tried to stop us with filth in the wells, and they couldn't. And they tried to stop us with soldiers again, and they couldn't do that, either. What have they got left?"

"They may have more fight left in them. They're tough," the general answered. "And then, if they keep losing, they stand siege in Yozgat. The place is supposed to be formidable."

"We'll find out how formidable it is," Grus said. Like Hirundo, he was looking south. Hirundo no doubt thought he was thinking of the city where the Scepter of Mercy had lain for so long. And so he was, but he was also looking farther south still, toward the Argolid Mountains. What would the Banished One do if—no, probably when—the Avornan army encircled the city? *We'll find out,* Grus thought again.

Pouncer knew what to do, every step of the way. King Lanius watched as the moncat proved as much in the city slice he'd had Tinamus design and build. "Look at him go!" Lanius exclaimed.

"He's a remarkable animal, Your Majesty," Collurio agreed. "It's been a . . . a privilege working with him."

"You started to say something else," Lanius told him. "What was it? A pleasure? But you didn't say that."

"No, I didn't. The moncat pushes back too hard to make it a pleasure," Collurio said.

After a few heartbeats, Lanius shook his head. "I don't think that's quite right. It's just that, well, a moncat is a cat. Pouncer will do what Pouncer wants to do, not what we want him to do. The trick is to get the miserable creature to want to do what we want him to do—and not to knock him over the head with a rock when he doesn't want to do it."

"Yes—and that last," Collurio agreed with a weary smile. "Anyone can tell you've had some experience with animals, Your Majesty."

"And with children," Lanius said.

That made the trainer laugh. "And with children," he agreed. "Oh, yes. Children, though, mostly grow out of it. Beasts never do."

"True enough." But Lanius was thinking about Ortalis, and about how much beastliness he'd never grown out of. Collurio might have heard this or that about Ortalis; palace gossip always leaked out into the streets of the capital. The animal trainer didn't have to live with the prince, no matter what he'd heard. As far as Lanius was concerned, that made Collurio the lucky one.

Pouncer kept on with the routine it had learned. It knew where to go and what to do to earn each new reward. The moncat knew how to reverse its course, too. Lanius kept looking away from Pouncer and up into the sky. No hawks. No eagles. Not even a jay scolding people for being people. Just a few small white clouds drifting on a warm, lazy breeze.

"I'm glad you're here, Your Majesty. We're just coming to the hard part now," Collurio said. "Crinitus and I are going to start widening the distances between rewards. We'll set them out in every other usual place, so the moncat will have to go twice as far between them. Then we'll double the distance again, and so on until we have what you want."

The trainer only knew what the king wanted. He remained unsure why Lanius wanted it. Lanius didn't enlighten him. The less the trainer knew, the safer he was—and the safer Pouncer was. Collurio had already drawn the Banished One's interest. If the exiled god looked his way again . . .

"Have you had any more dreams?" Lanius asked. "Has Crinitus had any?"

"Dreams?" Collurio looked blank for a moment, but only for a moment. "Oh, *those* dreams! No, the gods in the heavens be praised, I haven't. That one was plenty to last me a lifetime. I don't *think* my son has. If he had, I expect he would have said so."

They returned to the business at hand the next morning. As Collurio had said he would, he put out only half as many rewards as usual for Pouncer. When the moncat got to where the first one should have been, it looked around in surprise on discovering the treat wasn't there. After a brief pause, though, it went on to where the next treat should have been—and was.

Collurio breathed a sigh of relief. "You're always afraid they'll just sit down and lick themselves when they run into something different," he said. "I didn't really expect that, but you can't know ahead of time."

Pouncer hesitated whenever a reward was missing, but kept on with the routine to get the ones that were there. When Collurio put the moncat through its paces again later in the day, it went straight from reward to reward, scarcely even slowing at the sites that had held treats but did no more.

"He's figured it out!" Lanius said happily.

"Looks that way," Collurio agreed. "Like I told you, we'll keep going until he's good and used to doing it this way, then stretch the distance between rewards again. We're going in the right direction, Your Majesty."

Lanius nodded. "Yes," he said. "I really think we are."

King Grus fanned himself with a fan made of peacock feathers. It was not only gorgeous but, in this sweltering weather, highly practical. Anything that stirred the air was welcome. Even now, with the sun sinking down in the west, it was hotter than it ever got in the city of Avornis.

"Your Majesty?" A sweating guardsman stuck his head into the pavilion.

"What is it?" Grus asked.

"One of our scouts just rode into camp. I think he's got himself a high-and-mighty Menteshe with him."

"Oh, he does, does he?" With a grunt, the king heaved himself up off the stool where he'd perched. "Well, I suppose I'd better come see what the fellow wants, then, hadn't I?"

He had no idea who the nomad would be or which faction he represented. Whatever the answers to those questions were, Grus could guess what the man would want—would demand, probably. He would tell Grus that the Avornans had to go back over the Stura, and that they must not join with whichever faction he didn't happen to favor. The Menteshe knew only one song, though they tried to disguise that by singing it in different keys.

"Your Majesty." The nomad bowed low before Grus.

And Grus found he recognized him. "Good day, Qizil son of Qilich. What does Prince Sanjar want with me?" he inquired.

The Menteshe bowed again, lower this time. "I am honored that you remember me, Your Majesty."

"Oh, yes. I remember you. And I know Sanjar's men have attacked mine this year. What have we got to say to each other?"

"When we last spoke, Your Majesty, you mentioned something in which you were interested." Qizil didn't name the Scepter of Mercy. Did that mean he was too close to Yozgat? Or was he too close to the Banished One's lair in the Argolid Mountains?

It didn't really matter. Whether Qizil named it or not, Grus knew perfectly well what he was talking about. "Well?" the king asked. "You're right. I am interested. Does Sanjar have it?" If the concubine's son had stolen the Scepter from his unloving half brother, Grus was ready to deal with him. Grus would have made almost any bargain for the Scepter of Mercy.

But, regretfully, the Menteshe emissary shook his head. "No, I must tell you that it still rests in Yozgat. But my principal will join his men to yours in the effort to take the city and the—prize."

Grus bowed. "My thanks. That is generous of Prince Sanjar, but it would be more generous if things were different. The way they are, the Banished One could make them turn against us without warning, the way they did when they fought us not long ago. Then it was Sanjar's men and Korkut's all together, and all against my army."

To his surprise, Qizil looked embarrassed. "That . . . was not what we expected to happen, Your Majesty. Our own shamans are looking into it."

"Are they?" Grus was surprised all over again. This was the first time he'd ever heard of Menteshe working against the Banished One's wizardry. He didn't know whether to believe it, either.

"They are. We are not puppets on strings. We are not thralls." Pride rang in Qizil's voice. "We serve the Fallen Star because we choose to serve him. If the choice is not ours—well, maybe we will choose differently."

"You tempt me," Grus said. "It's a pity you don't tempt me

quite enough. If I could be sure you were your own men and would stay your own men—that might be different. But the way things are, my men can't trust Sanjar's men at their side or behind them. And so I think we'll just have to go on by ourselves."

"This could be the worst mistake you ever make," Qizil warned.

"Maybe," Grus said. "But it could also be one of the smarter things I've done lately, and so I'm going to do it. If you ever persuade me you're really broken free of the Banished One, we may have something to talk about. Until then, I'm afraid we don't."

Qizil winced at the name the Avornans gave the exiled god. That told Grus he might not be happy with his ultimate overlord, but he wasn't ready to break away from him, which meant Sanjar wasn't ready to break with the Banished One, either. It would have been nice if things were different.

"I will take your words back to my sovereign," Sanjar's ambassador said.

"Yes, do," Grus said. Unfortunately, to his way of thinking, Sanjar was only Qizil's superior; the Banished One remained his sovereign—and Sanjar's, too. They could see they were less free than they wanted to be, but they could not yet see how to get away.

After dismissing Sanjar's envoy, Grus summoned Pterocles. He told the wizard what Qizil had said. Pterocles stayed silent for some little while. "That *is* interesting," he said at last. His voice sounded far away; he was plainly still deep in thought. "I wonder what the Menteshe could do to block the Banished One's spells if they set their minds to it. They know his magic much better than we do."

"Than most of us except you do, anyhow," Grus said.

"Oh, I'm sure he gets into their minds sometimes, only to help them with their spells, not to knock them down," Pterocles said. "They ought to know him from the inside out, too, so to speak."

"What would a warding spell against him be like?" the king asked.

Pterocles started to laugh. "If I knew, Your Majesty, I'd use one," he said. "Since I don't know, since I'm just guessing, I'd say it would be something like the spell that frees thralls. Same principles, anyhow—probably a different way of using them."

"That sounds as though it ought to be true—which doesn't mean it is, of course." Grus plucked at his beard as he considered. "Would you do well to leave that spell written out someplace where the nomads might find it?"

"You *do* ask fascinating questions," Pterocles breathed. He paused again in thought. When he came out of his study, he said, "The way it looks to me, Your Majesty, that sword has two edges. Letting the Menteshe learn exactly how we free thralls might help them do something against the Banished One. The other edge is, it might help them—or him—figure out how to counter our spell. I'll do it if you order me to, but not unless you do."

Grus grunted. Now he had to do some studying of his own. In the end, he said, "No, I won't order you to do it. You're right—the risk that they might find a way to fight our spell is real, and we can't ignore it. For now, it's too important. But if we win this campaign, it gives us something to think about doing next, so we won't forget about it, either."

"I hadn't even begun to think about what happens next," Pterocles said.

"Neither had I, but we need to," Grus said. "Once we free the serfs, we ought to help the Menteshe build barriers against the Banished One." *Maybe the Scepter of Mercy will help*, he thought. *But even if it doesn't, we should try*. Aloud, he went on, "We'll still have trouble with them, no doubt, but it'll be trouble like we have with the Thervings—ordinary human trouble. It won't be the kind of trouble we have now."

"That would be good," Pterocles said seriously.

"It would, wouldn't it?" Grus' smile was wistful. "If I only had to worry about ordinary, human troubles . . . Yes, that would be wonderful. Well, here's hoping."

"Make way for His Majesty!" Lanius' guardsmen bawled as they rode into the city of Avornis. "Make way! Make way!"

People scrambled to clear the streets. Lanius wished the troopers wouldn't make such a fuss. He'd told them as much, but they refused to listen to him. Anyone who thought a king gave orders that were always instantly obeyed had never been a king.

"Look! It's the king!" People shouted and pointed, as though seeing him could somehow make a difference in their own lives. And then someone yelled, "Hurrah for King Grus! Beat those Chernagors!" In a heartbeat, everyone was cheering and applauding.

Lanius, by contrast, was fuming and steaming. Not only didn't the people know who Avornis' current foe was, they didn't even know who *he* was. And then, to his own surprise, he started to laugh. Like any king, he'd had wistful thoughts of living a normal life, of going through the streets of his own capital unrecognized. Well, here he was, going through the streets of his own capital, and he certainly seemed unrecognized. This was as close to anonymity as he was ever likely to come.

The palace battlements and, not far away, the heaven-leaping spire of the great cathedral dominated the city skyline. The closer Lanius came, the taller they seemed. He smiled as he got ready to fall back into the routine of palace life. The country holiday had been pleasant, but this was home.

Servants bowed and curtsied when he went up the broad stairway and into the palace. "Your Majesty!" they exclaimed. "Welcome back, Your Majesty!"

"It's good to be back," Lanius answered, over and over again. He beamed at the servants. They knew he wasn't King Grus. He'd never thought that was any special reason for which to admire them, but he did now.

"You'll want a bath, won't you, Your Majesty?" one of the servants said.

That was probably a polite way of telling him he smelled of horse. He couldn't smell it himself; he'd been too close to it for too long. But he nodded. "Thank you very much. A bath would be wonderful."

And it *was* wonderful—a big copper tub to soak in, with plenty of hot water to wash away the stinks and the kinks of a journey on horseback. They brought him wine, too, and put the cup where he could reach it without getting out of the tub.

He was thinking regretfully about getting out and getting dressed when the door to the bathing chamber opened yet again. This time, though, it wasn't another servant with a pitcher of hot water. It was Sosia.

"I hope you had a nice stay in the country," she said, politely if not enthusiastically.

"Thank you—I did," Lanius answered.

"I hope it wasn't *too* nice." Her claws came out, just for a moment.

"Not like that," he said truthfully, though he would have said the same thing even if it hadn't been true. "It's good to see you again," he added, also truthfully. "How are you?"

"I'm going to have a baby."

"Oh," Lanius said, and then, "Oh!" That wasn't the way he'd thought she would answer his question. "I want to give you a hug," he went on, "but I'm afraid I'd soak you if I did."

"You could dry off first," Sosia suggested.

Lanius still didn't much want to come out of the tub, even though he'd been in there for a while. For a baby on the way, though, he put what Sosia wanted first. Out he came. She handed him a towel. He rubbed himself more or less dry, then took her in his arms.

She let out a small squawk. "I thought you'd put some clothes on!"

"Why?" he asked, genuinely curious. He didn't let go of her. In fact, he held her tighter. "What better way to celebrate?"

Sosia squawked again. "In here?"

"It's as good a place as anywhere else," he answered, rising to the occasion. "Do you think the tub is big enough for two?"

"I think you're out of your mind," his wife said. "What if the servants walk in on us?"

"Then they'll have something brand-new to gossip about." Lanius kissed her. "The best way to keep them from walking in on us is to hurry."

"The *best* way to keep them from walking in is not to start in the first place." She tried to sound severe, but her mouth couldn't help turning up at the corners. "You really *are* out of your mind."

"I know." He kissed her again, and steered her toward the gently steaming tub.

They managed. They did hurry. It was more awkward than

Lanius thought it would be, and more water slopped onto the floor than he'd expected. But they had finished and were both dressed by the time a servant did come in.

"Sorry . . . I was so sloppy," Lanius said. He'd almost said, *Sorry we were so sloppy*. That would have given the game away.

The servant only shrugged. "You put towels down, anyways," he said. "That's something. Won't be a lot of mopping to do."

"Good," Lanius said. He steered Sosia again, this time toward the door. "A baby!" he repeated.

"It does happen," she said, and then giggled. "If I'd caught this time instead of before, I might have had a mermaid." Lanius laughed, too. Sosia turned serious again. "I hope it's a boy."

"So do I," Lanius said. "If it's a girl, though, we'll just try again, that's all." Ortalis had said the same thing after Limosa had Capella. They had tried again, and now they had Marinus.

Sosia hesitated in the hallway, then asked, "You don't have any bastards I don't know about, do you?"

"No. By the gods, no!" Lanius said. "What brought that on?"

"Mother thinks Father may have another one out in the provinces somewhere," Sosia answered bleakly. "She's not sure, but some things she's heard make her think so."

"I don't know anything about that," Lanius said. Grus had kept it a secret from him as well as Estrilda—if it was true. And if it was, and if Grus could keep secrets like that . . . *Good*, Lanius thought. *The way things are, good.*

# CHAPTER NINETEEN

Quite a few Menteshe moving around in front of us, Your Majesty," a scout reported to King Grus. "Don't know what they're up to, but they aren't likely to be there because they like the weather."

"No, I wouldn't think so." Grus turned to Hirundo. "This is—what?—the fourth such report that we've gotten this morning. They're getting ready to hit us."

"Did you expect they'd just blow us a kiss and wave us on to Yozgat?" the general replied. "We both figured they had another fight left in them after we beat them the last time. Now we get to see what their great General Bori-Bars has learned— and what we've learned, too. Doesn't that sound like fun?"

To hear him talk about it, it almost did. Grus said, "I'd sooner they'd run away, if you want to know the truth. Anything that makes this whole business easier is fine with me."

"I don't think they're going to run away, worse luck," Hirundo said.

"I don't, either." Grus' gaze sharpened. "In that case, why don't we run away instead?" Hirundo stared at him. He spent some little while explaining. When he was done, he asked, "Do you think we can bring that off?"

"We'll have to hurry if we want to try." Hirundo started to laugh. "Things will get lively if we do—I'll tell you that." Grus nodded. Hirundo asked. "Do you want me to give the orders?"

"If you'd be so kind," Grus said. Hirundo started yelling.

Horns started blaring. Avornans started riding and marching in what seemed like every direction at once. Such apparent chaos usually had order behind it. Grus hoped it did here.

He assumed it did, and called for Pterocles. Getting the wizard's attention in the midst of the commotion Hirundo was stirring up took some doing, but the king managed. He said, "I want you to block any unmasking spells the Menteshe throw this way."

"I'll do my best, Your Majesty, but we haven't set out any masking spells," Pterocles said, puzzlement in his voice.

"You know that, and I know that, but I don't want the nomads finding out," Grus said. "Send back whatever they aim at us. That will give them something to think about, eh?"

"I'll do my best, but this business doesn't come with a guarantee," Pterocles said. "Some of their wizards know what they're doing. That little affair by the river not long ago could have been much worse than it was."

"If they realize you're blocking them, they'll concentrate on beating down what you're doing, won't they?" Grus asked.

"That's what I'd do, anyhow," Pterocles replied.

"So would I. Let's hope they do, too," Grus said. Pterocles scratched his head. If his own wizard was confused, the king could hope the shamans serving Bori-Bars or whoever was in charge of the Menteshe would be, too.

Along with Hirundo and some of the royal guardsmen, he rode forward in the center of the Avornan battle line. Avornan outriders returned to the main body, driven back by the nomads. Roiling dust ahead hid the main force of the Menteshe. Before long, Grus could make out horsemen through the dust they stirred up. "They haven't lost their spirit—that's plain enough," he said.

"They wouldn't be so much trouble if they didn't have nerve," Hirundo said. "But we've already given them two good beatings this summer. If we can manage one more . . ."

"We'll know pretty soon," Grus said.

Before long, arrows began to fly. The Menteshe shouted their ferocious war cries. The Avornans yelled back, roaring out their kingdom's name and King Grus'. Grus didn't know if that raised their spirits, but it never failed to lift his.

A Menteshe arrow hissed past his ear. Behind him, somebody groaned. *That could have been me,* he thought, and shuddered. Even in the best-planned battles, so many things could go wrong. *Do I care if we win if I'm not there to see it? Well, I hope we do, but I'm afraid this campaign will fall to pieces without me.*

He didn't have time to wonder whether that was his vanity talking. The Menteshe seemed to have forgotten the Avornans had trounced them twice in recent weeks. By the way they pressed forward, they might have been the ones who'd done all the winning lately.

And the Avornans, who seemed taken aback by the nomads' aggressiveness, began to drift toward the rear. After shouting and cursing at them, Hirundo turned to Grus and said, "Your Majesty, looks like it's time to retreat."

"It does, doesn't it?" Grus said. "Falling back from the Menteshe . . . They're going to push us hard. They'll want to see if they can break us."

"They'd better not," Hirundo said. "That would be downright embarrassing." It would be worse than embarrassing, but Hirundo always looked on the bright side of things.

Grus guided his gelding back to the north. More and more Avornans were riding in that direction. The Menteshe shouted louder and more ferociously than ever. They pressed the Avornans harder—and Grus' men retreated faster. That encouraged the nomads to press them harder still.

Retreat turned into something that looked a lot like rout. Only a stubborn rear guard kept the Menteshe from smashing the Avornan army to pieces. Even the men in the rear guard kept on retreating for all they were worth. The Menteshe, having lost their earlier fights with the Avornans, pushed hard now, intent on doing the hated foes in front of them as much harm as they could. Any soldiers worthy of their weapons would have done the same.

It ruined them.

Because they had an enemy in front of them, they paid no attention to what lay off to the side—until the stone-throwers and dart-throwers sitting in the shadows cast by a grove of olive trees all opened up at once, throwing them into confusion.

Before the Menteshe had a chance to recover, most of the heavily armored royal guardsmen—who'd waited patiently in the olive grove—set spurs to their horses and thundered forward.

Horn calls rang out through what had been the retreating Avornan army, and the Avornans retreated no more, but went over to the attack. When they did, Grus and Hirundo, who were riding side by side, reached out at the same time and clasped hands with each other. A deliberate retreat was one of the hardest things in war to bring off. When an army pretended to fall back, it all too often started falling back in earnest. But the Avornans turned around and struck as fiercely as Grus could have hoped.

The Menteshe broke. Caught with a blow at their flank and suddenly and unexpectedly assailed from the front as well, they fled in all directions. Escape was the only thing that seemed to matter to them. If they could get away . . .

A lot of them couldn't. A lot of them went down to the guardsmen's lances or were hacked out of the saddle by their swords. At close quarters, Avornan archers could hold their own with the Menteshe, too, and they filled the air with shafts, shooting as fast as they could.

Nomads threw down their weapons and did their best to surrender. As on any battlefield, giving up was a risky business. With their fighting blood up, not all Avornans felt like taking prisoners. And a few Menteshe pretended to surrender and then started fighting again, which did neither them nor their comrades any good.

"Bori-Bars!" The shout went up not too far from Grus. "We have Bori-Bars!"

Grinning, the king clasped hands with Hirundo again. That was one of the things he'd most hoped for. Capturing the able general weakened the nomads. And now the Avornans would be able to question him. Who was his commander? Korkut? Sanjar? The Banished One?

Pterocles pointed at Grus. "I know what you were doing."

"Do you?" Grus said. "I often wonder myself."

"You can't get away with being coy, not this time," the wizard said. "You wanted me to fight the Menteshe so they'd do everything they could to break through my spells—and so they wouldn't do anything else."

"Who, me?" Grus said.

"Yes, you." Pterocles did his best to look severe. "And they were pounding on me, and I was doing everything I could to fend them off, and that only made them pound harder. But we weren't really masking anything after all."

"They never found that out, did they?" Grus asked. Pterocles shook his head. The king grinned again. "That was what I had in mind."

"You know how to get what you want, don't you?"

"I'm not sure yet," Grus answered, the grin slipping as fast as it appeared. "We'll know better as this campaign wears along, won't we?"

Before Pterocles could say anything, a soldier called, "Your Majesty, here's Bori-Bars!" The Menteshe general was still mounted on his rough-coated little horse. His hands were tied in front of him, his feet tied together under the horse's belly. He had a cut over one eye that splashed his swarthy face with blood and an expression that said he wished he were dead.

"Do you speak Avornan?" Grus asked. Reluctantly, Bori-Bars nodded. The king said, "You make a dangerous foe."

"So do you, Your Majesty." The Menteshe scowled. "I hoped you would be the one with ropes." He raised his hands a little.

"Life doesn't always give us what we hope," Grus said, and Bori-Bars nodded again. Leaning forward in the saddle, Grus asked, "Who is your master?"

"At the moment, you are," Bori-Bars answered sourly.

Grus bowed in the saddle. "Well, so I am. But who gave you the orders to attack my army?"

"No one did," Bori-Bars said. "My scouts spotted your men. It looked to be a good place to hit you. It *was* a good place to hit you. But you turned out to be sneakier than I expected. You fought that battle the way one of my folk might. Who would have looked for such a thing from an Avornan?"

"For which I thank you." Grus bowed in the saddle again. "But for whom did you command that army? Who is your superior?"

"I reckon no man my superior." Pride rang in Bori-Bars' voice.

"You are being difficult." Grus exhaled in exasperation. "I will point out to you—once—that you are in a poor position to be difficult. Now then—does that army you commanded owe allegiance to Korkut, or to Sanjar, or to the Banished One?"

"We all owe allegiance to the Fallen Star. Him I will reckon my superior." Bori-Bars still sounded proud. Grus did not understand that and did not particularly want to understand it—it struck him as being proud one was a slave—but he had also seen it from other Menteshe.

It was one more thing he would have to think about another time. "Do you also follow Korkut, or do you also follow Sanjar?"

"I follow the Fallen Star," Bori-Bars said.

"And no one else?" Grus asked. The captured general repeated himself. "If that's yes, then I know of Menteshe who don't like it," Grus told him. "I know of Menteshe who are working against the sorcery that makes it so. I know of Menteshe who want to follow their own will first, and who don't care to be sent halfway to thralldom."

That got through to Bori-Bars. His eyes flashed. "You know of my folk who would turn against the Fallen Star? I say you lie."

"I say you don't know what you're talking about," Grus replied. "I could name names. They would be names you know. But what would be the point? The names will do you no good, not after I send you back to Avornis. You have many, many more questions to answer." He nodded to the men who'd captured Bori-Bars. "Take him away. Put him in the compound with the rest of the captured Menteshe officers, but don't let him speak to them or they to him."

"Yes, Your Majesty," they chorused.

Away went the Menteshe general. Grus summoned the Avornan officer in charge of that compound. He was a stolid, middle-aged fellow named Lagopus. He blinked several times when Grus told him, "I want you to let Bori-Bars escape tonight."

"Your Majesty?" Lagopus dug a finger in his ear, as though wondering if he could have heard right.

"Let him escape. Don't be obvious about it—don't let him know you're letting him—but do it," Grus said. "He knows some things now that will make the Menteshe quarrel among themselves, but only if he gets away. He's the sort who will be looking for a chance. Make sure you give him one."

"Yes, Your Majesty. Just as you say." Lagopus was nothing if not dutiful. He saluted and went back to that compound. He would do as Grus told him. Bori-Bars would get away. And then . . . they would see what they would see.

Princess Limosa curtsied to King Lanius when she came up to him in a palace hallway. The serving woman behind Limosa carried little Prince Marinus. "Hello, Your Majesty," Limosa said. "How are you today?"

"Pretty well, thanks," Lanius answered. "Yourself?"

"I'm fine," she said. "I'm very pleased you and the queen are going to have another baby." She really did sound as though she meant it. Maybe she was blind to the politics all around her. Or maybe she just thought that, with Prince Crex, the succession—at least if it passed through Lanius—was already assured.

"Thank you. So am I. Of course, Sosia will have to do the work," Lanius said.

Limosa laughed. "That's the truth!" she exclaimed. "I think women forget how hard it is after every birth. If they didn't, they wouldn't have more than one baby, and then where would we be?"

"Gone," Lanius said, which made Limosa laugh again. He walked past her and held out his arms. "Let me see Marinus."

The maidservant put the baby in his arms. Marinus stared up at him. The baby was at the age when he smiled at anything and everything. By the way he looked up at Lanius, the king made him the happiest baby in the world just by existing. His little pink hands reached out . . .

Lanius jerked his head back in a hurry. "Oh, no, you don't, you little rascal! You're not going to get a handful of my beard. My children have already done that, and I know how much it hurts." Everything he said around Limosa could turn awkward, even something as innocuous as that. She relished pain. Hastily, he went on, "I think he looks more like you than like Ortalis."

"Yes, I do, too," Limosa answered. If the other thought occurred to her, she gave no sign of it. She went on, "Ortalis isn't so sure. He thinks Marinus has his nose."

Lanius looked down. The baby's nose was the small, mostly shapeless blob common to about eight babies in ten. "Where's the rest of it, in that case?" the king inquired, which sent both Limosa and the serving woman into a fit of the giggles.

"I'll take him back if you like, Your Majesty," the woman said. He handed her Marinus. The baby's face clouded up. He started to cry. Lanius didn't think that was a testimony to his own personality. Marinus sounded fussy and cranky. The maidservant began rocking him in her arms. Sure enough, his eyelids started to sag. "I'll wait until he's sound asleep, then put him in his cradle," the woman told Limosa.

"That will be fine, Pica," Limosa said.

She and Lanius chatted. She did most of the chatting, as the king wasn't overburdened with small talk. He didn't mind; most people did more talking than he did. After a couple of minutes, Pica carried Marinus away. By then, the baby wouldn't have noticed anything short of the ceiling dropping on him.

A little while after that, Limosa said, "I do go on and on."

"No," Lanius said, which wasn't strictly true. In fact, she did go on and on, but he didn't mind. "It's very interesting." That *was* true—she picked up most gossip before it got to him.

"You're kind to say so." Limosa looked around. Lanius understood that glance, having used it a good many times himself—she was seeing whether any servants were close enough to overhear. Satisfied none was, she went on, "And you're kind for not thinking me—stranger than I am." Now her gaze went down to the mosaic tiles on the floor.

"Stranger than you are?" For a moment, Lanius was puzzled. In every way he could think of but one, Limosa was ordinary enough. When he remembered the exception, of course, it made up for a lot of the rest. He felt like looking down at the floor himself. "Oh. That."

"Yes. That." Limosa's chin lifted defiantly. "Well, you are, because you don't." She paused as though sorting through whether that was what she really meant. Lanius needed to do the same thing. They both decided at about the same time that she *had* gotten it right. Relief in her voice, she went on, "You don't act like you think I'm some sort of a monster or something."

"I don't," Lanius said, which was true. He would have said the same thing about Ortalis, and sounded just as sincere—and he would have been lying through his teeth. About Limosa, though, he did mean it. Despite her husband, despite her father, he had nothing at all against her. He tried to figure out why, and to put it into words. The best he could do was, "You just—like what you like, that's all."

"Yes, that really *is* all." Her eyes glowed. "You see? You do understand. Oh! I could just kiss you!"

He could tell she meant it. And, if the look on her face meant what he thought it did, things could easily go on from there after a kiss. The idea of putting a cuckold's horns on his unloving and unlovable brother-in-law had a certain delicious temptation to it. But Lanius was too relentlessly practical to take it any further than being tempted. An affair with a serving girl annoyed nobody but Sosia, and both he and the kingdom could deal with that. An affair with a princess carried much more baggage. Nor did he think Ortalis would wear horns gracefully. On the contrary.

And so, as gently as he could, Lanius said, "I thank you for the thought, but that might not be a good idea."

Limosa's eyes fell open. Maybe she saw for the first time where that kiss might lead. Her cheeks turned the color of iron just out of the forge. "Oh!" she said again, in an altogether different tone of voice. "You're right. Maybe it isn't."

Gently still, Lanius added, "Besides, what you like isn't . . . what very many people like."

She turned redder yet, which he wouldn't have believed if he hadn't seen it. In a faintly strangled voice, she said, "That isn't *all* I like."

Lanius was willing to believe her. She wouldn't have borne Capella and Marinus if she hadn't done other things, and they were things she was likely to like if she did them. But exactly what she liked and didn't like wasn't really his business, or anyone's except hers and perhaps Ortalis'.

She must have realized that, too, because she squeaked, "Please excuse me," and hurried away. Lanius stared after her. He sighed. Maybe they would be able to talk more openly with each other from now on. Or maybe they wouldn't be able to talk at all. Time would tell, nothing else.

"Time will tell." Lanius said it out loud. It was true of so many things. He wanted to know whether Sosia would have a boy or a girl. Time would tell. He wanted to know how Grus' army was doing down in the Menteshe country. Time would tell. He wanted to know if Grus would reclaim the Scepter of Mercy. Time would tell. He wanted to know what the Scepter could do in the hands of a King of Avornis. Time would—or might—tell.

"But it won't tell soon enough!" Lanius said that out loud, too. He wanted to know all those things *now*. He didn't want to have to wait to find out. News from Grus might be only minutes away. Lanius hoped so. He surely wouldn't have to wait more than days for that. With the others, though, he would have to be more patient.

He'd had a lot of time to learn patience. Snaking through the archives had helped him acquire it. So had years of being altogether powerless. If he hadn't been patient then, he might have gone mad. He laughed. Some of the people in the palace probably thought he had, although, he hoped, in a harmless way.

And patience had paid. Now he had more power than he'd ever expected, more power than he'd ever dreamed of in those first few years after Grus put the crown on his own head.

"Your Majesty! Your Majesty!"

The call brought Lanius' head up like a hunting hound's. "I'm here," he said. "What's going on?" Good news? Bad news? Scandal? One thing was certain—it wasn't Pouncer stealing a spoon from the kitchens. But had another moncat finally found Pouncer's way out of the chamber?

"A courier's looking for you, Your Majesty," a maidservant answered.

"Well, bring him here, by the gods!" the king exclaimed. If this was news from the south, time would tell very soon indeed.

When he saw the courier, he thought the man had news from Grus. The fellow had plainly ridden hard. But the message he gave Lanius had nothing—or rather, not much—to do with events south of the Stura. A plague had broken out in the town of Priene, on the coast. The city governor asked the king to send wizards to help put it down.

"I can do that," Lanius told the courier. "I *will* do that, as fast as I can." Priene was an out-of-the-way place, a backwater where things happened slowly if they happened at all. The pestilence that had been such a worry along well-traveled routes during the winter was getting there only now.

Lanius called for pen and ink and paper. He wrote a message to the people of Priene, telling them help was on the way. Then he wrote a message to Aedon the wizard, telling him either to go to Priene himself or to send another wizard familiar with the spell he'd used to cure Queen Estrilda. *Knowing the inconvenience of this request, I promise the reward will be commensurate to it,* he finished.

Once both messages were on their way, Lanius started laughing again. Time would tell him what he wanted to know, all right, but at its pace, not his.

"By the gods!" Grus said softly. "Will you look at that?"

Hirundo looked south with him. The general spoke a word no Avornan general had ever used before in sight of the thing of which he spoke. "Yozgat."

"We're here." Grus shook his head in wonder. "We're really here. I can hardly believe it."

"Well, you'd better, because it's true. Now all we have to do is take the place." Hirundo made it sound easy. Maybe it was, compared to advancing from the Stura all the way to Yozgat. Compared to anything else? Grus didn't think so.

They were still three or four miles from the city that held the Scepter of Mercy, the city that had been Prince Ulash's capital for so long, the city that now belonged—however tenuously—

to Prince Korkut. The drawbridge over the moat was down; the gates were open. Tiny in the distance, Menteshe horsemen were riding into Yozgat. The warriors inside had plenty of time to close the gates before the Avornans drew near enough to threaten the place.

Grus got his first look at the fortifications he would face, and liked none of what he saw. Trabzun, the year before, hadn't been easy. Yozgat, by all the signs, would be harder. Its walls were higher and better built; that was obvious even from a distance. Inside the city, tall towers would make formidable strongpoints even if the Avornans forced an entry. And the palace—on a hill near the center of the town—plainly doubled as a citadel. If what Lanius said was right, that citadel housed not only the reigning Menteshe prince, whoever he happened to be, but also the Scepter of Mercy.

The king made himself smile. "If it were easy, somebody would have done it a long time ago. But we've already done a lot of hard things. One more? By now, one more hard thing should be easy for us."

He knew he was talking more to cheer up his men than for himself. He also knew he was making things simpler than they really were. Taking Yozgat wouldn't be one hard thing to do. It would be scores, hundreds, thousands of hard things. They would have to surround the city, have to fend off whatever attacks Menteshe outside the walls made on them, have to force a breach in the walls, have to defeat the garrison, have to storm the citadel . . .

"One more hard thing," Hirundo said. "That's just right." The soldiers who heard him would believe him. Grus gave him a sharp look. If Hirundo hadn't just said, *You must be out of your mind,* nobody ever had. But the general's face was as innocent as that of a graying, bearded, scarred, lined, leathery child.

"We'll put some stone-throwers upstream along the riverbank," Grus said. "Curse me if I want the Menteshe sneaking supplies in there by boat."

"Sounds reasonable. We ought to put some downstream, too, in case they try to row up against the current," Hirundo said.

"Olor's beard!" Grus exclaimed. "All these years on horse-back and I've finally learned to ride. And now here you are, thinking like a river-galley captain. What is this world coming to?"

"Beats me. Whatever it's coming to, I wish it would hurry up and get there," Hirundo said.

As the Avornan army neared Yozgat, the drawbridge rose. The heavy chains that drew it up rattled. After it rose, a massive iron portcullis thudded down in front of it. Grus muttered to himself. The city of Avornis had such fortifications, but he wished Yozgat didn't.

Not all the Menteshe outside Yozgat had gotten in before the defenders sealed off the city. Most of the ones left out there on the plain galloped off. A few rode at the Avornans and shot off the arrows they had in their quivers. Hirundo sent bands of scouts to outflank them. Some of them noticed and fled before the scouts could block their escape. Others, less lucky or less alert, didn't get away.

A herald with a flag of truce came up onto the wall when the Avornan army drew near enough for him to shout out over the moat. In good Avornan, he called, "Prince Korkut commands you to leave this city. If you leave it at once, you may go in peace. Otherwise, the full weight of his wrath, and of the Fallen Star's, will fall on you."

Despite mutterings from his guardsmen—who did their best to make sure with their stout shields that no Menteshe could pick him off at long range—Grus rode up to the edge of the moat and shouted back. "Let Prince Korkut give me one present, and he is welcome to keep his city and his land. I will go home to the Kingdom of Avornis straightaway. I swear it in the names of King Olor and Queen Quelea and the rest of the gods in the heavens."

"We care nothing for those foolish, useless gods," the herald replied. "But say your say. What would you have of His Highness?"

"The Scepter of Mercy," Grus said. Korkut had turned him down the year before. Then, though, the Avornans were far from Yozgat. Now they moved to surround it even as Grus parleyed with Korkut's man.

"He told me you would say this," the herald shouted. "The answer is no, as it has always been, as it will always be."

"Then my answer is also no," Grus said. "The fight will go on. When Sanjar is prince over Yozgat, he will show better sense." That was probably untrue, but it should give Korkut something new and unpalatable to think about. Yozgat was being cut off from the outside world. The defenders couldn't be sure Sanjar hadn't made common cause with Grus.

"You will be sorry," the herald said, and ceremoniously lowered the flag of truce.

"Get back, Your Majesty!" three guardsmen said at the same time, and with identical urgency in their voices. As soon as that flag of truce went down, the Menteshe did start shooting. Arrows thudded into shields near the king. One guard and one horse were wounded before Grus and his men got out of range.

He wished that hadn't happened, but he didn't know what he could have done to stop it. If the Menteshe in Yozgat wanted to parley, he had no choice but to talk to them. There was a chance they would surrender the Scepter in exchange for his withdrawal. He had the feeling Korkut might have done it if he didn't fear the Banished One.

*Well, let him,* Grus thought. *I'll show him he'd better fear Avornis, too.*

Avornans shot back at the Menteshe on the walls of Yozgat. The Menteshe, with stronger bows and the advantage of height, had the better of that until Grus' artisans got some dart-throwers in position and started skewering them. Korkut's men did not seem to have any of those up on the walls.

Hirundo said, "I think I'd better get the outer ditch and palisade made before the inner ones this time."

"Oh? Why is that?" Grus answered his own question, saying, "Because every nomad south of the Stura is liable to be heading this way just as fast as he can ride?"

"Not *every* nomad, Your Majesty." Hirundo pointed to the walls of Yozgat. "A lot of them are already here."

"So they are. That's a relief, isn't it?" Grus said. They both laughed. If they didn't laugh, they would start worrying. Grus knew he would start worrying very soon anyhow. He looked toward Yozgat. "I wonder how much food they've got in there."

"Wonder how much we can scrounge off the countryside, too," Hirundo said. "If we knew this stuff ahead of time, maybe we wouldn't have to fight the battles. Since we don't, we do."

Grus thought about that. After he worked it through, he nodded. "Right," he said, and then, "I think."

"Don't fret, Your Majesty." Hirundo grinned at him. "Let Korkut fret. Let the Banished One fret. Do you think they're not? You'd better think again if you do. When was the last time they had to figure out what to do with an Avornan army besieging Yozgat?"

"If this isn't a first for Korkut, he's a *lot* older than I think he is," Grus observed, which made Hirundo laugh. Grus added, "It's been a long, long time for the Banished One, too. We're giving him something to think about, anyway."

Korkut kept his archers busy on the walls, making things as hard as they could for the Avornans. That impressed Grus less than it might have. If he'd intended to try to storm Yozgat right away, a strong, aggressive defense would have mattered more. As things were, it just meant the Avornans set up their inner perimeter a little farther from the wall than they would have otherwise. Even so, soldiers and engineers went about their business with unflustered competence. This wasn't the first siege for most of them.

The king's pavilion rose between the inner and outer perimeters. Hirundo's tent and Pterocles' went up nearby. So did the one that Otus shared with Fulca. The ex-thrall bowed to Grus. "It makes me happy to see the Menteshe beaten, Your Majesty," he said. "For so long, I did not know they could be."

"For a long time, I didn't know they could be, either, not south of the Stura," Grus said. "You have Pterocles to thank for that."

"I have Pterocles to thank for *me,*" Otus said. "I have Pterocles to thank for my woman—even if she does tell me what to do."

"That can happen," Grus said. "Do you tell her what to do, too?" When Otus nodded, the king clapped him on the back.

"Then things are pretty near even, sounds like. That's about how they ought to be."

He was glad to go to bed that night. He liked staying in one spot more and more as he got older. Not having to break camp and travel in the morning had a strong attraction for him. Even a siege camp could come to resemble a home as he spent time there.

But he was anything but glad when, sometime in the night, the Banished One appeared before him in all his fearful majesty. "You will not enter Yozgat. You shall never set foot in Yozgat. This I tell you, and tell you truly," the exiled god said.

When that bell-like voice resounded inside Grus' head, not believing it was almost impossible. Grus did his best. "I'll take my chances," he replied.

"They will bring you sorrow." Again, the Banished One left no room for doubt or disagreement.

Instead of disagreeing, Grus tried to deflect. "Life is full of sorrow. Facing sorrow is part of what makes a man."

The Banished One's laughter might have been a lash of ice. "What do you know of sorrow, wretched mortal? I was cast down from the *heavens* to this accursed place. Shall I rejoice in it? When you know exile, you will understand—as much as a flea understands a dog."

"I don't intend to be exiled, thank you very much." Grus managed such defiance as he could.

All he won was more scorn from the Banished One. "As though what a man intends matters! It will be as I say it will, not as you intend."

Grus woke then, with the usual shudders after confronting the Banished One. The exiled god had sounded even more certain than usual. His certainty was part of what made him so terrible—and so terrifying. *He's lying. He wants to confuse me. He wants to trick me.* Telling himself that was easy for Grus. Believing it? Believing it came ever so much harder.

# CHAPTER TWENTY

The dispatch rider handed Lanius the letter from his waxed-leather message tube, then bowed and departed. Lanius broke the seal and began to read. As usual, Grus came straight to the point. *Your Majesty,* he wrote, *We have surrounded Yozgat, and we are laying siege to it. All goes as well as possible. With the gods' help, the Scepter of Mercy will soon be in Avornan hands once more.*

"We have surrounded Yozgat." Lanius read the phrases aloud so he could savor them. "We are laying siege to it. Soon to be in Avornan hands."

He had been waiting to hear those phrases ever since Prince Ulash's sons squared off against each other. That seemed a long time now—until he thought about how long the kingdom had been waiting for them. Four hundred years. A long, *long* wait, but one finally over.

Lanius shook his head. The wait was almost at an end. When a King of Avornis actually took up the Scepter of Mercy, then it would be over. Not until then. He had no trouble imagining all the things that still might go wrong.

He called for pen and ink and parchment. He had no doubt Grus could imagine everything that might go wrong, too. Now, though, now was not the time to dwell on such things. *Congratulations,* he wrote, and then, after a pause, *Your Majesty. All Avornis is proud of what you have achieved, and hopes you may achieve more still. Is it time to begin what we discussed when you were here in the north this past winter?*

He sealed the letter and sent it off. He wanted it to get to Grus as fast as it possibly could. There was no room for jealousy, not about this.

Realizing he shouldn't be the only one in the palace who had such excellent news, he hurried toward the bedchamber to tell Sosia. On the way there, he came up to Ortalis and a captain of the guards. The officer's mailshirt clinked as he bowed to Lanius. The king bowed back, more than a little absently. To Ortalis, he said, "Your father is besieging Yozgat down in the south."

"That's very good to hear, Your Majesty," the guard captain said.

"Yes, very good." But Ortalis sounded much less impressed than his soldierly companion. Looking down his nose at Lanius, he said, "Makes training a moncat pretty tame, doesn't it?"

He laughed uproariously. The guardsman looked as though he didn't know whether to laugh, too, or to look embarrassed. He tried doing both at once; what came out was a distinctly uneasy chuckle.

As for Lanius, he didn't think he'd been so angry since Grus announced he was appropriating more than his share of the crown. The hand that wasn't holding the letter from Grus now bunched into a fist. Instead of trying to wipe the smirk off Ortalis' handsome face, though, Lanius stormed away. Ortalis laughed again. So did the guard captain, but he still sounded nervous.

"Quelea's mercy!" Sosia exclaimed when Lanius thundered into the bedchamber. "What happened to you? You look like you want to murder someone." Without a word, he thrust Grus' letter at her. Once she read it, she seemed more bewildered than ever. "But this is *good* news. Or am I missing something?"

"No, it's good news, all right." Lanius' growl made it seem anything but. He summed up what Ortalis had said, and the way Sosia's brother looked and sounded while he said it.

"Oh," Sosia said once the bile had poured out of him. She shrugged helplessly. "You know what Ortalis is like. I'm sorry, but he *is* like that, and nobody can do anything about it. If you let him see he's gotten your goat, he's won."

She was right. Lanius knew as much. He passed off most of

Ortalis' gibes with a smile and a nod—if his brother-in-law didn't see him angry, he had less incentive to sting again. "This was just too raw to ignore," he muttered.

"It shouldn't have been." Sosia was doing her best to seem quiet and reasonable, the role Lanius usually took for himself. She continued, "It's not even so much that he was wrong, even if he *was* rude. Training that moncat *doesn't* seem like much next to besieging Yozgat."

"Not you, too!" Lanius shouted. Sosia stared at him in astonishment complete and absolute. He was as furious as she'd been when she caught him with each new serving girl. She was usually the one who yelled and threw things. Now he looked around for the closest missile, and she was lucky he didn't find one ready to hand.

"What's the matter?" she asked helplessly. "What did I say?"

"You're as bad as your brother!" Lanius roared. He didn't calculate that to wound, but it did the job. He rushed out of the bedchamber and slammed the door behind him.

Servants scattered like frightened little birds when they saw his face. If they hadn't scattered, he would have walked over them or through them. Once he got to the archives, he stormed in as fiercely as he'd swarmed out of the royal bedchamber. He slammed that door behind him, too. The boom echoed through the vast hall.

Once the echoes faded, he found himself in the midst of silence. Whatever waited outside couldn't touch him here. He knew what he'd done for Avornis. Grus also knew what he'd done for Avornis, even if the other king sometimes needed reminding. If no one in the palace knew . . .

*It's because you haven't told anyone here,* Lanius thought. He knew why he hadn't, too. The less he said, the less other people knew, the better for the kingdom. The better for the kingdom, yes, but the harder for him. He'd just painfully run into that. Until he ran into it, he didn't realize how hard it would be.

Soldiers made great swarms of hurdles from brush and branches. They piled them out of fire-arrow range of the walls of Yozgat.

Grus didn't know if he was going to try to storm Korkut's capital. If he did, he would need some way to cross the moat. Hurdles, he thought, gave his men the best chance.

The Menteshe had already tried to run barges piled high with sacks of grain under the walls. The Avornans had captured some and burned others. A few had managed to unload their supplies.

That wouldn't happen anymore—or Grus hoped with all his heart it wouldn't, anyhow. Now, along with the stone- and dart-throwers by the riverbank, he had boats on the river, too. They weren't proper river galleys. They were what his men could capture and what his carpenters could knock together with the timber they found locally. They floated, and he could fill them with archers and spearmen. As far as he knew, the Menteshe didn't have any river galleys in these parts, either. Up until now, why would they have needed them here?

Korkut's men seemed alert. They shot from the top of the wall. Every so often, one of their arrows would hit an Avornan. Grus' artificers set up more and more catapults that bore on the walls. Every so often, one of their darts would pierce a Menteshe or one of their stones would smash a man or two flat. Neither side did the other much harm. Each reminded the other it was still in the fight and still serious about it.

Grus' engineers began digging to see if they could undermine Yozgat's walls the way they had with Trabzun's. They reported to him with long faces. "Won't be easy, Your Majesty," one of them said. "Soil's pretty soft, and the water from the moat seeps on down. I don't see how we can keep a tunnel dry."

He listened, he thanked them, and then he summoned Pterocles. After describing the problem, he asked, "What can you do about it?"

The wizard frowned. "I'm not sure I have a spell strong enough to shore up the bottom of a moat. Even if I did, it wouldn't be something I could keep the Menteshe from noticing. There are quiet magics and loud ones, if you know what I mean. That sort of thing couldn't be louder if I yelled at the top of my lungs."

Grus grunted discontentedly. He'd asked for miracles from Pterocles, and he'd gotten a lot of them. *No* wasn't what he wanted to hear. He asked, "Could you come up with something new?"

"Maybe," Pterocles said. "Do you want to send me back to the city of Avornis and let me do somewhere between six months and six years of research? By the time I'm done, I may have something worthwhile. I *may,* mind you—I can't promise anything."

That was *no* again, a polite *no,* but *no* all the same. Grus liked it no better than he had before. "Do you think any of the other wizards with the army will give me a different answer?" he inquired.

"Some of them may," Pterocles answered. Grus brightened—until the sorcerer went on, "I don't think they'll be telling the truth if they do, though. But some people do like to let you think they can do more than they really can."

That was depressingly true. Grus had seen it more times than he could count. Just to check, he called in several other wizards and asked what they could do about the moat. Sure enough, one man promised everything but to drink it dry with a hollow reed. Grus asked him several pointed questions and found out he knew less than he pretended.

Quailing, the wizard asked, "What are you going to do to me, Your Majesty?"

"I ought to give you a good kick in the backside for wasting my time," the king answered. "Go on, though—get out of here. I've seen that you can cure thralls. Stick to that. If you want to tell tales, tell them to your grandchildren when you have some." Chastened, the wizard hurried away.

Once he was gone, Grus called Hirundo and said, "I'm afraid we're going to have to do it the hard way."

"I didn't really expect anything else, Your Majesty," the general replied. "Did you?"

"Well, I hoped for something better, anyhow." Grus eyed Yozgat's formidable defenses. "Breaking in won't be easy."

"If it were easy, somebody would have done it a long time ago," Hirundo said. "One way or another, we'll come up with something."

As usual, Grus admired his optimism. Also as usual, the king had trouble matching it. But his own spirits rose when he got a letter from Lanius telling him Sosia was expecting another baby. Up there in the north, life went on. And one reason it went on was because of what he was doing down here. Even if he didn't take the Scepter of Mercy, the Menteshe would be too busy on their own soil to trouble Avornis for a long time to come.

Grus shook his head. That wasn't the right way to look at things. He was giving himself a comfortable excuse for failing. He didn't need that, and neither did the army. He hadn't come all the way down to Yozgat to fail. One way or another, he and the army *had* come up with something, again and again and again. Once more? Why not? Maybe Hirundo had the right idea after all.

But Grus also knew he hadn't been exaggerating or sounding a note of gloom and doom. Breaking into Yozgat *wouldn't* be easy. The city was well fortified, and the defenders seemed in good spirits—or maybe they just feared what the Banished One would do to them if they let the place fall. Either way, they weren't going to throw down their bows and their spears and surrender, however much he wished they would. He would have to get them out and get his men in.

"How?" he wondered aloud. He couldn't go under the moat—that seemed all too clear. His soldiers couldn't sprout wings and fly, either. He didn't even waste his time and Pterocles' asking about such impossibilities. That left storming the city, which wasn't impossible in the same sense of the word as the other two choices, but which didn't look very promising, either.

*Or we can starve the Menteshe out—if we* can *starve them out,* Grus thought. He had no idea what his chances there were. He did know keeping his own army supplied would be none too easy. The nomads would do everything they could to disrupt grain shipments from the north. They would probably burn or trample as many nearby crops as they could, too.

*If it were easy, somebody would have done it a long time ago.* Hirundo had grinned as he said that. Grus wasn't grinning. Taking Yozgat *wouldn't* be easy. He had to hope it wouldn't be impossible. More than that—he had to find a way to make sure it wasn't impossible.

At the moment, he had no idea what that way was.

*Don't you think you should have had a better plan before you came this far?* he asked himself. The only answer he could come up with was, *I didn't expect Yozgat to be quite so tough.* That was true, but didn't seem good enough.

Inside Yozgat stood the formidable princely palace that also served as a citadel. Even if the city itself fell, the citadel could hold out for . . . well, who could guess how long? And the Scepter of Mercy . . . was in the citadel, of course. Where else would it be?

Grus shook his head. He'd come so far. He'd done so much. No King of Avornis since the Scepter was lost had even come close to what he'd done. Freeing so many thralls south of the Stura would complicate the nomads' lives for years to come, if not for generations. And yet, if he had to go back to the city of Avornis without the Scepter, he would have failed. That was why he'd come.

The Menteshe knew it, too. He could feel that. If he went home without the Scepter of Mercy, he would never see Yozgat again. He didn't know why he was so sure, but he was. *Now or never,* he thought unhappily.

Maybe this was what the Banished One wanted him to feel. Maybe the exiled god was trying to lure him into something foolish, something rash. Maybe—but he didn't think so. Something on the wind told him that whatever would happen would happen *soon*.

He looked down at the hair on his arms. A lot of it had gone gray while he was looking in some other direction. Gray or not, though, it prickled up as though lightning were in the air. It also thought something important was on the way. Before this campaigning season was over, Avornis would have an answer.

A good answer? The right answer? For now, he had to hope so.

Marinus smiled up at Lanius and reached out with pink, chubby hands. Not for the first time, the king jerked his head back from the baby in a hurry.

Ortalis laughed at him, saying, "That's why I trim my beard closer than you do—less to hang on to."

"My children don't grab and yank anymore," Lanius said, though he'd worn it long even when they did.

"Ah, but you're going to have another one." Ortalis looked at him sidelong. "Marinus there got you back into bed with my sister."

"No," Lanius said, though the answer to that was *yes*. He sent Ortalis a sidelong glance of his own. His was wary; for Ortalis to mention the succession even glancingly was out of the ordinary, and anything out of the ordinary was liable to be dangerous. Anything that had to do with Ortalis was also liable to be dangerous; he still steamed at how Grus' legitimate son had wounded him not long before.

Ortalis laughed again. Lanius would have preferred almost any other sound. The laugh tried to hide fear and mockery and scorn, and magnified them instead. "You or me?" Ortalis said. "Your son or my son?"

There it was, out in the open, naked and bleeding. Lanius tried to make light of it. His laugh was—he hoped—easier than his brother-in-law's. "I don't know why *we're* worrying about it," he said. "Your father will have set it up to work the way *he* wants it to."

He should have hated that idea. He wanted to be his own man, or at least to have the illusion that he was his own man. But the notion that Grus was firmly in charge held attractions, reassurances, of its own. It made him think of how things might have been if his own father had lived longer.

Slowly, Ortalis shook his head. Now he was the one who said, "No," and he meant it with every fiber of his being. "No," he repeated in a soft voice, but one no less certain for that. "My father is not going to run this. Once he's gone, by the gods, he's *gone.*"

"What are we going to do about it, then?" Lanius asked. "I don't want to go to war with you. Whenever the kingdom has a civil war, it loses no matter who wins."

"We'll settle it, the two of us," Ortalis answered. But he didn't say how he thought they should settle it, or what sort of settlement it might be. Instead, he scooped up his baby son, who giggled. "My father won't have anything to do with it. Not a thing, you hear me?"

"I hear you," Lanius said, almost as though he were gentling a wild animal. He felt that way. Ortalis seemed to think it was more important that Grus not be involved in the succession than who ended up succeeding. That made no sense to Lanius, but plainly it did to his brother-in-law.

"All right." Ortalis breathed heavily, his nostrils flaring each time he inhaled. "That's how it's going to be. *We'll* take care of things. *He* won't." He carried Marinus away.

Lanius was glad to see him go. Sweat trickled down the king's sides from his armpits. He hated confrontations. He didn't do them well, and he didn't relish fights or arguments of any kind. And this one . . .

What he'd wanted to scream at Ortalis was, *Not now! You thick-skulled dunderhead, not now! This isn't the time for these things. Wait until we know what happens in the south, for better or for worse.*

Would Ortalis have listened if he'd shouted something like that? He didn't think so. Ortalis was a master of timing—of bad timing, that is. He saw what he wanted and he grabbed for it. He didn't think of anything past that. *Sometimes I wish I didn't, either,* Lanius thought.

He needed a while to realize Ortalis hadn't threatened him. Ortalis hadn't threatened Grus, either. He hadn't sounded friendly, but how could anyone sound friendly talking about the succession? All Grus' legitimate son had said was that he and Lanius would have to settle things after Grus was dead. How could anyone disagree with that?

When Lanius told Sosia what Ortalis said, her eyes lit up. She might have been Ortalis spotting a deer on the hunt. "Write that down and send it to my father," she said. "Write it down just the way you told it to me. As soon as his orders get back here, Ortalis will end up in the Maze, and that will be that."

"Why?" Lanius said. "It really was harmless."

"If Ortalis is worrying about the succession, it's not harmless." Sosia spoke with great conviction. "A scorpion couldn't be more dangerous. A snake couldn't be. Write to my father. He'll say the same thing."

But Lanius shook his head. "Not now. He has more important things to worry about."

"More important than this?" Sosia didn't believe a word of it.

"More important than this," Lanius said firmly. "If the army is outside of Yozgat, that's more important than anything." He started to say that Ortalis could overthrow him and the siege would still be more important. He started to, but he didn't.

Sosia looked down her nose at him even as things were. She looked very much like her brother then, which she didn't usually do. Lanius hated the thought, which didn't make it any less true. Now Sosia was the one who started to say something but didn't. He knew what it would have been—something rude about Pouncer. Ortalis would have said it. He *had* said it. Still, not hearing it but watching her think it hurt almost as much as her shouting it would have.

Lanius made himself shrug. He knew what he'd done. And he knew what he'd written to Grus. Now all he had to do was wait for the other king's reply—and hope it was the one he wanted to hear.

For once, Grus looked to the east, not the south. The walls of Yozgat dominated the horizon, all the more so when silhouetted against the lightening predawn sky. Everything seemed quiet on the walls. Grus had done everything he could to keep the Menteshe and the Banished One from learning when he would order an assault. He hadn't known himself. Every night before going to bed, he'd tossed two coins. On the night he first got two heads . . . That had been last night. He'd left his pavilion then, told Hirundo, "Tomorrow," and gone back to get what sleep he could.

And now tomorrow was here.

He turned to Hirundo, who stood beside him. "Are we ready?"

"If we're not, it isn't because of anything we haven't done up until now," the general answered. With each moment of growing light, the gilded armor he and Grus wore seemed to shine more brightly.

"Then let's go," Grus said.

Nodding casually, Hirundo walked over to the trumpeters waiting nearby. He set a hand on the closest one's shoulder and spoke in a low, casual voice. The trumpeter and his comrades raised their horns to their lips and blew the call for the attack. A heartbeat later, other musicians all around the encirclement relayed the call to the waiting men.

The soldiers sprang into action as though they were performing some elaborate dance. Dart- and stone-throwers started shooting at the top of the wall, trying to clear the Menteshe from it. Archers ran forward to get into range and added ordinary arrows to the mix. Men flung hurdles into the moat, to give attackers and scaling ladders purchase for the assault on the walls.

"Let's go! Let's go!" sergeants screamed. "Keep moving, gods curse your stupid, empty heads!"

More slowly than they might have, the Menteshe realized Grus' men were trying to storm Yozgat. Their own horns rang out, on harsher, brassier notes than the ones Avornan trumpets used. Grus could hear their guttural shouts of alarm, and their own officers and underofficers shouting commands and advice probably not much different from what his men were using. Anyone who didn't hurry in an attack was liable to be in trouble, from the enemy or from his own side.

The thud of stones smacking against the wall was like a giant landing haymaker after haymaker. Engines groaned and clunked as artificers tugged on windlasses and loaded new stone balls and darts onto them. They clacked and swooshed and bucked when the missiles flew off against Yozgat.

"Forward the ladders!" Hirundo shouted.

Was it too soon? Had enough hurdles gone into the moat to support the ladders and the men who would climb them? Grus thought he would have waited a little longer before giving the command. But he also knew he might have been wrong. Hirundo had keen judgment for such things.

"Come on!" the king yelled. "You can do it!"

He hoped they could do it. Now the sun climbed up over the horizon, spilling light across the countryside. Avornans started swarming up a ladder. The Menteshe at the top of the wall pushed it over with a forked pole. The soldiers on it shrieked as they fell back to earth.

Heavy rocks crashed down on other climbing soldiers. The Menteshe greeted others with boiling water and red-hot sand. A few men gained a lodgement on top of the wall—but not for long. The defenders swarmed over them and overwhelmed them before they could be reinforced. Grus cursed. He knew he was too old to lead a charge up a ladder. He knew it, but he wished he were leading one just the same.

Hirundo was watching the fight as intently as he was—and had sworn as loudly and as foully when the Menteshe stamped out the Avornan foothold at the top of the wall. Now, his mouth as tight as though he were trying to hold in the pain of a wound, the general turned to the king and said, "I don't think we're going to be able to get up, Your Majesty."

Grus had already begun to fear the same thing. Even so, he asked, "What about the far side of the wall, the one we can't see from here?"

"Horns would have brought us the news," Hirundo said.

"Hmm." Grus knew that, too—at least as well as Hirundo did. He was looking for excuses to go on with the attack. "No chance at all, you say?"

"If we'd been able to hang on to that little stretch where we made it onto the wall for a minute—then we'd have a chance, and a good one," the general replied. "The way things are? No. We're just throwing men away, and we're not getting anything much for them."

Another scaling ladder went over. Faintly, the frightened cries of the falling Avornan soldiers came to Grus' ears. They might have proved Hirundo's point for him. Grus swore again. Hirundo set a sympathetic hand on his shoulder. "These things don't always work out just the way we wish they would."

"No, eh? I never would have noticed," Grus said. Hirundo chuckled. Grus kicked at the ground and kicked up a cloud of dust. That didn't get him anywhere. He kicked up another one. Then his shoulders slumped. "Order the retreat, curse it."

"I'll do it." Hirundo spoke to the trumpeters. The mournful horn calls rang out. Slowly, sullenly, the Avornans pulled back from the walls of Yozgat. At first, the defenders seemed to think the withdrawal was a trick. When they realized that it wasn't, that Grus' men really were retreating, they whooped and jeered the way any soldiers who'd driven back their foes would have done.

Grus said several other things he wouldn't have if things had gone better. He kicked up almost enough dust to hide Yozgat. He wished a dust storm like the one that had afflicted his army would sweep down on Prince Korkut's fortress. But that storm hadn't been natural. The Banished One wouldn't inflict anything like it on a fortress his men held.

"Shall we get ready to try it again, Your Majesty?" Hirundo asked. "Next time, we may catch 'em napping."

"Yes, so we may," Grus said. "But if we don't, how much will it cost us? How long can we go on trying to storm the walls before we throw our own army away or ruin its spirit?"

"That's always an interesting question, isn't it?" Hirundo said. "You can't know the answer this soon, or I don't think you can. But we ought to be able to tell before we get in trouble pushing the men too far."

"Yes, we ought to," Grus agreed bleakly. "Will we, though?"

Before Hirundo could answer, a courier who smelled powerfully of sweat and of horse came up and saluted, saying, "Excuse me, Your Majesty, but I've got a letter from, uh, the other king for you."

"Have you?" Grus said, amused in spite of himself. Even after all these years, ordinary people didn't always know what to make of the arrangement he'd made with Lanius. Well, he didn't always know what to make of it himself, either, even after all these years. He held out his hand. "I'm always interested in seeing what King Lanius has to say."

"Here you are." The rider handed him the message tube. He opened it, took out the letter, broke the seal, unrolled the sheet, and began to read. Lanius wrote in large letters he had no trouble making out at arm's length. And the question the other king asked . . .

Grus started laughing before he paused to wonder what was funny. The question wasn't unreasonable, especially in light of what had just happened in front of the walls of Yozgat—in front of them, yes, and briefly on top of them, but not beyond them. If the Avornan army had gotten beyond them, then Lanius' question wouldn't have needed answering so urgently.

As things stood, Grus wasn't in much of a position to say he had any better ideas than the one Lanius had come up with. All he'd thought of was trying more and more assaults on the walls, in the hope that one of them worked. That was a hope, but no more than a hope. Lanius' scheme wasn't guaranteed, either—far from it. But the Menteshe would be looking for more of the same from the Avornan army. Whatever else you could say about it, Lanius' scheme wasn't more of the same.

In spite of himself, Grus started laughing again. He called for pen and ink. "By the gods, we'll see who's laughing when I'm done," he said as he wrote.

Tinamus bowed to King Lanius. "Hello, Your Majesty," the builder said. "May I please speak with you in private?"

"I don't see why not," Lanius replied. "Why don't you come out into the garden, then, and tell me what's on your mind?"

Something obviously was. Tinamus looked pale and worried, as though he hadn't been sleeping well. Guards came out with him and the king, but stayed far enough away to let them talk without being overheard. Butterflies fluttered from flower to flower. Sometimes Lanius liked to come out as dusk was falling, when buzzing, humming hawk moths replaced the butterflies.

The garden's beauty was lost on Tinamus. His clever hands twisted and writhed. They might have had lives—unhappy lives—of their own. "I hardly know where to begin," he said.

"Many people think the beginning is one of the better places," Lanius remarked.

His sarcasm flew right over Tinamus' head. Hands still clutching each other, the builder asked, "Have you ever had—bad dreams?"

"Oh," Lanius said. Half a dozen words, and everything was clear—clearer to him, probably, than it was to Tinamus. "Yes, by the gods, I have. So the Banished One finally decided to visit you, too, did he?"

Tinamus looked astonished, then flabbergasted. "How could you possibly know that?" Tinamus demanded.

"You asked me if I've had bad dreams. The only dreams that are *that* bad are from . . . him," Lanius said. "What did he tell you?"

"That he was going to punish me for building what I built

for you," Tinamus answered. "That I deserved to be punished, because I was making a nuisance of myself."

"Congratulations," Lanius said somberly.

That struck home—struck home and angered Tinamus. "You shouldn't joke at other people's misfortune," he said.

"I wasn't. I wouldn't. I'm not," Lanius said. "But if the Banished One cares enough about you to send you a dream, you've done something he doesn't like. And what's so bad about that?"

"Building a fancy place for your whatdoyoucallit—your moncat, that's right—to run?" Tinamus exclaimed. "That's crazy. The Banished One would have to be out of his mind to worry about it even for a heartbeat."

"The Banished One is a great many things, most of them unpleasant," Lanius said. "Out of his mind, he is not."

Tinamus shook his head in stubborn disbelief. "He must be—either that or he's in my dreams for something that has nothing to do with what I built for you, no matter what he said."

King Lanius supposed that was possible. He didn't know everything Tinamus had done. But he found it about as likely as Ortalis putting away his whips and giving up his hunting. The king said, "Do you know Collurio the animal trainer?"

"I don't think I've met him. I know his name—but I suppose a lot of people here know his name." Tinamus' eyes grew sharper. "Hold on. Didn't I hear somewhere that he's training animals for you?"

"I don't know whether you heard it or not, but it's true." Lanius bent down to sniff a yellow rose. The flower was beautiful. As usual, though, he thought the red ones smelled sweeter. He turned back to Tinamus. "Here's something you probably haven't heard—he's also had dreams from the Banished One."

"An animal trainer?" Tinamus' eyes widened. "By Olor's beard, Your Majesty, why?"

"Because he's doing something the Banished One doesn't like. So am I, and I've had those dreams. And so are you—and now you've had them, too." Lanius held out his hand. "So you see I meant it when I congratulated you."

The architect looked at the king, looked at his outstretched hand, as though he couldn't believe what he was seeing and hearing. Even after he clasped the proffered hand, he still looked and sounded bemused. "An animal trainer. Me. Why should the Banished One care about the likes of us? You're the King of Avornis, Your Majesty. At least it makes some kind of sense that he would worry about you."

"Glad you think so," Lanius said dryly. "There are plenty of people who would say that all I ever do is play with animals and poke around in the archives, and so nobody ought to worry about me at all—not even people, let alone the Banished One."

Now Tinamus stared at him in a new way. Lanius realized the builder hadn't expected to hear anything like that from him. Lanius shrugged. Tinamus was getting all sorts of surprises today. After a dream from the Banished One, a complaint from the king most likely wouldn't loom so large. And, sure enough, Tinamus asked, "What—what do I do—what *can* I do— if . . . if *he* visits me again?"

"You can't do much," Lanius answered, "except remember that he can't hurt you in one of those dreams. He can scare you until you almost wish you were dead, but he can't hurt you. Otherwise, I would have died a long time ago, and so would some other people."

Tinamus nodded. "All right, Your Majesty. Thank you. That *does* help—some, anyhow. Uh, do you mind telling me who else, besides you and the animal trainer?"

"You might have less trouble from *him* if you didn't know." Lanius waited to see whether Tinamus would press him even so. The architect said not another word. The king wasn't the least bit surprised.

# CHAPTER TWENTY-ONE

Whenever wagons reached the Avornan army besieging Yozgat, Grus let out a sigh of relief. The Menteshe did their best to harass his communications with the north. Sometimes that best was alarmingly good. In theory, he controlled everything between Yozgat and the Stura. Theory was wonderful. In practice, the nomads could nip in and raid when and as they chose.

To make them regret it, he ordered a special wagon train to come down to Yozgat. The wagons didn't carry sacks of wheat and beans. Instead, archers lay under the usual canvas covers. It was an uncomfortable trip for the men, but not an unprofitable one. Sure enough, the nomads attacked the wagons and the riders escorting them.

As always, the Menteshe were fierce and dashing and intrepid. They charged the wagons as though they were wolves and those wagons full of raw meat. Very often, that kind of charge routed the escorts and let the Menteshe do as they pleased with the wagons and the men who drove them.

Very often—but not this time. Avornan officers shouted words of command. Off popped the canvas covers. Up popped the archers, who hadn't had an easy or pleasant time of it in hiding. They were ready to make the Menteshe pay. They poured volley after volley into the onrushing nomads at close range.

The Menteshe, those who survived the trap, galloped away

even more wildly than they'd advanced on the wagon train. Word of the ploy must have spread fast, because after that attacks on the wagons eased for a while. When the triumphant archers came into the lines around Yozgat, Grus gave every one of them a bonus of twenty silverpieces.

Meanwhile, the siege ground on. Grus decided against another all-out assault on the walls. The defenders had been too tough for him to find success at all likely. Instead, he tried something different. He had soldiers who spoke the Menteshe language shout to the men besieged in Yozgat that they could freely leave the city if they surrendered, and that the only thing they were defending was Prince Korkut's vanity.

He didn't expect immediate results—a good thing, too, for he didn't get them. He hoped the trapped nomads would start talking among themselves and eventually decide they didn't have much chance of getting out alive if they kept on fighting.

"They've got to be worried in there—don't they?" he asked Hirundo.

"Nobody *has* to be anything," the general replied, which wasn't what Grus wanted to hear. Hirundo did add, "I tell you, though, Your Majesty—if I was cooped up in there, *I'd* be worried."

That was more like it. "I was thinking the same thing," Grus said. "Maybe they'll turn on Korkut. Maybe they'll even do it before . . ." His voice trailed away.

"Before what?" Hirundo asked.

"Before we try something else," Grus said—an answer that was no answer.

Hirundo, nobody's fool, realized as much at once. "What sort of other things have you got in mind, Your Majesty? From what you and the engineers and Pterocles have said, undermining the walls doesn't look like it'll work. I'm ready to try to storm them again whenever you give the word, but I don't know how good our chances are there. Or . . ." He snapped his fingers and grinned at the king. "You've figured out some way to give our men wings after all."

"I wish I had," Grus said. "It would make this business of war a lot easier—until the Menteshe and the Chernagors and the Thervings figured out how to fly, too."

"There's always that," the general agreed. "It wouldn't take long, either. But what *have* you got in mind, if they're not shipping wings down from the city of Avornis?"

Grus found himself oddly reluctant to go into detail. He shook his head. *Reluctant* wasn't the right word. *Embarrassed* came much closer to the truth. "When I start—if I start—I'll tell you, I promise," he said. "Right now . . . well, who knows if . . . he's listening?"

"I know what you're telling me. You're telling me you don't want to talk about it," Hirundo said. "You've come up with something strange, haven't you? I bet I know what it is. I bet it's something King Lanius dredged out of the archives, isn't it?"

"No," Grus said. "That it isn't. I can tell you the truth there, and I'll take oath on it if you like."

Hirundo only shrugged. "Never mind, Your Majesty. If King Lanius isn't getting strange, then I expect *you* are. I'm not so sure I want to know about that." Still shaking his head, he walked off.

Grus laughed. If Hirundo had really worried about the state of his wits, the general wouldn't have been shy about saying so. Hirundo was rarely shy about saying anything. For now, he seemed willing to believe Grus knew what he was doing. Grus wished he were so sure of that himself.

After he went to bed that night, the Banished One appeared to him in a dream. Seeing those coldly perfect features before him, Grus had another wish—that there was a better word to described these manifestations. *Dream* didn't begin to do them justice.

"You plot against me," the exiled god declared without preamble.

"Well, of course I do." Grus saw no point in denying it.

"You think you can outsmart me." The Banished One fleered laughter. "As well think a cat can outsmart you. You are nearer to a cat—you are nearer to a worm—than you are to me."

He was probably right about that. Grus had never partaken of divinity. All the same, plenty of cats had outsmarted him at one time or another. He didn't say that to the Banished One.

Having the exiled god thinking along those lines was the last thing he wanted. All he did say was, "I'll take my chances."

"You raise up serpents behind you, and you know it not," the Banished One said.

"I'll take my chances," Grus repeated stolidly. The less he gave, the better.

"Whatever you seek to bring against me, I will seize it before it reaches you."

"Maybe." Grus knew he was still asleep. He felt himself shrugging all the same, as though he and the Banished One really were face-to-face and not separated by miles and by the barrier of consciousness. "If you could do everything you say you can, though, you would have conquered Avornis a long time ago."

"You will see what I can do. You will see what your own flesh and blood, your own kith and kin, can do. And may you have joy of it." More laughter burst from the exiled god. Grus woke up with sweat running down his face. His heart thudded as though it would burst from his chest.

Slowly, ordinary awareness returned. A lamp burned inside the pavilion, casting a dim, flickering light and filling the air with the smell of hot olive oil. Grus got to his feet. A mosquito whined.

He cocked his head to one side and listened. Here and there, men talked quietly. A little farther off, a horse—or possibly a mule—snorted. It was the middle of the night. Everyone and everything with any sense was asleep.

The sentries outside Grus' pavilion had to stay awake and alert. One of them spoke in a low voice to the others. After a moment, Grus made out what he was saying. The king laughed softly. He'd first heard that joke when his beard was no more than fuzz on his cheeks. Some things grew new again for each generation.

He pulled his nightshirt off over his head and put on tunic and baggy breeches again. The nightshirt was more comfortable, but he would scandalize the guards if he stayed in it. When he stepped out of the pavilion into the darkness beyond, he scandalized them anyhow. "What are you doing up, Your

Majesty?" one of them demanded, as though he were a toddler caught running around in the night by its mother.

"Bad dream." Grus' answer sounded like the one a toddler might give, too.

"You should go back to sleep." But the sentry couldn't pick him up and put him into bed, the way a mother could with a wandering little boy. When the king walked out into the night, his guardsmen could only accompany him at a discreet distance.

Grus looked toward the walls of Yozgat. Torches flickered along them. In the light those torches cast, he could see men moving here and there. He'd thought about a night attack against the Menteshe in the city. That didn't look like a good idea. The defenders seemed much too alert. *What a shame,* he thought.

He hadn't planned to go over to Pterocles' tent, but his feet had a mind of their own. He wasn't astonished when the tent flap opened and the wizard came out, either. Pterocles was in *his* nightshirt—he didn't care what people thought. Nor did he seem surprised to see Grus. "Hello, Your Majesty," he said; they might have been meeting at breakfast.

"Hello." Grus also sounded matter-of-fact. "Bad dream?"

"Yes, as a matter of fact," the sorcerer said. "You, too, I gather?"

"That's right." Grus nodded. "He's . . . annoyed at us." He managed a wry shrug. "Breaks my heart."

"Mine, too." Pterocles also tried to seem casual. He didn't have such good luck. "Uh—do you know *why* he's annoyed at us?"

"I have some idea, yes," Grus admitted.

Pterocles sent him an annoyed look. "Would you care to tell me why?"

"Because we're trying to get the Scepter of Mercy back."

Now annoyance turned to exasperation. "Thank you, Your Majesty. I already suspected that. Why is he particularly annoyed now?"

"Because we're going to try something new and different," Grus replied.

"Aha! Now we come down to it," the wizard said. "*What* are we going to try that's new and different?"

"Certainly is warm tonight, isn't it?" Grus said.

He waited for Pterocles to splutter and fume. That was one of the more engaging spectacles of camp life. But Pterocles disappointed him. All he said was, "Since I'm alleged to be a sorcerer, and even a fairly decent one, don't you think I have the right to know?"

Grus smiled. "Why, when this has nothing to do with sorcery?"

"I see." Pterocles' bow was a masterpiece of sarcasm. "You're just going to walk in, pick up the Scepter of Mercy, say, 'Thank you very much, Your Highness,' to Prince Korkut, and saunter on out again."

"As a matter of fact," Grus answered, "yes."

Lanius was putting the finishing touches on a sketch when Ortalis came into the little north-facing audience chamber he was using as a studio and looked over his shoulder. "What's *that*?" Grus' legitimate son asked.

"What does it look like?" Lanius said.

"A mess." Ortalis rarely bothered with tact. After further study, he added, "It's not the city of Avornis. What's the point of drawing anywhere else?"

"I thought it was interesting. I wanted to draw a place that wasn't anything like this one here," Lanius said.

His brother-in-law grunted. "Well, you did that, all right. It doesn't look anything like anywhere. So you made it up out of your head, did you?"

"You might say so." Lanius hadn't said so. He'd just agreed that Ortalis might. He waited to see whether Ortalis would notice.

To his relief, Ortalis didn't. He said, "You come up with the weirdest ideas sometimes," and walked away.

That suited Lanius fine. He went back to the sketch, pausing every now and then to check with the ancient manuscript he'd taken from the archives. He laughed softly. When he started drawing, back in the days when Grus didn't trust him at all, he'd done it to sell sketches and make a little extra silver. He'd done moncats then, not cityscapes.

He stepped back and looked at this one. Ortalis was right. It didn't look a bit like the city of Avornis. What he really needed to be sure of was that those three towers were properly aligned. He'd done the best he could, going by what this manuscript and a couple of others told him. If they were wrong . . . If they were wrong, he'd wasted a lot of money and effort and time, that was all.

When he had things the way he wanted them—the way he was convinced they ought to be—he wrote Grus a letter, explaining exactly how the other king should use the sketch. He put both his artwork and the letter into a message tube. "Pass the word on to others who take this south—you may be troubled by bad dreams," he told the courier to whom he gave the tube.

"I'm not afraid of dreams, Your Majesty," the man replied. "I don't think anybody is, at least after he grows up."

"These dreams will frighten a grown-up," Lanius said firmly. "Pass the word along. I'm not imagining this. They won't hurt you, but you won't know what being frightened is until you've had one."

"All right, Your Majesty." The courier sounded more as though he was humoring him than anything else, but that was all right, as long as he remembered what Lanius told him.

But then he was gone, and Lanius couldn't do anything but worry. He went over to the great cathedral to pray to the gods in the heavens. He didn't know how much good that would do, but he didn't see how it could hurt.

Of course, when the King of Avornis visited the great cathedral, he didn't go alone. Guardsmen accompanied him. So did a secretary, to write down whatever he said that might need writing down. And he couldn't simply visit and pray. He had to be announced to the arch-hallow. In his crimson robes of office, Anser looked every inch a holy man. When he came up to talk with Lanius after the king finished praying, the guards and even the secretary withdrew to a discreet distance.

"You don't look very happy, Your Majesty," he said.

"Truth to tell, I'm not." Lanius didn't feel he could go into detail; like Sosia and Hirundo, Anser was one whom the Banished One had not troubled with visits in the night.

"I know what you need to do," the arch-hallow said now.

"Oh? What?" Lanius asked.

Another man in the red robes would have spoken of cleansing his spirit, of setting aside his will and accepting the decrees of the gods. Anser? Anser said, "You ought to go hunting. Nothing like hunting to take your mind off things."

Lanius didn't laugh. He'd always known Anser wasn't the spiritual leader Avornis needed in a time of trouble. He wasn't what the kingdom needed—but he was what it had. And Avornis had done some great things with him as arch-hallow. How much he had to do with all that was liable to be a different question.

"You really should," he persisted. "Yes, even you. I know you don't care about the hunt, but how can you not like the woods?"

"If *you* liked the woods any better, you'd grow hair all over and start going around on all fours," Lanius said. Anser laughed good-naturedly. The king went on, "Besides, I really can't right now. Too much is going on down in the south. I can't leave the palace."

"Why not?" Anser asked. "Nothing you do up here will change the way things go down there, will it?"

*I hope it will,* Lanius thought. Aloud, he said, "I want to *know.*"

"Well, all right." The arch-hallow sounded patient and amused, both at the same time. He also sounded very much like his father, which amused Lanius. Anser went on, "If you've got to keep up with everything every hour of the day and night, you can send couriers out from the woods to the palace. That way, you won't hear the news *much* later than you would if you stayed here. And I don't suppose the riders would spook the game very much." He sounded like a man making a formidable sacrifice, and no doubt thought he was.

Because he worked so hard to meet Lanius halfway, the king didn't see how he could say no without sounding rude. "All right. You've talked me into it," he said, and Anser grinned enormously.

"Good. Let's go. I'll meet you in front of the palace as fast as I can change clothes and call my beaters," he said. Any excuse for getting out of the city was a good one, as far as he was concerned. His ecclesiastical duties worried him not even for a moment.

Laughing, Lanius held up a hand. "Let's make it first thing tomorrow morning," he said. "I don't know about you, but I have some things I need to take care of before I leave."

"Spoilsport." But Anser was laughing, too. "All right, Your Majesty—tomorrow morning it is. You'd better not give me any excuses then, that's all I've got to say, or I'll get up in the pulpit and start screaming about heretics."

If he'd meant that, Avornis would have needed a new arch-hallow. Leading clerics who got up in the pulpit and caused kings trouble had to be replaced. Otherwise, they thought they were the ones running the kingdom. Arch-Hallow Bucco had, back when Lanius was a boy. For a while, he'd been right—he'd led the regency council. He hadn't led it any too well, unfortunately.

But Anser had no ambitions along those lines. If ruling Avornis would have meant all the hunting trips and all the deer he wanted, he might have taken the idea more seriously. As things were, not a chance.

"Have fun," Sosia said when Lanius told her where he was going. "You're not chasing serving girls when you go out with Anser." If he wasn't doing that, she didn't mind whatever he did.

He nodded. "No, that's your brother."

Sosia grimaced. "I didn't mean like *that*," she said. If Ortalis chased serving girls through the woods, he was as likely to shoot them for the fun of it as he was to do anything else with them.

"Tonight, I'll show you what *I* do for fun," Lanius said.

"Oh, you will, will you?" Sosia gave him a sidelong look.

He did, too, and enjoyed it as much as he'd hoped. By all the signs, his wife did, too. After a last kiss, they both rolled over and fell asleep. The next thing Lanius knew, he was looking into the Banished One's inhumanly handsome face. "Worm, you think you can trick me!" the exiled god roared.

"How could I do that?" Lanius said, as innocently as he could. "I'm only a man. You must know so much more than I do, anything I try will be plain as day to you."

"Do you mock me? Do you *dare* mock me? You will pay for that!"

"I'm already paying for so many things," Lanius said. "After all of them, what's one more?"

"My curse shall fall all the more heavily upon you and your miserable joke of a kingdom, all built of mud and straw and sticks." The Banished One sounded ready to explode with fury. How long had it been since anyone had the nerve to twit him? Since he was cast out of the heavens? Lanius wouldn't have been surprised.

Somehow, the exiled god didn't leave the king quite as terrified as usual. Or maybe Lanius realized, even in a dream, that having the Banished One angry at him was liable to be better than having him angry at Grus. All Lanius' mental faculties were intact, as they always were in dreams the Banished One sent. That usually made those dreams worse for him. Here, now, he turned it to his advantage. "I know why they sent you down to earth," the king said.

"*Do* you?" The Banished One seemed to lean toward him. Even if Lanius was less frightened now than he had been in some other dreams, that alarmed him. In a deadly voice, the Banished One asked, "Why?"

"Because you're a bore," Lanius' dream-self said.

The Banished One's roar of fury was so enormous, Lanius thought for a moment that it was a real sound, not an imaginary one. He burst from sleep as though shot from a stone-thrower, the way he'd gotten used to doing when escaping one of the exiled god's dreams. Sweat ran down his face and trickled along his sides from his armpits. His heart drummed madly.

"What's the matter?" Sosia asked, sleep blurring her voice.

"Bad dream." Lanius' answer, as usual, was true but inadequate.

"You've had a lot of those lately." His wife sounded as sympathetic as she could around a yawn.

"Maybe I have." Lanius knew he had. The Banished One sensed he was doing something out of the ordinary, and tormented him because of it. So far, the Banished One hadn't worked out what the king had in mind. More than anything else, Lanius wanted that very partial ignorance to go on.

Sosia patted the pillow. "Well, go back to bed." She yawned again.

"Later, maybe." As usual after one of these jolts, Lanius was too excited to sleep. He got up and started for the door. He'd put a hand on the latch before noticing he was naked. *That* would have given any servants going through the palace corridors in the middle of the night something to talk about.

He slipped on the lightest, plainest robe he had, one made of a blend of silk and linen. No one would expect him to wear a heavy robe of state at whatever hour this was. He opened the door, slipped out, and closed it behind him as quietly as he could.

The palace was dim and quiet. Only a few torches were lit, which saved fuel. A little moth fluttered around one of the ones that still flickered. It would be sorry if it flew into the flame.

*And what about me?* he wondered. *Am I flying into the flame when I go against the Banished One?* Many before him had burned themselves up. He didn't think he would. But how many of the others had thought so? Hadn't they been sure they were doing something wonderful, something that would make Avornans remember their names until the end of time? Of course they had. The only trouble was, they'd been wrong. He had to hope he wasn't.

Someone came around the corner. It was Ortalis. He seemed as surprised to see Lanius as Lanius was to see him. "Oh, hello," Grus' son said. "What are you doing up at this time of night?"

"I might ask you the same question," Lanius said. "As for me, I had a dream that woke me." That would do. He didn't want or intend to go into details.

One of Ortalis' eyebrows lifted in surprise. "Did you? As a matter of fact, so did I."

"Really?" Lanius was not only surprised but also frightened. A dream bad enough to get Ortalis out of bed was likely to come from the Banished One. Why would the exiled god want to send Ortalis dreams? For no good reason—Lanius would have staked his life on that. Cautiously, he asked, "Was the nightmare very bad?"

"Nightmare?" Ortalis gaped at him as though he'd suddenly started babbling in Thervingian. "Nightmare?" he repeated; he might not have believed his ears. "This was the most wonderful dream I ever had in my life."

"Was it?" Lanius said, surprised all over again.

"It certainly was!" Ortalis had never spoken of anything, even hunting, with such enthusiasm before. Lanius laughed at himself. He'd jumped to a good many wrong conclusions. This looked to be one of the wrongest. *Well, good,* he thought.

"Here you are, Your Majesty." A weary-sounding courier handed Grus a message tube.

"Thanks," the king said, and then, sympathetically, "Have any trouble coming down here?"

"Did I ever!" The courier got livelier remembering. "This bunch of nomads started chasing me, and I was afraid they'd catch me before I could get to our next little fort. But then this *other* bunch of Menteshe came out from the side, and I really thought I was a goner. Instead of going after me, though, they pitched into each other, and I got away."

"Good for you!" Grus said. "Nice to know the civil war between Korkut and Sanjar is still going on."

Knowing that was especially nice after Bori-Bars had led the army of both princes' backers against the Avornans. Maybe the Banished One didn't bother uniting the Menteshe unless something more important than one courier was at stake. Or maybe Sanjar's shamans really had worked out a way to keep him from doing that. Grus hoped so.

"I had bad dreams all the way down, too," the courier said. "But the gods in the heavens watched over me and kept me safe."

"No doubt," Grus said, doubting. How often did the gods in the heavens pay any attention to what went on down here in the material world? Not often enough. But, even if Grus had trouble staying confident in them, he didn't want to damage the other man's faith, so he let it go at that.

He opened the message tube and drew out the letter inside.

Another sheet came out with it. Grus unrolled that one first. It was a sketch of a town, as seen from outside. Grus blinked. He'd known Lanius could draw, but he hadn't had any idea the other king was this good.

He started to give his attention to the letter, then looked back at the sketch again. From that sketch, his eyes snapped to the walls of Yozgat. "By the gods!" he muttered. Lanius was not only better than he'd thought, but *much* better than he'd thought. There could be no doubt about it—the other king had produced an outstanding portrait of a city he'd never seen.

Lanius had made mistakes. The texture of the stone didn't quite match that of Yozgat's walls, and the proportions of the towers were subtly off. But it was unmistakably Yozgat.

More than a little reluctantly, Grus rolled up the sketch and broke the seal on the letter. When he finished reading it, he shook his head in reluctant admiration and respect. The letter was as precise as the sketch—and, like it, had a few details that weren't quite the way they were supposed to be.

As with the sketch, those didn't worry Grus. They just reminded him that Lanius was human—for all his cleverness, he didn't see everything there was to see. Noting as much relieved Grus. He decided there might still be some point after all to *his* having a share of the crown.

And, here, he saw very clearly what needed doing. He went over to Pterocles' tent and stuck his head inside. "Oh, good," he said. "You're here."

"No, not really," the wizard answered. "But I do expect to get back pretty soon."

"Er—right," Grus said. "You were wondering how we would get the Scepter of Mercy out of Yozgat."

"Something like that had occurred to me, yes," Pterocles agreed. "You told me it was none of my business, though." Resentment stuck up all over him, like spines on a hedgehog.

"Well, it may be after all." Grus thrust Lanius' letter at him. "Here—read this and tell me what you think."

Pterocles obeyed. The more he read, the more astonished he looked. When he was finished, he blurted, "That's the craziest thing I ever heard of."

"Just what I said when King Lanius told me about it last

winter," Grus replied. "Suppose we forget it's crazy, though. Suppose we look at what chance it has of working. More than a little, wouldn't you say? Here, look at this, too." He showed Pterocles Lanius' sketch of Yozgat.

"Olor's beard!" the wizard exclaimed, recognizing it at once. "That's—amazing, isn't it?"

"Pretty much so," Grus said. "He's never even gone as far as the Stura, let alone anywhere near here."

"He's got it down, though. Every place where it matters, he's got it down," Pterocles said, and Grus nodded. Pterocles asked, "Where do I come into all this?"

"I don't know for certain, but I'll tell you what I had in mind," Grus said, and he did.

Pterocles stared, then burst out laughing. "Yes, I can do that," he said, laughing still. "Come to think of it, you don't need me to do that. The clumsiest, most fumble-fingered drunken excuse for a wizard in the world could do that."

"Well, I don't know the clumsiest, most fumble-fingered drunken excuse for a wizard in the world, and I do know you," Grus said reasonably. "I still think you'd do a better job than he would, too."

"For this? You might be surprised," Pterocles told him.

"Maybe I might be, but I'd better not be, if you know what I mean." When Grus wanted to, he could sound every inch a king.

Pterocles bowed in acquiescence. "Yes, Your Majesty. Let me know when."

"I will. Obviously, not yet," Grus said.

"Yes. Obviously." Pterocles started a chuckle, but this time didn't quite finish it. His voice was altogether serious as he said, "You know, Your Majesty, I'm a little surprised—maybe more than a little surprised—that letter and that sketch made it down here safely. They had to cross an awful lot of ground the Menteshe can raid before they did."

"Funny you should say that." Grus told him the story of the courier's narrow escape from the nomads.

"That's . . . interesting," Pterocles said thoughtfully. "And it's even more interesting that the two bands of Menteshe should have squabbled with each other, don't you think?"

"I did, as a matter of fact," Grus answered. "When I heard that, it made me wonder whether Sanjar's wizards really had worked out a spell to keep the Banished One from taking control of them. That envoy said they were going to try it, but I would be lying if I said I'd believed him."

"A possibility. Definitely a possibility."

By the way Pterocles said it, it wasn't a possibility he took seriously. "What were you thinking?" Grus asked him.

"Well, it did occur to me . . . If the gods in the heavens were going to meddle in the affairs of the material world, that's the way they might go about it. A little bit of confusion at just the right time would go a long way, and who could prove anything afterwards? Not even—him." The wizard looked south, toward the Argolid Mountains.

So did Grus. Was the Banished One gnashing his teeth down there because his henchmen hadn't caught that courier? It did seem possible. Did it seem likely? Grus pointed at Pterocles. "If—he—can't prove anything, you can't, either."

"Oh, I know that, Your Majesty," Pterocles said cheerfully. "But it does give us something to think about, doesn't it?"

Grus' wave encompassed the palisade surrounding Yozgat. "I've already got plenty to think about, thank you very much." He paused. "It would be nice, though, wouldn't it, to believe the gods in the heavens were paying a little bit of attention— just a little bit, mind you—to what's going on down here?"

"We'll see how things turn out," Pterocles said. "That may tell us something, one way or the other."

"Yes, it may," Grus said. "Question is, will it tell us anything we want to hear?"

"We'll find out," Pterocles said.

"Very good." Grus laughed and bowed. "As long as you stick to that, you can prophesy about anything."

"Being patient is a good start to the secret of all wisdom," Pterocles said.

"No doubt you're right. It's also one of the hardest things for most people to manage." Grus shook his head. "No—that's wrong. Most people can't manage it. Take me—I can hardly wait until I get to go on." He looked down at the sketch Lanius had sent. "I know what I can do in the meantime. I can go around Yozgat until I find the place where this matches up best with what I really see."

"Good," Pterocles said. "Then you'll be ready, or as ready as you can be. I didn't know the king—uh, the other king—could draw so well."

"Neither did I," Grus admitted. "Lanius . . . will surprise you every now and then."

He set out on a circuit of the Avornan lines, carrying the sketch and looking from it to the walls and the city beyond them every fifty paces or so. The other king said in his letter that he'd been as precise as he knew how. Grus believed him. Lanius was precise even when he didn't particularly aim to be. When he did, he was bound to be very precise indeed.

He was bound to be—and he was. Grus looked up from the sketch to the walls after another few steps, then slowly nodded to himself. He rolled up the sketch again. He needed to go no farther. "Here," he said. "Right here."

# CHAPTER TWENTY-TWO

L anius paced through the palace in an agony of anxiety. Every time a courier came in, he met the man and snatched the message tube out of his hands. Every time the message turned out to be something ordinary from the provinces, the king snarled in frustration. Lanius was not usually given to snarling. People sent him odd, even frightened, looks.

Rumors didn't take long to start swirling. People talked about him when they didn't think he was listening. Sometimes, though, he was just around a corner in the corridor. Some of the servants thought he and Sosia had had another fight.

Other servants were convinced he'd either quarreled with a new mistress or gotten her pregnant. Since he didn't have a mistress at the moment, that wasn't true, either. If they'd known he was worrying about whether a letter and a sketch had gotten down to Yozgat safely, they would have been convinced he'd lost his wits.

But Lanius couldn't help being snappish. The servants walked softly around him. Had his temper been of a different sort, he might have enjoyed stirring up alarm in the palace and punishing people when they did anything wrong, no matter how small. As things were, he regretted their fear when he noticed it.

Three days later, the letter he'd been waiting for finally came. He all but tackled the courier who handed him the message tube. When he recognized the royal seal on the letter, he whooped. When he broke the seal and unrolled the letter and recognized Grus' strong, simple script, he whooped again.

*Your Majesty, with the gods' help I have your letter and your sketch,* the other king wrote. *I may even mean that instead of sticking it in for the sake of padding or decoration. The sketch is quite good, good enough to be used for its intended purpose. When all else is in readiness, we shall go forward. And, because the gods watched over what you last sent me, I dare hope they will go on looking out for our endeavors.* His signature was a hasty scrawl nothing like the rest of his handwriting.

"Ha!" Lanius said, and then, "Ha!" again.

"Is the news good, Your Majesty?" the courier asked.

"The news is very good," Lanius answered. "Yes, by Olor's beard, very good indeed." He fumbled in his belt pouch. As usual, he never knew what in the way of money he would find there. A handful of silver seemed to do the job. He pressed it on the courier, saying, "And this for the good news."

"I thank you, Your Majesty." The man bowed and left.

For a little while, Lanius was as happy as he had been anxious. Some of the serving women exclaimed among themselves, guessing—wrongly—why he seemed so pleased. However mistaken, their guesses were funny and lewd, and Lanius once more had trouble not laughing out loud when he overheard them.

But his worries came back sooner than he would have liked. Grus had gotten his letter and the sketch that went with it—good. The other king would have had a harder time going forward without them. But, by themselves, they weren't enough to let him go forward. Until Lanius knew he could . . . well, what was there to do but worry?

Grus eyed the newcomers to the siege line around Yozgat with no small curiosity. The two men closely resembled each other, but for a generation's difference in age. Each of them had a long face and a big nose. The older man's mustache was shot with gray, the younger one's just losing the downy look of youth. They even stood alike. They both had a slightly stagy manner, as though they never stopped performing.

And, at the moment, they both put down cups of wine as fast as they could. The older man said, "Begging your pardon, Your Majesty, but if we'd known the trip down here would be the way it was, I don't think you could have found enough gold in the world to get us to make it."

"Why is that, Collurio?" Grus asked, though he suspected he already knew the answer.

The animal trainer drained his cup before replying. He filled it again from the jar of wine in Grus' pavilion. "Why?" he repeated. "I'll tell you why—because I thought we were going to get killed a dozen times, that's why."

"Only a dozen?" his son murmured.

"Well, I don't know. I lost track after a while," Collurio said. "It all started when a log hit the boat we were in while we were crossing the Stura and almost pitched us into the river. By the gods in the heavens, I don't know what I would have done—I never learned to swim."

"Ah?" Grus said. "How were you saved?"

"Well, the rowers pulled like madmen, and the log swung a little right at the last instant, so it smacked into the very back of the boat—"

"You mean the stern," Grus said, thinking, *Landlubber.*

"Whatever you call it." Collurio wasn't inclined to be fussy. "Anyhow, the log just glanced off, you might say, and swung us around, but it didn't tip us over."

He'd had no reason ever to learn the word *capsize.* Grus didn't suppose he would want a vocabulary lesson now. The king didn't think that log had come sliding down the Stura by accident. He hoped it hadn't swerved at the last instant by accident, either. "What happened next?" he asked.

Collurio nudged his son. "You tell it, Crinitus."

"All right," the younger man said. "That was when the wagon had to run for a fort about half a bounce ahead of the Menteshe."

"That was the first time, you mean," Collurio said.

"Well, yes." Crinitus nodded. "The first time. But a few lancers rode out from the fort, and for some reason the nomads didn't keep coming after us. They must have thought the soldiers were going to pitch into them. It didn't look to me like there were enough Avornans for that, but I'm not going to complain, believe me."

"Neither will I," Collurio said. He looked at Grus. "I thought the same thing my son did. It was nothing but Queen Quelea's mercy that saved us."

*I hope you're right,* Grus thought. What he said was, "I gather you had some other narrow escapes?"

"A wagonload of 'em," Collurio said, and laughed at his own wit. "Some of the riders and drivers we talked to said those kinds of things happen all the time. If they do, though, I don't see how anything ever gets here, and that's the truth."

"Sometimes things don't," Grus said. "I'm glad the two of you did. And, meaning no offense to you, I'm even gladder the moncat did."

Collurio scratched his plowshare of a nose. "King Lanius kept going on and on about how the beast was more important than I understood. I would have told him he was daft if he wasn't the king—I probably shouldn't say that to you, should I, eh, Your Majesty?"

"I've had the same thought about King Lanius now and again," Grus replied, "but I have to admit I've been wrong more than I've been right."

"It could be. Yes, it could be," Collurio replied, pouring more wine for himself and Crinitus. He and his son would be drunk in short order if they kept that up. He went on, "Other thing besides him being king that made me keep my fool mouth shut was *those* dreams. You know about *those* dreams, Your Majesty? King Lanius said you did."

"Oh, yes." Grus raised his own winecup in salute to the animal trainer. "I do know about *those* dreams, and I know who sends them, too. Welcome to the club. There aren't very many of us. We're the people who worry *him*." He looked south, toward the Argolid Mountains.

Collurio shuddered. "His Majesty—His other Majesty, I mean—told me the same thing. I'll tell you what I told him— I could do without the honor."

"I wish I had one of those dreams." Crinitus sounded resentful at being left out.

"Don't." Grus and Collurio said the same word at the same

time. Grus went on, "With a little luck—and I think with only a little luck now, not the great slabs of it we would have needed a while ago—with a little luck, I say, *he* won't have much chance to trouble us like that anymore."

"How's that, Your Majesty?" Collurio sounded like a sorely perplexed man. "I've tried and I've tried, but I just can't cipher it out. Why did we fetch the moncat down to the walls of Yozgat?"

If Collurio couldn't see it, then—with that little bit of luck—the Banished One wouldn't see it, either. Pterocles had been taken by surprise when Grus explained it. Pterocles, in fact, had been completely astonished. "Why?" the king said. "I'll tell you why."

"Please!" This time, Collurio and Crinitus spoke together.

"To take the Scepter of Mercy, that's why," Grus said.

The two animal trainers, middle-aged and young, looked at him with identical expressions. Their faces both said, *Your Majesty, you're out of your mind.* Grus' biggest worry was that they were liable—indeed, were much too likely—to be absolutely right.

Again, Lanius waited anxiously for word from the south. He wanted to be sure that Pouncer (and, not quite incidentally, Collurio and Crinitus) had reached the Avornan works surrounding Yozgat. Unless he was wrong, and unless the Banished One and the Menteshe were better fooled than he thought, they would do everything they could to stop the moncat and its trainers. If they did . . .

*If they do, I'll start over with a different beast—and with different trainers,* the king thought. *No, I'll start over with several moncats, and send them down separately.*

That was a good idea. The more he looked at it, the more he wished he would have done it this time instead of letting everything rest on Pouncer's furry shoulders. But Pouncer had advantages over all the others. They would have taken longer to learn what they needed to know—what he hoped they needed to know.

If something went wrong this campaigning season, though, would he ever have the chance to send more moncats south of the Stura? Would Grus be able to lay siege to Yozgat again? La-nius couldn't be sure. All the same, he had the feeling this was Avornis' best chance, maybe Avornis' only chance.

Having that feeling only left him more anxious to learn what was going on down there in the south.

Even if Pouncer had gotten to Yozgat safely, that was no guarantee the moncat would succeed. Lanius was acutely con-scious of how old the descriptions of the city he'd used were. He couldn't do anything about that; they were the newest ones he had. If not for the archives, he wouldn't have had any. Street plans changed little, even after the Menteshe held a town for many years. He'd seen that proved after the siege of Trabzun. He had to believe it held true for Yozgat as well.

Lanius tried his best not to show his excitement whenever a courier came into the palace, and not to show his disappoint-ment when the couriers would hand him messages that had nothing to do with what was going on around Yozgat. It wasn't easy, and got harder as day followed day with no news from the south.

*Whatever I hear doesn't really matter,* he told himself. *It will only be word of what's already happened, and I won't be able to do anything about it one way or the other.* That was true, but it was cold consolation. He wanted to feel, he wanted to *know,* that what he'd done made a difference.

If it made a difference. That was the other side of the coin, the side he didn't want to think about. One way or the other, he'd find out.

When Grus finally did send a letter, it told him less than he wished it would have. Grus gave a good reason for that, but still left Lanius frustrated. After the usual greetings, the other king wrote, *You will be pleased to hear that your two intrepid ani-mal trainers and the animal they trained have gotten here safely. This is after adventures that put to shame those of your recent letter and sketch.* He described some of them, then went on, *However dangerous the journey, they* did *arrive safely, which I take as a good sign. Maybe the gods in the heavens are paying a little attention, a very little, to the material world after all. I dare hope.*

*We now wait for a moonless night. Once we have it, we will find out if we are smarter than we think or only better at fool-ing ourselves—or letting ourselves be fooled.* His signature fol-lowed.

Looking at the date on the letter, Lanius saw Grus had writ-ten it two weeks earlier. Then, the moon had been swelling toward full. Now it was shrinking toward new. Grus had his moonless nights, if he wanted them.

Maybe Grus had already done what needed doing. Maybe word was on the way. Lanius hoped it was. He also hoped Olor and Quelea and the rest *were* paying attention to what went on down here, as the other king suggested. The Banished One pretty plainly hadn't wanted Lanius' letter and sketch or Collu-rio, Crinitus, and Pouncer to make it to Yozgat. Just as plainly, they had made it. If the gods in the heavens hadn't helped them, who had? No one at all? Lanius couldn't believe that, not with the Banished One trying to stop them.

Again, he wasn't sure what the gods could do here. The ma-terial world wasn't their proper sphere. Of course, the gods hadn't intervened directly. Olor hadn't hurled a thunderbolt. Quelea hadn't spread flowers over the landscape to distract the Menteshe. What did seem to have spread was confusion—and confusion wasn't material.

"Exciting times ahead," Lanius murmured. He hoped they would be exciting. After a moment, he shook his head. He hoped they would be exciting in the right way. Even if the Ban-ished One triumphed, there would be plenty of excitement. But it wouldn't be the kind Avornis wanted to know.

*We'll find out soon,* the king thought. He wondered whether he would be able to sense the change if things went well. Then he wondered whether he'd be able to sense the change if they went dreadfully wrong. *We'll find out,* he thought again. Or maybe he'd already found out, and the answer was no.

"I'll find out if I find out," he said, and laughed. When he found out, he'd know how much he really had to laugh about—if he had anything at all.

"Black as the inside of a sheep," Collurio muttered.

"Not quite that bad," Grus said. But then, the animal trainer had lived almost his entire life in the city of Avornis, where torches and lamps and candles always burned to hold night at bay. This was dark enough, and more than dark enough. Only stars shone in the sky. No campfires burned anywhere near the king and his comrades. A few torches shone up on Yozgat's walls, but the Menteshe didn't use their light to peer out. The city's defenders just wanted to be sure they could see any Avornans unexpectedly joining them on the walls.

Grus laughed almost inaudibly. They would have company up there for a little while, all right. But it wouldn't be the kind of company they were looking for—Grus hoped with all his heart it wouldn't be, anyhow—and it wouldn't hang around for long.

"Everything ready?" the king whispered. When no one told him no, he nodded to himself and said, "Let's try it, then."

Soldiers quietly moved sharpened timbers aside to make a gap in the palisade. Other soldiers laid a gangplank over the ditch surrounding the fence of stakes. Grus, Collurio, Crinitus, and Pterocles waited before crossing. Looking over at Yozgat, Collurio said, "The other king really did know this slice of the city, didn't he? The towers he drew in the sketch are just in the same place as the ones in Yozgat."

"Is everything inside this part of the city the same as it is in the slice he had Tinamus build?" Crinitus asked.

"Good question," Grus said. "I don't know the answer to that. I don't think King Lanius *knew* the answer to that. He hoped things hadn't changed too much, and so do I. Before much longer, we'll see."

As though his words were a cue, Avornan archers and siege engines far around the line started shooting at Yozgat. Grus' men had been doing that almost—but not quite—at random for several days now. The Menteshe responded much as the king hoped they would. They sent men to the threatened stretch and didn't worry much about any other part of the wall.

"Now," Grus said. He and the trainers and the wizard crossed the gangplank and hurried toward the moat. Collurio carried Pouncer's cage. Crinitus and Pterocles were in charge of a long, thin pole. Carpenters had made it up in sections in the capital, and other woodworkers had joined the sections together once the animal trainer brought it down to Yozgat.

When they got to the edge of the moat, Grus stared up toward the wall. No one up there seemed to be paying any attention to what was going on outside the city. Pterocles noted the same thing, saying, "Looks quiet enough."

"Yes." Grus nodded. "We're going to try it. Gentlemen, if you'd be so kind . . ."

Crinitus and Pterocles angled the pole up toward the top of the wall. At last, after what seemed much too long, the far end of the pole tapped against the crenellations up there. "Anyone hear that, do you think?" Crinitus asked anxiously.

No shouts came from the wall. No Menteshe came over to grab the other end of the pole. "Everything seems all right," Grus murmured. "Why don't you let the moncat out of the cage, Collurio?"

"I'll do it," the animal trainer answered, also in a low voice. He fiddled with the door to the cage. As it swung open, he said, "I hope the trip down here hasn't made the beast forget what it's supposed to do. That happens sometimes, and we had an awfully long trip."

"Only one way to find out," Grus said.

Pouncer let out a musty meow. It wasn't quite like the noises ordinary cats made, but was closer to those than anything else. The moncat poked its head out of the cage as though unsure such liberties were allowed. When no one shouted at it or poked it to make it withdraw, it came all the way out of the cage, stretched—and settled down on the ground to lick its backside. "Miserable thing!" Crinitus exploded, and made as though to prod it with his foot.

His father stopped him. "Let the beast be," he said. "It has to tend to itself before it can tend to what we want of it."

Pouncer stopped grooming itself. Grus could tell the moment when the moncat noticed the pole. The animal made a small, interested noise. The moment Collurio heard that, he made a small, pleased noise. Pouncer went up the pole. With what were essentially hands on all four limbs, the moncat was less graceful than ordinary cats on the ground. As soon as it started climbing the pole, though . . . The moncat gripped with forefeet and hind feet, and rose faster and more skillfully than Grus would have imagined possible.

"Gods be praised!" Collurio breathed. "It still knows what it's supposed to do."

*No wonder he sounds relieved,* Grus thought. If the animal balked, who would have gotten the blame? That wouldn't have fallen on Pouncer. After all, a moncat was only a moncat. It would have landed on Collurio and Crinitus.

"Up to the top and on the wall," the younger trainer said. "I can't feel its weight on the pole anymore."

"Up to the top and into Yozgat," Grus said. He hoped Pouncer went into Yozgat, anyhow. If the moncat chose to amble along the wall instead, who could say what would happen? Maybe one of the Menteshe up there would find a new pet. Or maybe, since the city was under siege, one of the plainsmen would find supper. But Grus couldn't do anything about that now. It was up to Pouncer—and, maybe, to Pterocles. Grus turned to the wizard. "Are you ready?"

"Yes, Your Majesty." The wizard gave Grus an ironic bow. "You need me for this spell about as much as you need to break an egg by dropping the great cathedral on it."

"That's nice," Grus said placidly. "You told me something like that before. I've got you, this way I don't have to tell anybody else about what we're doing, I know you're up to it, and you'll do a good job of breaking that egg."

Along with his usual sorcerous paraphernalia, Pterocles had several small chunks of raw mutton wrapped in cloth in his belt pouch. He held one of them in the palm of his left hand. In his right hand he held an arrowhead shot from the walls of Yozgat. "Same trick I used outside of Trabzun, only with a new twist," he remarked. "The law of contagion means the arrowhead that had been inside Yozgat is still connected to the place."

He began to chant in a low voice no one on the walls could have heard. When he broke off, the bit of mutton vanished from his hand. "It's inside the city?" Grus asked. "It's where it's supposed to be?"

"Yes, Your Majesty—right where the moncat is supposed to find it," Pterocles answered patiently. "I told you, a hedge-wizard could move this meat around as well as I can."

"Just keep doing it," the king said. "If it's so easy it offends your dignity, well, maybe I'll have you do something harder next time, that's all."

Pterocles repeated the spell again and again. Piece after piece of mutton disappeared. By the wizard's murmured comments, Grus gathered that each one was going deeper into Yozgat. Collurio and Crinitus knew just where in the model of the city Pouncer was accustomed to getting his rewards as he went through his routine. As closely as Pterocles could, he was putting mutton in spots that corresponded to those.

The wizard started the spell yet again, then paused. "Your Majesty, this one will go close to the citadel. There are sorcerous wards in place. If I penetrate them, I may alert the wizard who set them. Shall I put the meat there anyhow?"

"No!" Grus wasn't sure he was right, but he didn't hesitate. "The moncat will go on anyhow, I think, and I don't want to alert the Menteshe. No matter what, I don't want to alert the Menteshe. We may have to try this again, and surprise will help if we do."

"As you wish." Pterocles accepted his decision. A big part of what made a king a king was getting people to accept his choices. Of course, if they accepted too many that were wrong . . .

"I think this is good. I hope it is," Collurio said. "The moncat is a clever beast. Even if some rewards are missing, it will usually go on, expecting to find the rest. I have seen as much."

"Thank you," Grus told him. But he'd made his choice for reasons mostly different from the one the trainer had given. He thought he would have made it even if Collurio had told him something else.

"I'll place these other bits on the way back, then," Pterocles said. "I wish I knew just where in Yozgat Pouncer is now."

"Nothing we can do but wait," Grus said. However true that was, he didn't like it. Sooner or later, the Menteshe were bound to notice his companions and him, to say nothing of the pole that led up to the wall . . . weren't they? Alert men should have noticed them already. Maybe, just maybe, the gods were helping to keep the defenders from noticing what was going on under their noses. Or maybe the Menteshe weren't alert because they didn't think the Avornans could put men on the walls without their knowing it.

And they were right. The Avornans *couldn't* sneak men up onto the walls of Yozgat. But the Menteshe hadn't thought about moncats. They'd probably never heard of them. What they didn't know . . . might give them a surprise.

Off on the other side of the city, the sounds of skirmishing went on. Grus heard a sharp thud as a stone smacked into the wall. Distant shouts said the Menteshe didn't like that. But the walls were well made. Stone-throwers could pound them for a long time—maybe forever—without knocking them down.

Bats and nightjars came into sight every now and then when they swooped close to torches to snatch insects out of the air. They paid the fighting no attention; it meant no more to them than the taste of a moth meant to Grus. He wondered whether he ought to envy them.

It was the dark of the moon. Nothing but starlight would be in the sky until the sun came up. Even though Grus knew as much, he found himself looking toward the east. That was nothing but foolishness; if his senses hadn't told him dawn was still far away, the positions of the stars as they wheeled through the sky would have.

"How much longer?" Crinitus asked.

"However long it takes," Grus answered. "Until the moncat comes back, or until we're sure it won't."

Collurio pointed not east but south. "What's that?"

For a moment, Grus thought it was a red star he hadn't spied before, throbbing down there just above the southern horizon. As he'd moved from the Stura to Yozgat, northern constellations hung lower in the sky, while southern ones climbed higher and a few stars he'd never seen before came into view. But then he realized this wasn't a star. He thought of a great leaping flame, but that didn't seem quite right, either. "I don't know what it is," he said at last.

Pterocles looked at the pulsing point of scarlet light, too. "Isn't that about where . . . he's supposed to have his lair in the Argolid Mountains?"

Grus considered. "Yes, I think it is," he said at last. "But why can we see it now? It's never lit up like that before."

"Maybe he's never had anything much to worry about up until now," Pterocles said. "Maybe . . ."

"Olor's beard," Grus whispered, awe in his voice. If Pouncer had penetrated the defenses that would have stopped the boldest human thief far from his goal . . . Oh, if Pouncer had . . . !

No sooner had the thought crossed Grus' mind than Yozgat went wild. It seemed as though all the Menteshe in the town started shouting at one another at once. All Grus could see was the top of the wall. That made him grind his teeth in frustration, for it meant he could get only the vaguest idea of what was going on down in Yozgat itself.

Things on the wall were lively enough. Menteshe ran this way and that. They were all yelling at the top of their lungs. Some of them carried torches; others didn't. He got to see one spectacular pratfall, as a plainsman with a torch tripped over someone or something. The man fell with a splat. His torch flew out and down and hissed into extinction in the moat.

That, luckily, was some way down the wall from where the King of Avornis, the animal trainers, and the wizard stood. Not even the falling torch threw much light on them. None of the Menteshe seemed to have any idea they were there. None of the plainsmen seemed the least bit interested in what was happening outside of Yozgat. All their attention focused on whatever had gone wrong within the walls. That the commotion inside might be connected to the Avornans outside didn't look to have crossed their minds.

"I wish somebody had told me the city would go crazy while the moncat was inside it," Collurio said worriedly. "I would have trained the beast to be used to the noise and the fuss. This way, it may scare him out of doing what he's learned."

That was the last thing Grus wanted to hear. *Lanius, you thought of everything else. Why didn't you think of this, too?* But he didn't—he couldn't—really blame the other king. Lanius had taken an idea no one else would have come up with and made it real. *And so have I, by the gods. So have I,* Grus thought. "We've come this far," he said. "With any luck at all, we'll be able to go as much further as we need."

More shouts rang out inside Yozgat. Somebody bellowed

what was plainly an order. Someone else yelled what was just as plainly defiance. Iron clanged on iron. Wounded men shrieked. Did they have any idea why they were fighting one another? Grus wouldn't have bet on it.

That wasn't his worry. It was theirs—and the Banished One's. *His* worry was Pouncer. Where was the moncat? What was it doing? Was it doing anything past hiding from the chaos all around or maybe chasing a tasty-smelling southern mouse? Grus didn't know. He couldn't know, even if he could guess and hope. Not knowing gnawed at him.

The base of the pole stirred, there in the dirt by the edge of the moat. Pterocles and Crinitus both grabbed it, both steadied it. Either the Menteshe had found the other end at the edge of the wall and were starting to pull it up or . . .

Grus peered toward the top of Yozgat's works. "There's Pouncer!" he said—as joyous a whisper as he'd ever used.

Down came the moncat, quick and graceful as ever. Was it holding something in one of its clawed hands? Lanius had grumbled when it stole spoons from the kitchens in the palace. What had it stolen now, and from where?

"Mrow," the moncat said as it left the pole for solid ground. It glared at Collurio. He took a piece of mutton from Pterocles.

"No, let me," King Grus said, and solemnly handed out the last reward. And, as Pouncer ate, Grus took the Scepter of Mercy into his own hands.

# CHAPTER TWENTY-THREE

Y ou!" The Banished One's bellow was full of rage and
desperation and despair. "You thief! You bandit! You
brigand! You have taken that which is mine, that to
which you have no right. Do you think you can flout me so?"

In Lanius' dream, he looked at the exiled god. As always,
the Banished One's countenance seemed perfectly beautiful,
perfectly calm . . . or did it? Wasn't that the faintest trace of a
frown line by the side of his mouth? It marred his inhumanly
cold magnificence as a broken window might have marred a
building.

And, no matter how impassioned the Banished One
sounded, he wasn't telling the truth, not as Lanius understood
it. "Years ago, you took what belonged to Avornis," the king
replied. "How can you complain when we do what we have to
do to get it back?"

"It is not something mortals deserve to have. It is not something mortals should profane with their touch," the Banished
One said furiously.

Lanius shook his head. The motion felt completely real, although, as always when he faced the Banished One, he knew
he was dreaming. "You are the one whose touch profanes it,"
Lanius said. "If you could use it, if you were meant to use it,
you would have been able to hundreds of years ago. It is not
yours. It does not belong to you. It is not for you."

"It is my key to regaining the heavens," the Banished One

·

said. "It is mine—*mine,* I tell you! With it in my hands, the so-called gods who cast me down cannot hope to stand against me."

"But it's no good in your hands, is it?" Lanius said. "It's no good at all to you. You can't even pick it up. While a—" He broke off. He did not want to tell the Banished One a moncat could do what the exiled god could not. He didn't know whether Pouncer was still inside Yozgat or had succeeded in escaping the city. No point to saying anything more than he had to, and a great deal of point to telling the Banished One as little as he could.

Luck—or, just possibly, the protection of the gods in the heavens—stayed with him. The Banished One was so agitated, he didn't notice Lanius' hesitation and didn't probe for what might have caused it. "It should be mine. It must be mine. It shall be mine!" the Banished One shouted.

"It belongs to Avornis again," Lanius said. "It always was ours, even if you'd stolen it. We can use it. We can—and we will."

*Grus will use it,* Lanius thought, there in the middle of his dream. Even then, that irked him. *He'd* realized Pouncer, who stole kitchen spoons, might steal other things, grander things, if properly trained. *He'd* had Tinamus build a segment of Yozgat in the countryside. *He'd* hired Collurio to make sure the moncat learned what it was supposed to do. What had Grus done that compared, that gave *him* the right to wield the Scepter of Mercy?

No sooner did he ask the question than he also answered it. Grus had led the Avornan army from the Stura south to Yozgat. Without him, Pouncer couldn't have gotten within a couple of hundred miles of the Scepter. That might give the other king a certain claim on the talisman, mightn't it?

"You don't know *how* to use it," the Banished One said. "I could show you. . . ."

"I'm sure you could," Lanius said dryly. But the exiled god, so sensitive to tone most of the time, did not seem to notice that dryness now. The Banished One eagerly leaned forward—eagerly, that is, until Lanius added, "I'm sure you could—for your own purposes, but not for ours."

The Banished One drew back. More small lines appeared on the visage that was usually smooth as polished marble. "Die, then!" he thundered. "Die, and imagine anyone who comes after you will ever know your name."

Instead of dying, Lanius woke up. As always after facing the Banished One in a dream, he needed a moment to realize he was safe, and the confrontation was over. Sosia muttered something beside him. "It's all right, dear," he said. This time, he dared hope it really *was* all right.

He'd wondered whether he would know when and if Pouncer stole the Scepter of Mercy. He still had to wait for a courier to come up from the south. That would take a while. This time, though, he had the answer with or without the courier.

He also had something new to wonder about. Grus had always said he cared more about the Scepter of Mercy than he did about capturing Yozgat. He'd said it, yes, but did he mean it?

*I suppose that will depend on how well he's able to use the Scepter,* Lanius thought, and shook his head in slow wonder. Use the Scepter? Had he ever really believed he would think such a thing? He'd hoped so, yes. He'd done everything he could to bring this moment about. But had he really, had he truly, *believed* it would come?

For his very life, he couldn't say for certain.

He got out of bed. Sosia muttered again, but kept on breathing deeply and regularly. Gray predawn light leaked through the drawn shutters. Down in Yozgat, he supposed it would still be dark. Summer days were shorter in the south. By contrast, they had more sunshine down there in the wintertime. Things had a way of evening out. Lanius nodded again. Yes, things had a way of evening out, even if it sometimes took centuries.

The king left the royal bedchamber smiling to himself. He was the only one in the whole city of Avornis who knew what had happened down in the south. That almost made him want to thank the Banished One. Almost. The exiled god hadn't let him know to do him a favor.

*I could show you. . . .* Lanius shivered. No, the Banished

One hadn't had his good, or Avornis', in mind with a suggestion like that.

A sweeper paused and bowed as Lanius came up the hallway. "You're out and about early, Your Majesty," the old man said.

"Not as early as you are," Lanius answered. The sweeper smiled and nodded and went on with his work.

Lanius wandered. When he looked out through the windows, morning twilight brightened minute by minute. Flowers in the gardens went from gray to their proper blues and reds and golds. A few birds began to sing—not as many as would have in the early spring, but enough to sweeten the morning. More sweepers bowed and curtsied as Lanius went by. Distant shouts from the kitchens said the cooks were getting ready for a new day.

Someone came around the corner—Ortalis. "Good morning, Your Highness," Lanius said, adding, "You're up early." It was truer for Ortalis than it had been when the sweeper said it to him; Grus' legitimate son was often fond of lying in bed longer than most.

Ortalis made a horrible face. "Nightmare," he said. "One of the worst I ever had. Everything in ruins." He shuddered.

"I'm sorry." Lanius found himself meaning it, which surprised him. "My dreams were . . . not so bad." Had he ever imagined he would say such a thing after seeing the Banished One? He knew he hadn't. But was it true? Without a doubt, it was.

Morning's first sunbeam came in through the window. A new day began.

A new day began. Inside Yozgat, chaos still seemed to reign. Grus wondered whether civil war had broken out among the Menteshe. They'd opened a couple of postern gates and crossed the moat on gangplanks to raid the Avornan works around the city, but hadn't staged the all-out attack he'd feared. Maybe they could see such an assault was hopeless no matter how enamored of the Banished One they were.

That—well, that and a certain thieving moncat—left the Scepter of Mercy in Grus' hands.

He stared at the talisman in . . . *awe* was the only word he could think of, but it struck him as much too mild. The reliefs on the golden staff were so fine, he didn't see how any merely earthly, merely human artisan could have shaped them. They showed the gods in the heavens with a liveliness, an intimacy, that had to speak of personal knowledge—and how could any merely human artisan hope to come by that?

The great blue jewel atop the Scepter shone and sparkled with a life of its own. Grus could not imagine a sapphire that size. Besides, the color was wrong for a sapphire, and no sapphire—indeed, no earthly jewel he knew of—possessed that inner fire. Where could it have come from? Probably from the same place as that intimate knowledge of the gods.

Wherever it came from, the staff was plainly solid gold. And a solid gold staff of that size should have made the Scepter of Mercy much, much heavier than it was. How had the moncat ever carried it out of Yozgat? Without much trouble, evidently. And Grus had no trouble lifting it. When he did, in fact, it hardly seemed to weigh anything at all.

Lanius had said something about that. Grus scratched his head, trying to remember. For those who would use it rightly, the Scepter was light—it *made* itself light. Those who would do otherwise with it couldn't lift it at all. The Banished One himself had never found a way to wield it.

Having it was one thing. Wielding it . . . But why had it let itself come into his hands, if not for him to wield it? *Do I have the strength?* Grus wondered. *Can I do this? Should I do this?*

He hesitated. But if he did not have the strength, why had he—and Lanius, and the Kingdom of Avornis—gone through so much to reach this moment? If these years of effort had any point, it was that he *should* wield the Scepter of Mercy.

He swung the Scepter toward the south, toward the Argolid Mountains, toward the Banished One. It still seemed feather-light in his hands, which encouraged him. *This is what I ought to be doing,* he thought. He turned the jewel this way and that, like a dowser casting about for water.

And, as a dowser felt where to dig a well, so Grus knew the instant he aimed the Scepter of Mercy at the exiled god. Power crackled up his arms, as though lightning had struck nearby.

The hair at the back of his neck stood up, also as though he found himself in the middle of a thunderstorm. During dreams, he'd known the Banished One was strong. But he'd never understood *how* strong the Banished One was while he dreamed. Now the king encountered him with all his own faculties intact, and was amazed at what he'd done in those dreams.

Along with that astounding power, he took the measure of the Banished One's hatred—for him, for the material world, for the gods in the heavens who had cast him down to the world. But, under that hatred, the Scepter also showed him the Banished One's fear.

Had he not known of it, he would have had a hard time believing it was there, for his own fear was great as well. But the Scepter's revelation helped him pluck up his courage. "Now we meet while I am awake," he said.

*What if we do?* the Banished One said sullenly. Grus couldn't hear him the way he did in dreams, but had no trouble understanding what he meant. *You are a thief. You will not come to the end you look for, no matter what you do with* that. *I have told you the same thing before, and told you truly.*

Grus thought the Scepter of Mercy would let him know if the exiled god were lying. He got no sense of that now. He shrugged. How much did it matter? Not nearly as much as keeping the Banished One within some kind of reasonable limit. "Hear me," he said, and the Scepter made sure the Banished One *did* hear him.

Rage came back through the Scepter. *Who are you—what are you—to speak to me so?*

"I am the King of Avornis," Grus said. "You and yours have tormented my kingdom since time out of mind. I am going to call you to account for it. Do you understand?"

By way of answer, he got back another blast of fury, this one strong enough to stagger him. But that fear underneath it remained. The Banished One was sure Grus *could* call him to account. If the Banished One hadn't been sure, Grus wouldn't have been so sure himself.

"Do you understand?" he repeated, and something went out with his words, something that said the Banished One had better understand.

*I hear you.* The Banished One might have been a chained dog running out and discovering, suddenly and painfully, the length and strength of the chain.

"Then hear this. From now on, you will not order or encourage the Menteshe to go to war against Avornis. You will not order or encourage the Chernagors to go to war against Avornis. You will not order or encourage the Thervings to go to war against Avornis. You will not aid any of these folk, or any others, in their wars against my kingdom. By the power of the Scepter of Mercy, I order you to obey."

The Banished One's laugh could still flay. *Very well, little man. I shall do as you require of me here. Just as you command, so shall it be. And it will do you less good than you think.*

He was liable to be right. The Menteshe, the Chernagors, and the Thervings could find reasons of their own to war against Avornis. They didn't need the Banished One to spur them on. But Grus said, "I'll take the chance. And, by the power of the Scepter of Mercy, I order you to abandon all spells that make men into thralls, or that sap the will of men so they do not know or fully understand what they are doing, such as the ones you used on the Menteshe when Korkut's men and Sanjar's attacked mine together."

*You dare demand this?* the Banished One said furiously. *Do your worst, for here I shall not hearken to you.*

"I mean it," Grus said. "That is my command. You will make it so." He exerted his will. He exerted it—and the Scepter of Mercy magnified it. By himself, he couldn't have hoped to prevail. The Banished One would never even have noticed his will, let alone yielded to it. The Banished One hadn't noticed his will, or Lanius', as they mounted the campaign that yielded Avornis the Scepter of Mercy. That the exiled god hadn't was perhaps his greatest failing.

He fought back now with all his formidable strength. Opposing him was like opposing the wind, the sea, the storm. His anger and his power buffeted Grus. The king struck back. Thanks to the Scepter, he could feel the Banished One wincing when his blows landed. It was a contest where the two enemies never touched, where many miles separated them. But it reminded him of nothing so much as two strong men standing toe-to-toe smashing each other in the face until one of them either fell over or, unable to stand the battering anymore, gave up.

A shudder—that was what it felt like, anyhow—from the Banished One made Grus shudder, too, in involuntary sympathy. *Enough!* the exiled god cried. *Enough! I will do as you say. That accursed thing you carry is a torment like a lash of scorpions!*

He told the truth. The Scepter of Mercy let Grus be sure of it. The King of Avornis let out a relieved and weary sigh. The Scepter had let him win the contest of wills, but hadn't been able to disguise that it *was* a contest, and a hard one. He felt as though he'd been pounded from head to foot.

"You could do so much good in the world," he said wearily. "Why do you work evil instead?"

Now only incomprehension greeted him. *I do good,* the Banished One answered. *I do that which is good for me. Of other goodness, I know nothing.*

Again, the Scepter told Grus he meant it. *No man is a villain in his own eyes,* the king thought. Much experience with rebels and brigands had taught him as much. *It must be the same for gods. Too bad.*

He wondered if he could use the Scepter's power to show the Banished One the error of his ways. He tried—and felt himself failing. Nothing he did made the exiled god see his point of view. It was not a matter of giving orders and enforcing obedience. He would have had to change the Banished One's essential nature. And that seemed beyond even the Scepter of Mercy.

Would he be able to figure out how to make the Scepter do more than he had on this first try? Would Lanius? Who could say? One thing was sure—now they would have the chance. For centuries, Kings of Avornis had had to do without.

Since he couldn't change the exiled god's nature now, he decided to work with it instead. "Remember," he said, "the game is more even now. We have the Scepter, and this time we intend to keep it. If we have to, we'll use it again."

*I am not likely to forget,* the Banished One said. *Strength is strength. Power is power. Who would have thought* men *could do such a thing?* He might have been a man talking about moncats.

Who would have thought Pouncer could do such a thing? Lanius had, and he'd made Grus see the possibility, too. Pouncer was less than a man, much less, but Lanius hadn't underestimated the beast. Grus and Lanius were less than gods, much less, but the Banished One hadn't fully taken into account what they *could* do. And now the exiled god was paying for it. When had he last had to pay? When his ungrateful children cast him down from the heavens?

Grus had always wondered who had the right of that, whether the one who had been Milvago the god deserved to spend—eternity?—trapped down here in the material world. He still didn't know. He doubted he would ever know. But now he had a stronger opinion than he'd had before.

*Be thankful you did not push me further, little man,* the Banished One said. *Even that accursed Scepter will only go so far.*

Maybe he didn't realize Grus had already discovered as much. And maybe that was just as well. A lion tamer could put his beasts through their paces, and they would obey him. Did that mean the man, even backed by his whip, was stronger than a lion? Every so often, a lion forgot its training—or recalled what it was. And when that happened, a lion tamer got eaten.

"Yes, no doubt it will," Grus said, not showing the Banished One the alarm he felt. If a lion tamer showed fear, his beasts would be on him in a heartbeat. Still boldly, the king went on, "You would do well to remember you have limits of your own."

The burst of rage that came through the Scepter of Mercy then made his hair stand on end. That was literally true; it rose from his scalp, as it might have done if lightning struck close by. And he knew that what he felt was only the tiniest fraction of what the Banished One sent his way. The Scepter brought it down to a level a mere man might grasp without being left a mindless idiot afterwards.

With what would have been a petulant shrug from a man, the Banished One in effect turned away, breaking the channel between himself and Grus. Grus let him go. The king had done what he'd set out to do. He looked down at the Scepter, which he still held in his right hand, and shook his head. That he held it . . . If he'd imagined he ever would when he first took the throne, he'd have been sure he was doing nothing but exercising his imagination.

He walked out of his pavilion into the morning sunlight once more. The guards in front of the tent bowed very low. They didn't usually do that for him—they took him for granted. They gave their respect to the Scepter of Mercy. Pterocles waited out there, too, and Collurio and Crinitus, and Hirundo—and Otus and Fulca.

Grus laughed. They were all waiting to see how he'd done—or to see if he'd survived. He held up the Scepter of Mercy. The sun made the jewel sparkle as though alive. When Grus looked at the sun, he was amazed to see how low in the eastern sky it still stood. By the way he felt, the confrontation with the Banished One might have gone on for hours. In fact, though, it had lasted only a few minutes.

When Grus didn't speak right away, Pterocles and Otus and Collurio all asked, "Well?" at the same time, and in identical anxious tones.

That made Grus want to laugh again. He didn't. This was a serious business, as no one knew better than he. "Very well, and I thank you," he said. "I have met the Banished One, and he has no choice but to obey the Scepter of Mercy." He held it up again. The jewel sparkled once more. Maybe that wasn't the sun glancing off it. Maybe it really did have an inner fire, an inner life, of its own.

They crowded around him then, exclaiming and congratulating him. So did the pavilion guards. Hirundo took the liberty of slapping him on the back. Grus didn't mind at all. The general, a practical man, asked, "What did you squeeze out of him?"

"First, he won't help or incite any of our neighbors to war on us again," Grus answered. Everyone who heard him cheered.

He did wonder whether that pledge was good for all time. He wouldn't have bet on it. If the Scepter was ever lost again, or maybe even if Avornis had a king who lacked the will or the strength or whatever it was that he needed to use the Scepter as he should . . . In that case, the exiled god might well stir up trouble once more. But Grus did dare hope that evil day, if it ever came, lay many years away.

"You said *first*," Pterocles remarked. "That should mean there's a *second*, maybe even a *third*." He waited expectantly.

"There is—a second, anyway." Grus nodded. "He will no longer make or back up spells of thralldom, or even the weaker sort of mind-dulling magic he used on the Menteshe this campaigning season."

This time, Otus and Fulca cried out louder than the rest. She threw her arms around his neck and kissed him on the cheek. He enjoyed that liberty more than the one Hirundo had taken, and squeezed her for a moment before letting her go. He wondered if he could have gotten more from her, and wouldn't have been surprised. A little regretfully, he put the idea aside. He'd enjoyed himself with a good many women, before and after he was married, but he'd never tried to sleep with a friend's wife. He thought that record worth keeping.

"Is there a third?" Pterocles asked.

"Aren't those two enough?" Hirundo said.

"Those two *are* enough," Grus said. "The Banished One . . . is what he is. I don't think even the Scepter of Mercy can make him anything else. The only way he'll ever change is by deciding he wants to or has to, if he ever does. If he hasn't for this long, I don't suppose he will any time soon."

He looked at the Scepter again. Did the fault lie in it, or in the Banished One, or in his own ignorance of how to use it? He didn't know. Thanks to that ignorance, he couldn't know, not now—maybe not ever. But he wouldn't have been surprised if all three were involved.

"What happens next?" Hirundo asked. "Are you going to go on with the siege of Yozgat? Or is the Scepter of Mercy enough?" He eyed it with something not far from awe of his own. After a moment, he resumed. "Heading for home might be better. The sooner we can get it back to Avornis, the less chance the Menteshe have of stealing it again." After another pause, he added, "The choice is yours, Your Majesty. I know that. I was just—thinking out loud, you might say."

"I understand. I've been thinking about the same thing—only more quietly," Grus said. Hirundo made a face at him. The king went on, "I think we will go back. I told Korkut he was welcome to this place if he gave up the Scepter, and I meant it."

"It's all right with me," Hirundo said. "I just hope the Banished One doesn't whip the nomads into a fit to get it back, that's all."

"He can't. His Majesty made sure he couldn't," Pterocles pointed out. He also kept staring at the Scepter of Mercy. Some of his expression was awe like Hirundo's; the Scepter naturally brought it out. But his face also showed intense curiosity. He wanted to know what all the Scepter could do and how it did it.

That worried Grus for a moment, but only for a moment. He was sure of one thing—the Scepter would not let itself be used wrongly. If the Banished One hadn't been able to do that, Pterocles wouldn't be, either. Grus said, "We'll need to be careful no matter what. The Menteshe will probably strike at us whether the Banished One whips them on or not. They really do worship him."

"I'll do everything I can, Your Majesty," Hirundo promised. "I suppose it's possible they can beat the whole army. You can have my head, though, if they catch us by surprise."

If the Menteshe caught the Avornans by surprise, *they* would probably have Hirundo's head, and Grus', too. Grus didn't point that out. Instead, he gestured with the Scepter. By the way everyone's eyes, even his own, followed it, he couldn't have found anything more effective to do. He said, "Let's get ready to go home."

The soldiers wouldn't be sorry to break off the siege. Most of them liked having campaigned much more than they liked campaigning. Since Grus felt the same way, he couldn't get angry at them for that. And they would likely stay healthier on the move than settled down here. Fluxes of the bowels and other sicknesses cut short more sieges than enemy soldiers did.

"When we first met—when you were a river-galley skipper and I ran a troop of horsemen—did you ever dream it would come to . . . this?" Hirundo asked.

"No," Grus answered. If he tried to say yes, Hirundo wouldn't need the Scepter of Mercy to know he was lying. He pointed at the general. "How about you?"

"Me? Back then, all I worried about was driving the

Menteshe out of the kingdom. It seemed like plenty, too—plenty and then some."

"It did, didn't it?" Grus agreed. Hirundo sketched a salute and went off to start readying the withdrawal from Yozgat.

"Your Majesty?" Otus asked, and then paused. Only when Grus nodded did the former thrall go on, "Did you really mean that, Your Majesty? Thralldom is gone? All the thralls are themselves again?"

"I . . . think so," Grus answered cautiously. "When we go back, we'll send out riders to villages where our wizards have never gone. We'll find out for sure then. But that was the promise I got from the Banished One. I don't believe he can break a promise he makes through the Scepter."

"This is good. This is gooder—*better*—than anything I can think of." Otus looked at the Scepter, then toward the south. When his eyes swung back to the king, they had a twinkle in them. "I would kiss you, too, but I know you like it better from Fulca."

Grus laughed. "Well—yes," he said, and Otus laughed with him. The world seemed fresh and new and wonderful. When was the last time he'd had *that* feeling? After his first girl, maybe. He shook his head. As far as he could see, this was even better than that, and he'd never imagined anything could be.

*What's left for me to do?* he wondered. In the short run, several things needed taking care of. He knew what they were. He intended to deal with them. But after that? Once he'd recovered the Scepter, wasn't everything else an anticlimax? *I'll worry about it when I get back to the capital,* he told himself. *I've had plenty of worse things to worry about, by the gods.*

One of the things that needed taking care of now was a talk with Korkut. He approached the moat under flag of truce, but with enough shieldsmen and other guards to make sure the Menteshe couldn't hope to break the truce and kill him. When he called for Korkut, one of the defenders who understood Avornan shouted back, asking him to wait. He waved to show that he would.

The Menteshe prince came up onto the wall half an hour later. "What do you want?" he called in his fluent Avornan.

"You know I have the Scepter," Grus said.

"I know it, ah, disappeared," Korkut answered bleakly. "If you say you have it, I will not call you a liar, though you could show it to me."

"No," said Grus, who'd left it in his pavilion under guard. Bringing it anywhere near the wall would have been all too likely to tempt the Menteshe to attack to get it back. "I have it. Believe me or not, as you like. The Scepter is what I came for. I told you that before. Since I have it, I'm going home. As far as I'm concerned, you're welcome to Yozgat. Your loving half brother may have a different idea about that, but the two of you are welcome to each other, too."

"You are—going home?" Korkut sounded as though he couldn't believe his ears.

"I said so from the beginning," Grus answered. "If you'd handed me the Scepter then, we never would have had a siege to begin with. But you need to know I'm leaving because I want to, not because I have to. We've won every stand-up fight against the Menteshe. We can win one more—or three or four more—if we have to."

"Can you fight the Fallen Star, thief?" Korkut asked.

"Yes," Grus said bluntly. "I can, and I have, and if I need to I will again." That made the Menteshe who understood Avornan stir on the wall, as he'd hoped it would. The rest would stir, too, once they'd translated it. Having said what he'd come to say, he went back inside the Avornan palisade. When he looked toward Yozgat again, Korkut was still up on the wall, staring out after him. *Well, well.* Grus smiled. *Now he has something brand new to think about. Good.*

More waiting. Lanius had always thought he was a patient man. He'd had to be patient. He'd been shoved into the background several times in several different ways. Even if Pouncer had succeeded down in Yozgat, he would stay in the background. Grus would get the credit, and Grus would deserve . . . a good deal of it, for he would be the one who wielded the Scepter of Mercy.

But he never would have had the chance to wield it if Lanius hadn't had the idea to train Pouncer to steal it.

Things had happened down in the far south. The dream the

Banished One had sent made him sure of that. But he still wanted a human source for the news, a source he could pass on to others. Not having one yet made him itch worse than sitting in a bathtub full of fleas would have.

He buried himself in the archives so he wouldn't snap at whoever was unlucky enough to run into him. He expected that Grus and Collurio and Pterocles and Hirundo and Otus—maybe especially Otus—were rejoicing down there outside of Yozgat. He wanted to have a palpable excuse to rejoice himself. He wanted to run through the palace corridors whooping and waving his arms and kissing everybody he met—old men with brooms, serving girls (if Sosia didn't like it, too bad—but he would kiss her, too), fat cooks, Chernagor ambassadors (not that any Chernagor ambassadors were around right now, but the longer he waited for a letter, the more chance they had to show up), his children. Ortalis? He had to think about that, but in the end he nodded. He'd even kiss Ortalis.

But he couldn't, not just on the strength of a dream. He needed something written down in a man's hand. He ached for that—and he didn't have it.

As long as he didn't, he buried himself in tax registers that would have stupefied him in ordinary times—and he didn't stupefy easily. While he was concentrating on them, though, he wasn't thinking about anything else.

He learned that his great-great-great-grandfather was a thief and a cheapskate and a man any reasonable person would hate on sight. There were several uprisings in those days. Lanius' ancestor put them down with ferocious brutality and then taxed the rebels even more to make them pay for the cost of suppressing them. The king thought that, if he'd been alive in his multiple-great-grandfather's day, he would have wanted to revolt, too.

And yet his own father—a stern, hard man himself—would have probably put down the uprisings about the same way. And Mergus was a pretty good king, as far as Lanius could judge. The more you looked at things, the less simple they got.

One afternoon, someone knocked on the heavy doors that closed the archives off from the rest of the palace. Lanius jumped and swore. He'd trained the servants not to bother him in here unless it was the end of the world.

Maybe it was.

With that in mind, Lanius didn't shout at the apprehensive servant waiting outside. "Yes? What is it?" he asked in his usual tone of voice.

Relief blossomed on the man's face. "Your Majesty, there's a courier up from the south waiting to see you."

"Up from the south? From south of the Stura?" Lanius asked, and the servant nodded. "Well, you'd better take me to him, then," the king said.

The servant took him to the courier, who waited in an anteroom with a cup of wine and a chunk of brown bread. The man jumped to his feet and bowed. "Your Majesty, I was to give you this first," he said, and handed Lanius a rather crumpled scrap of parchment.

Lanius recognized Grus' firm hand at once. *Please don't eat the man who carries this if he bothers you while you're in the archives,* the other king wrote. *The news he carries will be worth the hearing.* A flush rose all the way to the top of Lanius' head. Grus knew him much too well.

"All right. You're eating here. You're not being eaten," Lanius said, and the courier managed a nervous smile. Lanius held out his hand. "Give me this news King Grus says you have."

His fingers trembled as he broke the seal on the letter the courier took from his tube. Now it would be official. Now the world could know. There was the other king's script again. *The moncat fetched it,* Grus wrote without preamble. *I have it. I've used it. It's even more astonishing than we hoped it would be. I'm bringing it back to the city of Avornis. It belongs to the kingdom again.* Lanius didn't run and whoop after all. He knew too much joy for that. He just stood there, smiling while tears ran down his face.

# CHAPTER TWENTY-FOUR

Before, whenever Grus found himself near the south bank of the Stura, the north bank had always seemed much farther away than the width of the river should have suggested. It was as though he were leaving a different world, one that hated him and did not want him to escape.

He didn't get that feeling now. Maybe it had always been his imagination, but he didn't think so. He'd noted it too often for that.

He turned to Hirundo, who rode beside him. "When we get back into Avornis proper with the Scepter of Mercy, all this will truly start to seem real," he said.

"It already does to me," the general replied. "When the Menteshe didn't come after us in swarms to try to take the Scepter back, that's when I knew for sure you'd taken care of things."

"The Banished One couldn't set them in motion against us. He *couldn't*." Grus repeated the word with amazement in his voice. "And there are no more thralls. None, not as far as I can tell."

"Doesn't look that way," Hirundo agreed. Thralls weren't his chief worry. He cared much more about bad-tempered horsemen with double-curved bows. "The nomads raided us a few times, harried us a little—but that's all." He sounded amazed, too.

Ferries moved back and forth across the Stura. "Do you

know what we're going to have to do one of these days? We're going to have to bridge the river," Grus said. Hirundo eyed him as though he'd gone mad. But there had been bridges over the Stura before the Menteshe came. Why not again?

Hirundo had no trouble putting his objections into words, asking, "Do you really want to give the Menteshe a free road into the kingdom?"

"If they're their own men, if they're not the Banished One's cat's-paws, why not?" Grus said. "I'd rather trade them than shoot arrows at them all the time."

"I'd like to do a lot of things," Hirundo said. "That doesn't mean I'm going to do them, or even that I ought to do them. The nomads are dangerous even as their own men."

Grus stared at him. Usually the king was the one with the calm, cool, gray good sense, and Hirundo the smiling optimist, always sure things would turn out for the best. Here they'd reversed roles. Hirundo had spent his whole career worrying about the Menteshe as enemies; he didn't have an easy time changing the way he'd thought for so long. Grus could do it. But then, he had an advantage—he'd held the Scepter of Mercy in his hand.

Instead of a bridge, a river galley waited to take them over the Stura to Cumanus. That seemed fitting. He'd started his rise to the crown as captain of a river galley. Now he would bring the Scepter back to Avornis in one.

He held the talisman as he boarded the galley, and savored the awe on the faces of officers and oarsmen. When he began to savor it perhaps too much, the Scepter seemed heavier, as though warning him that, while it deserved all the respect they gave it, he didn't. He laughed. Humility evidently walked hand in hand with mercy. Well, fair enough.

At the captain's order, the oarmaster called the stroke. He used the tap of a drum to help the men at the bow hear the rhythm. It was all as familiar to Grus as a pair of old shoes. He could have given the commands himself. The skipper was a young man. Did he remember the days when Grus had walked the deck on a ship like this? Had he even heard of those days?

And did this young skipper have the same kind of ambition as Grus had once known? Did he dream of wearing the crown himself one day? Whatever he dreamed of, it wouldn't be as big as bringing the Scepter of Mercy back where it belonged. From now on, Kings of Avornis and those who longed to be kings would have to have smaller goals. The big one, the one that had eluded so many for so long, was finally done.

The galley arrowed across the river. The wharves and piers of Cumanus drew ever closer. Then, very smoothly, the ship came up to a pier. A sailor tossed a line to a waiting longshoreman who made the bow fast to the pier. By the river galley's stern, another burly longshoreman was doing the same.

"We're here, Your Majesty," the captain said softly, as though Grus wouldn't have noticed without being told.

"By the gods, we are," Grus agreed. Yes, with the Scepter of Mercy in his hands, those first three words were something more than a common figure of speech. Olor and Quelea and the rest of the gods in the heavens might not care much about what went on in the material world, but they'd cared enough—or worried enough—to give mankind the Scepter.

"Let out the gangplank," the skipper said, and grunting sailors scrambled to obey. The captain bowed to the king. "Go ahead, Your Majesty."

"Thanks," Grus said, and he did. The gangplank echoed under his boots. It shook a little from the motion of the river on the boat. The thudding continued when Grus stepped off the gangplank, but the motion ceased. He walked toward the open gate in the wall alongside the river. He wanted to be on true Avornan soil at last.

There. Now his boots thumped on hard-packed, sandy dirt. *I've done it,* he thought. *I've brought the Scepter of Mercy home.*

Soldiers trotted toward him. For an anxious moment, he wondered if he ought to have a sword in his hand, not the Scepter. If the Banished One had somehow suborned those men . . . Enormous grins on their faces, they crowded around him, shouting congratulations.

From behind him, Pterocles said, "Everyone rejoices to see the Scepter of Mercy return to its homeland."

"So it seems." Grus would have guessed the Scepter legendary at best to most people, or more likely all but forgotten.

He seemed to be wrong. Memory of the talisman and its power survived in more places than the palace in the city of Avornis.

Shadow swallowed him as he went through the gate. Then he was in the sunshine again, and inside the walls of Cumanus. That was another milestone. He saw more ahead—bringing the Scepter of Mercy into the capital, and then bringing it into the palace. Avornis had waited four hundred years to see that day.

"Your Majesty!" That wasn't a shout of congratulations. It was a woman's voice, high and shrill and urgent. She struggled to force her way past soldiers and plump officials, and wasn't having much luck.

"What is it?" Grus called to her. He gestured with his free hand to let her pass. No one seemed to notice. Then he gestured with the Scepter, and people scrambled to get out of the woman's way. He didn't know how it did what it did, but he couldn't doubt that it did it.

She fell to her knees before him. When he helped her up, mud stained her shabby wool skirt. She said, "Help me, Your Majesty! My little daughter has a terrible fever. She'll die if she doesn't get better soon. Can you . . . Can you use the Scepter to save her?"

"I don't know," Grus answered. The only thing he'd used the Scepter of Mercy for was putting the Banished One in his place and making him stay there. This . . . This struck him as more merciful. "Take me to her," he told the woman. "I'll do what I can."

"Quelea's blessing upon you," the woman said. "Come with me, then, and hurry. I only hope she'll last until we get back there."

Grus did go with her, soldiers and Pterocles and Hirundo and abandoned officials crowding along behind them. The woman led him through a maze of alleys to what was nearer a hovel than a proper house. That didn't surprise him; neither her clothes nor the way she talked suggested any great wealth. She threw open the door and pointed ahead.

Inside, the place was cleaner than Grus would have expected. The little girl lay on what was plainly the only bed. She writhed and muttered as fever dreams roiled her. The mother was right—she wouldn't last long, not like that.

"Please," the woman said.

Not certain what he was going to do or how he was going to do it, Grus pointed the Scepter's blue jewel—no, it was not a sapphire; it was ever so much brighter and more sparkling than the finest sapphire anyone had ever seen—at the sick girl. "Queen Quelea, please make her well," he said—and nothing happened.

When he confronted the Banished One, he'd felt power thrum through him. He didn't feel that now. He didn't feel anything special at all. Very plainly, neither did the dying little girl.

When he confronted the Banished One, he hadn't called on the gods in the heavens at all. He'd used the Scepter of Mercy to focus and strengthen his own will, his own determination. He tried that now, *willing* the sickness to leave the girl. *Something* thrummed along his arm. The hair on it stood, again as it might have with thunder and lightning in the air.

The little girl sat up in bed. By the way her mother gasped, that was a separate miracle all by itself. "Mama," the girl said. "I'm thirsty, Mama." She pointed at Grus. "Who's this old man in the funny clothes?"

With another gasp, the woman said, "She doesn't mean anything bad by it, Your Majesty. She's only six."

"It's all right." Grus stroked his beard. "This will never be dark again. And I *am* wearing funny-looking clothes."

"I'm thirsty," the girl repeated. "And I'm hungry, too. Can I have some bread and oil and some figs?"

"I'll get them for you, dear, and some watered wine with them." Her mother dashed away and returned with the food and drink. When she saw how the girl ate and drank, she burst into tears. "I don't have much, Your Majesty. Whatever you want of me, though—anything at all—it's yours." She dropped to her knees in front of him once more.

He raised her up. "If I take anything for helping a little girl, I don't deserve to wear these funny clothes, do I?" he said gently. *I don't deserve to carry the Scepter of Mercy* was what went through his mind at the same time.

"Queen Quelea bless you! King Olor bless you!" she choked out between sniffles.

"It's all right. I'm glad I was able to do something, that's all."

When Grus tried to call on Quelea, the queen of the gods gave him nothing. She might as well not have been there up in the heavens. So Grus thought, but only for a moment. Yes, he'd succeeded by exercising his own will, not through her. But how had the Scepter of Mercy come to the material world, if not through the gods in the heavens? It wasn't the product of some human wizard of bygone days, and no one had ever been mad or arrogant enough to claim it was.

"More!" the little girl said, as imperiously as though she and not Estrilda or Sosia were Queen of Avornis.

As the woman turned toward the kitchen again, Grus said, "I don't think you need me here anymore. Take good care of her, and I hope she stays well from now on."

"Thank you, Your Majesty," the woman said. "I'm sure she will. How can she help it, once the Scepter has blessed her?"

"To be honest, I have no idea. There are a lot of things I don't know about the Scepter of Mercy—a lot more than I do know, as a matter of fact," Grus told her.

She looked at him as though she couldn't believe her ears. "How modest you are, Your Majesty!" she exclaimed, and then, "Who ever thought a king could be modest?"

That made him proud. His pride made the Scepter of Mercy perceptibly heavier. It didn't want him thinking what a wonderful fellow he was, at least not for reasons that had anything to do with it. He'd never been particularly modest, no matter what this grateful woman thought. He never had been, no, but now maybe he would have to be.

"Is everything all right, Your Majesty?" a guardsman called from outside the sad, shabby little house.

What would make everything all right here? About five times as much money as the woman had now. Grus couldn't just come out and say yes without making that woman liable to mock him—and without making himself deserve it. "Everything is—well enough," he said.

"Everything is wonderful!" the woman said. "Wonderful!" She kissed Grus on the cheek. Then she went over and kissed her little girl, who seemed as well and happy and bouncy as though she'd never been sick a day in her life.

Out in the street, the guardsmen and Pterocles were laughing. Grus hoped the little girl's mother never figured out why. The king's men knew his reputation, and at least wondered if the woman had given her all to pay him back. She'd offered it, all right, and he'd turned her down. *Maybe I'm growing up at last,* he thought. *Some things you do because they need doing, not because of that.*

Pterocles and the soldiers grinned at Grus when he came out. "Did you make the little girl feel better, Your Majesty?" a guardsman asked. "Did you make her mother feel better, too?" More laughter.

Grus also grinned. "The Scepter of Mercy cured the girl," he answered. "Seeing her better made the mother happy. And," he added hastily, "that's the *only* thing that made her mother happy."

The guards leered. They went right on teasing him as he walked back toward the riverside. Pterocles asked, "The Scepter of Mercy cured the little girl?"

"Yes, once I figured out what to do," Grus replied.

"I would have thought calling on Queen Quelea would do the trick," the wizard said.

"I thought the same thing, but that turned out to be wrong," Grus said. "The gods in the heavens really don't do much, or seem to want to do much, in the material world. When I used my own will instead of calling on Quelea, the girl got better."

"Interesting. Worth remembering," Pterocles said. "Of course, if it weren't for the gods in the heavens, the Scepter of Mercy wouldn't be here in the material world for us to use."

"That also occurred to me," Grus said. "I'm not going to try to get above my station. If I do, the Scepter probably won't let me use it at all." He eyed the talisman, as though wondering if it would agree with him.

Pterocles bowed to him. "Your Majesty, I don't think anyone will quarrel with you over how you've used the Scepter and how you will use it. I don't see how the Scepter itself could judge that you've done anything wrong, either."

"I hope not," was all Grus said. He didn't think the Scepter of Mercy would find he'd done anything wrong. About the rest of what the wizard had said . . . He wasn't so sure of that. Lanius would probably have ideas of his own about the Scepter and what to do with it. Lanius always had ideas; that was what he was best at. Here, the other king might well be entitled to see how those ideas went, too. If not for Lanius, the Scepter would still be inside Yozgat and the Avornans still besieging the place with no guarantee of success.

Grus wondered whether bringing home the Scepter of Mercy would impress Ortalis. He sighed. If the Scepter didn't impress his legitimate son, nothing ever would. Of course, on the evidence, it was entirely possible that nothing would.

Lanius climbed aboard one of the royal steeds—a sturdy gelding, not a stallion—to ride out of the city of Avornis and greet King Grus and the Scepter of Mercy. A few stalls down in the royal stables, Prince Ortalis was mounting a much livelier steed.

The great cathedral had its own stables. Its horses, no doubt, were greatly improved since Arch-Hallow Anser donned the red robes. Lanius couldn't help thinking someone holier should have worn those robes, so as to give the Scepter a proper blessing. But the Scepter seemed to have done just fine for itself regardless of who put on the arch-hallow's regalia.

Not far away, Prince Crex whooped with excitement. He would ride his own pony out to greet his grandfather, and couldn't have been prouder if he'd gone campaigning against the Menteshe himself.

Better still—as far as Crex was concerned, anyhow—Princess Pitta, being younger than he was and a girl besides, would ride out with Queen Sosia in a litter. That Crex had done that himself more than once did nothing to convince him it wasn't a babyish way to go.

"I think you're ready, Your Majesty," Lanius' groom said after checking the horse's trappings one last time.

"Let's go, then," Lanius said. He and Crex and Ortalis all emerged from their stalls at about the same time. Crex waved to his father. Lanius waved back. He also nodded to Ortalis.

However little he loved his brother-in-law—which was putting it mildly—he did try to be civil.

Ortalis nodded back. "So the Scepter of Mercy really is coming here, is it?" he said.

"Unless your father's been telling a lot of lies in his letters, it is," Lanius answered. "After more than four hundred years, it's finally coming home."

He thought the number would impress Ortalis. It certainly impressed him. But his brother-in-law only shrugged. "If we've done all right without it for all this time, I don't see why everybody's making such a fuss about getting it back now."

"We finally have a real weapon against the Banished One," Lanius said. "Why do you think the Menteshe stole it in the first place?"

"The Menteshe are way off . . . wherever they are," Ortalis said vaguely. Lanius was shocked and astonished to realize he didn't know, or care, whether the nomads lived to the south, the north, the west, or even the east, where Avornis had no neighbors save the sea. Ortalis went on, "Wherever they are, they aren't about to bother us here."

Against such invincible ignorance—and, worse, indifference—where could Lanius begin? Nowhere. Nowhere that he saw, anyway. He decided not to try, saying only, "Well, everyone else is pleased about it. You'll want to go along, won't you?"

"I'm here, aren't I?" Ortalis said irritably. "I'm not going to let my old man say I was off hiding somewhere when he came back. He'd score points off me for years if I did that." His chuckle was less than pleasant. "Unless I score 'em first, anyway."

"What's that supposed to mean?" Lanius asked.

"Never you mind," his brother-in-law answered. "We're going to ride out and celebrate the day, right? Yahoo! Huzzah!"

Lanius didn't think he'd ever heard less sincere celebration. But, again, it was much too late to repair the long-ruined bonds between father and son. He just said, "Come on, then," and rode out of the royal stables.

"I think Uncle Ortalis would rather be doing something else," Crex said.

"I think you're right, son," Lanius agreed. "Sometimes, though, even grown-ups have to do what they have to do, not what they want to do." Crex looked as though he wanted nothing to do with such an unpleasant notion.

Mounted guards riding in front of the royal party bellowed, "Clear the road!" The people of the capital obeyed slowly when they obeyed at all. Lanius didn't think he would have wanted anybody bellowing at him, either. He doubted the cavalrymen's officers would be interested in hearing anything like that.

Eventually, and despite more bad-tempered shouting, he and Crex and Ortalis took their places outside the city of Avornis. Arch-Hallow Anser joined them a few minutes later, followed by the women of the royal family.

Off in the distance waited a pair of horsemen. When the royal family was assembled, one of the men rode toward Lanius and his kin. The other sent his horse trotting back around a stand of apple trees and out of sight.

"Your Majesty!" called the rider who approached the king. "Your Majesty, King Grus and the rest will be along directly."

"Good," Lanius said.

The brief stretch while he waited was enlivened when Tinamus the builder hurried out to join them. "So sorry, Your Majesty," Tinamus mumbled, and stammered out a tale of woe about oversleeping, getting sidetracked on his way to the gate, and a dozen other small catastrophes.

"Never mind." Lanius waved aside all the apologies. "You're here now, and that's all that really matters."

No sooner were the words out of his mouth than a detachment from the army that had besieged Yozgat came into view. After the standard-bearers rode Grus and his companions. Hirundo was easy to spot. So was Pterocles, because he bounced along on a mule instead of a horse (no great horseman himself, Lanius had more than a little sympathy for the wizard). When the party came a little nearer, Lanius recognized Otus and Fulca, who rode behind the other king.

And there were Collurio and his son. Between them rolled a wagon that carried a cage. Lanius smiled. There was Pouncer, up near the front of things. The only trouble was, the moncat probably didn't want the honor.

A flash of blue light drew Lanius' gaze back to Grus. The other king carried the Scepter of Mercy in his left hand. Awe trickled through Lanius. *I had a hand in bringing that back here. I really did.*

"Is that the Scepter?" Sosia asked.

"That's the Scepter," Lanius answered.

"And that silly moncat stole it out of Yozgat?" his wife persisted.

"Pouncer did it, yes," Lanius said. "I don't suppose the Banished One thought the moncat was silly, though."

Sosia thought about that before nodding. "I suppose not," she said. "And having him do that was your idea?" Proudly, Lanius nodded. Sosia looked from the Scepter to the wagon carrying the moncat to Lanius again. "Nobody else would have come up with it—I'm sure of that."

Was she praising him, or was that something less? Lanius wasn't sure and didn't feel like asking. Nor did he have to. Grus broke out of the lead group and rode up to him. The Scepter of Mercy looked more magnificent the closer it got. "Your Majesty," Grus called.

"Congratulations, Your Majesty," Lanius answered. That was as much praise for Grus as it was for the Scepter. The other king had to know as much.

Then Grus did something Lanius didn't expect. He held out the Scepter of Mercy, saying, "Here. You take it for a bit. You did as much to bring it back to Avornis as I did."

"Me?" Lanius' voice rose to a startled squeak. No, he hadn't thought the other king would let him set a hand on it.

Understanding him perfectly, Grus gave him a wry smile. "One of the things you find out, once you've got the Scepter, is that you have to live up to having it. Do you know what I mean?"

"No, not altogether," Lanius admitted, "But I think I'm about to find out." He accepted the talisman from Grus.

It was lighter than it looked. He'd thought it would be from what he'd read about it, but holding it still came as a surprise. It didn't make him feel suddenly stronger or smarter than he had been a moment before. But it did make him feel *larger,* as though he and his kingdom were mysteriously merged. He could also sense the Banished One, off in the distance—not that it seemed so far from here to the Argolid Mountains, not with the Scepter in his hand. He didn't try to say anything to the exiled god; from all he knew, Grus had done everything that needed doing there. Slowly, he said, "Thank you. I begin to understand."

Then, even more slowly, but with firm determination, he handed the Scepter of Mercy back to Grus. "Thank *you*," the other king said. "I wondered if you would keep it for yourself."

Lanius shook his head. "No. I won't tell you it didn't cross my mind, because it did. But you have to be able to give the Scepter of Mercy away to deserve to hold it, don't you?"

"I thought so. That's why I handed it to you," Grus answered. "I hadn't put it quite that neatly, though, even to myself. You think straight." He suddenly grinned. "And you think crooked, too. If you didn't, the Scepter would still be sitting down in Yozgat."

"It took both of us," Lanius said.

Grus nodded. "Ride with me, Your Majesty, and we'll show the Scepter to the people of the city together."

"I'll do that." Lanius had wondered whether Grus would try to shove him into the background while celebrating the Scepter's return to Avornis. Now he realized the other king couldn't very well do that. To deserve the Scepter of Mercy, you had to live up to the ideals it stood for. That would take some getting used to, to put it mildly.

Trumpeters blared out fanfares as the two Kings of Avornis rode into the city of Avornis side by side. Grus held up the Scepter of Mercy with his right hand, Lanius with his left. People lined the streets and cheered. "Hurrah for the Scepter!" they shouted, and, "Hurrah for beating the Menteshe!" and, "Hurrah for beating the Banished One!" and, "The gods in the heavens love us!"

Did the gods in the heavens love the Avornans? Or did they just fear the exiled Milvago? Lanius had no idea. If he were to guess, he would have guessed the latter, but he knew he would only have been guessing. Nobody in the material world—except perhaps the Banished One—really understood the gods in the heavens, and the Banished One was not inclined to be objective about them.

Behind Grus and Lanius, Arch-Hallow Anser sang a hymn of thanksgiving. The two kings smiled at each other. No, Anser wasn't particularly pious; anyone who knew him knew that. But his heart was in the right place. Just now, that seemed to count for more.

Lanius wanted to look back over his shoulder to see what Ortalis was doing. Having Ortalis behind him made him nervous. He told himself he was worrying over nothing. He told himself, yes, but he couldn't make himself believe it.

Then he told himself Ortalis wouldn't try anything outrageous with the whole city of Avornis looking on. That felt more reassuring.

Instead of going on to the palace, Grus led the procession to the great cathedral. "We ought to give the gods in the heavens a prayer of gratitude," he said. "It's the least we can do." With a wry grin, he added, "And it's probably the most we can do, too."

"Yes, it probably is," Lanius agreed. "You're right, though—we ought to do it. If they don't care, well, we can't help that."

Most people in the Kingdom of Avornis—including Arch-Hallow Anser—knew less about the gods in the heavens than did the two kings. Knowing less, most people took the gods more seriously than Lanius and Grus did. No throb of reproof stung Lanius after that thought crossed his mind, even though he still had a hand on the Scepter of Mercy.

He glanced over to the Scepter. It was beautiful—perhaps even supernaturally beautiful—but its beauty wasn't what caught his eye. There it was, in his hand and Grus', but he could still believe he didn't take King Olor and Queen Quelea and the rest of the gods seriously.

He nodded to himself. Yes, he could believe that. The gods had given mortals one marvelous talisman and then, by all appearances, forgotten about it and forgotten about mankind. It had been up to the two kings to figure out how to reclaim it after it was lost for so long . . . hadn't it? If the gods had intervened in that, they'd done it far too subtly for anyone to notice.

"The moncat! The moncat! The gods love the moncat!" some people in front of a saddlery shouted as first the two kings and then Pouncer's cage went by.

Olor and Quelea and the rest had reason to love Pouncer, considering what the beast had done. But had they loved it before? Had they made it love going into the kitchens and stealing spoons? Had they given Lanius the idea that an animal which stole spoons might also steal a Scepter? He didn't think so, but how could he prove he was right to doubt it?

He couldn't, and knew as much. Once the notion occurred to him, he also knew he would spend the rest of his life wondering.

People cheered as Prince Ortalis rode through the streets of the city of Avornis. The only trouble was, they weren't cheering him. All the cheers were for his father, whom he hated and feared, and for his brother-in-law, for whom he'd always felt an amused contempt.

He wasn't amused, not anymore.

As for the Scepter of Mercy, what was the point of making such a fuss over a bauble Avornis plainly didn't need? How many years had it been gone? Lanius had told him, but he'd forgotten. Lots, though—he knew that. Had the kingdom fallen apart because it wasn't there? Of course not.

He'd tried explaining to Lanius what was only plain sense. The king hadn't wanted to listen. He'd babbled all sorts of mystical nonsense instead. Ortalis knew it was nonsense, but he hadn't felt like arguing. Life was too short.

He wondered just how he was so sure Lanius was spouting nonsense. It seemed obvious, but why? Maybe it had something to do with the dreams he'd had lately. Lanius had dreams, too, but he didn't seem to enjoy his. Ortalis wondered what was wrong with Lanius, anyhow.

How could anybody not enjoy dreams that showed him as the most powerful man in the kingdom, able to do whatever he wanted to whomever he wanted? They seemed so real, too, as though they were actually happening. And the voice—the Voice—that guided him through them didn't detract from that realism. Oh, no—just the opposite. It made everything seem sharper, more intense.

He could almost hear the Voice now, even though he was awake. He knew exactly what it would be telling him. There were his father and Lanius, riding out in front of him. They were both hanging on to the Scepter of Mercy. *They* thought it was important, even if he didn't. Since they did, shouldn't they have let him share it with them?

The question answered itself, at least in his mind. Of course they should have. But would they? No. They weren't even letting him get anywhere near it. Was that fair? Was that just? Not likely!

"Moncat! Moncat! Hurrah for the moncat!" people shouted. Ortalis didn't think that was fair, either. A stupid animal got the applause, but what did *he* get? Nothing.

His father probably thought he would be happy riding along here. Hadn't his father kept him from doing anything when it came to running the kingdom? Hadn't his father even tried to keep him from getting married? That was the truth, all right—no use trying to pretend anything different.

And hadn't his father sucked up to Lanius for all he was worth? That was the truth, too—the truth from Ortalis' eyes, anyhow. His father treated Lanius more like a son than he did his own legitimate offspring.

*I've got a son of my own now,* Ortalis thought. *Anybody who thinks he won't wear the crown—wear it after me, by the gods!—had better think again.*

The blue jewel that crowned the Scepter of Mercy sparkled in the sun. It drew all eyes to it, including Ortalis'. *I don't care if it's important or not,* he said to himself. *If they think it is, they should give me a share of it. They should, but they won't, because they want to keep it all to themselves.*

Was that really his own voice inside his head, or was it *the* Voice? He wasn't sure one way or the other. It didn't really matter. His voice and *the* Voice were saying the same thing.

After what felt like forever and a stop at the cathedral for what seemed no good reason, the procession finally got back to the palace. Ortalis slid down off his horse with a sigh of relief. He was glad to let a groom lead the animal away.

People went right on making much of his father and Lanius. Nobody paid any attention to him. He might as well not have existed. His father probably would have been happier if he didn't.

Well, he still had some friends, anyhow. Times like this showed him who they were. A guard captain named Serinus came up to him and said, "Pretty fancy show—if you like that kind of thing, anyway."

Ortalis made a face. "Just between you and me, I could live without it."

"I'll bet you could, Your Highness," Serinus said sympathetically. "Did they ever give *you* the attention you deserve? Doesn't look that way, not to me. Hardly seems right."

"Sure doesn't." Another friend of Ortalis', a lieutenant named Gygis, came up in time to hear Serinus finish.

"Question is, what can we do about it?" Ortalis said. The three of them put their heads together.

# CHAPTER TWENTY-FIVE

King Grus sat on the Diamond Throne, the Scepter of Mercy in his right hand. When he rested his arm on the arm of the throne, the base of the Scepter fit perfectly into a small depression there. He smiled to himself. He'd noticed that depression before, but he'd never really thought about why the throne had it.

Up the central aisle of the throne room toward him came a big, burly Therving named Grimoald. He had a hard, ruddy face, a thick, graying tawny beard, and graying tawny hair tied back in a braid that was not the least bit effeminate. Coupled with the wolfskin jacket he wore, he looked almost as much like a beast as a man.

The royal guardsmen in front of the throne must have thought the same thing, for they bristled like dogs scenting a wolf. Grimoald, however, affected not to notice that. He bowed low before Grus. In good if gutturally accented Avornan, he said, "Your Majesty, I bring you greetings and congratulations from my master, King Berto of Thervingia."

"I am always happy to have King Berto's greetings, and I send him my own," Grus replied. "I am also happy that his kingdom and mine have lived side by side in peace for so long, and I hope they go on living in peace for many years to come."

He meant every word of that. Berto's father had come much too close to conquering Avornis. King Dagipert had also almost succeeded in marrying Lanius to *his* daughter, which would have left him the dominant influence in the kingdom and his grandson, if he had one, probably King of both Avornis and Thervingia. Berto, however, was peaceable and pious by nature—proof, if proof was needed, that sons often differed greatly from their fathers.

Berto's ambassador bowed again. "You are gracious, Your Majesty. My sovereign sent me here as soon as word reached him that the Scepter of Mercy had come back to the city of Avornis after its, ah, long absence. I see the news was true." He stared at the Scepter with poorly disguised wonder. His eyes were blue, though not nearly as blue as the gem topping the talisman.

"Yes, it is true," Grus agreed. "King Lanius and I both did everything we could to bring the Scepter out of Yozgat. Between us, we managed." He might have bragged of his own accomplishments. He might have, yes, if he hadn't been holding the Scepter of Mercy. It didn't approve of boasting, at least not about matters involving it.

Even his modesty was plenty to impress Grimoald. "His Majesty, King Berto, has a favor to ask of you, if your kindness stretches so far," the Therving said.

"I would hear it first," Grus said. He was glad to find the Scepter didn't keep him from being normally cautious.

"Of course," the envoy said. "My king wonders whether he would be welcome if he made a pilgrimage here to see the Scepter of Mercy with his own eyes."

"He would be very welcome," Grus said, not hesitating for even a moment. "Nothing would make me happier than entertaining him here. King Lanius has met him, I believe. I have not had the privilege, though I did meet his father." They'd tried to kill each other, too, but he didn't mention that.

Grimoald's eyes glinted. He was old enough to remember the days when Thervingia and Avornis fought war after war. Maybe he longed for those days. Grus wouldn't have been surprised if a lot of Thervings did; they had always been a fierce folk, and it would likely take more than the reign of one peaceable king to make them anything else. But they hadn't risen against Berto, not once in all the years since he succeeded Dagipert.

Whatever Grimoald's opinion of days gone by might have been, he made a good, solid diplomat. Bowing to Grus once more, he said, "I shall convey your generous invitation to His Majesty. I am sure he will be eager to make the journey."

"Good," Grus said. "And of course there will be gifts for an envoy on such welcome business."

Grimoald bowed yet again. "You are much too kind, Your Majesty. I expected nothing of the kind."

"Well, whether you expected it or not, it's my pleasure," Grus said. Gifts for ambassadors were commonplace—as Grimoald no doubt knew perfectly well. Elaborate custom regulated the ones between the Chernagor city-states and Avornis. Arrangements with Thervingia were less formal, which meant Grus could be more lavish if he chose. Here, he did choose. Grimoald struck him as an able man, one he wanted well disposed toward him and toward his kingdom.

The Therving said, "You can be sure I will do everything I can to make Avornis appear in the best possible light." He understood why Grus was giving him presents, then. Good.

After Grimoald had made his final bows and left the throne room, Grus descended from the Diamond Throne. "A King of Thervingia visiting here?" said one of his guardsmen, a veteran—the soldier was perhaps forty-five, not far from Grimoald's age. "Not hardly like it was in the old days, and that's the truth. If Dagipert had, ah, visited here, he would've torn the palace down around our ears."

"Yes, the same thing crossed my mind," Grus answered. "And do you know what else? I'll bet it crossed Grimoald's, too. He had that look in his eye."

"D'you think so?" the guardsman said. "Well, I wouldn't be surprised. I wonder if we tried to murder each other, him and me, back when Berto's old man sat on their throne."

"It could be," Grus said. "Here's one more thing, though." He paused. The royal guardsman nodded expectantly. Grus continued, "It's better this way." The guardsman nodded again, this time in complete agreement.

Lanius approached the Scepter of Mercy furtively, almost as though he were sneaking up on it. He wasn't really, of course.

He couldn't, not when so many guardsmen watched it all the time. No one was going to make off with it again, not if the two Kings of Avornis had anything to say about it.

The guardsmen bowed and saluted their sovereign. Lanius nodded back, trying to hide his apprehension. He closed his hand on the Scepter and lifted. Up it came from the velvet cushion on which it rested. Lanius breathed a silent sigh of relief and set it down again.

"That's a marvelous thing, Your Majesty," a guard said.

"Yes, isn't it?" Lanius agreed. He didn't tell the guardsman—he didn't intend to tell anyone—the Scepter had let him pick it up even though he'd sneaked a serving girl into the archives. Whatever it expected of Kings of Avornis, it didn't insist on sainthood. He hadn't been sure. Had things turned out the other way, he would have been as penitent as he could—and he would have put the maidservant aside. Maybe that would have been enough. He could hope so, anyway.

"Is it really true that one of your moncats stole the Scepter out of Yozgat?" the guardsman asked.

"It's really true," Lanius said solemnly. "And if you don't believe me, you can ask Pouncer."

The soldier started to nod, then stopped and sent him a look somewhere between quizzical and aggrieved. Lanius smiled to himself as he went on his way. He didn't want people taking him for granted.

King Grus came around the corner. "What are you looking so pleased about, Your Majesty?" Grus asked. "The Scepter?"

"Well, yes, in a manner of speaking." Lanius looked back over his shoulder to make sure the guardsman couldn't hear, then explained how he'd confused the man.

He got a laugh from Grus. "You never know—maybe the moncat would tell him," the other king said.

"Maybe Pouncer would," Lanius agreed. "With that beast, you never know for sure until you see what happens."

"Maybe the gods in the heavens *were* working through him," Grus said. "We'll never know, not for certain."

"Maybe." But Lanius went on, "I can't imagine a better disguise for a god than a moncat."

That made Grus laugh again. "No doubt you're right. At

least the Banished One didn't get into him." The other king was joking, but Lanius felt a chill all the same. The Banished One probably *could* have done something like that. Why hadn't he? The only answer that occurred to Lanius was that, if the exiled god despised people, wasn't he likely to despise animals even more?

Lanius didn't say that out loud. No dreams had troubled him since the Scepter came back to the capital, but who could say how long the Banished One's reach was even now? Instead, the king changed the subject. "So Berto truly is coming? It's been a long time since I've seen him. I was still a boy."

"Berto's really coming. Yes, indeed." Grus nodded. "Grimoald should be back in Thervingia by now, telling him we'd be glad to see him. And you're one up on me, because I've never set eyes on the man. Dagipert . . . Dagipert's a different story."

"In all kinds of ways," Lanius said, and Grus nodded once more. Lanius went on, "It's funny, you know, that Berto's more pious than we are." He thought of his sport with the serving girl. The Scepter of Mercy had forgiven him—either that, or found there was nothing that needed forgiving. "Of course, he knows less than we do, too." He mouthed Milvago's name, but didn't say it aloud. "A good thing, too," he finished. "If Thervingia had pitched into us while we were fighting the Chernagors or the Menteshe . . ."

"Yes, that's a nightmare right there, isn't it?" Grus said. "I worried about it for a while after Dagipert died. I couldn't believe that iron-handed old tyrant would have a son who cared for nothing but praying. Only goes to show you never can tell, doesn't it?"

"It does indeed." Lanius favored Grus with a brief but speculative glance.

To his acute embarrassment, his father-in-law burst out laughing one more time. Grus aimed an accusing finger at him. "By Olor's beard, I know what you're thinking. You're thinking you're looking at another iron-handed old tyrant."

"You're not a tyrant," Lanius blurted. Grus laughed harder than ever. Lanius got more embarrassed than ever.

"Oh, dear," Grus wheezed at last. "The worst of it is, you're not even slightly wrong. I'm never going to be young again, that's for sure. And the Chernagors and the Menteshe and a good many Avornan nobles will tell you what an iron-handed rogue I am. Come to that, those Avornan nobles will likely call me a tyrant, too."

"*I* didn't," Lanius said virtuously.

"So you didn't," Grus agreed. "And the Scepter of Mercy doesn't think I'm a tyrant, either, or it wouldn't let me pick it up. And do you know what? I care more about what it thinks than I do about any Avornan noble."

Lanius had no idea whether the Scepter *thought* in manlike terms. He was inclined to doubt it. But he knew what the other king meant all the same. "Oh, yes," he said, remembering his relief of a little while before. "The Scepter is an honest judge."

Grus smiled. "Do you want to know something funny?"

"I would love to know something funny," Lanius answered.

"Right this minute, I hardly know how to be king," his father-in-law said. "We haven't got any enemies. The Chernagors are quiet. The Menteshe are quiet. The King of Thervingia isn't just quiet—he's coming here on a pilgrimage. Even our nobles are quiet. What am I supposed to do? Sit on the Diamond Throne and twiddle my thumbs?" He started twiddling them even though he wasn't on the throne.

"There are worse troubles to have," Lanius said, and started twiddling his own thumbs. Grus chuckled. Lanius went on, "Enjoy the quiet while you can, because it won't last. It never does. The Chernagors will get bored not being piratical. Sooner or later, Korkut or Sanjar is bound to win that civil war. Then the Menteshe will start trying to take bites out of what we've won south of the Stura, and maybe on this side of the river, too. They don't need the Banished One to make them want to raid us."

"This thought had already crossed my mind," Grus said.

"Things won't stay quiet forever inside Avornis, either," Lanius added. "Somebody with a lot will decide that, however much he has, it isn't enough. And he'll blame you—or maybe me—for that, and he'll start making trouble. I don't think it'll happen tomorrow, but I don't think we'll have to wait very long, either."

"That all sounds sensible. You usually do make good sense, Your Majesty. So I'll have things to worry about again, will I? My heart wouldn't break if I didn't," Grus said.

"I'm sorry, but I'm afraid you'll have to. Things work that way," Lanius said.

Grus only shrugged. "Do you know what else? After bringing the Scepter back, getting excited about any of them won't be easy." Lanius thought the other king was joking, then took a second look at him and decided he wasn't.

In Ortalis' dream, he held Avornis in the palm of his hand. The kingdom was his, and rightfully his. He didn't know what had happened to his father or to Lanius, but they weren't around to give him trouble. He did know that.

"You see?" the Voice told him. "You can do it. Don't let anyone tell you that you can't do it. This kingdom belongs to you. They may try to keep you from taking what's yours, but they won't get away with it, will they?"

"No!" dream-Ortalis said.

"Avornis is yours, and Marinus' after you. Isn't *that* right?" the Voice asked.

"You'd better believe it is!" dream-Ortalis answered.

"And if they do try to steal your birthright? What will you do then?" the Voice inquired. "What *can* you do then?"

"Punish them!" dream-Ortalis exclaimed.

"How would you do that?" the Voice asked, as smoothly and suavely as though it were at some elegant reception.

Ortalis' response was anything but elegant. "With whips!" he shouted. "With whips, until they scream for mercy. Or maybe I'd take them out to the woods and . . . and *hunt* them! Yes, maybe I'd do that!" Excitement surged through him. His father and Lanius and even Anser had kept him from ever really hunting people. In his dreams, though, it was perfectly all right. In his dreams, in his *special* dreams, everything went just the way he wanted.

"Once you caught them, you could mount their heads on the wall of the royal bedchamber," the Voice mused. "They would look good there."

"They might," Ortalis murmured. "Yes, they just might."

"Might what?" Limosa asked, breaking off the dream and returning Ortalis to everyday reality. It seemed much less real than the bright, vivid scene he'd just left. His wife, oblivious, went on, "You were talking in your sleep."

"Was I?" Ortalis blinked, there in the darkness of his bedroom. The brilliant light by which he'd seen things in his mind's eye was gone, gone. Yet the sense of excitement he'd felt in his dreams remained. There was excitement, and then there was excitement. "Maybe I was thinking I might do . . . this." He reached for Limosa.

She squeaked as his hands roamed her. "What? In the middle of the night?" she said, as though the very idea were a crime against nature. She shoved him away.

When she did something like that, it only excited him more. "Yes, in the middle of the night," he said, and began to caress her again.

If she'd kept on struggling, he would have taken her by force. He enjoyed that, though it appealed to Limosa less than the special thrill of the whip. But she must have decided he was going to do what he wanted whether she came along or not, and that she would have a better time coming along. Instead of trying to fight him off, she began to stroke him in turn and to urge him on.

He needed very little urging. He drove home, again and again, until Limosa gasped and shuddered beneath him. A moment later, he spent himself, too. "Maybe you should talk in your sleep more often," Limosa purred.

"Maybe I should," Ortalis said. He stood up, used the chamber pot, and lay down again. Sleep came quickly, but all his dreams were ordinary.

When he woke up the next morning, he felt vaguely cheated. Not even Limosa's smile, bright as the sunshine outside, could drive that feeling away from him. In his dreams, his special dreams, he was everything he was supposed to be, and everything went the way he wanted it to. And the Voice was there, urging, explaining, supporting. The Voice seemed more real and more full of character than most of the people he knew in the clear light of day.

He called a servant, and told the man to have his breakfast

and Limosa's brought to the bedchamber. "Yes, Your High-ness," the man said, and hurried away.

"You don't want to eat with the king?" Limosa asked.

"No, not today," Ortalis answered, and let it go at that. She meant Lanius, of course. But Ortalis' father was back in the palace, too, and the prince especially did not want to eat with him.

"I hope His Majesty won't be offended," Limosa said.

"It'll be all right." Ortalis didn't much care whether it would or not. But he thought it would. Lanius was soft. Even when he was slighted, he hardly seemed to notice most of the time.

Ortalis laughed. *I know better than that,* he thought. He never forgot an insult. *One of these days, I'll pay everybody back for everything.* Lanius, Anser, his father—everyone. He was starting to get the feeling that that day wasn't so far away, either.

A knock on the door said breakfast had arrived. Ortalis took the tray from the servant and brought it back to the bed. It wasn't anything fancy—barley porridge enlivened with chopped onions and chunks of sausage, with wine to wash it down—but it was good, and it filled the belly.

Limosa put on a tunic and a long skirt. "I'm going to see how the children are," she said.

"All right," Ortalis answered. "Better Marinus' howling while he's teething should keep a nursemaid up half the night than that it should bother us."

"Well, yes," Limosa said, "but plenty of people who don't have the money for nursemaids have children, too. They must get through teething and sick babies by themselves, or there wouldn't be any more people."

"Gods know how they manage it," Ortalis said.

"What will you do today?" Limosa asked.

"Beats me," Ortalis said cheerfully. He lay down on the bed again. "Maybe I'll just go back to sleep." He hoped he could. He wished he could. The kingdom of his special dreams and the seductive soothing of the Voice were ever so much more at-tractive than the mundane reality of the Kingdom of Avornis.

His wife's sniff told him that wasn't what she'd wanted to hear. "They're your children, too," she said pointedly.

"I'll be along in a while," he said. If that didn't make her happy, too bad.

She knew better than to push an argument very far with him. "All right," she said, and left the bedchamber.

Ortalis did lie down again. But, no matter how he tried, sleep would not come.

From the city of Avornis, the Bantian Mountains were barely visible—a purple smear on the horizon on a clear day, a smear that vanished with the least fog or haze. Here on the frontier between Avornis and Thervingia, the mountains' saw-backed shape defined the boundary between land and sky.

King Grus and his soldiers waited for King Berto to cross over the border. Grus had waited with soldiers for King Dagipert to cross the border, too. Then he'd waited—and waited anxiously—to do battle. Now the soldiers were an honor guard.

One of his guardsmen pointed east. "Here come the Thervings, Your Majesty," the man said.

Grus shaded his eyes with the palm of his hand. "You're right," he said after a moment. "Is that Berto, there in the middle? The one whose beard is going gray?" He wasn't sure just how old Berto was. Older than Lanius and younger than he was himself, but that covered a lot of ground.

"I think so, Your Majesty," the guardsman replied. "Yes— I'm sure it is. He's wearing a coronet."

Even as he spoke, the King of Thervingia's gold circlet flashed in the sun. Grus nodded. "Well, so he is. He doesn't have very many men with him, does he?" The troopers who rode with Berto were far fewer than the men accompanying Grus. If he'd wanted to . . . But he didn't. If Dagipert had given him a chance like this, he would have been sorely tempted. Dagipert, of course, had been far too canny ever to make such a mistake.

Chuckling, Grus remembered his last meeting with Berto's father. They'd each rebuilt part of a bridge over the Tuola River, a bridge that had long been cast down to help keep the Thervings out of the heartland of Avornis. They'd spoken across a gap too wide to let either reach the other with a weapon. And after the parley, Avornans and Thervings wrecked what they'd built.

These days, the bridge over the Tuola stood again. Grus had crossed it on the way to the border. Therving traders and Avornan merchants went over it every day. Soldiers—soldiers in arms, anyhow—didn't seek to cross it. That was why it stood again.

Berto had almost reached the granite pillar that marked the border. Dagipert had knocked that pillar over not long after the start of his reign, but it too stood once more. Grus waved to the approaching King of Thervingia. "Welcome, Your Majesty!" he called, first in Avornan, then in Thervingian. He didn't speak much of the latter, but he'd made sure to learn that phrase.

"Thank you, Your Majesty," Berto answered, first in his own tongue, then in almost accentless Avornan. He kept on using Grus' language as he continued, "I am glad to enter your kingdom as a peaceful pilgrim."

"And we are glad to have you here." Grus rode up to the pillar, but not an inch beyond. He held out his hand. Berto took it. His clasp was stronger than Grus had expected. He might not be a warrior, but he was no weakling.

Berto rode past Grus and into Avornis. "It's been many years since I've seen your capital," he said, and smiled. "This time, my people won't have to besiege it to let me get inside."

Grus smiled back. "You've always been welcome to visit, Your Majesty, as long as you didn't try to bring your whole kingdom along."

"Here I am," Berto said. "I think the men I have with me will be plenty. In fact, I think I could have come alone and been as safe as though I'd stayed at home—maybe safer. Any man who could use the Scepter of Mercy, any man who could bring it back from the south, would not betray his trust with a guest."

*And what am I supposed to say to that?* Grus wondered. The first thing that came into his mind and out of his mouth was, "You do me too much credit."

"I don't think so," Berto said. "The Scepter of Mercy!" His gray eyes went wide with what Grus slowly recognized as awe. "Real proof that the gods in the heavens care about us and care for us."

"Well, so it is." Grus didn't mention that it seemed to him to be proof the gods in the heavens didn't care about the material world very much. If they had, would they have let the Scepter stay lost for so many centuries? Would they have let so many generations of thralls live and die one short step above beast-hood? Grus suspected they worried more about the Banished One and his chances of storming into the heavens again than about Avornis or Thervingia or anything else merely human.

He didn't say any of that to Berto. If the other king wanted to believe in merciful gods who watched over him, why not? Grus wished he could do the same.

"Shall we go on, then, Your Majesty?" Berto said.

"I am at your service, Your Majesty," Grus replied. He waved to his men. They all swung their horses back toward the east, back toward the city of Avornis. Dust kicked up from the animals' hooves as they began to walk. Grus smiled again. Going places at a walk was a pleasure, a luxury, all by itself. He'd spent a lot of years trying to get from here to there in a tearing hurry. Right this minute, he didn't have to, and he wanted to savor the sensation of slowness.

Cattle and sheep grazed in the meadows. Farmers tended their fields—harvest time wasn't far away. When Dagipert warred against Avornis, this province west of the Tuola had been a ravaged wasteland, fought over and plundered by both sides. Peace had a lot to be said for it.

"I've always wanted to meet you," Berto said. "My father admired you greatly."

"Did he?" Grus hoped he didn't sound too surprised. "I always had great respect for him, too." In less polite language, that meant, *He scared the whey out of me.* "He was a formidable man."

"He would say, 'The cursed Avornans found somebody who knew what he was doing, and just in the nick of time.'" Berto's voice was mild, on the border between tenor and baritone. He deepened and roughened it to give a pretty good impression of the way his father had sounded. He went on, "I mean no offense—that was how he talked. And he'd say, 'If not for that miserable Grus, I'd have Avornis in my belt pouch.'"

Dagipert had come close as things were. Grus said, "Both sides spilled a lot of blood and a lot of treasure. You should always be able to fight at need, but you shouldn't go looking for the need all that often."

"I agree," Berto said, and said no more.

Once again, Grus wondered how he would have done if he'd had to worry about Thervingia along with the Chernagors and Menteshe. *Not very well,* he thought. Yes, who would have imagined the ferocious Dagipert could have a peaceable, pious son? Grus sent a sudden, startled glance upward. *Maybe the gods in the heavens did.*

"What is it?" Berto asked.

"Nothing," Grus answered. Then, because he was an honest man (except sometimes when he was talking to his wife), he added, "I don't think it's anything, anyway." It certainly wasn't anything he or Lanius or Pterocles would be able to prove. The most they would ever be able to do was wonder.

To his relief, King Berto proved incurious. "All right," he said, and let it go at that. The two sovereigns and their retinues rode deeper into Avornis.

The gates to the city of Avornis stood open. Lanius waited on his horse not far outside the one that faced west. Beside him, looking much more comfortable on horseback, sat Anser. The arch-hallow had other things than horsemanship to worry about today. "I'm not used to riding in these robes," he muttered. The crimson vestments of his office were indeed a far cry from the hunting clothes he usually chose when he got on a horse.

"Can't be helped," Lanius said. "King Berto expects you to look like a holy man."

"I know. I'll do it," Anser said. "He doesn't know just what he's getting, though, does he?"

"He's getting the arch-hallow," Lanius told him. "That's all he has to worry about." He looked down the road that led to Thervingia, the road along which so much trouble for Avornis had come in years gone by. The dust from Berto's followers and Grus' had been visible for some little while. Now he could make out the horses that were kicking it up. "They won't be long."

"So they won't," Anser agreed. "I'll show Berto the great cathedral, and then he'll go over to the palace and slobber on the Scepter of Mercy."

That was inelegant, which didn't make it any less likely to be true. Up rode King Grus and King Berto. Grus bowed in the saddle and nodded to Lanius. "Your Majesty, I am pleased to present to you His Majesty, King Berto of Thervingia."

Lanius held out his hand to Berto. "We've met before, Your Majesty."

The Therving had been smiling before. His smile got broader now. "Why, so we have. I was not sure you would remember."

"Oh, yes," Lanius said, although in fact he could not recall Berto's face. "Welcome to the city of Avornis." He waved back toward the open gate. "You are welcome here."

No Therving, not even the mighty Dagipert, had ever forced his way into the capital. But Berto hadn't tried to force his way in; he came in peace. He was looking from Anser to Grus and back again. More than Ortalis back at the palace, Anser favored his father. Berto didn't remark on it, not out loud. All he said was, "I am honored to make your acquaintance, Most Holy."

"And I yours, Your Majesty. I hope the gods in the heavens looked over you on your way here and gave you a safe and pleasant journey." Though not an especially holy man, Anser could sound like one when he had to.

"Yes, thank you," Berto said. "I so look forward to seeing the great cathedral once more — and then, perhaps, if all of you would be so kind, the Scepter of Mercy itself?"

"Without a doubt, Your Majesty," Lanius said. Grus nodded. Anser's expression was full of I-told-you-so.

Along with his followers, the two Kings of Avornis, the arch-hallow, and the men who had ridden with Grus, King Berto rode over the drawbridge and entered the capital. Local citizens came out to cheer him. The older ones no doubt had fearful memories of less friendly Therving visits to the neighborhood of their city, but Dagipert had been dead for a good many years now. Palace officials made sure the crowd was friendly, sometimes with small bribes. That had been Grus' idea; Lanius, who wouldn't have thought of it himself, admired it all the more because he wouldn't have.

King Berto pointed toward the great cathedral's spire, a landmark that stood out more than the palace's disorderly sprawl. "It's as splendid as I remember, leaping to the heavens," Berto said. "Will the arch-hallow lead a service for me?"

"Of course, Your Majesty. I would be honored," Anser said smoothly. And when they got inside the cathedral, he did a perfectly capable job of saying the required prayers and chanting the hymns that went with them. How deeply he felt what he was doing—indeed, whether he felt it at all—was a different question, but, with luck, not one that occurred to the King of Thervingia.

The more obvious question had occurred to Berto. "He looks like you," he murmured to Grus during a lull in the services.

Lanius wondered how the other king would handle that. "D'you think so?" Grus answered, his voice bland. But then he relented. "He *is* my son, Your Majesty, but on the wrong side of the blanket, if you know what I mean."

"Ah. Yes. Of course." Berto did his best to look worldly-wise. "You seem to have found a good place for him here, for I can tell how much he loves the gods."

That meant Anser made a better actor than Lanius had suspected. If Berto had spoken of the chase . . . There, the arch-hallow's enthusiasm was altogether unfeigned. Well, Anser had earned some good hunting with his performance here today.

Berto bowed and knelt and prayed and chanted with un-feigned enthusiasm of his own. Lanius tried his best to match, or at least to appear to match, the King of Thervingia's piety. He noticed Grus doing the same thing. His eye slid to the Thervings who'd accompanied their king to the city of Avornis. They also did not seem to be merely going through the motions. Maybe they were as sincere as Berto, or maybe, like courtiers everywhere, they simply had the sense to follow him in whatever direction he went.

"Coming here does my soul good," Berto said when the service ended. "This wonderful building reminds me how important the gods are to us all. You Avornans are so lucky, to be able to worship here whenever you please." He paused. Lanius and Grus both nodded politely. Neither said anything. Berto went on, "Would it be . . . could it be possible for me to see the Scepter of Mercy now?"

"Of course, Your Majesty," Lanius and Grus said together. Lanius added, "The palace is only a short walk away."

Queen Estrilda waited at the entrance. So did Queen Sosia, with Crex and Pitta. And so did Prince Ortalis and Princess Limosa, with Capella and baby Marinus. King Berto was unfailingly polite to the rest of the Avornan royal family. It was plain, though, that they interested him not in the least. And why should they have? Next to the Scepter of Mercy, they were only . . . people.

Lanius hoped the servants had gotten all the trophies won in battle against the Thervings out of sight. He didn't want to remind Berto how often their kingdoms had clashed in days gone by.

Guardsmen drew themselves up to stiff attention as the three kings came up to the Scepter of Mercy. "How beautiful it is!" Berto whispered. "That jewel . . . Yes, you *are* lucky, all of you. You tempt me to go to war to carry it back to Thervingia." He laughed. "That is a joke, my friends. No one who does not serve the Banished One could want to take the Scepter away from its proper home."

If it was a joke, Lanius found it far from funny. He thought of a way to test it. He lifted the Scepter of Mercy and handed it to Grus, hoping the other King of Avornis was thinking along with him. And Grus was. Most ceremoniously, he passed the Scepter to Berto.

The King of Thervingia gasped at the honor the Avornans had done him. And it *was* an honor. But it was also a test. If he wanted to steal the Scepter, wouldn't it sense as much and not let him hold it? So Lanius reasoned, anyhow.

But King Berto had no trouble holding the Scepter. An exalted look spread over his face. "In my hands," he murmured. "In *my* hands . . ." He bowed deeply to Lanius and to Grus, then returned the Scepter of Mercy to Lanius. "I prove myself worthy of it by giving it back."

At that, Lanius and Grus both bowed to him. "We realized the same thing, Your Majesty," Lanius said respectfully. "If the Scepter has a secret, that is it." And it was a secret the Banished One would never, ever understand.

# CHAPTER TWENTY-SIX

Ortalis was convinced that if he'd been any more bored, he would have been dead. His father and Lanius and the visiting barbarian were making such a fuss over the Scepter of Mercy, he more than half wished it would have stayed down in Yozgat. Had his father—had anyone—ever made such a fuss over *him*? He didn't think so.

Lanius, of course, was crazy for old things, and now he had his hands on something as old as the hills. It all made Ortalis want to yawn. So the Scepter was here. Kings could pick it up and do things with it. *When I'm king, I'll pick it up and do things with it,* Ortalis thought. *Until then, who cares?*

"Do you like to go hunting?" Ortalis asked Berto at a feast the evening after the King of Thervingia came to the palace.

Berto paused to gnaw the meat off a roasted duck drumstick before answering, "Not very much, I'm afraid, Your Highness. I find prayer and contemplation more pleasant ways to pass the time."

"Oh," said Ortalis, who found prayer and contemplation even duller than all the unending chatter about the Scepter, if such a thing was possible. He thought for a moment, then tried again, asking, "What do you like in a woman?"

"Well, piety, to begin with," Berto said, and Ortalis gave up. Even if the Therving had no . . . special tastes, he could have come up with something more interesting than *that*. But he made his answer seem the most natural thing in the world.

Once more, Ortalis fought to stifle a yawn. He reached for another chunk of duck himself. The dead bird had to be more interesting than the Therving.

"What of you, Your Highness?" Berto asked. "How did you aid your father and your sister's husband in recovering the Scepter of Mercy?"

"In . . . recovering it?" Ortalis could hardly believe his ears. He couldn't have cared less about getting the Scepter back. As far as he was concerned, the Banished One was welcome to it. But King Berto would have dropped the leg bone if he'd said that. The only thing he did say was, "Well, any way I could, of course."

That did the job, and with room to spare. The King of Thervingia beamed at him and raised his winecup in salute. "Spoken like the true son of a great father!" He gulped down the sweet red wine.

So did Ortalis, who needed little excuse, or sometimes none at all, for some serious guzzling. A serving girl poured his cup full again after he drained it. He smiled at her. She quickly found something to do somewhere else. He laughed; he'd drunk enough to make even that funny. He wanted to tell Berto that of course he was Grus' true son, that Grus' bastard son was a nice enough fellow but of no real consequence. He wanted to, but he didn't. To Grus, *he* was of no real consequence himself. He knew that—knew it and hated it.

"I'll show him," he muttered. "I'll show *everybody*, I will."

"What's that, Your Highness?" King Berto asked. Why wasn't he too drunk to pay attention to someone else's private mutterings?

"Have you ever listened to a voice? A Voice, I mean?" Ortalis said in return. "A Voice that told you—that showed you— the way things were supposed to be?"

Berto frowned, which made his bushy eyebrows almost meet above his long, straight nose. "Are you talking about your conscience? I know I try to listen to mine. I am only a man. I do things I wish I hadn't later on. But I do try."

They both used Avornan, but they didn't speak the same language. Ortalis was no more talking about his conscience than he'd thought of looking for piety in a woman. He almost told

Berto so to his face, just to see the barbarian splutter. But something—maybe even the Voice—warned him that wouldn't be a good idea.

He endured the rest of the banquet, then staggered off to bed. After blearily kissing Limosa half on the mouth, half on the cheek, he fell deep into sodden slumber. And then, as he'd hoped he would, he dreamed.

The dream felt and seemed more real than reality. These dreams always did. He looked out on the world the way it should have been. The biggest difference was that it was a world that recognized Ortalis as its rightful lord and master. The Voice said, "They mock you behind your back."

When the Voice said something, there was no room for doubt. "Oh, they do, do they?" Ortalis growled. "Well, I'll show them. I'll show them all. You just see if I don't."

"Time grows short," the Voice warned. "Chances grow few. You would do well to seize the ones you have."

"I will. Oh, I will," Ortalis said. "You don't need to worry about that. I'll take care of everything—just wait and see."

"Are your friends your true friends?" the Voice asked. "Are your enemies lulled and drowsy?"

Ortalis thought of Serinus and Gygis, and of the other young officers he'd cultivated since Marinus was born. "My friends are my true friends," he answered. "They know where their hopes lie."

"Good," the Voice said smoothly. "And your enemies? *Are* they lulled?"

At that, Ortalis laughed a raucous and bitter laugh, there in the middle of his dream. "Why should they need lulling? They don't think they do, not from the likes of me."

For a dreadful moment, he wondered if the Voice would laugh, too—laugh at him, not with him. But it didn't. Instead, it said, "Well, then, the time is coming, and coming soon, don't you think?"

"What time?" Ortalis asked, and the dream showed him. It was better than he'd imagined, better than he could have imagined before the Voice started speaking to him in the night. The time was coming soon? He could hardly wait.

\* \* \*

Grus and Pterocles and Otus stood staring at the Scepter of Mercy. Grus could understand why King Berto had traveled so far to see the great talisman. If it had come to Thervingia, he thought he might have traveled there to see it himself. But it was here in the city of Avornis, and he could look on it, he could *use* it, whenever he liked. Somehow, that pleased him less than he'd thought it would. Maybe being able to leave it, as Berto had done, was better than keeping it.

Otus didn't think so. A smile on his face, the former thrall said, "It freed my folk." He shook his head and bowed to Grus and Pterocles. "Well, no. You two freed my folk. But the Scepter made sure they will stay free."

"So it did," Grus said. And the Scepter *had* let him impose his will on the Banished One. With it in his hand, he'd been, for a little while, as great as—greater than—the exiled god. He had been . . . but now, again, he wasn't. He snapped his fingers.

"What is it, Your Majesty?" Pterocles asked.

"Where do I go from here?" Grus had a question of his own.

The wizard frowned. "I don't understand."

"Where do I go from here?" Grus repeated. At last he *did* understand at least some of what was troubling him. "Where?" he said yet again. "What's left for me to do, after I've done *this*?" He pointed to the Scepter.

"Why, live happily ever after." That wasn't Pterocles but Otus. He went on, "By the gods in the heavens, if anyone's ever earned the right, you're the man."

Slowly, Grus shook his head. "This isn't a fairy tale, I'm afraid. I wish it were. I've spent a lot of years matched against the Thervings and the Chernagors and the Menteshe and our own nobles. I've fought and I've schemed and I've plotted. Lanius worked out how to get the Scepter back from Yozgat, and I went and did it. I did it, and I used the Scepter the way you said, Otus—and now what can I possibly do for the rest of my days that will matter even a tenth as much?"

"Oh," Pterocles said softly. "Now I see."

Otus still looked puzzled. He had what he wanted—his soul to call his own and his woman to call his own, too—and he was content. What Grus had was the certain knowledge that he'd already done the greatest deeds of his life. He was proud of them, yes, but they made everything that might come after feel like an anticlimax.

And how many years of anticlimax did he have to look forward to? No way for him to be sure, of course. Perhaps the gods in the heavens were sure of such things. If so, keeping it to themselves was one of the few kindnesses they showed mortal men.

Grus turned away from the Scepter of Mercy. Getting what you'd always wanted your whole life long was wonderful. Having it in front of you and knowing you would never want anything as much again as long as you lived—and also knowing that nothing you did want would be of any great consequence next to what you already had—was daunting.

For a moment, he imagined he heard laughter far off in the distance. Then he realized he wasn't imagining it; it was a servant somewhere halfway across the palace. A sigh of relief escaped him. He'd feared it was the Banished One, getting the last laugh after all.

He looked south, as he'd hardly done since coming back to the city of Avornis. Suppose the exiled god had gotten what *he* always wanted. Suppose he'd been able to master the Scepter of Mercy and regain rule in the heavens. Would he have lived happily ever after? Or would even limitless domination have palled after a while? Grus didn't know, of course. By the nature of things, he couldn't know how things would have gone for the Banished One. But he knew how he would guess.

It also occurred to him that the Banished One didn't know how lucky he was, not to have gotten his heart's desire. He could go on scheming and plotting and trying to come up with ways to get the Scepter of Mercy out of the hands of the Kings of Avornis. That wouldn't be so easy now, not since Grus had enjoined him against using any of the surrounding peoples against the kingdom. But the exiled god could keep on trying. Since he *hadn't* gotten his heart's desire, his existence still held purpose.

Grus wished he could be sure the same held true for his own.

Lanius also found himself wondering what to do now that the Scepter of Mercy had returned to Avornis. He was better than

Grus at finding ways to occupy his time. He wrote a long, de
tailed account of King Berto's visit to the capital. He feare
Crex wouldn't read the account; his son hadn't shown much in
terest in *How to Be a King*. But even if Crex never did glanc
at it, it would stay in the archives. Some other king might fin
it useful one day—or, if not that, it might help keep the futur
king awake on a long, warm summer afternoon. That was im
mortality, of a sort.

Immortality of another sort made Sosia's belly bulge. Laniu
hoped for a second son. Things would feel . . . safer if Crex ha
a brother. And who could say? Maybe the new child woul
have the scholarly temperament Crex lacked.

Sosia didn't worry about any of that. "I want this baby t
come out," she said. "I'm tried of looking like I swallowed
pumpkin. I'm even tireder of squatting over a chamber pot god
only know how many times a day."

"I'm sorry," Lanius said. "I can't do anything about that."

She sent him a glance half affectionate, half annoyed. "Yo
did have something to do with this business, you know."

"Well, yes," he admitted.

"I just wish Queen Quelea had found a better way to g
about it," his wife said. She eyed him again. "Can the Scepte
of Mercy do anything about *that*? It would be a mercy if
could."

"I don't know, but I wouldn't think so," Lanius answered
flabbergasted. "There's nothing in the archives about using
for anything like that, anyhow."

Sosia sighed. "I might have known. Of course, me
*wouldn't* think to use it against the pangs of childbirth. They'r
*men*." She brightened, but only for a moment. Then gloom re
turned. "Their wives would have thought of it, though. I'm sur
of that. So I suppose you're right. Too bad."

Remembering the cries he'd heard from women in labor, La
nius found himself nodding. "I'll use it when your tim
comes," he promised. "I'm sure of one thing—it can't hu
you."

"Thank you," Sosia said. "You do care about me, when—"

"Of course I do," Lanius interrupted.

But Sosia hadn't finished, and she intended to. "When you'r

not thinking about old parchments in the archives, or about your moncats—"

He tried interrupting again. "If it weren't for Pouncer and things I found in the archives, we wouldn't have the Scepter of Mercy. I don't think we would, anyway." Grus *might* have been able to break into Yozgat, but even the other king didn't think it would have been easy.

Sosia waved Pouncer—and the Scepter—aside, too. "*Or* about your serving girls." That was where she'd been heading all along.

The funny thing was that, even if she didn't—and wouldn't—understand as much, she was right to lump the maidservants with the documents and the animals. They were a hobby. He enjoyed them, but after Cristata he'd never conceived a passion for any of them. But that wasn't what Sosia wanted to hear. Lanius knew exactly what she wanted to hear, and he said it. "I'm sorry, dear."

"A likely story." She didn't look too unhappy, though. That *was* what she'd wanted to hear, and he couldn't very well say anything more.

He was in the archives later that day—by himself—when rustling behind a cabinet way off in a dim corner of the room showed he wasn't quite by himself after all. He thought he knew what that rustling meant, and he proved right. In due course, Pouncer came out. The moncat walked up to the king and dropped most of a mouse at his feet.

"Mrowr," Pouncer said, as though making sure Lanius understood the magnitude of the gift. As far as the moncat was concerned, this was more important than the Scepter of Mercy. The Scepter had just been a thing. A mouse was *food*.

"Yes, I know what a wonderful fellow you are," Lanius said. He scratched the moncat behind the ears and at the sides of the jaw and gently rubbed its velvet nose. In due course, Pouncer rewarded him with a rusty purr. That was about as big a reward as any cat ever gave. It made Lanius wonder why people kept them. He supposed the dead and mangled mouse on the floor represented a partial answer, but it didn't seem enough.

He never had found out how Pouncer got out of the moncats' room and roamed the narrow passages within the palace walls. Since Pouncer—and the Scepter of Mercy—returned to the city of Avornis, he'd stopped looking. That was his reward to Pouncer.

"Mrowr," Pouncer said again, and looked down at what remained of the mouse.

Lanius, being well trained by then, knew what was expected of him. He stroked Pouncer and praised his hunting talents some more, and then picked up the little corpse (fortunately, what remained included a tail, not too badly chewed). After holding it for a moment—which seemed to mean he would eat it if he only had the time—he gave it back to the moncat. Pouncer took the dainty in its clawed hands and ate another few mouthfuls. Lanius turned his head away.

He didn't miss the mouse. If Pouncer ate all the mice in the archives, he would have been delighted. But he didn't want to watch the moncat do it. That squeamishness had a lot to do with why he was such a reluctant hunter, too. Anser and Ortalis both found it funny.

He didn't mind Anser's teasing. Considering Ortalis' tastes, he was in a poor position to chide anybody about anything. That didn't stop him, of course. If it had, he would have been a different sort of person altogether. *Too bad he's not,* Lanius thought, and went back to an old tax register.

Hirundo bowed as he came into the small audience chamber where King Grus sat. "Thanks for seeing me, Your Majesty," the general said.

"As though I wouldn't!" Grus said, and waved him to a stool. "Here, sit down and make yourself at home. A servant is com— Ah, here she is now." The serving girl set a tray with wine and cakes and a bowl of roasted chickpeas on the table. After pouring wine for Grus and Hirundo, she curtsied and left.

Hirundo's gaze followed her. "Pretty little thing," he murmured. He raised his silver goblet in salute to Grus. "Your good health, Your Majesty!"

"Same to you." Grus returned the salute. "We're both pretty lucky, for people our age. Most of the parts still work most of the time."

"That's not bad." Hirundo scratched his beard, which was not quite as gray as Grus'. "A lot of people my age are dead."

Grus chuckled, not that it was anything but truth wrapped in a joke. He ate some of the chickpeas, then washed them down with more wine. That meant he got to the bottom of his goblet. After he poured it full again, he asked, "Well, what's on your mind?"

Before answering, Hirundo got up and shut the door to the audience chamber. When he came back, he slid his stool closer to Grus'. In a low voice, he asked, "Your Majesty, who are your son's friends?"

Grus frowned and scratched his head. The idea that Ortalis *had* friends was enough—more than enough—to bemuse him. His legitimate son was not an outgoing sort. "I don't know," the king said. "What are you driving at?"

"Maybe nothing," Hirundo said. "In that case, I'll beg his pardon, and yours, too. But do you remember him hanging around with these guards officers before we went off to fight south of the Stura?"

"He hunts with some of them—I know that," Grus said.

"Not with all of them," Hirundo said, which was true enough. "Do you really want him wasting time with them? What if he's not wasting it, if you know what I mean?"

"I know what you mean," Grus answered; the same thought had occurred to him. Even though it had, the king had trouble taking it seriously. "Ortalis likes hunting and . . . some other things." Grus didn't care to talk about those, although Hirundo knew what they were—come to that, half the city of Avornis knew what they were. "I've never really thought he liked politics."

"You might want to think again, then, Your Majesty," the general said. "People who don't like politics don't make friends like that."

"No?" Grus raised an eyebrow. "Who would Ortalis make friends with?" *If he makes friends at all.* He didn't—quite— say that out loud. Instead, he went on, "Priests? Not likely, not unless they're like Anser and enjoy going after deer. Scholars? He never cared for his lessons. I wish he'd cared more, but he didn't. Maidservants?"

Hirundo grinned at that. "Well, who doesn't?"

Some of Ortalis' dealings with maidservants might have started out in a friendly way, but that wasn't how they'd ended. Still, Grus said, "As far as I know, he hasn't done anything like that since he married Limosa. I wanted to clobber him with a rock when he did marry her, but it really looks like he loves her." The idea of Ortalis' loving anyone but himself was even more curious than the idea of his making friends.

"She . . ." Hirundo's voice trailed away. Grus had no trouble figuring out what the general would have said. *She lets him do what he wants to her. She even likes it when he does.* Every word of that was true, too. All the same . . .

"I think there's something more to it," the king said. "He's been different since she had a girl, and he's been quite a bit different since she had a boy."

"Ha!" Hirundo stabbed out a triumphant forefinger at him. "There! You said it yourself, Your Majesty. He *has* been different, and he has different friends, and you ought to look at him in a different way."

That made good logical sense. Grus realized as much. Logic or no logic, he couldn't do it. He could imagine his son being dangerous in a fit of fury. Anything that required planning? He didn't think so. Going hunting the next day was about as far as Ortalis' planning reached.

The more dubious Grus looked, the more insistent Hirundo got. He said, "For all you know, Limosa's egging him on."

"Maybe," Grus said, not wanting to laugh in his old friend's face. He couldn't see anyone leading Ortalis around by the nose. He'd never had any luck doing it, anyhow; he knew that.

Of course, he'd always tried to lead Ortalis in the direction he himself wanted his son to go. It never occurred to him that Ortalis might be easier to lead in the direction *he* wanted to go, or that the dreams he and Lanius had always perceived as nightmares might seem something else again to his son. And they were leading Ortalis, too. . . .

Even in their bedchamber, behind a door that was closed and barred, Limosa's voice was the barest thread of whisper. "Are you sure you want to go through with this?"

"I have to," Ortalis whispered back, even more softly. Limosa worried about Grus because he'd sent her father to the Maze. Ortalis worried about Grus because his father had been there scowling at him, shouting at him, hitting him, for as long as he could remember. Why Grus had felt he needed to do those things was forgotten. That Grus had done those things never would be, never could be. Ortalis went on, "It's for Marinus' sake."

"Of course it is," Limosa said. "He's not just robbing you. He's robbing your whole line, that's what he's doing. And all because of—"

"Lanius," Ortalis finished for her. He whispered his brother-in-law's name, too. Somehow, that let him pack more scorn into it, not less. "All he does is sit around and *read* things all day, *read* things and play with his miserable animals. And for him—for *him*—my own father's going to disinherit me, disinherit his grandson, too. Oh, no, he's not, by the gods."

That some of his own actions—and inactions—might have given Grus reason to prefer Lanius to him never once crossed his mind. Even if it had, Limosa or, more likely, the Voice in his dreams that were better than dreams would have talked him around. He wouldn't have needed much persuading; like most people, he saw himself in the best possible light.

Limosa saw him in the best possible light, too. She leaned over and kissed him. "When you put on the crown, you'll show everybody what being king is really all about. You'll be the best king Avornis ever had. You'll pick up the Scepter of Mercy and . . . do all sorts of good things with it." Her imagination failed her, there at the end.

"Of course I will." Ortalis tried to sound confident, too. He really would rather have forgotten all about the Scepter. Now that it was back here, he didn't suppose he could, not permanently, but he still wanted to.

He cursed well *could* forget about it for the time being. He kissed Limosa, too, kissed her hard, and kept on kissing her until he tasted blood. She whimpered in mixed pain and pleasure. They were always mixed for her. Giving them was always mixed for him. If the two of them weren't made for each other, no couple ever had been.

"Oh, Ortalis," she murmured when at last their lips separated. He caressed her roughly and took her even more roughly. "Oh," she said again, softly, when he went into her. A few minutes later, the sounds she made were altogether unrestrained. Ortalis laughed, there on top of her. Then he groaned as though he were the one under the lash—a place he'd never had the least interest in being.

If palace servants—or his father's spies—heard noises like that, they wouldn't think twice about them. They might be jealous, but that kind of jealousy didn't worry Ortalis. On the contrary—it made him proud.

After they'd used the chamber pot and gotten back into their nightclothes, Limosa teased him, saying, "You're going to act just like a man. You're going to roll over and go right to sleep."

"You do that as often as I do," he said, which was true. But his yawn declared she hadn't been wrong, either.

He went out hunting the next morning. He didn't invite Anser, though his half brother had been his chief hunting partner for a long time. Not all the men he did invite had reputations as enthusiastic followers of the chase. They were, however, all enthusiastic followers of Ortalis. To Grus' legitimate son, that counted for much more.

One nice thing about the hunt was that it seldom roused suspicion. If you went out and came back with lots of carcasses, you'd had a good day. If you went out and came back with next to nothing, the most anybody would say was, "Oh, bad luck!" If anything besides hunting happened while you were out there . . . Well, who was likely to find out?

With his henchmen gathered together, Ortalis could ask them, "Are we ready to move when the time comes?"

"Your Highness, we are." Serinus spoke with what sounded like complete confidence and assurance. The other young officers in the royal bodyguard nodded.

"Will your men follow you no matter what orders you give them?" Ortalis persisted.

"Your Highness, they will." Again, Serinus sounded very sure. Again, his fellow officers nodded. Ortalis could never have gotten so many of them together in the palace without stir-

ring up more gossip than he wanted. Out here in the woods, nobody was likely to pay any attention to what he did.

He said, "You've told me what I most needed to hear. The
time is coming soon. I know I can count on you to do your
duty."

*The time is coming soon.* A year or two earlier, he wouldn't
have been able to imagine saying those words. He never would
have had the nerve. Truth to tell, he wouldn't have had the will,
either. But things had changed since then. He had a son now, a
son and heir. That made him look differently—as opposed to
indifferently—on his place in the bigger scheme of things. And
he had his dreams. The Voice made him think of his place in the
bigger scheme of things, too, and that his place ought to be bigger as well.

"Soon?" Some of his followers sounded pleased. A few
sounded alarmed. Ortalis knew what that meant. It meant he
had some fair-weather friends, men who would suck up to a
prince for the sake of whatever advantage that might bring, but
who wouldn't back him when it counted.

He glanced toward Serinus and Gygis. They both nodded.
They were his most reliable followers. He could count on them
to make sure none of the others got cold feet at a bad time.

"Soon," he said firmly. "It will be fast. It will be smooth.
And then things will go on as they were meant to."

"Let's give three cheers for King Ortalis!" Gygis called.

Everyone in the hunting party did cheer, too. Ortalis beamed
at Gygis. Good to know who the clever ones were, and that was
very clever indeed. Now they'd all cheered him as king. They
couldn't say they hadn't had any idea what he was thinking
about. And they would have a harder time withdrawing from
this plot.

"When the time comes, do we deal with both of them together, or just the one?" Serinus asked.

"Just my father. He's the one who's always been trouble for
me," Ortalis said venomously. "We don't need to worry about
Lanius. He's been my old man's lapdog for years. Why should
he be any different for me?"

Several young officers chuckled. Serinus sketched a salute.

"However you want it, Your Majesty, that's how it'll work. I just needed to find out."

"Fair enough," Ortalis said. The more he heard himself called *Your Majesty* and *King Ortalis,* the better he liked it. People should have been calling him things like that a long time ago. If Grus had to share the throne with somebody, he should have shared it with Ortalis, not with the weedy good-for-nothing who'd sat on it beforehand.

"What will you do when you're king, Your Majesty?" one of the guards officers asked eagerly.

"Why, I'll do—" Ortalis broke off. Despite having lived in the palace for many years, he had only a vague notion of what his father did when not harassing him. He gave the best answer he could. "I'll do all kinds of really neat stuff."

That seemed to satisfy the guardsman. "I bet you will, Your Majesty!" he said.

Serinus pulled a flask off his belt and yanked out the stopper. "Here's to the new king!" he said. Most of the officers had flasks of their own. They drank the toast, and passed wine to the few men who hadn't brought any. Ortalis had his own flask. As he drank the red, red wine, he imagined it was his father's blood. It would have been even sweeter if it were.

A knock on the bedchamber door in the middle of the night always meant trouble. Grus knew that. Good news would wait until sunup. Bad news? Bad news cried out to be heard right away.

"What do they want?" Estrilda asked sleepily.

"I don't know." Clad in only his nightshirt, Grus was already getting out of bed. "I'd better find out, though." He walked over to the door and asked, "Who's there? What's the word?"

"It's Serinus, Your Majesty," said the man on the other side, and Grus relaxed, recognizing the captain's voice. Serinus went on, "A courier's just come in from the south. Some kind of trouble down there—I don't know exactly what, but it didn't sound good."

"Oh, by the gods!" Grus exclaimed. And it might have been by the gods, too. Had the Banished One found some way around the concessions Grus had forced from him with the

Scepter of Mercy? Were the Menteshe kicking up their heels even without any help from the exiled god? Or had some ambitious and stupid noble decided this was a good time to rebel? "I'm coming," Grus added, and unbarred the door. "Where is this fellow, anyway?"

"Near the front entrance, Your Majesty," Serinus answered. "He's hopping around like he's got to run for the jakes any time now."

"He can do that *after* I've talked to him," Grus said. "Come on. What are you waiting for?" He hurried up the corridor.

So did Serinus, who hadn't really been waiting for anything. A couple of squads of soldiers, all of them armed and armored, fell in with the guards officer and the king. But for their thumping boots and jingling chainmail, the hallways in the palace were very quiet. Grus wondered what the hour was.

He also suddenly wondered why, at whatever hour this was, so many soldiers should appear as though from nowhere. Suspicion flared in him. "What's going on here?" he demanded.

"This way, Your Majesty," Serinus said as though he hadn't spoken.

"Wait a minute." Grus stopped. "For one thing, you didn't answer me. What *is* going on? And, for another, this isn't the way to the front hall."

"Well, so it isn't." Serinus smiled. It was not the sort of smile Grus wanted to see—more the sort a wolf would have worn just before it sprang. The young officer bowed to Grus. "But you see, Your Majesty, that's part of what's going on." He nodded to the soldiers. The ones who carried swords drew them. The ones who carried spears pointed them at Grus. "You can come along with us quietly or" —he shrugged— "the servants will have to clean a mess off the floor. Up to you."

"You can't do this!" Grus blurted. "You can't expect to get away with it, either."

"Oh, but we can. And we do. And we will." Serinus sounded as though he had all the answers. At the moment, he certainly had more of them than Grus did.

"Where do you aim to take me?" Grus asked. In his nightshirt, without even an eating knife on his belt—without even a belt!—he couldn't do much about it no matter where it was.

His best hope was that somebody would come by and notice this . . . this kidnapping. But no one except Serinus and his men seemed to be up and about.

"Why, to the Maze, of course." Serinus certainly had the answer to that question. "You've sent enough people there yourself. High time you find out what it's like, don't you think?"

Grus thought nothing of the sort. Still more outraged than afraid, he filled his lungs to shout for help. Some of the soldiers saw him doing it. They shook their heads. A couple of them brandished their weapons. He didn't shout.

"Smart fellow." Serinus nodded approval. "They say blood is so hard to get out from between these little mosaic tiles." His voice lost its good humor and assumed the snap of command. "Now get moving. If anybody sees us and tries to stop us, you'll be the one who's sorriest. I promise you that."

Believing him, Grus did get moving. He couldn't help asking, "Who put you up to this? King Lanius?"

Serinus laughed uproariously. So did his henchmen. "By the gods in the heavens, no," the officer answered, laughing still. "We serve King Ortalis."

"King—?" Associating his son with sovereignty was so ridiculous, Grus couldn't do it even now. He wanted to laugh himself, at the absurdity of the idea. He wanted to, but he couldn't. Ortalis and these men evidently didn't think it was absurd. *I should have paid more attention to Hirundo,* Grus thought, much too late for it to do him any good.

Serinus and the soldiers hustled him out of the palace. They bundled him onto a horse and tied his legs beneath him. They had horses, too. Out of the city they rode, as slick as boiled asparagus.

# CHAPTER TWENTY-SEVEN

"Y our Majesty, the other king wants to see you in the small dining room as soon as you can get there," a guard outside Lanius' chamber told him as soon as he opened the door.

"Does he?" Lanius said around a yawn. The soldier nodded. Lanius yawned again, then asked, "Did he tell you what it was about?"

"No, Your Majesty, but I think you'd better hurry. I've got the feeling it's important," the guard answered.

He knew more than he was letting on. Lanius didn't have to be a genius to figure that out. The king wondered if he ought to press the soldier. In the end, he decided not to. He would find out soon enough from Grus. He wondered what had happened. The other king hadn't summoned him like this in quite a while.

Scratching his head, Lanius went to the room where he usually ate breakfast. Ortalis sat there, sipping on a cup of wine and fidgeting a little. "Oh, hello," Lanius said. "The guard must have gotten his signals crossed. I thought your father would be here."

"What did he say?" Ortalis asked. The silver goblet shook in his hand—not very much, but enough for Lanius to notice. "What *exactly* did he say?"

Lanius thought back. He prided himself on being able to get things like that straight. "He said the other king wanted to see me in here as soon as possible." That wasn't word for word, but it caught the meaning well enough.

Ortalis nodded and smiled—a surprisingly nervous smile for so early in the day. "Good. He did get it right then," he said. "That's what I told him to tell you, all right."

"What *you* told him to tell me?" Lanius' wits weren't working as well as he wished they were.

"What I told him to tell you, yes." Ortalis sounded a little more confident this time. Without rising from his stool, he struck a pose. "I'm the new King of Avornis."

"You're what?" No, Lanius wasn't at his best. He didn't laugh in Ortalis' face, but held back only by the tiniest of margins. "What's happened to your father?" That worry was the main thing that made him not show everything he was thinking.

He waited for Ortalis to tell him Grus was desperately ill, or even that he'd died in the night. Grus had seemed in good health the last time Lanius saw him, but the other king wasn't a young man. Such things could happen, and happen all too easily.

But, a certain ferocious glee in his voice, Ortalis answered, "I packed him off to the Maze, that's what."

Now Lanius frankly stared. "You . . . sent your father to the Maze?" He couldn't believe it. Grus had overcome every foe in sight, from rebellious Avornan nobles to King Dagipert of Thervingia to the Banished One himself. How could he possibly have fallen to his own son, a far less dangerous opponent?

As soon as Lanius asked himself the question that way, the likely answer became clear. As far as Grus was concerned, would Ortalis have been a visible opponent at all? Grus had always made allowances for his legitimate son, and never taken him very seriously. He had to be regretting that now.

"You'd best believe I did," Ortalis growled. "He had it coming, too. This is *my* kingdom now, by Olor's beard."

"Yours?" Lanius said. "What about me?"

"What about you? I'll tell you what about you," his brother-in-law answered. "You can be king, too, if you want. You can go on wearing the crown, if you want. Whenever my old man said, 'Frog,' you'd hop. As long as you keep on hopping for me, everything will be fine." He smiled, as though to say he was sure Lanius wouldn't mind an arrangement like that.

Back when Grus first put the crown on his own head, all the power *had* been in his hands. Lanius had been a figurehead, nothing more. Grus would have gotten rid of him if he could have done it without inflaming people by ending Avornis' ancient dynasty. He hadn't even bothered pretending anything different.

Little by little, though, Lanius had gathered bits and pieces of power into his own hands. Grus' going out on campaign so often hadn't hurt things, not one bit. Grus had needed someone who could run things here in the capital while he was away. To whom else would he have given the job? Ortalis? Ortalis hadn't wanted it. And so it came to Lanius, and more and more came with it.

Had Ortalis ever bothered to notice Lanius really was a king in his own right? It seemed unlikely.

Lanius almost asked him, *And what happens if I don't feel like hopping?* He almost did, but he didn't. The look on Ortalis' face gave him all the answer he needed. *If you don't, I'll hurt you. I'll enjoy hurting you, too. Have you got any idea how much I'll enjoy it?*

What Lanius did say was, "I'll work with you the way I worked with your father on one condition."

"Condition?" Ortalis' face had been ugly before. It got uglier now. "What kind of condition? You don't tell me what to do, Lanius. No one tells me what to do now. I've had a bellyful of that from everybody."

"This isn't much," Lanius said, which might have been true and might not have.

"What is it, then?" Suspicion still clotted Ortalis' voice.

"If the Scepter of Mercy accepts you, I will, too," Lanius said. "Your father could use it. So can I. If you can, too, then I know you'll be good for Avornis, and I won't say a word about anything at all." After a moment, inspired, he added, "And the soldiers will want to see that you can wield it, too. They spent a lot of time and a lot of work and a lot of blood bringing it back from the Menteshe country, you know."

Odds were Ortalis knew nothing of the sort. He hadn't

wanted to know anything about the Scepter. But he just laughed now. "Is *that* all you want?" he said. "Sure, I'll do that. Like the Scepter cares who's holding it! Whenever you want, I'll do it, and the soldiers can stare as much as they please. Does that suit you, Your Majesty?" He made a mockery of Lanius' title.

"That suits me fine, Your Majesty." Lanius also mocked his title, but Ortalis never realized it.

Lanius wondered whether he really would, whether he really could, accept Ortalis as King of Avornis if the Scepter of Mercy did. *If the Scepter does, what choice have I got?* he asked himself. However little he liked it, he didn't see that he had any.

Grus had been through the Maze many times—always on the way to somewhere else. He'd sent people here for good, but he'd never imagined he would come here for good one of these days himself.

The Maze was, when you got right down to it, a dreary place. River turned to swamp turned to mudflat. It was heaven on earth for mosquitoes and gnats and midges. Grus supposed it was also pretty good if you happened to be something like a heron or a turtle or a frog. If you were a man . . . The Maze was green enough, but most of it was a sickly green, not a vibrant one. Besides being full of biting bugs, the air smelled stagnant.

"You won't get away with this," Grus told his captors as they rowed him along in a small boat.

"Seems to me we already have," the officer in charge of them answered calmly. "As soon as we got you out of the city of Avornis without running into trouble, the game was ours. We'll pack you away in a nice, quiet monastery, and the outside world can start forgetting about you. People get forgotten all the time."

"And suppose I don't feel like becoming a monk?" Grus asked.

The officer—his name was Gygis—only shrugged. "Then we tie something heavy to your hands and feet, we find a place where the water's a little deeper than usual, and we dump you over the side. Our worries are over either way. You figure out what you want."

"*Ortalis* gave the orders for this?" Grus couldn't believe his son had brought off such a smoothly efficient coup.

"Of course. Who else?" Gygis seemed innocence personified. That made Grus wonder whether he and his fellow officers were the tail or the dog in this plot. Could they use Ortalis for a figurehead? Why not? Grus had used Lanius as one for years. Gygis went on, "So what'll it be? The monastic life or a short one? You'd better make up your mind in a hurry."

No one had told Grus what to do like that since his father died. He noticed Gygis wasn't calling him *Your Majesty*. In spite of himself, Grus laughed. He'd wondered what he had left to do as king after recovering the Scepter of Mercy. Maybe the answer was *nothing* all along.

"Well?" Gygis demanded, obviously suspicious of that laugh. "Which way do we do it?"

"With the choice you gave me, being a monk looks better and better all of a sudden," Grus answered. And that was, perhaps, truer than either he or Gygis fully realized.

Ortalis' henchman grinned a crooked grin. "You see? You're not a fool after all."

*Oh, yes, I am,* Grus thought. Lanius wrote Ortalis was keeping dangerous company. Hirundo came and warned him about his son. Everyone saw trouble coming except him. And everyone was right, too. *I always was too soft on Ortalis.*

"Plenty of people before you have made the same choice. Nothing to be ashamed about," Gygis said, trying to be soothing. "Why, when you get to the monastery, you'll probably run into people you know."

*People you sent away,* he meant. "Oh, joy," Grus said in distinctly hollow tones.

Not many people lived in the Maze of their own accord. There were some fishermen, some trappers, a few men who gathered herbs and sold them to healers and wizards, and a few more who did a variety of things they tried to keep dark from Avornis' tax collectors. Every so often, as Grus' boat made its way through those tricky channels, someone would watch for a while from a boat of his own or from a hummock of ground slightly higher and drier than most.

A couple of the larger hummocks boasted real villages.

Grus' boat gave those a wide berth. Monasteries sprouted like toadstools on smaller patches of more or less dry ground. Some of them were for people who wanted to get away from the world and contemplate the gods at their leisure. Others—more—were for people put away from the world and invited to contemplate the gods instead of being executed and finding out about them with no need for contemplation.

Grus' captors took him toward a monastery of the latter sort. The structure seemed more like a fortress than anything else. Its outer walls looked at least as formidable as the ones Grus had faced at Yozgat. But these works were designed to hold people in, not out.

Gygis cupped his hands in front of his mouth and hallooed when the boat approached those frowning walls. One of the men atop them shouted back. "We've got a new friend for you!" Gygis yelled.

"Who's Grus angry at now?" came the reply.

Gygis laughed. Sitting there beside him, Grus didn't think it was so funny. "You'll see when we bring him in," Gygis said.

A rickety little jetty stuck out into the stream. One of Gygis' men tied up the boat. He looked at Grus and jerked a thumb toward the monastery. "Out you go."

Out Grus went. After sitting in the cramped boat for a couple of days, his legs had a low opinion of walking, but he managed. Gygis and his men made sure Grus went nowhere but toward the monastery.

He and they had to wait outside while a stout portcullis groaned up. Were those monks turning the windlass that raised the chains attached to the portcullis? Who else would they be?

A plump man in a shapeless brown wool robe met the newcomers just inside the portcullis. "Well, well," he said. "Who have we here?"

"Abbot Pipilo, let me present your newest holy man," Gygis said with a broad, insincere smile. "His name is Grus."

"Grus?" Pipilo stared first at Gygis, then at the suddenly overthrown king. "Olor's beard, it *is* Grus! How did Lanius manage that?"

In spite of himself, Grus started to laugh. Even in the gloom of the fortified gateway, he could see Gygis turn red. The officer said, "King Ortalis now holds the throne with King Lanius. You would be well advised to remember it. He is my master, and I serve him gladly."

"Until something happens to him, or until you see a better deal for yourself," Grus said. "That's how you served me."

"King . . . Ortalis?" Pipilo said. "Well, well! Isn't *that* interesting?" He gathered himself, then nodded to Grus. "Come in, come in. You're safe here, anyhow."

"Huzzah," Grus said.

Pipilo laughed. "It may not be everything you hoped for, but you'll agree, I think, it's better than a lot of the things that could have happened to you with your son taking the throne." Since Grus couldn't argue with that, he kept quiet. Pipilo went on, "Forgive me for saying this, but I think I ought to remind you that here you'll just be another monk. If this little domain has a sovereign, I am he."

He didn't sound as though he was rubbing Grus' nose in that—only reminding him, as he'd said. And Grus did need reminding. His word had literally been law for years. Having someone else tell him what to do would be . . . different.

"I hear what you're saying," he answered carefully.

That made the abbot laugh again. "By which you mean you don't want to believe it. Well, nobody can blame you for that. You just got here, and you didn't want to come. But you *are* here, and I have to tell you you're unlikely to leave, and so you should try to make the best of it."

*How could anyone make the best of* this*?* Grus wondered. He kept that to himself for fear of insulting Pipilo. The abbot beckoned him forward. Grus followed Pipilo into the monastery. Gygis and his henchmen must have gone back to their boat, for the portcullis creaked down again. With it in place, Grus was trapped here, but he felt no more imprisoned than he had with the iron gate still up.

"First thing we'll do is get you a robe, Brother Grus," Pipilo said. "You'll feel more at ease when you look like everybody else. It will be warmer than that nightshirt, too. You were taken by surprise, I gather?"

"Oh, you might say so." Grus' voice was as dry as he could make it. Pipilo chuckled appreciatively. "How did you become a monk?" Grus asked him, meaning, *I don't remember sending you here.*

"As a matter of fact, I've been here since the very end of King Mergus' days," Pipilo replied, understanding what he hadn't said as well as what he had. "I was a young man then, but he thought I had too much ambition. I dare say he was right, or I wouldn't have risen to become abbot, would I?"

One ambition he evidently didn't have was escape. Even if he had had it, it wouldn't have done him much good, so he was just as well off without it. A vegetable garden filled much of the monastery's large courtyard. Some of the monks weeding and pruning there looked up from their labors to stare at Grus. They wore brown robes with hoods like Pipilo's. Grus would have felt as out of place here in his royal regalia as he did in his nightshirt.

Wearing that nightshirt didn't keep him from being recognized. A man of about his own age with a wild gray beard came up to him and wagged a finger in his face. "See how it feels, Your Majesty? Do you see?"

"That will be enough of that, Brother Petrosus," Pipilo said. "You did not care to have people revile you when you first joined us here. Kindly extend Brother Grus the same courtesy you wanted for yourself."

Grus' former treasury minister didn't care to listen. "Is Ortalis king now?" he demanded of Grus, who couldn't help nodding. Petrosus chortled. "Then I'll get out! I know I will! Limosa will see to it."

Would Ortalis listen to Petrosus' daughter about this? He might, certainly, but Grus had his doubts. And he didn't want Petrosus to think he could get away with anything. He said, "Listen, my former friend, if Ortalis will send his own father into exile, why would he care even a copper's worth about his father-in-law?"

Petrosus scowled at him. "Because I wouldn't tell him what to do every minute of the day and night."

"No?" Grus laughed, not pleasantly. "Do you know how many scars he's put on your daughter's back?" He didn't tell Petrosus that Limosa had enjoyed getting her welts. Maybe

Petrosus already knew about his daughter's tastes. If he didn't . . . Grus was aiming to hurt him, but that went too far.

"And that will be enough of that from you also, Brother Grus," Pipilo said with the air of a man who had the authority to give such orders. "Brother Petrosus, kindly return to your gardening." Petrosus went, though his face was crimson and he ground his teeth in fury. That he went proved to Grus what a power Pipilo was here.

The abbot led the king to a storeroom where, as promised, a monk issued him a brown robe and a pair of stout sandals. The robe was as comfortable as anything he'd worn. The sandals would need breaking in.

A bell rang. "That is the call to midmorning prayer," Pipilo said. "We gather together at daybreak, midmorning, noon, midafternoon, and sunset. Come along, Brother. You are one of us now, and this is required of you."

"Is there any way I can get out of it?" asked Grus, who had trouble imagining the gods in the heavens paying much attention to prayer.

"It is required," Pipilo repeated. "Anyone who does not conform to the rule here will find his stay much less pleasant than it might be otherwise."

With that not so veiled threat ringing in his ears, Grus followed Pipilo to the chapel. Monks streamed in from all over the monastery. It held more of them than Grus had expected. He was relieved to see they weren't all men he'd sent into exile here. That would have made his stay even less pleasant than it was liable to be otherwise. All he could do now was try to make the best of things.

"Welcome, brethren, welcome," Pipilo said from the pulpit. "A new brother has joined us today, as some of you will already know. Please welcome Brother Grus to our ranks."

"Welcome, Brother Grus!" the other monks chorused. Some of them actually sounded as though they meant it. Others stared at him with the same vindictive relish Petrosus had shown. He could read their faces with no trouble at all. *Here is the man who put me here, and now he's here himself,* they were thinking. *Let's see how he likes it!*

Whatever they were thinking, they got no chance to say it to

Grus' face. Abbot Pipilo led them in prayers and hymns to King Olor and Queen Quelea. Grus knew the prayers and the words to the hymns. Coming out with them was easier than staying silent. He didn't think they would do any harm. On the other hand, he didn't think they would do any good, either.

When the prayers ended, the monks went back to their labors. Grus looked around, wondering what to do next. Pipilo came up to him. "This way, Brother, if you please," he said. Shrugging, Grus followed.

Pipilo took him to the kitchens. They were almost as large as the ones for the royal palace. The abbot introduced Grus to Brother Neophron, the chief cook. "Have you had any practice working with food?" Neophron asked.

"Not for a good many years," Grus answered.

Neophron's sigh made several chins wobble. Like most cooks who were good at their job, he was a hefty man. "Well, why don't you start off peeling turnips and chopping them up?" he said. "You can't do much harm there."

Several baskets of white-and-purple turnips stood on a counter. With another shrug, Grus got to work. *From the Scepter of Mercy to this,* he thought. *Thank you, Ortalis.* After a while, though, he found he minded the work less than he'd expected. It wasn't exciting, but it struck him as worthwhile. He was helping to feed people, himself among them. How could that be bad?

After half an hour or so, Neophron casually strolled over to see how he was doing. The chief cook nodded, which also made the flesh under his jaw shake. "I've seen neater work," he said, "but that comes with doing it. You're willing enough, by Olor's beard."

Grus got a break for noontime prayers and then for the midday meal. It was quite plain: bread and cheese and beer. But there was enough of it. The monks ate at long tables in a large dining hall. Grus recognized fewer men than he'd expected. *Not* recognizing them, and not being recognized by them, came as something of a relief.

After lunch, Grus went back to the kitchens. He cut up more turnips, which went into great pots of stew for supper. He washed dishes. He chopped firewood. Along with the turnips, the stew had barley and onions and peas and beans and, for flavor, a little sausage finely chopped. A cook who served it in the palace would have been on the street the next minute. For soldiers in the field, though, it would have done fine. It filled Grus up.

The cell to which Pipilo led him after sunset prayers was just that. It was barely big enough to turn around in. The latrine was down the corridor. His nose would have told him which way if Pipilo hadn't. The bed was a straw-stuffed pallet on a ledge at the back of the cell. The wool blanket was rough and scratchy, but it was thick.

Grus lay down. The only light came from a distant torch. The straw rustled under him. He'd slept very little the night before in the boat with Gygis. He'd worked hard since coming to the monastery. He yawned. He could have lain there brooding and plotting. He fell asleep instead.

Sosia was furious, and didn't even try to hide it. "He can't do this!" she snarled at Lanius in the near-privacy of their bedchamber. "He *can't*! You're not going to let him get away with it, are you?"

"Well, as long as the soldiers do what he tells them to, and as long as the people here don't start throwing rocks at him whenever he sticks his nose outside the palace, I'm not sure what I can do," Lanius said reasonably. "How long that will be, I don't know. Not too long, I hope."

"*I'll* throw a rock at him if he sticks his nose anywhere near me!" Sosia said. "My own brother! My brother did that! *My* brother did it to *my* father! Some fine family we turned out to be, isn't it?"

Lanius aimed to go on looking at the bright side of things as long as he could. "He sent your father to the Maze," he said. "He didn't do anything more than that, and I suppose he could have. He hasn't done anything to either one of us, and he hasn't done anything to the children."

His wife's hands automatically went to her belly, as though to protect the new life growing there. "He'd better not! He'll be sorry if he tries!"

"Well, he hasn't, and he could have done that, too," Lanius said. "If he hasn't, it probably means he doesn't want to."

"He'd better not," Sosia repeated darkly. "King Ortalis!" Her laughter had a hysterical edge. "Olor's beard, Lanius, he hasn't got any more business running this kingdom than one of your moncats does."

*He has less business running the kingdom than Pouncer does, I think. Pouncer was able to pick up the Scepter of Mercy. Can Ortalis?* Lanius kept that to himself. It wasn't that he didn't want Sosia to know about his doubts. They might have helped set her mind at ease. But she might have let her brother know about them. Lanius didn't want Ortalis having any idea that he had doubts. He wanted his brother-in-law confident that he could handle the Scepter.

If Ortalis wasn't confident, if he thought something might go wrong, or if he thought Sosia thought Lanius thought something might go wrong, he'd invent some excuse not to try to take it in his hands. He might be able to get away with that, too, at least for a while.

*What if he stands in front of the Scepter of Mercy, sets his hand on it—and up it comes?* That was Lanius' . . . oh, not quite nightmare, but worry. If the Scepter judged Ortalis worthy of being King of Avornis, Lanius knew he would have to do the same, as he'd said he would.

And then his long, slow, patient, often painful task would have to start all over again. He'd needed years to win back even a fraction of the kingship from Grus. Would he have to begin anew with Ortalis, who would probably be even more suspicious of him than Grus had been? Could he steal out of the shadows an inch at a time again?

Grus in the Maze! Grus in a monastery! Lanius tried to imagine that, but the picture didn't want to form in his mind. Grus was made for giving orders. If he was suddenly made into a monk, he'd have to take them instead. How would he like that? Would he be able to do it at all? Lanius had a hard time believing it.

He wondered if he ought to tell Ortalis about *How to Be a King.* He shrugged. *If the Scepter accepts him, maybe I will.* Ortalis could use a book about how to rule Avornis. Lanius thought Sosia was right—her brother had no idea on his own. But would he care to look at it, or would he only laugh?

Ortalis, from what Lanius had seen, got few ideas of any kind on his own. The ones he did have often involved hurting people or beasts. How had he pulled off such a neat, smooth usurpation? It was almost as though he'd had someone else, someone competent, whispering in his ear all the way through it.

"Your Majesty," the Voice whispered. King Ortalis had liked hearing that from his subjects the past few days. He liked just about everything about being king—he'd especially liked sending his father to the Maze. But most of all, he thought, he liked hearing the Voice acclaim him.

As always, what he saw in these dreams was better than what he saw in real life. The sky was bluer. The sun was brighter. The air smelled sweeter. The land was greener. And, in these dreams, the Voice told him what a wonderful fellow he was. And when the Voice told him something, he had to believe it, because how could a Voice like that lie?

"Your Majesty," it whispered again, caressingly. "You see, Your Majesty? Everything went just the way you hoped it would."

"Yes," Ortalis murmured. "Oh, yes." He wriggled with pleasure. Nothing compared to this, not even taking the lash in his hands.

The voice might have said, *Everything went just the way I told you it would.* That would have been as true. Without the Voice urging him on, Ortalis never would have had the nerve to move against his father. The price for failure was too high. And he *would* have failed; he could feel it. He wasn't very able most of the time, and was miserably aware of it. But with the Voice behind him, with the Voice seeing things he missed, he hadn't made a single mistake. And so he was King of Avornis, and his father was . . . a monk. Good riddance, too!

"Now all I need to do is take care of the stupid Scepter, and then I'll be king for—a long, long time," he said happily. He'd almost said, *for the rest of my life,* but he didn't want to think about life ending. He wanted to think about doing what he wanted, and about making everybody else do what he wanted.

He wondered which he would enjoy more. *Both,* he thought, and wriggled again.

"Take care of . . . the Scepter?" the Voice asked after a longer pause than usual. Maybe Ortalis was imagining things (well, of course Ortalis was imagining things—this was a dream, wasn't it?), but it didn't seem quite as smooth as usual.

"That's right," Ortalis said. "It's nothing, really. I've got to keep Lanius happy, that's all. He can pick up the stinking thing, and my miserable excuse for a father could pick up the stinking thing, so now I'll pick up the stinking thing, too, and then I'll go on doing what I was going to do anyway."

"You—agreed—to this with Lanius?" No, the Voice didn't sound smooth anymore. It didn't sound happy, either. If Ortalis hadn't known better, he would have said it sounded angry and disgusted.

He nodded even so, or his dream-self did. "Sure. Why not?" he said. "One more stupid thing to take care of, that's all."

Suddenly, the sun in his dreamscape wasn't just bright. It was *too* bright. The sky was still blue—as blue as a bruise. The leaves on the trees remained green—the green of rotting meat. The air smelled of carrion, and carrion birds flew through it— toward Ortalis.

"You fool!" the Voice cried thunderously. "You idiot! You imbecile! You ass! Better to kill Lanius, better to *slaughter* him, than to play his games!"

"But everybody expects it now," Ortalis protested. Trying to tell the Voice something it didn't want to hear was much tougher than going along with everything it said. He did his best to gather himself. "Don't worry. I can do it."

"Lanius tricked you—that cowardly wretch," the Voice growled. "Better, far better, you should have slain him when you pushed aside your father."

"I don't think so," Ortalis said. "His family's given Avornis kings for a long time. There'd be trouble—big trouble—if I knocked him off. Even my old man never had the nerve to do that."

He made the Voice backtrack. He never understood what a rare achievement that was. "All right," it said grudgingly. "*All right.* If you must be soft, then I suppose you must. I thought you would have enjoyed the killing, but if not, not. Still, you would have done better to send him to the Maze along with Grus."

"Maybe," Ortalis said, not believing it for a minute. Lanius in the palace could be a puppet, but he was still visibly king. That was how Grus had worked things. Ortalis' father could go to the Maze and stop being king without having too many people pitch a fit. He was only a usurper himself, if a highly successful one. But if Lanius went into exile . . . Riots didn't come to the city of Avornis very often. Ortalis wasn't sure enough soldiers would go on backing him to keep him safe if people rioted for Lanius.

The Voice sighed a heavy sigh. The dream-landscape around Ortalis came back toward what it had been—but not quite far enough back. Nor was the Voice back to its usual smooth self when it said, "I suppose we shall just have to hope for the best—but oh, what a feckless fool you are!"

Ortalis woke with a start, with his eyes staring, with his heart pounding, with cold sweat all over his body. His father had awakened like that—just like that—a good many times. So had his brother-in-law. Either of them could have told Ortalis exactly why he felt the way he did, exactly what—or rather, whom—he'd been confronting. They could have, yes, but he'd sent the one away and estranged the other. He had to try to figure things out on his own—but he, unlike Lanius, had never been much good at figuring things out.

Limosa stirred beside him. "What's the matter?" she asked muzzily.

"It's nothing. Go back to sleep. Sorry I bothered you," Ortalis answered. "I—I had a bad dream, that's all."

That wasn't all, and he knew it. What he didn't know was how many times his father had told his mother the same things, and how many times his brother-in-law had told his sister. He didn't know they'd been lying each and every time, either. He did know, and know full well, he was lying now.

"Poor dear," Limosa muttered, then started to snore again.

Ortalis lay awake a long, long time. Eventually, though, he fell asleep once more, too—a small miracle, though he also did not know that. What he did know when he woke was that the world around him looked better than it had for some time. He had a less highly colored memory now of the country of his dreams.

He drank several cups of wine with breakfast—*to fortify myself,* he thought. Limosa beamed at him. He looked away. He didn't feel like being beamed at, not this morning. After he lifted the Scepter of Mercy, after he held it in his hand, after he showed Lanius and his father (though his father wouldn't be there to see it) . . . *And after I show the Voice,* he thought. The Voice, after all, had found him imperfectly wonderful. Therefore he found it imperfectly wonderful as well, and much in need of showing.

His followers—he would not think, let alone say, such a vulgarism as *henchmen*—were among the officers gathered around the Scepter. *They* all looked confident. And here came Lanius. Ortalis wondered if he *should* have Serinus and Gygis and the rest of his—his *followers*—pack Lanius off to a monastery after the Scepter was his. Maybe the Voice hadn't had such a bad idea there after all.

"Well," Ortalis said lightly, "let's get it over with." No one else even smiled. Other people were much more serious about this . . . this folderol than he was. It was all foolishness and a waste of time. Ortalis knew that. If his somber subjects didn't, he'd show them by . . .

He set his right hand on the Scepter of Mercy. It felt like ordinary metal under his hand—cool and hard, but warming rapidly to his touch. He lifted—or rather, he tried to lift. The Scepter might have held the weight of the world. Ortalis tried to lift again—and, grunting with effort, failed again. Strain as he would, the Scepter of Mercy refused to budge.

"It will not accept him," an officer—one of *his* men—said, even as he strained. All the guardsmen, even Serinus and Gygis, turned to Lanius and bowed very low. "Your Majesty!" they chorused.

# CHAPTER TWENTY-EIGHT

Lanius had been crowned when he was still a little boy. Now, at last, he truly *was* King of Avornis. No one could tell him what to do, and there were no rival candidates. Ortalis had eliminated the last two, though he'd intended to take out only one.

"Your Majesty!" The officers wasted no time acknowledging him. Serinus, who'd been strongest for Ortalis, bowed almost double. "How may we serve you, Your Majesty?"

"I think you had better lay hold of my brother-in-law," Lanius said reluctantly. They did, not without a scuffle. Lanius eyed his brother-in-law with bemusement. "What shall I do with you?"

Ortalis' reply was colorful but not altogether relevant. Even some of the guardsmen, who used obscenity as a bad cook used salt—too much, and without even thinking about it—seemed impressed. Lanius knew he heard words and combinations he'd never run into before. He tried to remember some of the better ones in case he ever needed them.

When Ortalis ran dry at last—it took a while—Lanius said, "I know what seems fitting. I am going to send you to a monastery, the same way you sent your father to one."

He rapidly discovered Ortalis hadn't used up his store of bad language. Lanius marveled that the table and other fixtures in the Scepter's room didn't catch fire. "And your stinking horse, too!" Ortalis roared.

"That will be enough of that," Lanius said. "Take him to his bedchamber and confine him there."

"Yes, Your Majesty," the guards officers said, and they did. Lanius watched to make sure men he was confident were loyal to him outnumbered the officers who'd cozied up to Ortalis over the past few months. He didn't want his brother-in-law spirited out of the palace, out of the city of Avornis, so he could cause more trouble.

A couple of minutes later, a woman's screams erupted from the direction of the bedchamber. Lanius sighed. Limosa must have discovered that her husband had had what Lanius thought to be the shortest reign in the history of Avornis. He recalled there had once been an arch-hallow who died of joy on learning of his promotion, but no king had ever ruled for only a handful of days.

"How may we serve you, Your Majesty?" asked one of the officers still standing near the Scepter of Mercy.

After a moment's thought, Lanius answered, "Summon Hirundo and Pterocles to the throne room. I will meet them there in half an hour." He paused again, then added, "Pick some soldiers you can rely on and confine Serinus and Gygis in a place where they can't escape and can't communicate with their closest comrades."

"Yes, Your Majesty!" Several officers saluted and dashed off to do Lanius' bidding. Was it just that they wanted to make sure to seem loyal? Or was it that, since he could handle the Scepter and Ortalis couldn't, no one doubted he was the only legitimate king? It looked that way to him.

The guards officers who hadn't raced away in one direction or another escorted Lanius to the throne room. Servants bowed or curtsied as they passed him. "Your Majesty!" they murmured. They sounded much more sincere than usual. Had news traveled so fast? One of them said, "Much better you than Ortalis, Your Majesty!" so evidently it had.

After Lanius sat on the Diamond Throne, the men in his escort bowed low. He wondered if they would knock their heads on the floor for him, the way supplicants were said to do at the courts of some of the Menteshe princes. To his relief, they didn't.

Hirundo reached the throne room before Pterocles. He too bowed himself double before Lanius. "Your Majesty!" the general said, and then, "Am I to understand you're His only Majesty right this minute?"

"So it would seem," Lanius answered. "How does that sit with you?"

He tried not to show that he worried about the answer. Hirundo was popular with the soldiers. If he wanted a crown for himself, he had a real chance of taking it. But he said, "Suits me fine. I've always been loyal to the dynasty, and I don't aim to quit now."

"Good. Thank you," Lanius said.

"So Ortalis couldn't make the Scepter work for him, eh?" Hirundo said, and shook his head without waiting for an answer. "Can't tell you I'm very surprised. Never a whole lot of what you'd call mercy in him."

"No, I'm afraid not," Lanius agreed.

"What happens next?" Hirundo asked. "Are you going to bring Grus out of the Maze?"

"I . . . don't know." Lanius had wondered about that, too. He was saved from saying more when Pterocles came up to the throne and bowed to him. He nodded to the wizard. "Ah. Here you are."

"Here I am indeed, Your Majesty." Pterocles bowed again. "Very much at your service, I might add. I've tried to stay out of the way the past few days—"

"So have I, as a matter of fact," Hirundo broke in. "Wasn't so much worried about Ortalis, you understand, as I was about some of the young pups who ran with him. They might have wanted to see if they could bite an old hound's backside, and he wouldn't have told 'em it wasn't a good idea. . . ."

"No," Lanius said. "I don't suppose he would."

"But the wizard's right," Hirundo said. "We *are* at your service, Your Majesty. Better yours—much better yours—than *his*." He did not name Ortalis, not this time, but then, he had no need to.

"Much better yours," Pterocles agreed. "I wondered if the Scepter would put up with him. Since it didn't . . . well, that says everything that needs saying, doesn't it?"

"Everyone thinks so," Lanius said. "I don't think we'll ever see another king who can't pick it up." Had that been so before the Menteshe seized the Scepter? He couldn't remember reading anything in the archives that said it had. But then, would birds have written in detail of the air through which they flew? The chroniclers of bygone days must have felt the same about the Scepter of Mercy. Why go on about what everybody already knew?

Sounding apologetic for being so persistent, Hirundo asked, "Uh, Your Majesty, what *are* you going to do about Grus?"

At almost the same instant, Pterocles asked, "What are you going to do about Ortalis, Your Majesty?"

"I don't have to make up my mind about Grus right away," Lanius answered, and he knew more than a little relief when both the general and the wizard nodded with him. He went on, "I know exactly what to do with Ortalis, though. . . ."

Ortalis slumped against the side of a boat. He would have said there were few worse postures in which to fall asleep—and he would have been right. But when exhaustion pressed, posture mattered less than he would have imagined possible. And so, despite the awkward position, despite the musty smells of the Maze all around him—and some of those smells worse than merely musty, too—sleep he did.

No sooner had he fallen asleep than he also fell into a dream. It was, he saw at once, one of *those* dreams, the dreams that seemed brighter, realer, *truer* than mere mundane reality. This dream, unlike the ones that had gone before, did not paint a whole world. No, all he saw was a face.

But what a face!—inhumanly calm, inhumanly cold, inhumanly beautiful. And the voice that came from the face was the Voice that had urged him on to the kingship . . . for a little while. "You failed me," the Voice said.

Instead of warming Ortalis, praising him, pushing him to do great things, the Voice made him feel even smaller, even worse, than he had before. "It's not my fault," he whined. "I did the best I could."

The Voice laughed, a sound like a lash of ice. "Yes, and that was our great mistake."

"What do you mean? What are you talking about?" Ortalis demanded.

"The best you could do—the best *you* could do—was not very good," the Voice said, still laughing that wounding laugh. "It was not good enough to satisfy the stinking Scepter, was it?"

"No." Ortalis didn't want to admit it, but what choice did he have? Failing had been bad enough. Failing with Lanius there to watch him do it was ten times worse. His miserable slug of a brother-in-law . . . Yet the Scepter of Mercy that refused *him* accepted Lanius without a qualm. Savagely, Ortalis said, "I should have killed that scrawny bastard while I had the chance!"

"Oh, *now* you see wisdom!" The Voice's sarcasm flayed worse than its laughter. "I suggested this, you will recall, but you did not care to hear me then. Oh, no. You were too *good* to hear me then. Too good, yes, but not good enough. I told you you would not be. Your best was not good enough, and never will be. Otherwise, *I* would not have been interested in you. But if you had done your worst, your very worst, you likely would still be King of Avornis today."

"I see it," Ortalis said miserably. "I see everything."

"I told your father his successor would not be able to lift the Scepter," the Voice said. "I told him, but he called me liar. Well, he has gotten what he deserves, and now you are getting what you deserve. I daresay he will have something sharp to tell you when you follow him into that selfsame monastery."

"What?" Ortalis yelped. Lanius hadn't said anything about that when he sent Ortalis into the Maze—a monastery, yes, but not *that* one. Ortalis hadn't imagined Lanius could come up with such an ingenious and nasty revenge. "I'd do almost anything not to see my father again."

"A little late to worry about it now, don't you think?" the Voice said. "You can also tell your father-in-law why you failed to recall him. I am sure he will be interested in hearing about that—and about the stripes on his daughter's back."

"Shut up, curse you!" Ortalis cried furiously. No, he didn't want to see Petrosus, either.

The Voice laughed. How the Voice laughed! "Your curses are worthless. You break wind with your mouth, little man— nothing more. But I have been well and truly cursed by those who knew exactly what they were doing, and who, catching me unawares and trusting—a mistake I shall never make again—had *just* the power to send me forth and to maroon me, accursed, in this material world. For believe me, otherwise I would not waste my time on such worms as you."

He laughed again, laughed and screamed at the same time. Ortalis woke there at the side of the boat, a cry of horror on his lips. "Shut up, curse you," said one of the rowers—the same thing Ortalis himself had told the Voice.

"But the dream—" Ortalis broke off in confusion. The dream was gone now. Here was reality, and was it much better? He discovered he was nodding to himself. Even going to face his father, even going to face Petrosus, was better than facing the being that owned the Voice. *Anything* was better than that.

A boot stirred him. "Shut up, I told you. Think you're still king? Not if you can't pick up the Scepter, you're not. Serves you right, by the gods in the heavens!" Was *that* better than facing the Voice? As a matter of fact, it was.

Grus' biggest surprise at the monastery was how little he minded being there. He was busy with either work or prayer most of the day, but the work wasn't of the sort that would have kept him from thinking. Peeling turnips or washing dishes or chopping firewood didn't take much in the way of brains.

Part of him said he should have been figuring out how to escape, how to get back to the city of Avornis, how to put the crown back on his own head. The rest asked a question he'd never asked before he recovered the Scepter of Mercy: *Why?*

Before, it would have been a question that got a serious answer. Something always wanted doing, and he'd always been, or seemed to be, the only man who could do it. The nobles of Avornis needed quelling? Who could keep them in line but a strong king? Nobody.

Dagipert of Thervingia wanted to make Lanius his son-in-law and turn Avornis into a Thervingian puppet kingdom? Again, who could guess what mischief might have sprung from that without a strong king to resist? Nobody.

Who could beat back the Chernagor pirates? Who could drive the Menteshe out of Avornis' southern provinces? Was Lanius up to the job? Not likely! Lanius had his virtues, but military prowess wasn't one of them. He was perhaps the *least* military King of Avornis of all time. (He would have known whether that was true better than Grus did himself.) If Grus hadn't tended to such things, who would have? Once more, nobody.

And there was the Scepter. Lanius was the one who'd thought of using a moncat to get into Yozgat and bring it out. That never would have occurred to Grus, not in a thousand years. But Yozgat lay a long way south of the Stura. Who besides Grus could have taken an Avornan army down to the Menteshe stronghold, besieged it, and given Pouncer the chance to sneak in? Nobody, yet again.

But now the nobles were cowed, the Thervings quiet, the Chernagors intimidated, the Menteshe divided amongst themselves, even the Banished One beaten for the time being, and the Scepter of Mercy back in the city of Avornis where it belonged.

All that being so, what did he have left to do?

He'd had the same thought before, after wielding the Scepter of Mercy against the Banished One. Then, it hadn't seemed so important. He would go back to the capital—he *had* gone back to the capital—and pick up the reins again. Whatever came along, he would deal with it. And if it turned out to be less exciting than beating back King Dagipert and less dramatic than recovering the Scepter . . . well, so what?

Grus had wondered whether Lanius would try to gather more power into his own hands. He'd never imagined Ortalis would. Royal power wasn't the sort that had ever interested Ortalis very much. But now that he had it . . .

Now that he had it, he was welcome to it, as far as Grus was concerned. If he had great things in him, he could let them out. Grus had trouble imagining that, but life was full of surprises. The brown robe he wore proved that. And if Lanius didn't care to see his brother-in-law ruling the kingdom in his stead, he could do something about it or not, just as he pleased.

*It's not my worry, not anymore.* That bothered Grus hardly at all. He'd spent a lot of years being worried, and he'd had a lot of important things to worry about. Was he going to get all hot and bothered over whether his son or his son-in-law ended up telling the rest of the Avornans what to do? After fending off

King Dagipert, after bringing back the Scepter of Mercy, what difference did something like that make?

Abbot Pipilo came into the kitchen where Grus was washing supper dishes. "You're fitting in here better than I thought you would, Brother," the abbot remarked.

"Am I? That's nice." Grus thought about it for a moment and then said, "This isn't so bad."

"I certainly don't think so, but then my station was far less exalted than yours," Pipilo said. "Some of your fellow monks are, ah, surprised you show so little distress at being cast down."

Grus knew exactly what that meant—Petrosus was perturbed that he wasn't weeping and wailing and tearing out chunks of his beard. "It's not so bad," he said again. "It's even—restful in a way, isn't it? I don't have to tell anybody what to do, and I know what I have to do myself."

The abbot bowed to him. "You will make a good monk," he declared. "If you outlive me, you may make a good abbot."

"I wouldn't want to," Grus replied. "I told you—I've spent almost my whole life giving orders. Enough is enough."

"I wonder if you'll say that a year from now, when your duties no longer seem like a holiday from kingship."

Pipilo was shrewd, no doubt about it. But Grus said, "I think I will. What's left for me to do back in the city of Avornis? Nothing I can see."

"I hope for your sake that you're right," the abbot said. "You'll have an easier time of it if you are. But you're one of the people I worry about going over the wall. You might manage it, and you might get back to the city of Avornis, too. I don't say that about many of the men here."

"Thank you for the compliment, uh, Father." Grus was still getting used to that; he hadn't called anyone *Father* since laying Crex, his own father, on the pyre. "But even if I did, who would care? Whether it's Ortalis or Lanius on the throne, he won't want me back."

Pipilo raised an eyebrow. "Some of your followers might."

Would Hirundo rise against a king from a younger generation? Would Pterocles? They might possibly, against Ortalis. Against Lanius? Grus found it unlikely. And besides . . . "How do you know my followers aren't on the way here, or to another monastery, or in a dungeon, or dead? If you use that kind of broom, you're smart to sweep out all the dust." Was Ortalis that smart? Who could guess for certain? Sooner or later, one way or another, Grus would find out.

With a shrug, Pipilo said, "Well, it will be as it will be," which no one could possibly argue with. He added, "I am taking up too much of your time," and went on his way, leaving Grus to the dirty plates and bowls and spoons. Grus shrugged and ran a rag across the next bowl.

If his calm perplexed the abbot, it really did infuriate Petrosus. And what infuriated Ortalis' father-in-law even more was the lack of any command releasing him from the monastery. "Your pup is as ungrateful as you are," Petrosus snarled to Grus.

The deposed king, walking through the monastery courtyard, paused and bowed to the deposed treasury minister, on his hands and knees in the vegetable garden. "I love you, too, Brother," Grus said sweetly.

"I'm not your brother, and I wouldn't want to be." Petrosus spat on the pile of weeds he'd uprooted.

Grus had had a brother, a younger brother, but the other boy had died when he was so young, he hardly remembered him. "Don't worry," Grus said. "I don't want you for one, either. But with these"—he flapped the sleeves of his robe—"it's not like we've got much choice."

Petrosus came back with yet another unpleasantry. Before Grus could answer, a sentry on the wall—a wall undoubtedly built more to keep the monks in than to keep intruders out—called, "Who comes?"

That sent everyone within earshot hurrying toward the gate. Petrosus jumped up from the vegetable plot and pushed past Grus without a harsh word. Grus wondered what was going on, but not for long. They were about to get a new monk, or maybe more than one. And they couldn't know ahead of time who the new arrivals might be. After all, a king had joined them the last time.

Whatever answer came from beyond the monastery, that tall, thick wall muffled it. Abbot Pipilo pushed through the crowd of monks. "Let me by, Brothers," he said. "Let me by. Tending to this is my duty." When men didn't get out of the way fast enough to suit him, he wasn't too holy to move them aside with a well-placed elbow to the ribs.

He slipped through the inner gate by himself, closed it behind him, and walked up to the portcullis. Grus could hear him parleying with the men who brought the new monk or monks. The abbot's voice rose in surprise, but after a moment he sang out, "Open!"

Grunting monks turned a capstan. Chain rattled and clanked as it wound around the big wooden drum. Squealing, the portcullis rose. Monks oiled the iron every day to keep it from rusting. They got to leave the monastery. Only men Pipilo trusted had the privilege. Grus wondered if he would ever gain it. In Pipilo's sandals, he wouldn't have trusted himself.

"Close!" the abbot called. The monks grunted again as they bent to the bars of the capstan, although lowering the portcullis was easier work than raising it.

After the great iron grill thudded home, Pipilo said something else, too low for Grus to follow it. The answering voice was high and furious. Grus stiffened. That couldn't be . . . He looked at Petrosus, who also stood there in frozen astonishment.

But it was. When the gate opened, Pipilo said, "Brothers, I present to you our new colleague and comrade, Brother Ortalis!"

Now Grus did some elbowing to get to the front of the crowd of monks. "Well, well," he said to his son. "What brings you here?"

Ortalis looked harried. Sullenly, he answered, "I couldn't pick up the miserable Scepter."

"Why am I not surprised?" Grus jeered, and then realized he really *wasn't* surprised. The Banished One had told him his successor wouldn't be able to. The exiled god had sworn he was telling the truth. He'd even offered to take oath by his ungrateful descendants, something Grus had never imagined from him. And he hadn't lied, or not very much. The one thing he hadn't said was that the man who failed to lift the Scepter of Mercy would be Grus' *long-term* successor. Lying by omission was often more effective than coming out and saying that which was not true. Grus knew as much. He also knew he shouldn't have been surprised to discover the Banished One did, too.

"*You* weren't going to let me have the throne at all," Ortalis said. "*You* thought Lord Squint-at-a-scroll would make a better king than I would."

"Yes, and by all the signs I was right, wasn't I?" Grus answered. "The Scepter of Mercy thought so, too."

His son—his one legitimate son—suggested a use for the Scepter of Mercy at once illegal, immoral, and painful. Several monks of more fastidious temperament gasped in horror. Ortalis went on, "And a whole fat lot of good your scheming did you. You think Lanius will call you back? Don't hold your breath, Father *dear,* that's all I've got to tell you."

"No, I don't expect him to call me back," Grus answered calmly. "The difference is, I don't care."

"You don't *care*? My left one, you don't!" Ortalis cried. "How couldn't you? You were *king,* by the gods! King! Now look at you, in that shabby brown robe—"

"It is a robe of humility," Abbot Pipilo broke in. "Soon, Brother Ortalis, you will wear one, too."

Whatever burned in Ortalis, humility had nothing to do with it. Ignoring the abbot, he raged on. "In that shabby robe, I tell you, mucking out the barn and pulling up weeds in the miserable garden. What joy!"

Shrugging, Grus answered, "They haven't let me weed yet. That seems to be work for men who've been here longer and know more about growing things. Brother Petrosus here gets to do that, for instance. I haven't had to muck out, either—not yet, though I expect I will. Mostly I've been peeling vegetables and washing dishes and helping out in the kitchens any other way the senior cooks need."

Ortalis gave his father-in-law such a venomous, even murderous, stare that whatever Petrosus might have said to him curdled in his throat. *Ortalis could have been much more formidable if only he'd worked at it,* Grus thought sadly. *But he never wanted to work at anything.* There, in a nutshell, lay the difference between his son and himself—between Lanius and his son, too.

As usual, though, Ortalis saved most of his spleen for Grus. "What's the matter with you?" he demanded. "Do they put poppy juice in the wine here?"

"It's mostly ale," Grus said.

"Good ale," Pipilo said. "We brew it ourselves, Brother Ortalis, if the craft interests you."

Except for a look on his face that said no craft interested him, Ortalis ignored that, too. He aimed a forefinger at Grus as though it were an arrowhead. "You're *happy* here!" he cried. By his tone, his own quirks sank into insignificance beside such a perversion. "*Happy!*"

And Grus found himself nodding. "As a matter of fact, I am."

"*How?*" The question from his son was a pain-filled howl.

"It's not that hard," Grus answered. "There's enough to do. There's enough to eat. There's nothing much to worry about. I've been wondering for a while now what I could do that would come close to what I've already done. I didn't see anything. If you've already done the biggest things you're ever going to do, it's high time somebody put you out to pasture. Maybe I ought to thank you."

"That is the proper attitude for a monk," Abbot Pipilo said approvingly.

Ortalis, by contrast, turned very red and seemed on the edge of pitching a fit. "Olor's beard!" he cried. "Do you think I would have sent you here if I thought you were going to *like* it?"

"No." Maybe Grus didn't completely have the proper attitude for a monk, for he couldn't resist a dig at his son and brief successor, saying, "And I'll like it even better now that you're here to keep me company."

Several monks laughed at that, Petrosus loud among them. Even Pipilo smiled. He said, "Come, Brother Ortalis. Time to cast aside the raiment of the outer world for the robe that makes all of us one, all of us the same in the eyes of the gods in the heavens."

What Ortalis had to say about the gods in the heavens was, to put it mildly, pungent and uncomplimentary. No one reproached him, not even the abbot. Grus would have bet quite a few of the monks had said similar things when they first came here. Maybe some of them still had those thoughts. But most would have been able to see by now that they couldn't do anything about them, so what was the point of holding on to them?

"Come, Brother," Abbot Pipilo said again. And, even if Ortalis still fumed and cursed, he came.

\* \* \*

Limosa dropped King Lanius a curtsy that bent her low. They were in Lanius' bedchamber, not the throne room, but she treated him with the greatest possible formality. And fear made her voice wobble when she said, "Y-Your Majesty."

"Straighten up," Lanius said impatiently. "You don't need to tremble like that. I'm not going to tie rocks to your feet and throw you in the river or stake you out for wolves—I promise you that."

"Thank you, Your Majesty." Limosa did straighten, but remained wary. "Uh—what *are* you going to do with me?"

"Well, that's what we're here to talk about, isn't it?" Lanius said. Listening to himself, he thought he sounded a good deal like Grus. That *well* at the start of the sentence gave him the chance to work out what he ought to say next.

"I'm no trouble to Your Majesty, not now," Limosa said. "With . . . with Ortalis put away, I'm no trouble to anybody."

"Well . . ." Lanius repeated. Yes, that was useful. "I'm not so sure. For one thing, you might want revenge. For another, you're mother to King Grus' grandchildren. You could plot for them, if not for yourself."

He thought Limosa would protest that she'd never do such a thing. He wouldn't have believed her, but that was the line he looked for her to take. Instead, she turned pale. "You wouldn't do anything to my children!"

"Not like that, no, of course not," Lanius answered. "I'm not a monster, you know." Did she? She'd been married to a monster of sorts, and loved him. What did *that* say?

"Of course not, Your Majesty," Limosa said softly. But what else could she say? If she told Lanius he *was* a monster, she gave him all the excuse he needed to prove it on her person. *I'm King of Avornis. I'm the only King of Avornis,* he thought—he was still getting used to that, for it was true for the first time in his life. *If I don't want to bother with excuses, I don't need them.* Limosa was thinking along with him, at least in part, for she added, "Whatever you do, I know you'll be just."

Plainly, she knew, and could know, no such thing. She hoped reminding him of the possibility would turn it into reality. Lanius drummed his fingers on his thigh. "You were Queen of Avornis for a little while," he said, perhaps more to himself than to Limosa. "How likely are you to forget that?"

"It wasn't my idea." Limosa almost spat out the words in her haste to set them free. Her voice went shrill and high. "It was Ortalis' plan—all his. I didn't want anything to do with it."

"No, eh?" Lanius said. She shook her head; her hair flipped back and forth with the vehemence of the motion. The king sighed sadly. One thing years at court did for a man—or maybe *to* him—they gave him a pretty good notion of when someone was lying. "I'm sorry, Your Highness"—he wasn't going to call her *Your Majesty,* not now—"but I don't believe you."

She'd gone pale before. Now she went white. "But it's the truth, Your Majesty! It is! How can I persuade you?" She dug herself in deeper with every panicky word.

Lanius sighed again. Grus had had to make choices like these much more often than he had himself. When Grus saw trouble ahead, he'd made the hard choice, too—made it with everyone but Lanius himself, in fact, and Ortalis. He'd eventually paid for trusting Ortalis to be harmless. Lanius eyed Limosa. Could she be dangerous? Yes, without a doubt. One more sigh, and then Lanius said what he thought he had to say. "I'm very sorry, Your Highness, but I'm going to send you to a nunnery."

"You can't!" Limosa gasped. "You wouldn't!" But Lanius could, and she could see he would. She went on, "I'd do any-thing—anything at all—to stay free."

How did she mean that? The way it sounded? That seemed likely. She was an attractive woman, but she didn't do anything special for Lanius, even if she had tempted him once. Even if she had, he could find plenty of others to do whatever he wanted, and they would be in no position to strike at the throne. "I'm sorry," he said again.

Limosa started to wail. As though that were a signal, a cou-ple of the king's guardsmen—all of them, these days, vouched for by Hirundo—came into the bedchamber. As they took Limosa's arms, she cried, "The children! What about the chil-dren?"

"They'll be well taken care of," Lanius promised. Marinus

and Capella were too little to pose any threat for years to come. And, with both their father and their grandfather overthrown, they would have no connection to the ruling house of Avornis by the time they grew up. He nodded to the guards. "She is to go to the nunnery dedicated to Queen Quelea's mercy in the Maze."

"Yes, Your Majesty," the men chorused. Limosa wailed louder than ever.

"It's the finest nunnery in the kingdom," Lanius said, and then, biting his lip, "It's the nunnery where Grus sent my mother after she plotted against him."

"I don't care! I don't want to be a nun!" Limosa shrieked.

"I'm afraid all your other choices are worse," Lanius told her. She gave him a terrible look. Trying to soften her, he went on, "I *am* sorry. I truly am. This isn't how I would have wanted things to work out."

"No? Why not?" Limosa said. "Out of everybody, you're the only one who's gotten just what he wanted."

That held some truth—probably more than some. Lanius would have been happy enough if Grus had gone on sharing the throne. Grus was better at some things—things like this, for instance—than he was himself. But he could do these things if he had to. He proved it, telling the guards, "Take her away."

"Yes, Your Majesty," they said again. Limosa screamed and clawed and scratched, all of which turned her departure into a spectacle but delayed it by not even a minute. As the din finally faded, Lanius called for a maidservant and said, "Please fetch me a cup of wine—a large cup of wine."

She curtsied, not as deeply as Limosa had. But then, she wasn't in trouble. She also said, "Yes, Your Majesty," and hurried away to do Lanius' bidding. *Everyone in the palace will be doing my bidding now,* he thought. He'd come across ideas he liked much less.

Sosia walked into the bedchamber while Lanius was still waiting for his wine. "Well," she said—maybe she'd borrowed the turn of phrase from Grus, too. "That must have been fun."

"Just about as much as you think it was," Lanius agreed. "I don't see what else I could have done, though. People get more ambitious for their children than they do for themselves."

"I'm not arguing with you—not about this, anyhow." Sosia made a very sour face. Lanius realized *she* wouldn't calmly accept anything he wanted to do. As if to underscore that, she continued, "You give me plenty of worse things to argue about."

The maidservant came in with the wine then—a large cup, as Lanius had asked of her. He thanked her less warmly than he might have if Sosia weren't standing there watching him. His wife's upraised eyebrow said she knew that perfectly well. The maidservant made haste to disappear. Lanius took a long pull at the cup. Then he sighed and shook his head. "Still doesn't get the taste of Limosa out of my mouth." He tried again with a longer pull yet.

"She made a nuisance of herself, all right," Sosia agreed, which was one of the larger understatements Lanius had heard lately. Sosia hesitated, then said, "May I ask you something?"

By her tone of voice, Lanius knew exactly what her question would be. He raised the winecup to his lips yet again. When he lowered it, it was empty, and he still found himself wishing for more. He did his best to keep that from his voice as he replied, "What is it?"

"What are you going to do about Father?"

He looked down into the cup. Despite his wishes, it stubbornly stayed empty. "I don't know," he said at last. "I don't have to do anything right away. He'll just have found out Ortalis isn't king anymore. Let's see what happens, all right?"

"You *are* the king," Sosia said. "In the end, it will be as you please."

*Why don't you feel that way about serving girls?* Lanius wondered. But serving girls, unlike this, weren't a matter of state. *Too bad,* he thought.

# CHAPTER TWENTY-NINE

It was a day like any other day since Grus came to the monastery. Along with the other monks, he was called out of bed early for dawn prayers. Then he ate breakfast. As usual, it was filling but bland. Neophron and the other cooks had either never heard of spices, didn't like them, or couldn't afford to put any in the barley mush. After breakfast, Grus went into the kitchens to wash earthenware bowls and mugs and horn spoons.

Prayer and work alternated through the day, work predominating. After what seemed not so very long, it was time for supper. As usual, a little sausage did go into the mush for the evening meal. So did some beans and peas. The mug of ale that washed things down was larger than the one at breakfast—not enough to get drunk on, but plenty to take the edge off a bad day. Grus' hadn't been bad, but it too got better.

Most of the time, Ortalis stayed as far away from Grus as he could in the dining hall. That suited Grus as well as it did his son. This evening, though, Ortalis chose to sit across from him. "We ought to eat better than this," Ortalis complained.

Grus shrugged. "It's enough. Even if it weren't, why are you telling me about it? I can't change things one way or the other."

"But I can, by Olor's prong!" Ortalis said—perhaps a dubious oath for a monastery. "I never wasted my time in the archives, or in the forest, come to that. When I went hunting, I went out to kill things, and I did. I could do it again."

"Maybe you could," Grus said. Anser had never complained about Ortalis' talent, only about his judgment in when to be bloodthirsty. With another shrug, Grus went on, "I'm not the one to tell you you can or you can't, though. If you want to convince somebody to let you go out, the abbot is your man."

"He won't listen to me," Ortalis said scornfully. "He'll think I'm trying to get away."

"He might," Grus agreed. "The same thought crossed my mind, you know."

"Why should it? You told me yourself—I'm in here for good," Ortalis said. "We all are. I'm used to it by now."

He didn't sound used to it. He sounded suspiciously hearty, like a man saying what he thought people around him wanted to hear. Grus sipped from his ale. That was good; the monks who brewed it did know what they were doing. He said, "The other thing I told you was, it's not in my hands. And it's not. The only one who can tell you yes—or even no—is Pipilo."

"I *will* talk to him, then. He'll see sense," Ortalis said. *He'll do what I want him to do,* was what he likely meant by that. He'd never been able to tell the difference between what he wanted at the moment and what was right.

Grus was not unduly surprised when Pipilo came up to him a few days later and said, "Your son has approached me about the possibility of going out and hunting for the larder. Is he as good an archer and stalker as he says he is?"

"I don't know how good he said he was, but he's pretty good, yes," Grus answered.

"He did sound as though he knew what he was talking about," the abbot allowed. "That is, of course, only one part of the issue at hand. The other is, were he to go beyond the walls, would he be tempted to abandon his monastic robe and try to return to the secular world?"

*Of course he would,* Grus thought. All he said was, "The two of us, I fear, are estranged. I cannot be just in judging him, and so I will not try. You have to decide that yourself."

"You're honest, anyhow," Pipilo told him.

"Most of the time, anyhow—when it looks like a good idea," Grus said. "Were you a married man before you came here?"

"I was." Pipilo nodded.

"Well, then." Grus stopped, as though no more needed to be said. By the way Pipilo laughed, he *had* said enough.

In the end, the abbot decided not to let Ortalis go out hunting. If Grus had been in his sandals, he would have decided the same thing. Ortalis blamed him for it. Grus had expected that, though not the full force of his son's fury. Storming up to him in the monastery courtyard, Ortalis shouted, "You're keeping me locked up in this stinking jail!"

"I had nothing to do with putting you here." Grus looked down his nose at Ortalis—not easy when his son was taller. "You can't say the same about how I got here. Do you hear me complaining about it?"

"No, but you're soft in the head or something." Mere truth wasn't going to dent Ortalis' outrage. "You told the warder—"

"The abbot, and you'd better remember it, or he'll make you sorry."

Ortalis rolled his eyes. "Who cares what you call him? The point is, the old blackguard won't let me go out. I know he talked to you about it. What other reason would he have for keeping me in here except that you told him to?"

"Maybe he has eyes of his own to see with?" Grus suggested.

"What do you mean?"

"Anyone who does have eyes knows you'd take off in a heartbeat if you got outside the walls," Grus said, more patiently than he would have thought possible. "Pipilo doesn't need me to tell him that. You tell him yourself, every time you breathe. If you want to know what I said to him, ask him yourself. I'm sure he'll give you the truth."

"Suppose *you* tell me, before I knock some teeth loose," Ortalis growled.

Grus had given his son a few beatings. They hadn't done what he'd hoped they would. Maybe he should have started sooner and given more. On the other hand, maybe he never should have started at all. If he and Ortalis fought now, Ortalis probably could beat him. "You won't believe me even if I do," he said.

"Try me," Ortalis said. Grus recounted the conversation with the abbot as exactly as he could. Ortalis snorted and rolled his eyes again. "You're right. I don't believe you." Instead of swinging at Grus, he stormed off.

Petrosus came up to Grus. "He *is* a charming fellow, isn't he?" said the former treasury minister.

"He's my son," Grus answered. "I'm tied to him however he is. You yoked your daughter to him when you didn't have to. What does that say about you?" *And she fell in love with him, where nobody else in the world could. What does that say about her?*

Petrosus glared at him. "You're still as charming as you were when your backside warmed a throne, aren't you?"

"No doubt," Grus said. "And you're still as ambitious as you were when you dreamed of a throne. Don't you see how foolish that is when you're *here*?"

"Not if I don't have to stay here," Petrosus said.

"Do you think Lanius will let you out? Don't hold your breath," Grus said. "You were the one who held back his allowance while I was campaigning. He's never forgotten that, you know."

"You told me to. I did it at your order!" Petrosus exclaimed.

He was right, of course. Back in those days, Grus had worried about any power coming into Lanius' hands. He'd kept the other king weak every way he could, including not giving him enough money. And what had that gotten him? At the time, it won him security on the throne. In the end? In the end, power came into Lanius' hands anyhow. Grus looked down at his own hands, and at the coarse brown wool on the sleeves of the robe he wore now.

"The difference between us is, I don't mind being here, and you do," Grus said.

"The difference between us is, you're out of your mind and I'm not," Petrosus retorted.

Grus shook his head. "The reason I don't mind being here is that I did everything I wanted to do, everything I needed to do, out in the world. Because of what I did, people will remember me for years after I'm gone, maybe even forever. Who will remember you, Petrosus?"

"After I'm dead, what difference does it make?" Petrosus

said, which also held some truth. But it held only some, and Petrosus proved as much by snarling curses at Grus and storming away. Grus looked after him and shook his head. The monastery wasn't as calm as he wished it were.

Lanius was grateful to Sosia for not nagging him about releasing Grus. Ever since they wed, she'd inclined more toward him than toward her father. She understood the reasons why he wouldn't want Grus to come back to the palace. Whether she agreed with them or not, she respected them enough not to be difficult over them.

But she didn't—or perhaps couldn't—talk her mother out of asking Lanius to order Grus out of the monastery. "Don't you owe him that much?" Estrilda said with the peculiar certainty older people often show when talking to younger ones. "Don't you, after everything he did for the kingdom? If he hadn't done all that, you wouldn't be on the throne now, you know."

"No, I suppose not," Lanius said. If Grus hadn't become king, if he himself had had to marry King Dagipert's daughter instead of Grus', the fearsome old King of Thervingia probably would have shoved him aside more violently and more permanently than Grus had.

"Well, then," Estrilda said, as though that were the only thing that mattered. "Don't you have any sense of gratitude?"

"Shall I be grateful that he put my mother in a monastery and never let her out?" Lanius inquired acidly.

"Certhia tried to kill him," Estrilda said, which was also true. "He never tried to kill her."

"Well, I'm not going to try to kill him, either. On that you have my word," Lanius said. If his gratitude ran no further . . . then it didn't, that was all.

"You're not listening to me." Estrilda sounded surprised—almost astonished. As wife to the more powerful king, she'd gotten used to people following her slightest whim.

"I am listening," Lanius said politely. "But I decide what to do now—no one else."

She stared at him. Plainly, he was sole King of Avornis now. If he weren't, why would she ask him to let Grus go? Just as

plainly, the idea that nobody could tell him what to do now
hadn't fully sunk in until this moment. Shaking her head, Es
trilda walked out of the audience chamber.

As Lanius and Sosia were going to bed that night, she said
"I am sorry about what happened earlier today. I told Mother
didn't think that would be a good idea, but she went ahead and
did it anyhow."

By then, Lanius had had the chance to gain a little perspec
tive on things. "It's all right," he said. "It could have been
worse, anyhow."

"Oh?" Sosia raised an eyebrow. "How?"

"She could have asked me to let your brother out, too, or in
stead."

"Oh," Sosia said again, this time on an altogether different
note. "That would have been awkward, wouldn't it?"

"No." He shook his head. "*This* was awkward, because there
could be reasons to let Grus out of the monastery. If she'd
asked the other, I would have said no and then thrown her out
if she asked me again." To keep Ortalis from coming out of the
monastery, he was ready to be as rude and stubborn as he had
to. That went against his usual nature, but so did what he felt
about his brother-in-law.

At least he wasn't afraid of offending his wife about Ortalis
Except for Limosa, Ortalis seemed to have alarmed everyone
who ever knew him. That included Sosia. She'd never made
any great secret of it, either. All she said was, "It's over. You
don't need to worry about it anymore."

But she was wrong. The next morning, a servant came up to
Lanius just as he and Sosia were finishing breakfast. "Excuse
me, Your Majesty, but Arch-Hallow Anser would like to speak
with you."

"Of course," Lanius said. "I'm always happy to see him.
Bring him in, and then fetch some wine for him, too." The ser
vant bobbed his head and hurried off.

Anser came in a moment later. Lanius blinked when he did
Anser was wearing his red formal robes, something he hardly
ever did when not conducting services in the great cathedral
"Your Majesty," he said, and bowed to Lanius. Turning to

Sosia, he repeated the words. He also bowed to his half-sister, not quite as deeply.

"Sit down," Lanius urged. As Anser did, the king went on, "I've got a servant bringing you wine. What can I do for you? You're not usually out and about so early if you aren't hunting."

Anser looked faintly embarrassed, which startled Lanius almost as much as the ceremonial regalia did. "I have a favor to ask of you, Your Majesty," the arch-hallow said. "I haven't asked many, have I?"

"You've asked so few, it almost makes me suspicious," Lanius answered. "Go ahead and ask, and we'll see what happens then." He wasn't foolish enough to promise to grant favors no matter what. Kings had gotten themselves in a lot of trouble with promises like that.

After a deep breath, Anser said, "Your Majesty, please let my father out of that monastery. If you do, I swear I'll never ask another thing of you for as long as I live—not even to go hunting with me, if you don't want me to."

"He would be pleased with you, to know you've asked this," Lanius said. "He would be proud of you, too."

"He did everything for me," Anser said simply. "Plenty of bastards don't even know who their father is. But he made sure I always had enough. And then when he got the crown . . . Well, look what he did. Do you think I'd be wearing this" —he flapped the sleeve of his robe— "if not for him?" He snorted to show how unlikely that was, then went on, "So you see, Your Majesty, I'd do anything for him, too. I'm not too proud to beg you to set him free. Please."

With some regret, Lanius shook his head. "I'm not going to do that. I'm sorry, but I'm not. I'm the King of Avornis now. I didn't expect to be, not until he'd lived out his days. Frankly, I thought I was sure to lose if I rose against him. Maybe I was wrong—who knows? But if I called him back to the city of Avornis, I couldn't very well do it without seeing the crown go back on his head, too, could I? You may think I'm heartless, but I just don't want to do that."

"I don't think you're heartless, Your Majesty. I would never think so," Anser said. "You'll do what you think you have to do, but please understand that I've got to do the same thing."

"I do understand that," Lanius said. "And I think it's sad that his legitimate son overthrew him and his bastard is pleading for me to turn the hourglass upside down again, but I can't change that."

"Neither can I. I wish I could," Anser replied. "Ortalis . . . Ortalis always knew he couldn't live up to his father, and he couldn't live up to what his father wanted from him. Me, I was further away. I didn't have to live up to anything at all. I was glad enough just to live, and to live pretty well."

Lanius thought there was a lot of truth in what his half brother-in-law said—a lot, but not enough. "Not being able to live up to what Grus wanted of him wasn't the only trouble Ortalis had," the king said. "That mean streak, that taste for blood and pain, was all his own."

"It was," Sosia said softly. "He always had it, as far back as I can remember."

"Well, I didn't know him then—or you, Your Majesty," Anser said to her. "I'll have to take your word for that." He turned back to Lanius. "But it doesn't have anything to do with why you should or shouldn't let my father come back. He didn't do anything to deserve what Ortalis did to him. I should say not! Look how much Avornis owes him. The Scepter of Mercy back again! Could anyone have imagined that?"

*I had something to do with it, too,* Lanius thought. He couldn't have done it without Grus, but Grus couldn't have done it without him, either. He said, "The Scepter accepts me, too, you know."

"Oh, of course, Your Majesty! I never said it didn't," Anser said quickly. "But . . ." He spread his hands. "You know what I mean."

"I do," Lanius said. "But I'm the king now, and I intend to stay the king for as long as I last."

Anser sadly bowed his head. "Then there's not much I can do about this, is there? Thanks for hearing me out, anyhow." He bowed to Lanius, then to Sosia, and left the room.

Sosia sighed. She quickly finished eating and also hurried out. She might understand why Lanius was doing what he was doing, but that didn't mean she liked it, either. Lanius sighed, too. He poured his own cup of wine full again, and then again after that. He wasn't a man in the habit of getting drunk before noon. Today, though, he made an exception.

Grus had won a promotion. From peeling turnips, he'd advanced to measuring out grain and beans and dried peas, pouring them into big iron kettles full of boiling water, and stirring the stews with a long-handled wooden spoon. It wasn't exciting work—he wasn't sure such a thing as exciting work existed anywhere in the monastery—but it was a step up. When Neophron offered it to him, he took it.

As long as he was in the kitchens or at whatever other work Abbot Pipilo set him, he was contented enough. It was something to do, something not too hard, something to keep him busy through most of the day. Things could have been worse.

When he wasn't at his labors, things *were* worse. He couldn't avoid Ortalis and Petrosus; the monastery wasn't big enough. Whenever he got near one of them, he got into a quarrel. He didn't start the arguments, but he didn't back away from them, either. If he hadn't backed away from King Dagipert or the Banished One, he didn't intend to back away from his son or a palace functionary, either.

After the seventh or eighth shouting match in the courtyard, he did go to see Pipilo in the abbot's office. Pipilo was scribbling something on a piece of parchment when Grus knocked on the open door and stood waiting in the doorway. "Come in, Brother," Pipilo said. "And what can I do for you today?"

His tone said, *Let's get this over with so I can go back to the important things I was doing before I had to deal with the likes of you.* Grus fought to hide a smile. Sure enough, the abbot was a king in his own little realm. Grus couldn't begin to remember how many times he'd used that same tone himself.

"Father Abbot, isn't this supposed to be a place of peace?" he asked.

"Of course, Brother," Pipilo answered. "But what a place is supposed to be and what it turns out to be aren't always the same. I wish I could tell you otherwise, but I don't think you'll say I'm lying."

"No, not at all," Grus agreed. "Still, I would like to be able to get through a day without at least one screaming row."

"I can see how you might, yes," the abbot said judiciously. "It was perhaps unfortunate that three men who have such strong reasons to disagree with one another were all gathered together in the same place."

"Perhaps it was." Grus went along with the understatement. "Is there any chance one or two of us might be moved to another monastery?"

Pipilo spread his hands, as though to show the limits of his domain. "I have not the authority to make such a transfer, Brother. It is possible to send a petition back to the city of Avornis, a petition I would endorse. But what my endorsement would do, if anything, I am not sure. This is the most, ah, secure monastery in the kingdom, which is why each of the three of you was sent here."

*Why each of the three of you will stay here,* he might as well have said. "By your leave, I will write that petition," Grus said. "The worst I can hear is no, and no leaves me no worse off."

"By all means, Brother. You may have parchment and pen for the purpose," Pipilo said. "And I wish you good fortune from it—not because I am not glad of your company here, for you have shown yourself a worthy monk, but because, if the king grants it, you will find more tranquility in your life."

"Tranquility," Grus murmured. He'd had a lot of things in his life, but, up until now, rarely that. Did the abbot really think him a worthy monk? Pipilo must have. He didn't need to keep Grus sweet. It was the other way around here. Grus hadn't had many finer compliments than that.

If only he didn't have to worry about Ortalis and Petrosus . . . Yes, he would write that petition, as soon as he could.

*Brother Grus to King Lanius—greetings, Your Majesty.* Lanius wasn't used to getting letters from Grus without the royal seal stamped in wax to help hold them closed. This one had no seal of any sort. As usual, Grus came straight to the point. *Here in this monastery,* he wrote, *Ortalis and Petrosus and I quarrel like so many crabs in a kettle with the water getting hot. I do not ask to be released from this place back into the world. I know you would say no at once. But could you please arrange it so the three of us are in three separate places? It would take a miracle for us to get along here, and miracles are in moderately short supply lately. I hope the kingdom runs smoothly. I know it is in good hands.*

"Well, well," Lanius said under his breath. Grus had never been a man to show self-pity, and he showed even less now than the king would have expected. Lanius would have granted his petition without the least hesitation . . . if he weren't in the strongest monastery in the Maze. He seemed content as a monk now, but how could anyone guess if he would stay that way?

And Ortalis had a claim on the throne—had held it, if not for long and not well. And Petrosus was father to a princess who'd briefly been a queen (and was now a nun) and was grandfather to a young prince and princess. All three men could become problems if they found themselves in a place easier to escape from than that monastery.

*It would take a miracle for us to get along here.* Lanius sighed when he read that again. It wasn't that he didn't believe it. On the contrary—it seemed much too likely. Ortalis had never gotten along with his father. Petrosus had no reason to.

"A miracle," Lanius repeated. A slow smile spread over his face. He didn't know if he had a miracle handy. On the other hand, he didn't know he didn't, either, and that was more than most men could say.

The guards in front of the Scepter of Mercy stiffened to attention when Lanius walked up. "Your Majesty!" they chorused.

"As you were," the king said, and the guardsmen relaxed. Lanius picked up the Scepter. Being able to pick it up encouraged him; as King Cathartes had written centuries before it was stolen, it would not let itself be used for anything unrighteous.

Lanius thought carefully about how to seek what he wanted from the Scepter. If he sought to make Grus and Ortalis and Petrosus suddenly love one another, he was sure his wish would go ungranted. There was such a thing as asking—and asking for—too much.

Up until now, he'd used the Scepter of Mercy for things that would obviously help Avornis as a whole. Chief among them was seeking better harvests in the lands the Menteshe had ravaged in their invasion before Prince Ulash died. Even with that help, he feared the southern provinces would still be a long time recovering.

This . . . This was something else. Whether he used the Scepter of Mercy or didn't, Avornis wouldn't change one way or the other. Few people outside the monastery would have any idea of what he'd done. This almost struck him as a task too small and trivial to bring to the Scepter's notice, as it were.

But there were small mercies as well as large ones. If Grus and Ortalis and Petrosus had to live together—and they did—couldn't they live together without rubbing one another raw every day of their enforced cohabitation? It didn't seem too much to ask. Grus particularly deserved peace and quiet, if that was what he'd found at the monastery.

Lanius aimed the Scepter in the general direction of the Maze. He wasn't sure that helped, but he didn't see how it could hurt. He shaped the idea behind what he wanted until it was clear in his mind. Then he sent it forth, out through his will, out through his arm, out through the Scepter.

He'd felt power thrum through the Scepter of Mercy when he used it to do what he could for the southern croplands. He felt it again now, but not nearly to the same degree. That made him smile at himself. Not even he believed this was as important as anything he'd done with the Scepter before. All the same, that didn't mean it wasn't worth doing.

"What did you do, Your Majesty?" one of the guardsmen asked as Lanius set the Scepter of Mercy back on its velvet cushion.

He smiled again, a little sheepishly. "I'm not quite sure. I hope I find out in a while." The guard smiled back, thinking he'd made a joke. The smile slowly faded as the man realized Lanius meant it.

Because Grus had always been in the habit of rising early, the call to sunrise prayer worked no great hardship on him. Even back in the palace, he would have been up soon anyhow. He rolled his eyes. From the Maze, the palace seemed farther than Yozgat had from the city of Avornis.

He'd gotten to Yozgat. He didn't think he'd get back to the palace. What still surprised him was how little that seemed to matter. He slid out of bed, belted his robe around him, and joined the stream of monks trudging down the hallway toward the chapel.

The sky was bright in the east as he walked across the courtyard, but the sun hadn't risen. Night's chill still lingered, though it wouldn't much longer. The day would be warm and muggy. The air was full of the damp, mostly stagnant smell that pervaded the Maze. A jay flew by overhead, screeching.

In their robes, monks often appeared interchangeable. Grus didn't notice he was walking only a few feet from Petrosus until he'd been doing it for some little while. The former treasury minister saw him, too, but didn't say anything. Neither did Grus.

*That could have been worse,* he thought as he went into the chapel. Along with the rest of the monks, he offered up the day's first hymns to King Olor and Queen Quelea and the other gods in the heavens. He sang with better conscience than he would have before the Scepter of Mercy came back to the city of Avornis. The gods probably didn't pay much attention to what went on here in the material world, but sometimes they did, and it mattered that they did. He hadn't been convinced that was so. Now he believed it.

When the service was over, the monks trooped into the refectory for breakfast. Grus took a bowl of barley porridge and a mug of ale from one of the servers, then sat down at a bench and a table just like all the other benches and tables in the large hall. Again, he wasn't as far from Petrosus as he wished he were. The other man left him alone. That suited him fine.

After breakfast, Grus went into the kitchens himself to wash dishes. That kept him busy for most of the morning. The head cook came over to watch him. "You sure don't mind work, do you?" Neophron said.

Shrugging, Grus answered, "Why should I? What else is there to do here but sit around twiddling my thumbs?"

"Some people would like that—you bet they would." Neophron laughed. "Never thought I'd have a king working under me, and that's the truth."

"You don't," Grus said. The other man raised an eyebrow. Grus continued, "If I were still king, I'd be back in the city of Avornis. Since I'm here, I'm a monk like any other monk." That was true enough; no one had tried to make life in the monastery any easier or any softer for him because of what he had been.

"Guess you're right," Neophron said after a little thought. "Well, I never figured I'd have somebody who used to be a king working under me, either." He eyed Grus to see if the formerly illustrious dishwasher would argue with that. Grus didn't. He just rinsed out another mug and set it on a rack to dry.

Once he'd leveled the mountain of earthenware, he went out into the courtyard. Petrosus was watering the garden. He eyed Grus, but again didn't speak to him. Petrosus had been snapping every time Grus came out of the kitchens. His silence seemed doubly welcome because it was so unexpected.

Here came Ortalis. He looked discontented—but then, he usually did. He minded work, but Abbot Pipilo didn't care whether he minded or not. He got it either way, and he got punished when he didn't do it well enough to suit Pipilo or whoever else was set over him. That did nothing to improve his temper.

He gave Grus a curt nod and kept walking. Caught by surprise, Grus nodded back. He and his son quarreled even more readily than he and Petrosus did. They had, anyway, ever since Ortalis' brief reign collapsed and he ended up here along with his father. Grus had looked for yet another barb from Ortalis. He scratched his head, wondering why he didn't get one.

After quiet persisted for a few days, Grus approached Pipilo in his office and asked him if he'd had anything to do with it. The abbot gravely shook his head. "No, Brother Grus, not I. I said not a word to either of them or to you, figuring whatever I said would do no good and might make things worse."

"It wouldn't have made them worse with me. All I want is peace and quiet," Grus said.

Pipilo smiled thinly. "One man's notions of peace and quiet are not always the same as another's." He held up his hand before Grus could reply. "I don't intend to offend anyone by saying this."

"Oh, you don't offend me, Father Abbot," Grus said. "I know that's true. Anyone who's had anything to do with more than a few people will know it's true."

The abbot smiled again. "Yes, you would have had that kind of experience before you, ah, joined us, wouldn't you? Well, Brother, if you've sent prayers up to the gods for tranquility, maybe you've had them answered."

"Maybe I have." Grus couldn't see how else he could respond to Pipilo, and he couldn't see where else to go from there. Since he couldn't, he bowed and left the office—which was, no doubt, just what Pipilo wanted him to do.

Even so, he grappled with the small problem—not that silence from Ortalis and Petrosus was a problem, even if the reason for their silence was—as stubbornly as he'd grappled with the problems King Dagipert or the Chernagor pirates posed for Avornis. Past their eventually delivering the Scepter of Mercy into his hands, he didn't see that the gods in the heavens listened to prayers very often, let alone answered them.

That left him shaking his head and laughing at the same time, which made his fellow monks send him puzzled, even wary, glances. He didn't care. He wondered whether any other monk in the long history of this monastery had ever had a less reverent attitude toward the gods in the heavens.

But if Olor and Quelea and the rest of the heavenly host hadn't inspired his son and his son's father-in-law to leave him alone, who or what had? Grus couldn't believe Ortalis and Petrosus had suddenly decided on their own to back off; that wasn't like either one of them, let alone both at the same time.

It was a nice puzzle. He realized he'd missed having something to ponder since he came here. Now he did, and found he was enjoying himself while he pondered. The more he did, the more perplexed he got. He didn't mind that; at least now he had something to wonder about.

Life at the monastery went on. One of the monks died—not an old man with a white beard, but one scarcely half Grus' age, of an attack of belly pain that led to fever. The surviving brethren, Grus among them, stood around his pyre and prayed that his soul might rise to the heavens with the smoke of his burning. *This will be my end, too,* Grus thought. The idea worried him less than he'd expected it to. He'd already lived a long life. And, while few people if anyone outside the monastery would remember poor Brother Mimus, his own name would last.

Though Ortalis went on leaving Grus alone, he got into a brawl with another monk. He broke one of his knuckles giving the man a black eye; the other man broke Ortalis' nose. Pipilo put them both on bread and water for a week. Dishonors were judged to be about even on both sides.

A couple of new monks came in. One of them, a skinny young man with a scraggly beard, really wanted to be there. He'd grown up not far away, and had wanted to join the monastery ever since he was a boy. Grus wondered how he'd like his wish now that he had it. The other was a city governor who'd thought living far from the city of Avornis let him get away with fattening his belt pouch. Grus was glad Lanius had proved him wrong, and took that as a good omen for his son-in-law's sole reign.

Lanius was a clever fellow, no doubt about it. Grus had always wondered whether the other king would be strong enough to rule on his own. He'd had his doubts about that. Maybe Lanius would prove him wrong after all.

And sometimes being clever sufficed. Grus was lying down on his thin mattress one evening when, instead, he sat bolt upright. The gods in the heavens surely couldn't care less if he and Ortalis and Petrosus squabbled. But the idea might bother Lanius, and the king knew there was trouble from Grus' petition. If he decided to pick up the Scepter of Mercy . . .

Would he use it for as small a thing as stopping a nasty quarrel? Grus nodded to himself, there in the darkness. Lanius didn't like unpleasantness. It was untidy. And he might well feel he owed Grus enough to make sure the other king got at least some peace now that he was king no more.

"Thank you," Grus murmured. He wasn't supposed to speak after lying down, but he wasn't pious enough to get upset at breaking a small rule, either. If one of the other monks had

caught him at it, he would have had to do something unpleasant for penance, but the brothers nearby were all snoring.

He nodded again. Now he was pretty sure he had an answer
to his riddle. The world wouldn't have ended even if he hadn't
gotten one—hardly!—but he still felt better knowing. Maybe
he wasn't so different from Lanius after all. He rolled over and
fell asleep.

# CHAPTER THIRTY

Lanius was amazed at all the correspondence Grus had dealt with. Letters addressed to the other king kept coming in weeks and months after Grus went to the monastery. Now Lanius had to deal with them.

Some of them didn't get dealt with; Lanius wasn't the administrator Grus had been. He consoled himself by thinking people would write again if anything really important fell through the cracks. Maybe he was right, maybe he wasn't. Either way, it made him feel better.

He did try to read everything that came in addressed to Grus. One letter, in a scrawl just this side of illiteracy, talked about how a boy named Nivalis was flourishing. It also complained—deferentially—that payment for the boy's expenses was overdue. It was signed by a woman named Alauda.

"Well, well," Lanius said, and then again, "Well, well." He'd never heard of Nivalis or Alauda.

So Grus had another bastard out there, did he? Did he? If he did, he must have fathered the boy when he was down in the south fighting the Menteshe. It wasn't impossible. Before sending money to a woman who might be trying to deceive, though, Lanius wrote to Grus in the monastery.

The answer came back as promptly as such things could. *Please pay her, Your Majesty*, Grus wrote. *The boy is mine, and I promised her she would not want. I do not care to be forsworn on something like this, and the expense is not large.*

*And besides, who knows what Nivalis may grow up to become?*

There was an interesting thought. The boy would know his heritage. His mother would make sure of that. He might come to the city of Avornis for an education, or to serve as a soldier. If he had any reasonable part of Grus' abilities, he could prove formidable. Avornis needed formidable people; there were never enough to go around.

And so Lanius wrote back to Grus, saying, *Have no fear. I will make sure your obligations continue to be met.* He ordered the treasury minister to send Alauda the usual payment. "Yes, Your Majesty," the man replied. Unlike Petrosus, he'd never given Lanius any trouble. "I delayed until I learned what your intentions here were."

He was smart enough to see he could have gotten into trouble for acting as easily as for not acting. Not acting could be mended. If he'd acted on his own, that would have been irrevocable, and would surely have landed him in hot water if he'd guessed wrong. He might not have been brave, but he'd been sensible.

"Fair enough," Lanius said. "From now on, the woman Alauda is to have her usual allowance, and you are to continue your usual discretion about it." He'd been so discreet, Lanius had had no idea that Sosia and Ortalis and Anser had another little half brother.

"Just as you say, Your Majesty, so shall it be," the treasury minister promised. "As long as I have instructions, I shall carry them out to the best of my ability." Without instructions, he would sit there and look up at the ceiling and gather dust; that was the corollary. But he was a useful and reasonably able official. Expecting someone in his place to have imagination, too, was no doubt asking too much.

"We'll let it go at that, then," Lanius said. Alauda and Nivalis were taken care of. Lanius wondered what the boy was like. Grus had never said a word about him. The other king had always been able to keep secrets. Had Grus ever seen his newest bastard? He might have been able to, traveling to or from the wars with the Menteshe. If so, though, he'd never given the slightest sign.

In due course, another letter came from the monastery. *Thank you for your generosity toward this boy. It shows you deserve to use the Scepter of Mercy,* Grus wrote. *Thank you also for using it to help bring peace among the monks in this place. Nothing less than the Scepter of Mercy, I am sure, could have eased the strife that flourished here.*

Lanius looked at that and slowly shook his head. Grus had no great amount of book learning. He was no scholar, and would have laughed at the idea of becoming one. But, as he always had, he saw how things worked. He got to the bottom of them. And when he did, he was rarely wrong. He certainly hadn't been this time.

Still bemused, Lanius summoned Hirundo. "What can I do for you, Your Majesty?" the general asked.

"Did you know Grus had a bastard son a few years ago?" Lanius asked.

To his surprise, Hirundo laughed. "Oh, yes. We were both in the tavern when he saw the boy's mother. Matter of fact, I saw her first. But he took a shine to her, so I backed off—he was king, after all. I've never set eyes on the boy, mind you, but I liked his mother."

"No one ever said anything about it," Lanius said.

"What's to say? These things happen." Hirundo shrugged.

Since Lanius knew it was only luck that none of the serving girls he'd bedded had conceived, he couldn't very well argue with that. He did say, "A king's bastard makes for . . . certain problems, you might say."

"Oh, no doubt about it," the general replied. "But Grus isn't king anymore, and it doesn't sound like he wants to be king anymore. Since that's so, I expect you'll be able to handle anything that comes up. Odds are nothing will—the boy'll likely be grateful for as much of a head start as he can get in life."

"I hope you're right." Lanius eyed Hirundo. A general could make for . . . certain problems, too. If Hirundo had risen in Grus' name, he and his longtime friend might well have prevailed. And if he'd rebelled in his own name, he also might have won. He was and always had been popular with the soldiers.

But he seemed content not to wear a crown. Maybe, watch-

ing Grus, he'd seen how much work being king really was. Lanius wondered what Hirundo would have done if he thought
Grus wanted to retake the throne. That, fortunately, seemed to
be one thing he himself and Avornis didn't have to worry about.

Hirundo probably knew what he was thinking. A general
also had to be a courtier. But if he did know, he gave no sign of
it. He just dipped his head and asked, "Anything else, Your
Majesty?"

"No, I don't think so," Lanius answered. Hirundo sketched
a salute and left the room. Lanius sat there scratching his head.
"Nivalis," he murmured. It wasn't a bad name—and, to his ear
at least, it didn't sound the least bit kingly. That made him like
it better.

Another day at the monastery, not much different from the one
that had gone before. The one that came after probably
wouldn't be much different, either. Grus didn't worry about it.
He'd seen enough ups and downs. Steadiness, right now, suited
him.

Some monks who'd spent much longer behind these frowning walls still couldn't abide it here. Petrosus wasn't the only
one who schemed to get a royal order, or an ecclesiastical one,
releasing him from his vows and letting him return to the secular world. Ortalis wasn't the only one who paced the courtyard
and the hallways like an animal in a cage too cramped to suit it.

A break in routine came when Pipilo summoned Grus to his
office. Grus tapped at the open door. "You wanted me, Father
Abbot?" he asked respectfully. Monks were supposed to respect their abbot. Grus *did* respect Pipilo. He knew how hard
being in charge of any community was. Pipilo did a good job
of running the monastery, and deserved respect for it.

He nodded to Grus now. "Yes. Come in, Brother, and close
the door after you." When Grus had, Pipilo said, "You do surprise me."

"Have I done something wrong?" Grus didn't believe he
had, but he often discovered the rules here by bumping into
them. From what he heard, he wasn't the only monk to whom
that happened.

But the abbot said, "No, no, no—not at all. Just the opposite in fact. I grow more amazed day by day at how well you fit in here."

"Thank you, Father Abbot." Grus couldn't resist adding, "I said I would."

"Yes, so you did," Pipilo agreed. "But people say all kinds of things. Some prove true. Some . . ."

Grus laughed. "Anyone would think you were a man who had some small experience in ruling men, Father Abbot."

That made Pipilo smile. "Maybe not as much as you, Brother, but yes—some. You were always a man who did so many things. Here, there aren't so many things to do. I thought you would be restless and bored. I thought you would want to go back to the secular world so you could do more."

"If this had happened to me a few years ago, I would have. I'm sure of that," Grus said. "No more, though. I'm content here."

"I see that," Pipilo said. "But how? Why?"

"What more do I need to do?" Grus said. "After all I've done, anything else would be an anticlimax. I'm not King of Avornis anymore, but my daughter is still married to the king. My son . . . Well, my son won't get any better than he is, no matter what I do. But my grandchildren are growing up, and my bastard boy is still arch-hallow. My family is as well set up as I could make it."

"And you have that other little bastard," Pipilo observed.

"Yes, I have Nivalis, too, though I'll never get to know him," Grus said. "I am sorry about that, but I wouldn't have gotten to know him even if I'd stayed king. My wife never quite found out about him." He took some modest pride in that, and knew it deserved no more.

"Congratulations—I suppose," the abbot said dryly. "The way it looks to me now, it's a shame you're older than I am and came to the monastic life so late. Otherwise, you'd be my likely successor. I told you that once before. I mean it more than ever now."

"Kind of you to think so, Father Abbot, but I told you I'd turn down the honor any which way," Grus replied. "That's part of why I don't mind being here, too. I've had a bellyful of telling people what to do."

"Have you really?" Pipilo sounded surprised again. "Most people never get enough of that."

Grus shrugged politely. "Maybe not, but most people don't get as big a dose as the one I had, either."

The abbot eyed him, then also shrugged. "I don't know whether I should believe you, but I do. And how do you like taking orders instead of giving them?"

"Not very much," Grus admitted. "No, not very much at all. But now that I know the routine and fit into it better than I did, people don't have to give me as many orders as they did when I first came here. I know what I need to do, and I do it."

Ortalis hadn't figured that out yet. He still tried to buck the monastery's routine. That, of course, landed him in more trouble than he would have had if he'd gone along at first. But Ortalis had never done anything the easy way, and it didn't look as though he would start now.

Pipilo must have known how Ortalis loved strife, for he asked, "Do you have any hints for dealing with your son?"

"Sorry, but no." Grus spread his hands, palms up. "If I did, don't you think I would have used them myself?"

"I meant no offense, Brother," Pipilo said. "I asked for the sake of peace and quiet here in the monastery. I know you prize them; I value them no less."

"I wasn't angry," Grus said. "I just know I didn't do as well with Ortalis as I wish I had. I truly don't know how much any one person can be responsible for what someone else turns out to be. I don't think anyone else knows, either, and I do think anyone who'll tell you he does is lying. But however much one person can be to blame for another, I'm to blame for Ortalis. I'm sorry. I wish he'd turned out better. But he is what he is, and that's all he is."

"It's remarkable how much he's calmed down toward you the past few weeks," the abbot said. "For that matter, you and Brother Petrosus seem to be getting along better, too. I'm glad to see it. Feuds in a place like this can cause a lot of trouble, because people can't get away from one another."

"I'm glad to see it, too," Grus said, and said no more than that. He couldn't prove Lanius had used the Scepter of Mercy to make sure he and Ortalis and Petrosus didn't feel the way

Pipilo had described; the king hadn't answered his comment about that. But nothing else made sense to him. Neither Ortalis nor Petrosus was one to back away from a quarrel. Come to that, neither was Grus.

"May I ask you one more question, Brother?" Pipilo said.

Grus bowed to him. "How can I refuse the holy abbot of this monastery anything at all? Don't I owe him obedience?"

"Quite a few of our brethren have no trouble refusing me any number of things," Abbot Pipilo replied with a laugh. "I have no doubt you could be among them if you chose. Well, here is my question, and do with it what you will. Suppose a river galley came up to the monastery tomorrow with an order signed by the arch-hallow or the king, saying you were released and could return to the world. What would you do then?"

"What would I do, Father Abbot?" Grus echoed. "I would be very surprised, that's what."

Pipilo sent him a reproachful stare. "You answer by not answering. Please don't evade, but tell me straight out—would you stay or would you go?"

"Yes," Grus answered, which made Pipilo stare more reproachfully still. Grus held up a hand, as though to ward off those sorrowful eyes. He said, "The truth is, I don't know what I'd do. And the other truth is, I don't expect that river galley, and I do think you'll be wasting your time if you expect it."

"All right, Brother," Pipilo said. Grus wasn't sure it was all right; the abbot liked things just so, and fumed when he couldn't get them that way. He went on, "I suppose I'll have to be satisfied with that. You may go."

"Thank you, Father Abbot," Grus replied. Any man who said he supposed he'd have to be satisfied was in fact anything but satisfied. Grus knew that perfectly well. He wondered whether Pipilo did, or whether the abbot hid resentment even from himself. Grus dared hope not; Pipilo knew well how other men work, and so he ought to have at least some notion of how he worked himself.

Bright sunshine in the courtyard made Grus blink until his eyes got used to it. Sparrows hopped in the garden. The monks argued about whether to shoo them out or not. Some said they ate grubs and insects, and so should be tolerated. Others in-

sisted they stole seeds, and so should be scared off. Both sides
were loud and excitable, no doubt because the question that
roused the excitement was so monumentally trivial.

Petrosus let them stay when they hopped near him. Grus
would have expected him to drive them away. He was the sort
who drove away everything that came close to him. If he let the
little birds come close, to Grus that was as near proof as made
no difference that they really did some good in the garden.

The next day, a river galley pulled up to the monastery. Grus
felt Pipilo's eye on him before the abbot went out to see why
the ship had come. Grus shrugged, as though to say he'd had
nothing to do with it—and he hadn't. He wondered what he
*would* do if that galley bore a release from this new life he'd
entered. He shrugged again. He still didn't know, and tried not
to worry about it.

One thing he did know—his heart didn't leap and fly at the
thought of escaping the monastery. He didn't hate the idea, but
he wasn't passionate about it, either.

If he had been passionate, he would have been disappointed.
The galley came not to let anyone out of the monastery but to
put someone into it. The new monk was a baron—or rather, a
former baron—named Numerius. Grus didn't remember his
face; he wasn't sure they'd ever met. He did know Numerius
squeezed his peasants for more than their due and paid his own
tax assessments late and often only in part. Now he'd gone too
far or done it once too often, and Lanius had made sure he
wouldn't do it again.

He came up to Grus. He was a big, blocky man with a red
blob of a nose and a bushy brown beard streaked with gray. "I
heard you were in here," he said. "I figured that other fellow
wouldn't give me any trouble." He sounded accusing, as
though his sudden arrival at the monastery were somehow
Grus' fault.

"Seems you were wrong, then, doesn't it?" Grus said. "By
all the signs, Lanius makes a perfectly good king."

"I figured he was just a figurehead," Numerius said. "That's
all he ever was."

"Now that you mention it," Grus said, "no."

"Huh?" The deposed baron gaped at him. "Come on. You

know better than that. You called the shots. That weedy little bugger did what you told him."

"He did when I took the crown," Grus admitted. "But he was only a boy then, on the edge of turning into a man. As time went by, he gave more and more orders, and they were usually good ones." He didn't admit how much that had worried him when it first started. Instead, he went on, "You shouldn't be surprised he can go on by himself now that he's the only king."

"Shouldn't I?" Numerius rumbled. "Well, I bloody well was when his soldiers swooped down on me. I never had a chance." He spat in disgust.

He wasn't the first baron who'd discovered the Kings of Avornis were serious these days about holding on to royal prerogatives. Several of his colleagues were in this very monastery. Maybe they could form a club.

Pipilo had let Numerius talk with Grus. Now, though, he said, "Come along, Brother. Time for you to get your robe and learn what will be required of you in your new station in life."

"I don't want to be a bloody monk!" Numerius roared.

"Your other choice was to be shorter by a head. I'm sure of it," Grus said. "I may be wrong, but I'd guess you didn't want that, either."

By the way Numerius glared at him, he would have been happy to see Grus shorter by a head. When Abbot Pipilo spoke to him again, his voice held more than a little sharpness. "Come along, Brother Numerius. I told you that once, and I am accustomed to obedience. No matter what you were before you came here, you are only one brother of many in this monastery. Many who are here came from a station higher than yours. Brother Grus is a case in point, and he is contented with his lot. Come along, I say."

Numerius came. He looked surprised at himself, but Pipilo, like a good general, could make himself obeyed when he wanted to. Hirundo had the gift. Grus did, too. It had to do with speaking in a tone that suggested nothing but obedience was possible.

Half an hour later, Numerius emerged in the plain brown robe of an ordinary monk. With his dirty but fine secular garb went a lot of his arrogance. As the abbot had said, he was just one among many now. The robe emphasized that, both to others and to himself.

Pipilo came out, too, and walked over to Grus. "I hope he will not trouble you as some of the other brethren did," he said quietly.

"I don't think so," Grus answered. "I wasn't the one who ordered him here, after all. I couldn't very well be, could I? I was already here myself when he got in trouble once too often."

"Once too often?" Pipilo's eyebrows rose. "You sound as though you knew him."

"No, not really. But I knew of him," Grus said. "He was always a man who would grab for everything he could—and for quite a few things he wasn't supposed to. I hope he won't cause you trouble."

The abbot smiled an experienced smile. "Men of that sort are not rare, here as in the wider world. I have met more than a few. If Brother Numerius proves troublesome, rest assured I have ways to bring him to heel."

"All right, Father Abbot. You know your business best," Grus said. *And it's not my worry. Not one bit of it's my worry,* he thought. He'd carried the worries, the weight, of the whole kingdom for many years. Now that burden was gone. Getting sent here had lifted it from his shoulders. He felt as though he were straighter and taller without it.

He almost owed Ortalis a debt for taking the weight away. The trouble was, Ortalis hadn't really intended to put it on his own shoulders. He would probably have ended up dropping it somewhere and watching moss grow on it.

Well, Avornis wouldn't have to worry about that. Lanius' shoulders were on the narrow side, but he was a conscientious man. When he saw a burden that needed lifting, he picked it up. And he wouldn't set it down until they laid him on his pyre.

And then Crex would pick it up, as long as he stayed healthy. If he didn't, Sosia was going to have another baby—maybe she'd already had it—and she could have more. One way or another, things would go on. He missed Estrilda, but a lot of that was habit, too.

*They'll go on without you,* Grus said to himself, tasting how that felt. A few years earlier, it would have troubled him enormously. Now? He found himself shrugging. Things would have gone on without him before many years passed any which way. A little sooner, a little later—what difference did it make? None he could see.

Realizing that, he also realized he had his answer to Abbot Pipilo's question. If that ship had come for him, he would have stayed in the monastery. What point was there to coming out again? Things would go on without him no matter where he was, so this made as good a place as any—better than most. Here he would stay.

Lanius took the latest letter from Abbot Pipilo to the archives himself. He wasn't sorry to get away from Elanus' crying. The new baby was healthy, but he cried more than Crex and Pitta had put together. *Or maybe I just don't remember. It's been a while now,* Lanius thought. Either way, he could escape to the archives. Sosia had no place like that to go, though serving women and a wet nurse gave her a lot of help with her new son.

Pipilo remarked that Baron Numerius' transition to Brother Numerius was not going as smoothly as it might have. The king didn't intend to worry about that. He doubted whether Numerius would ever escape from the monastery, which meant he had the rest of his life to get used to being a monk. If he'd paid his taxes and not tried to turn peasants into his personal dependents, he wouldn't have brought the change in way of life on himself. Since he had, he could just make the best of it.

One of these days, one of these years, one of these centuries, someone poking through the archives might come across the abbot's letter and the other documents about Baron Numerius' decline and fall. Lanius tried to keep all of them together, so some curious king or scholar in times to come could get the whole story. He wished some of his predecessors had followed the same rule. The archives held lots of unfinished tales, or at least tales where he'd found no ending. There were also some where he had no beginning, and others with the vital middle missing.

He closed the archives' heavy doors behind him. A smile stole over his face. *This* was where he belonged, as surely as Anser was made for the woods and the chase. The watery sunlight, the dancing dust motes, the slightly musty smell of old parchment, the quiet . . . What could be better? Nothing he'd ever found.

Pipilo's letter went into a case stuffed with documents on the struggle Avornis had had with its greedy nobles. Grus had started the struggle, and he'd won it. These days, the nobles recognized the superiority of the monarchy. The ones who hadn't were in monasteries or beyond human judgment.

No one before Grus had seen a problem in the rising power of the nobility—not even King Mergus, and Lanius' father had been both clever and ruthless. Grus had seen it, taken action against it, and done something about it. He deserved a lot of credit for that. Lanius wondered if chroniclers in years to come would give it to him.

"Between us, we made a fine king," Lanius murmured. He hadn't been able to come to the archives as often as he wanted lately. He'd been too busy dealing with royal affairs large and small. Grus would have handled a lot of them while he was still in the palace. Having someone else to handle them was the only reason Lanius could see even to think about recalling his father-in-law.

For the moment, he put aside all thoughts of royal affairs— even the ones about serving girls. He poked through the jumble of documents at random, looking for anything interesting he might turn up. He found mention of a small scandal involving his many-times-great-grandfather and a black-eyed maidservant. The arch-hallow of the time had preached a very pointed sermon in the great cathedral. Lanius wondered if his ancestor had had to put aside his lady friend. The archives didn't say— or if they did, the document with the answer wasn't with the rest. One more story without an end.

Lanius heard a noise. It came from somewhere in the bowels of the archives, from the cases and crates in the shadows near the edge of the enormous room.

"Pouncer!" he called. "Is that you?"

Calling a moncat usually did as much good as calling any other kind of cat. Every once in a while, though, you got lucky. Lanius did this time. "Mrowr?" Pouncer said blurrily.

"Come here, you ridiculous animal." Lanius knew that was

no way to talk to the beast that had brought the Scepter of Mercy out of Yozgat. He knew, but he didn't care. It was a perfectly good way to talk to a cat that was making a nuisance of itself—and Pouncer was.

He heard Pouncer moving through the archives, with luck, toward him. The moncat wasn't as quiet as it might have been; he could follow its progress by clunks and the occasional clank. Did that mean . . . ? Up until now, Pouncer hadn't raided the kitchens since coming back from the south—or hadn't gotten caught raiding the kitchens, anyhow.

Out came the beast. When Lanius saw it, he started to laugh. He couldn't help himself. Pouncer held a good-sized silver spoon in one small, clawed hand, for all the world as though it were the Scepter of Mercy. In its jaws, the moncat carried a dead mouse. No wonder that meow had sounded odd.

Plop! Pouncer dropped the mouse at Lanius' feet. The king knew that was an honor from the moncat, even if it was one he could have done without. "Oh, yes, you're a brave fellow, a hero among moncats," he said, which happened to be true. He could have called Pouncer a soup tureen full of giblet gravy and it wouldn't have mattered to the moncat, as long as he used the proper tone of voice. It had to sound like praise.

As soon as Lanius lifted the mouse by the tail, the moncat wanted it back again. Lanius knew that would happen; he'd seen it before. He scooped Pouncer up. The moncat shifted the spoon to its hind feet, which gripped just as well as its hands. That let those hands seize the mouse once more. Pouncer contentedly nibbled on its tail and began to purr.

*This* was the creature that had defeated the Banished One, that had returned the Scepter of Mercy to Avornan hands? Watching it, listening to it, the idea seemed absurd. But it was true.

"Come on, you preposterous thing," Lanius said. "You can keep the mouse, but you have to give back the spoon."

He cradled Pouncer in one arm and tried to take the spoon away with his free hand. The moncat hung on with both hind feet. Thanks to their thumbs, it hung on tight. He shrugged and gave up for the time being. The archives could wait. He needed to take the thief back to the scene of the crime.

He hadn't gotten even halfway before he almost ran into a cook. "Your Majesty!" she said, and then, "Oh! You've already caught the miserable beast."

"So I have," Lanius agreed. "Let's go back to the kitchens. Maybe you can trade some mutton for the spoon. Or if that doesn't work, we'll take it away there."

"Mutton!" The cook rolled her eyes. "That thing doesn't deserve mutton. It deserves a poke in the snout for being a nuisance and a thief."

"Oh, I don't know," Lanius said. "Pouncer *did* get the Scepter of Mercy out of Yozgat, remember. Maybe you could give the beast something for that, eh?"

The cook shook her head. "Who cares about some old Scepter? What's it ever done for me? That's what I want to know."

"We're not fighting the Menteshe anymore, and the Banished One isn't so much trouble," Lanius reminded her. "That's all on account of the Scepter of Mercy."

"Like the Menteshe were ever going to come up to the city of Avornis," the cook jeered. "Like the Banished One ever cared about the likes of me." She laughed at the idea.

And it *was* silly when you put it in such terms. Lanius couldn't deny it, and didn't try. "Sometimes things that help the kingdom a lot don't matter very much to some of the people who live there," he said. Pouncer bit off the mouse's tail. It dangled from the corner of the moncat's mouth for a moment. Then it disappeared.

When they got back to the kitchens, the head cook laughed to see Pouncer still clutching the silver spoon. Cucullatus' chins and belly wobbled as he laughed; he was fond and more than fond of what he turned out. "So you nabbed the thief, eh, Your Majesty?" he said. "More than the Menteshe ever did, by Olor's beard."

"Menteshe, Menteshe, Menteshe!" The woman who'd gone to get Lanius threw her hands in the air. "Why don't people talk about something important? The price of lard in the market square—*that* matters. But who cares about a bunch of foreigners, anyway?"

How many people all over Avornis felt the same way? More

than a few, probably. Lanius sighed. He couldn't even show her she was wrong; she didn't know enough even to realize how ignorant she was. Instead of trying, the king turned to Cucullatus. "Would you be kind enough to ransom the spoon with a bit of mutton?"

"I can do that," the head cook replied at once, though his underling sniffed. "Will the beast want it, though, what with its dainty there?" He pointed to what was left of the mouse.

"Who knows? All we can do is find out," Lanius answered. "You'll get the spoon back any which way." He tugged on it. Pouncer still didn't want to let go.

"Oh, I know, Your Majesty," Cucullatus said. "Let me go bring you that mutton. Be right back." Off he went. Off went the woman who'd gone to get Lanius, too. She plainly remained convinced she'd outargued the king.

The mutton was fresh, unsullied by either garlic or mint. The moncat meowed on smelling it. Maybe it was better than a murdered mouse. Lanius thought so, but he was no moncat. He got the silver spoon away from Pouncer while the moncat was distracted and handed it to Cucullatus. "Get it out of sight."

"Right you are." The cook tossed it into a bucket of sudsy water. That was perfect. Not only did the spoon disappear, but moncats liked getting wet no better than their ordinary cousins did.

Pouncer seemed torn between mouse and mutton, and ended up nibbling on each in turn. "Thanks for your help, and for the ransom," Lanius told Cucullatus. He explained why he thought Pouncer deserved it.

"What, Your Majesty? You think the Scepter of Mercy is worth a bit of mutton? Seems to me you set a pretty high price on it." Cucullatus' eyes twinkled.

"That's what I told him," said the woman cook who'd come after Lanius. "He didn't want to listen to me—oh, no."

Lanius' eyes met Cucullatus'. The head cook smiled and sighed at the same time, as though to say, *What can you do about some people?* The answer to that was simple. You couldn't do anything about some people. You had to make the best of them when there was a best to make, and put up with them when there wasn't.

Now Lanius was the one who sighed. He'd been King of Avornis since he was a little boy, and that was what he'd learned? Why hadn't he smoked fish for a living in that case?

When you got down to it, though, plenty of people went through their whole lives without ever figuring out anything so basic about their fellow men and women. If they had realized it, there would have been far fewer quarrels.

Lanius also had to put up with Pouncer. "I'm going to take the thief of Yozgat back to his chamber," the king said. "We'll see how long the beast stays there this time."

"As long as it feels like it, and not a minute longer," Cucullatus predicted. That told Lanius the head cook understood moncats as well as any mere human being was ever likely to.

Pouncer started wiggling even before Lanius opened the door. The moncat knew where it was going, and didn't want to go there. Lanius could put it in the room. Not for all his power could the king make it stay there.

After barring the door again, Lanius started back to his bedchamber. He needed to get away from Elanus every now and then, but he always felt bad about doing it. He hadn't gone far before someone called him. He wasn't too sorry to turn back. "Oh, hello, Otus. What can I do for you today?"

"Hello, Your Majesty." The freed thrall hurried up the corridor toward him. "I just wanted to thank you again for all you've done for my people south of the Stura. You and King Grus, I should say." He shyly bobbed his head.

"I'm glad we did it, and I know Grus was, too. Grus is, I should say." Lanius meticulously corrected himself. He went on, "Seeing you here, and Fulca, too, shows me every day that what we did was worthwhile."

Otus smiled. "Seeing Fulca every day—seeing her the way she's supposed to be, not like a brainless beast—shows me what you did was worthwhile." He bowed. "And I thank you for it, and so does she."

"Sometimes things work out the way you hope they would," Lanius said. "Not always, not even most of the time, but sometimes."

"They did here. You even paid the Banished One back.

That's worth everything, and two coppers more besides," Otus said.

"So it is," Lanius said. Sometimes things *did* work out. He'd gone from bastard to crowned king, from puppet to king in his own right. Thervingia and the Chernagors and the Menteshe had all harried Avornis. Now no enemy did. Even the Banished One was beaten, as Otus had said. Grus had had a lot to do with that. Lanius couldn't deny it, and didn't try. *But I had a lot to do with it myself,* he thought proudly. He had the biggest, hardest job in the world, and he'd grown to the point where he could do it and, he hoped, do it well. Slowly, he nodded to himself. No, not bad for someone who'd started out a bastard. Not bad at all. He headed back to Sosia and Elanus.

Kirsten pops in a tape labeled *Road Tunes* and cranks the volume. "Roll down your window!" she shouts over the screeching guitars and thudding bass.

The wind rips through the little car like a hurricane, and the miles peel away, layer by layer, beneath the sure ride of our tires. I slip on a pair of shades and undo my ponytail and let my hair fly free as Waynesboro becomes a fading postcard in our rearview mirror. Ahead of us, burned into the pavement, is a mosaic of undiscovered colors—the white peaks of snowcapped mountains; golden grasses; the cold blue of the Pacific; desert rust. Freedom is now. The eagle has left the nest. And while I soar high above, stretching my newfound wings, there's only one, solitary question spinning inside my head.

What's next?

Miranda's next stop?
An unexpected detour named Dustin.
Don't miss

## on the road

### Exit #3 TAKING CHANCES

Miranda's always been afraid of heights, but that was before she met Dustin. He's tall, blond, and gorgeous, and he wants Miranda to be his climbing partner on a huge mountain in Colorado. Even though she's terrified, Miranda can't bear to disappoint him. She just hopes he'll understand there's only one thing she's more afraid of than heights— and that's falling in love.

● ● ● ●